The Pennycandystore

Robert M. Dias

The
Pennycandystore

Robert M. Dias

Hathaway–Seymore Publications, Inc.

The Pennycandystore

Published by Hathaway-Seymore Publications, Inc.
411 Truman Avenue
Key West, FL 33040

Copyright © 2002 by Robert M. Dias
First Edition

Library of Congress Cataloging-in-Publication Data

Dias, Robert M.
        The pennycandystore/ by Robert M. Dias -- 1st ed.
        p.cm.
        LCCN 2002105428
        ISBN 0-9643434-1-X

        1. Terrorism--United States--Fiction. 2. Women
        presidents--United States--Fiction. I. Title.

PS3604.I375P46 2002   813'.6

Dedicated to the members of the United States armed services.

Bob Dias is co-author of
Franchising: The Investor's Complete Handbook,
a non-fiction bestseller, and ten trade books
which sold in bestseller quantities.
He lives in Florida with his wife, Jean.

What we all look for is a bastion of sanity in a world gone amuck.
Like you, I'm still in the hunt.

Bob Dias
December 25, 2001

1

To Anthony Voccio, Junior, the girl in his arms was just the Alka-Seltzer he needed. *Manny, Manny, Manny. How do I get rid of you,* he thought. The loud hard rock music stopped and the band launched into a slow one. Junior pulled Ginger in close. "I need a favor."

"Whatcha need, baby?"

Nodding toward his table, Junior said, "See my babysitter over there?"

"Manny."

"See that bulge in his coat?"

"Yeah."

"My car keys. We gonna get out of here together. I need'm."

She pressed herself tighter against him. "Together, you promise?"

"God as my judge."

"Hang in the john for ten minutes."

When the song ended, Ginger's young, well-formed body slid into Manny's well-padded lap. Before Junior returned, Manny's stubby fingers were working their way up her thigh. "You're such a naughty boy, Manny," she whispered as her fingers closed around the ring of keys. "Don't you go away now. I want to get rid of my pantyhose."

Anthony Voccio, Junior, was a sleazy punk who had already wrecked three cars while driving drunk. He'd walked away, but others hadn't been as lucky. Even in Rhode Island, where his father was a king, the judge had taken away his right to drive. Afraid her out-of-control son might kill someone, Junior's mother had berated her husband to assign their son a full-time driver. Manny had been chosen.

Handing Ginger a silver flask full of Crown Royal, Junior wheeled out of the parking lot throwing dirty slush in every direction. "Hold this."

At 50 miles per hour and without snow tires, the low-slung Mercedes coupe fishtailed every time they navigated a corner. Ginger stiffened and held on to the grab bar above the door. "Baby, you'd better slow it down some." Junior was in a funk and sweet words were not part of his vocabulary. "You wanna get out? Just say the word and you're gone."

Ginger saw the sign announcing they were entering a hospital zone with a 20 mph speed limit. As the coupe picked up momentum, she thought, *I had to pick a nasty drunk with no couth.*

The bus driver saw Kathryn Garboosian scurrying across the street, so he waited. She never made it. Junior had the flask tipped back and never saw her until it was too late. He was doing over 60 miles per hour when Ginger shrieked, "Stooooop!"

Arcing through the air seven feet above the street, Kathryn, a nurse, knew in the split second of last conscious thought before the speeding car struck her that she was not going to get any older and she wondered who would take care of Jake and her plants. She heard the unmistakable sounds of a happy kitchen and saw thousands of flickering candles dancing below her. She died painlessly, her slender neck snapped like that of a young sapling smote by too much wind. It had been her first day at a new job at Mercy hospital. Twenty minutes away, her husband, Jake, was driving home from his first day with the Providence Police Department.

With a minimum of fuss, Junior sat leadenly, working the cell phone until he reached his father. "Just a girl and a bus driver."

A minute later, he croaked, "I got it."

"Stay here." Ginger was still in shock and she wasn't going anywhere.

Junior lurched out of the car and headed toward the shapeless blob in the road. Missing the warmth of the car and pissed that his custom-made boots were getting ruined, he followed his father's instructions. He went through the motions of feeling for a pulse and covered her head with his leather jacket. As Junior knelt next to Kathryn Garboosian's stiff, lifeless body, his only response was a snide, "Hum." There wasn't the slightest doubt in Junior's mind that the whole incident would all go away.

2

Narrow, low ceilinged and dingy, the meeting room reeked of futility and inertia. Those present divided themselves into the natural order of things. Twelve homicide detectives filled the chairs near the windows while the support staff slouched on the bench seats along the corridor wall. Everyone knew why he or she was there, but nobody liked it. Even though it was a no smoking building, half the people gathered were sucking on cigarettes.

In the front of the room, Captain Donald Tenhagen looked out at the first snow flurries of the year. "Going to be a bitch of a storm," he muttered. Tall, with graying hair and a lean frame, the captain looked more rancher than cop. Under Tenhagen's command were forty-two detectives and twelve administrative staff. The detectives were split, unequally, into four squads that covered an assortment of felonies. Today's meeting was restricted to homicide personnel. "I've got 20 years in. What the hell's wrong with me?" He mumbled to himself, "I've done this dozens of times." To hide his trembling hands, he tucked them under his armpits and stared down at the traffic already piling up. To those watching, it looked like he was looking for his man. He wasn't. Since hiring the lieutenant, an ominous premonition had found a cozy crevice in Tenhagen's mind. Somehow, the new man was going to change his life in ways that would be painful and far-reaching. Five weeks earlier, he could have sent the voice away with a phone call. "Sorry, Lieutenant, my budget just got cut." Turning away from the window, Tenhagen strode to the podium and scanned his audience. "Looks as though the weather has delayed our new lieutenant. Be that as it may, we're all here, so let's clear the air. First off, I want you to know that our man didn't come looking for the job; we went to him. Nobody here was on the short list."

Her hair bouncing around, Detective Teresa Maggio almost made it to her feet before her partner pulled her down. Tenhagen paused, gave her a hard look and kept going. "Now, about Jerry Manfred. The lieutenant is going out on disability and will remain on sick leave until his papers clear."

A voice piped up from the front row. "Cap, what about a party?"

"Manfred told me he doesn't want a party and if there is one, he won't show up."

Ineffective but well liked, Jerry Manfred had run homicide for the last two years. The man they were all waiting on was his replacement.

"People, we've tried to resolve our problems without going to the outside. Unfortunately, the situation has only gotten worse. That's gonna change."

As the tension in the room grew, a veteran detective stood. "Cap, no disrespect, but just who is this new savior of ours?"

"Until we recruited him, Lieutenant Garboosian was a supervisory detective in New Haven. His reputation and stats are AAA-1. Anyone here thinks they're going to snow the man had better forget it. The lieutenant's a player."

No one was thrilled by the captain's remarks and the feeling of gloom-and-doom thickened and spread. Tenhagen was about ready to add a few more choice comments when the door opened. The man's absurd bulk filled the frame and they saw lots of wet brown hair matted down over a swollen face. Eyes shrouded by shaggy brows surveyed the room and came to rest on Tenhagen. "Nasty out there."

Encased in a drab topcoat that flared outward down to his ankles, the newcomer looked like he was wearing a tent. Complete silence enveloped the room and the only sound was the jingle-jangle of his unbuckled goulashes as he traversed the vinyl-tiled floor. Standing in front of Tenhagen, he smiled and held out a paw. "Captain, you got a serious parking problem." Unruffled, Tenhagen smiled back. "Jake, welcome to the Providence Police Department. People, your new boss, Jake Garboosian."

After some brief welcoming remarks and a parting handshake, Tenhagen strode out and left an eerie silence in his wake. Like a retired matador returning to the ring, Jake shed the oversized topcoat that enshrouded his impressive girth. Reading glasses were tethered from a piece of string strung around his head and a practiced hand moved instinctively to make sure they were still there. Reassured, he perched his considerable bulk on a corner of the speaker's table.

"First off, I grew up in Providence and my mother and sister still live here. For that reason alone, I'm glad to be back. That said, let's go around the room so I can put faces to the names on the roster."

The last detective took his seat and Jake resumed. "At this time, there's not a lot to discuss. We'll have more to talk about when we meet one-on-one. I'll have a meeting schedule posted by noon today. When we meet, please bring me up to date summaries on all your open cases."

This time, Detective Maggio shot up from her chair before her partner could react. "Lieutenant, look at the calendar. Christmas is only two weeks away and we're all pretty much buried. Updates take time."

Jake was unimpressed. "Make the time."

An undercurrent of unfriendly voices and deliberate shuffling of feet and chairs helped ease Maggio's pique, and by the time her backside hit wood, the dour cast on her face had faded. Responding to the babble, Jake had unbuttoned his coat to reveal a yellow polka-dot tie and a polyester shirt stretched so tight you could almost hear the fabric groan. With inordinate grace for a man his size, he slid off the table, glided to the speaker's lectern and brought a huge fist down on the pine top. "Cut the crap and listen up."

Because the detectives wanted to rise up in rebellion, the quiet that invaded the room seemed unnatural. Jaws agape, they leaned forward in anticipation. "Two weeks ago, I reviewed a copy of your latest stats and noted that your suicide/murder ratio was way out of whack. Curious, I checked the national stats. Guess what? The suicide rate here in Providence is three times higher than that of Vegas and that, detectives, is impossible."

Faces tightened.

"Rhode Island being the Ocean State, I figure, eh, it could be all that water. So I asked the captain to pull a half dozen suicides. At random, of course, so there's no bias. May I lose my taste buds if the first case doesn't scream murder? Wanna know why?"

No response.

"I'll tell you anyway. First off, there's no note. Second, photos of the scene show the poor bastard's clothes stacked neatly on a chair by the window with his pants on top. That's ass backwards, but there's another thing. No watch. In case you don't know, most suicides that dive remove their wrist watches beforehand. Eh, why ruin a good Rolex. It's not on the pile, the most likely place, and there's no watch listed in the inventory. The building's got a doorman, so I know the vic didn't live in a walk-up. Two thousand a month and he can't afford a watch? Jake, I say to myself, you'd better get your fat ass out to the scene."

"This is bullshit." A nattily dressed detective was out of his chair and shaking an accusing finger at Jake. "That case was a lock. The chain bolt was still fastened when we got to the scene. We needed bolt cutters to gain access. Nobody else was in that room."

"Detective, I like your suit, but I hate interruptions. Sit your ass down."

The detective looked around for support that wasn't there. Slinking down, he studied the lower spine of the man in front of him.

"Upstairs in the apartment, I asked the building manager about the new chain bolt." Jake paused, removed a pocket notebook and flipped to a page marked with a pink paperclip. "Quote: *The new chain bolt is identical to the old one. See there, the same screw holes were used to mount it.* With that in mind, I go out in the hall and try to fasten the chain from the outside. No luck. My hands are too big. I ask the new tenant to give it a try. Her hands and wrist are smaller and she fastens the chain in ten seconds flat. The woman's surprised, but the manager only shrugs. Quote: *Hell, Lieutenant, when those chain bolts were installed, they used a template that left too much slack in the chain. Half this building knows you can unfasten the chain from the hall. Husband comes home early from a business trip, the chain's on and the wife's in bed. That sort a thing happens all the time.*"

As the case detective slid lower in his chair, deep sighs flooded the room.

"Down in the lobby, I kibitz with the alert doorman who was on duty when tissue and bone hit the steel roof of the Lincoln. All my interviews are taped so this is another direct quote: *Unless there's someone who can walk through steel rebar and poured concrete, no one, and I mean no one, left this building after three o'clock. There's only one other exit and it has a tamper-proof crash bar that sounds a loud horn whenever the door is opened. It never went off.* According to the doorman's statement, the suicide jumped at twenty past three in the morning. Now, I gotta good feeling about this doorman because I've watched him operate from my car and know he's a lion tamer."

The frowns and raised eyebrows slowed Jake down a notch.

"Lion tamer. Someone who's alert and wary of strange cats. Ya got it?

Good. So, I ask my alert doorman if the vic had any women friends in the building. Quote: *You serious, he was a good-looking guy and a classy dresser. Drove a Porsche. She still lives on the eighth floor. Took it pretty damn hard.*

I come back with, *Did any of the cops ask about her?* Quote: *Nah, they asked how I'd fixed the time and I showed them my log. That's all?* Quote: *Yeah.* So, I ask you, what do we have?"

They all knew, but there were no hands.

"Detectives, we got a woman who not only killed her lover, but she had enough smarts and guts to stay put."

Jake waited a few beats to drive the point home. "There's more. The vic had to be high on something because she was able to lure him to the window. We'll never know what. Fifteen floors was enough to scramble his internal organs into a souffle and because it's classified a suicide, there's no autopsy, no blood work and no prints."

Except for natty dresser and the still pissed-off Maggio, heads had started nodding in the right direction.

"Now, the vic was found naked. How many suicides you know who jump naked? Stats say almost none. So it's likely he jumped her bones before she lured him to the window and pushed him out. The bed's all messed up and his clothes are scattered all over the place. That didn't look right, so she changed the bedding and stacked his clothes on a chair next to an open window. Satisfied, she stuffed the bedding and watch in a bag, fastened the chain bolt from the outside and scooted down the stairs to her place, free as the proverbial bird."

A strong gust of wind dislodged a loose rain gutter and it started to beat against the side of the brick building. Jake waited until the noise became part of the furniture. With an expression that was more curiosity than sarcasm, Jake thumbed his way around the room. "Anyone here see anything else out of kilter in this mixed bag we're examining?"

Some of the detectives traded anxious looks, others hung their heads.

"Come on, people, there's a major lapse of logic here. The man was naked. How many naked vics you see jump out of windows? That's right, it's too embarrassing."

Shaking his head in disbelief, Jake gave the Case Detective one of his stock deadpan looks. "Get a search warrant for the watch and bedding. If the watch isn't there, look through her address book until you find the lucky guy who's wearing it. As for the rest of you, statistics don't lie. There's a lot more of these slam-dunks in the files and I'm gonna find them all."

The room fell silent and before long, you could hear the splatter of the wind-driven snow flakes as they hit the cold panes of glass.

"Detectives, you're awash in cold cases and your closing rate is pathetic. Throw in a dozen bad suicides and the picture gets worse. Now, my methods work and you're going to use them. It's that simple. Fight me, and I'll bury you."

Stifling an impulse to scream and bash some of their incompetent heads together, Jake continued like he was chatting over coffee. "On the updates, you've got one week. No excuses. No exceptions. Anything else?"

When no one spoke up, Jake added, "For the record, I'm five-ten, weigh 272 and I don't like smoking. You're dismissed."

Except for Detective Maggio, there was a mass exodus. She stalked Jake, her green eyes flashing warning signs, but before she could say anything, the beeper on Jake's hip started to vibrate. With a cell phone to his ear, he mouthed, *We'll talk another time.* Stymied, Maggio turned abruptly and left in a huff. Left to himself, Jake smiled.

After hashing out the option of bringing down some union pressure, the detectives opted to let the *hard-ass fat man* eat himself to death. This was good news to Captain Tenhagen who was fed up with the status quo. The squad had been coddled by Jake's predecessor and they'd coasted along in blissful ignorance. To make matters worse, half of the detectives had gotten their gold shields through political patronage. An amused grin appeared on Tenhagen's face as he fancied the up-coming demolition derby. Unfortunately, the moment was short-lived, for minutes later the ominous feeling returned, only this time it was much stronger.

3

It had been a trying first day and Jake was thinking about a hot shower and the Chicken Marsala he was going to make. Like a lot of Greek men, cooking was his favorite work of the day. Pulling into the driveway, he hit the garage door opener. No car. His wife was not home. A practical man, he honed in on the most likely reason, the icy roads. Riding from scene to scene with his police radio on, he knew there had been a rash of serious auto accidents and he assumed that Mercy Hospital's emergency room was swamped. He also mistakenly supposed that since Kathryn was new, they'd probably kept her over. Still, it was getting dark fast and her absence made him uneasy.

Dripping on the entry rug, Jake wiped his feet and made for the rear of the house. Every board in the wood floor creaked from his bulk as he steered around the plant life that was Kathryn's passion. At the counter in his favorite room, the kitchen, he called the hospital. Told that Kathryn had already left, the first prickles of fear furrowed his brow. *Where is she?*

Wind gusts over 45 knots had come out of nowhere and the driving snow pelting the aluminum siding was making a dull machine gun-like sound. Jake finally reached the shift supervisor riding herd on dispatch.

"Dispatch, Olson."

"This is Lieutenant…"

Jake was furious. "Disconnected damn, damn, damn."

He was re-dialing when a loud bark at the kitchen door diverted his attention. *God, I forgot about Woofer.*

The sociable pound dog was wet and scared. Feeling guilty, Jake rubbed Woofer down and fed him some chopped steak and gravy. The dog was licking the bowl when the lights started to flicker. Moments later, a loud clap of thunder shook the wood-framed windows and everything went black. As he was groping around in the dark, Jake's cell-phone rang. The caller was Captain Tenhagen. A gray-faced basket case of a man put down the instrument. His beloved wife of ten years was dead, killed by a drunken driver whose license had been revoked. Captain Tenhagen laid it out. "It's a vehicular homicide. He's gonna do some time."

The patrolman dispatched to get Jake found a roly-poly man sitting on the floor hugging a spouted watering can and talking to a wall of plants. Hearing the toneless despair in Jake's voice, the officer turned off his flashlight and sat down in the dark. "Jesus, Mary and Joseph," he muttered to himself.

Six months after Kathryn Garboosian's funeral, Captain Tenhagen called Jake into his corner office. His voice was somber. "It was plea-bargained down to a misdemeanor."

"No license, three DUI's, speeding tickets up the ass and he walks. What's the read?"

Tenhagen paused, debating how far to go.

"The girl and the bus driver testified that Kathryn ran in front of Junior's car. Worse, no one can find the punk's blood test. Jake, he's Anthony Voccio's son."

Like most people who lived in New England, Jake knew about Anthony Voccio.

"How'd he work it?"

"My guess? The girl, the bus driver and someone in the lab got paid. We've never lost a blood sample."

"What about the judge?"

"It's possible."

"Kathryn was thrown over sixty feet. How'd they get around that?"

"Junior's attorney came up with a report that showed Kathryn could have slid on the icy pavement."

"The attorney and accident shlock who did the report. They have names?"

"Archie Pope. He's a good attorney and wired-in everywhere. I'm blank on the report."

Jake wanted out of the flimsy side-chair, but it held him like a corset two sizes too small. Seething, he lurched upward, leaving a wooden armrest dangling by a piece of cloth. Oblivious, he fixed two dark sockets of fire on Tenhagen's face and mouthed the words, *He got away with murder.*

Pinching his nose between two fingers, Tenhagen looked down and removed his glasses. "Repeat any of this and it's my job."

Jake's nod of understanding was almost imperceptible.

At the door, Jake turned. "What did he get?"

"A $2,500 fine. There's no license to take away."

"And the booze?"

"No blood tests, no proof and no mandatory rehab."

Jake's voice was bitter. "So, a little cash and some expert's hocus-pocus was all it took?"

Tenhagen sighed.

Lightheaded and nauseated, Jake closed the door and leaned against the far wall. *I need some fresh air.*

The police helicopter was tied down and the station house roof was vacant. Climbing the winding metal stairs had left him panting and he collapsed on a bench in the shaded waiting area. *I'm pathetic. What in hell did Kathryn ever see in me?* He'd always been a little heavy, but two years ago the intervals between his food binges all but disappeared. Finally, Kathryn had insisted that he see a psychologist.

At the start of his third session, he got the verdict. "Mr. Garboosian, you're 42 and roughly a third of your life has been spent dealing with death and mayhem. And after your promotion, your eating binges got more frequent, yes?"

"Yeah, after I made lieutenant."

"And you became a Supervisory Detective required to visit every crime scene."

"Yeah, that's what I do. Doc, please call me Jake."

"All right. Jake, all those visits, so filled with violence and death, have overloaded your psyche. Eating enables you to cope. It's your escape mechanism."

"What am I supposed to do, quit?"

"Either that or transfer to another division within the department."

"You're sayin' I'm beyond therapy?"

"One or two hours a week is not going to balance out the seventy plus hours you spend around death."

"Doc, this is a bitch."

"I know."

Informed of the diagnosis, Kathryn had come down hard. "Well, quit or wrangle a transfer. All that weight is going to kill you."

"To what, stolen cars? I'd have to take a downgrade."

"So, take a downgrade."

"My pension will take a hit."

"Forget the pension and look at how much we're spending on food."

Knowing it was a sensitive issue, Kathryn hadn't mentioned the expense of keeping up with three different wardrobes, lovingly labeled: Fat, fatter and ridiculous.

"There's gotta be something."

"Damn it, Jake, you've already tried every diet out there."

From his perch on the roof, Jake noted that the "o" in the deli take-out sign was missing. As his eyes began singling out the women on the sidewalk crowded with after work shoppers, his mind started churning again. *She must have been embarrassed; an attractive woman out in public with a baby elephant. She had to be. Funny that it never showed. A lot of women would have walked.* Overcome by a feeling of helplessness, he turned away and headed back to his office.

Charged with boundless energy, Maggio knocked on Jake's door. "It's open."

Jake was cracking open a window and she noticed that he was padding around in stocking feet. "Lieutenant?"

"Yeah." Jake's voice was raspy and his face was waxen and gray.

"You coming down with something?"

Jake answered despondently which worried Maggio since that was an emotion he had never shown before. "Yeah, I may be in the early stages of mankinditis, a not-so-rare malady that slowly cripples your will while it chips away at your soul. Wouldn't you know, there's no known cure."

"Lieutenant, you should call it a day."

"I'm going to sit here awhile and think about that. Hit the lights."

4

Snow covered the front lawn like a freshly washed baby blanket. On the porch of his mother's home, Jake was sweating as he swung an old broom at the dagger shaped icicles that were threatening to bring down his mother's rain gutters. Bareheaded and clad in an old flannel shirt, he hardly noticed the biting cold. He'd been working 16-hour days trying to block out Kathryn's death. Concerned, Tenhagen had counseled, "Jake, your staff is ready to flame out. You've got to slow it down."

"One more week."

"No, now. The numbers are way up and everyone from the mayor on down is delirious. I never thought I'd say this, but your squad needs a breather."

"Cap, we still have…"

"Jake, enough. Starting tomorrow, *everyone* works an 8 hour 5 day schedule."

"Yeah, you're right. We're pretty much there."

Shuffling inside, Jake found his mother in the living room. Her legs, with their varicose veins showing, were up on the couch. "Sonny, your ears are red."

"Don't worry, they'll thaw."

"I want you to know that giving your sister-in-law your house was a wonderful thing. If Kathryn were here, she'd be pleased."

"The boys are getting older and they're hellions. They need their own rooms and Liz needed that break. Besides, you were all alone."

"They're hellions because Steve's always working."

"With no rent to pay, he can cut back. Ma, ease up on Steve, he's one of the good guys."

"I know, but perhaps you could spend more time with the boys. To them, you're the world's greatest detective and they follow you around like shadows."

"Ma, it's the gun."

"Sonny, did I take my medications?"

"An hour ago, Ma."

"Can we visit Dad's grave?"

"Sure, how's ten tomorrow?"

"I'll be ready."

Providence had positioned itself as the Renaissance City, and the old Biltmore Hotel on Dorrance Street was a symbol of the city's renewal. Built in the roaring 20's, the hostelry had been thoughtfully renovated and it oozed Old World elegance and charm. Thanks to Jake, the Horn family: Steve, Liz and their two boys now owned a home. In appreciation, they were hosting a Christmas party at the Biltmore and Jake was the guest of honor.

Liz had spent the last few hours in the hotel's beauty shop and she had a new hairstyle. Upstairs, encased in a black, ankle-length dress, she sneaked up on her husband and gave him a hug. "Has your brother checked in?"

"Robert called. Horrendous traffic. They're going to be late. How are the boys doing?"

"Mrs. G has them under control. The Christmas excitement and gallivanting around town wiped them out. They're napping."

"Good, tonight's special and I want them bright-eyed and ready to enjoy!"

The Biltmore's Presidential Room featured gold crown moldings, antique furniture and original artwork. A company the hotel recommended had transformed the room in an afternoon. A cream-colored Christmas tree shimmering with hundreds of tiny white lights and various shades of shiny gold and silver garlands ruled one corner of the room and the pile of packages that encircled the tree had been wrapped to match the theme. To enhance the ceiling, over 800 tiny white bulbs entwined with garland were strung from wall-to-wall on monofilament fishing line. For the centerpiece, there was a magnificent ice carving of an angel that shimmered in the reflected glow of the long-stemmed candles placed near every place-setting.

"Steve, it's almost 8:30. We'd better get the lights on. The boys are getting antsy," Liz pleaded. "The late arrivals will understand."

"All right, how about if we do the lights and wait on the food?"

When Steve darkened the room and plugged in the Christmas lights, the effect was magical. The boys' unrestrained oohs and ahs mingled with the sound of *Silent Night* brought tears to Liz's eyes. Even Steve's best friend and his wife, the only non-family guests invited, inched closer together and locked hands. Woofer, a silver bell hanging around his neck, snuggled on a leather chair, bewildered by all the lights.

The Biltmore doorman was in a lousy mood as the white limo pulled up to the entrance of the hotel. It was the holiday season and his average tip for opening a door was still a buck. It never dawned on him that with his cadaverous face and pointed mustache, he loomed defiant. The squat, piggy-looking man with the camel hair topcoat changed all that as he pressed a fifty into the doorman's hand. "All right to park here for ten minutes?" Moving the bill as deep into his overcoat pocket as possible, the doorman bowed. "Sir, you take all the time you need."

The elegant looking woman was the same height as the piggy man who took her by the arm and steered her toward the lobby. Despite the cold, the woman was wearing a simple black dress with a single string of pearls and a shawl. The doorman noticed the expensive briefcase in her right hand as he studied her walk. *What's a good lookin broad doin with a scuzz like that?* His eyes wandered to the chauffeured limo and he thought he knew.

Serving the Horn party was a busboy and two crackerjack waiters. The hotel's banquet manager was talking quietly with one of them when he heard the door creak open. The elegant woman and piggy man entered the room and stood there for a long minute letting their eyes adjust to the dark. To the manager, they were guests.

The pair were professionals and there was no nervousness as the man opened his topcoat and the woman her briefcase. Steven Horn was nursing a scotch when his wife was driven against the wall, a mannequin with its mouth agape. Liz's body crumpled to the floor and Steve saw that the front of her dress was smoldering and turning red. He turned and held out his hands in a futile attempt to parry the lethal projectiles he knew were coming. A hailstorm of minute pieces of flesh peppered the air and Santa Claus red splashed the walls. The Christmas tree, its lights and its promise of joy extinguished, crashed loudly to the floor but the rowdy crowd in the hall and adjoining meeting rooms masked the noise. Since the walls were padded to make them sound proof, ricochets were nil.

The woman returned the silenced machine pistol to her briefcase and with the music cut off, the loudest sound in the room was the sound the locks made as she snapped the case shut. As they walked casually through the lobby, the woman took a fresh rose from a vase of fresh flowers set on a table in the center of the lobby. She stopped and brought the bloom to her delicately shaped nose. "Is good," she muttered to the piggy man.

The obliging doorman opened the car door and the man handed him a ready twenty. As they drove away, the doorman muttered, "Now there goes a sport." As the limo turned the corner into traffic, the partition separating the front and rear seats vanished and a bearded man sitting next to the driver snarled, "Well?"

"It's done."

The man's capped teeth flashed as he coughs. "*Da,* that is good."

As the partition slid back into place, the two pros were aware of the man's unearthly smile. Plagued by feelings of foreboding, they began planning for the worst. Their fate, however, had already been sealed.

Coping with the two hellions in the hotel during the day had worn out Jake's mother and she'd needed more time to get ready. As they waited for the elevator, Jake heard the wail of sirens. "Must be a big fire somewhere."

The hour between eight and nine was a busy time and their elevator made four stops before reaching the mezzanine. When the doors opened, Jake came face-to-face with Sergeant Maggio. Surprised, he asked, "What's going on?"

Maggio's response ducked the question. "Lieutenant, would you and Mrs. Garboosian please follow me."

The young patrolman stationed in the hall unlocked the Franklin Room but deliberately avoided any eye contact. Jake noticed and pressed Maggio. "Sergeant, for the last time, I want to know what in hell is going on." Then he remembered the sirens.

Maggio bought time by turning on lights and opening the curtains. She did not respond to Jake's query.

Sounds of the growing hubbub in the hallway outside the room filtered in and Jake saw that his mother was getting nervous. As he tried to reassure her, Sergeant Maggio turned away and keyed her radio. "They're here."

Jake heard her and asked, "Who's coming?"

"Lieutenant, Captain Tenhagen will be with us directly."

The Captain's ashen face told Jake that something dire had happened. "Jake, Mrs. Garboosian, I have some dreadful news. Four adult guests and two children were shot in the room reserved for your party. Four people from the hotel's staff were also in the room. There were no survivors. I'm terribly sorry."

Mrs. Garboosian pressed her face into Jake's pounding chest and he felt her frail body shudder. She looked up. "Sonny, the boys?"

Tenhagen shook his head.

Without warning, Mrs. Garboosian's body went limp. Maggio keyed her radio. "This is Maggio. I'm with the Captain in the Franklin Room, mezzanine floor. I need an EMT team and a doctor, stat! Look for me in the hall."

Paramedics gave Mrs. Garboosian oxygen and minutes later, a physician injected a mild tranquilizer. Later, at the hospital, her blood pressure skyrocketed. Alarmed, her doctor wrote orders for complete sedation.

With Jake unavailable, Captain Tenhagen took charge. During his years as a homicide detective, he'd seen hundreds of crime scenes, but none as macabre as the one he was now studying. Tenhagen could see the twisted bodies strewn helter-skelter around the room, but his mind refused to acknowledge the madness. To avoid a complete shut down, it became numb.

In the funeral parlor hush, the mere sound of rubber gloves being snapped on drew sharp looks from those already in the room. Three high-velocity bullets had thrown Tommy, Liz's youngest, against the Christmas tree, knocking it to the floor. He'd landed in a grotesque position on top of the presents, his straw-blond hair and new clothes wet with blood. Taking a table cloth from a service cart, Tenhagen moved the child's body and covered him. *Screw procedure,* he said to himself.

The ice carving of the angel, like the rest of the room was splattered with blood and with the ice starting to melt, it looked like the angel was bleeding. The crime scene stirred something in Tenhagen and he remembered the premonition he'd had after his first meeting with Jake. He wondered if the Biltmore was the end or another omen of worse things to come, Kathryn's untimely death having been the first. Woofer's whimpering broke the spell. Tenhagen motioned to a detective. "Phil, the poor dog is scared to death. Take him up to Jake."

When Steve's brother, Robert Horn and his family arrived, Sergeant Maggio escorted them to Jake's suite where he'd been drinking straight bourbon. After the wave of emotion subsided, Jake turned to Maggio. "Thanks for the update on my mother. It was very thoughtful."

Maggio nodded, but didn't say anything to keep the conversation going. However, Steve's grief-stricken brother, Robert, needed to talk. "Do you know *anything* yet?"

Sergeant Maggio looked over at Jake who shook his head. "We have some ideas, but I can't provide any details."

Robert wasn't satisfied. "Ten people have been wiped off the face of the earth and Mrs. Garboosian's in the hospital. What on earth…"

Jake touched Robert's arm. "Let it go. Her hands are tied."

Jake's usually gruff voice was now a whisper and he looked so totally drained that Maggio was having serious qualms about interviewing him. She also noticed the tremor in the hand that was holding his drink. Conscious of the fact that he was so over-weight and stressed, she proceeded cautiously. "Lieutenant, if I read some names, would you verify them as your guests?"

Jake nodded.

From a scruffy notebook, she began: "Elizabeth and Steven Horn and their children, Thomas and Lawrence. Phyllis and Joseph Singleton."

"Detective, the list is correct."

Vacant eyes stared back at her and she knew that to continue would be unconscionable. "Let's finish this up tomorrow, Lieutenant."

Having spent most of the night in his mother's hospital room, Jake returned to the Biltmore for a quick shower and a change of clothes. Tenhagen and Peter Hyde caught him as he was getting ready to leave. As the FBI's point man for the FBI's Russian Organized Crime Task Force, Hyde was an enigma. An Englishman, with an aristocratic bearing, Hyde had spent most of his career working out of the Bureau's London office. His transfer to Providence mystified everyone in the department including Tenhagen. A black man with graying hair and a salt and pepper mustache, Hyde's formal manner usually stamped him as an administrator instead of the seasoned field operative that he was.

After the introductions, it was obvious that it was Hyde's show. He flashed a straight-away smile and an unhurried voice said, "Jake, please accept my condolences and that of the Bureau. This is hellish matter, simply hellish. It must be a terrible strain for you."

"Thanks, Peter. I'm glad you're here, but I can't figure out why."

"I'm here because Russian Organized Crime, ROC, wants to expand into New England. Yesterday's…"

Tenhagen puts a hand on the agent's arm. "Peter, as you know, the Voccios have controlled the territory for as long as anyone can remember. Others have tried and failed. It doesn't make sense."

After fumbling with the combination lock on a new aluminum briefcase, Hyde finally got it open and handed out a memorandum. "This should shed some light on many of your questions, including the reason for my being stationed in Providence. For security purposes, some parts, including the list of recommendations have fallen victim to whiteout."

MEMORANDUM, FROM: (Deleted)

DATE: (Deleted)

SUBJECT: The expansion of Russian Organized Crime (ROC) into New England for the purposes of distributing illegal substances.

OVERVIEW: The Bureau is aware that ROC is planning to expand northward from their base in New York. Based on the factors outlined herein, it is my opinion that the ROC current boss, Valentine Petrovich, will conclude, as I have, that Rhode Island and Providence, in particular, represent the ideal stepping stones for entry into the vast New England market.

   Access and Transportation…Rhode Island has over thirty offshore islands with 400 miles of coastline dotted with hundreds of navigable inlets and harbors. Eight of New England's twelve Major Metropolitan Statistical Areas, MMSA's, are located within 75-miles of Providence. The state has two deep-water ports. One of them is located minutes from downtown Providence. The new $200 million state airport is predicted to boost passenger and freight traffic. The state is also sprinkled with small, out-of-the-way airfields which make ideal infiltration points. Amtrak service into Providence from Boston and New York is frequent and dependable.

Student Population... Providence is home to eight colleges and the largest student population for a given geographical area in the entire U.S. lies within a ninety minute drive from Providence's central core. In the Boston MMSA, just two schools, Harvard and MIT have a combined student enrollment that exceeds 30,000.

Opportunity for money laundering... The scope of ROC money laundering has increased dramatically in the last five years and banks in New York and New Jersey are under close scrutiny by the Federal Reserve. Rhode Island's financial institutions are not as closely supervised, and some of its banks are thinly capitalized. These attributes make the state's banks vulnerable, low-risk takeover targets for the cash-rich Russians.

In addition to his money laundering activities for the gangster-politicians who have and still continue to strip Russia of its productive assets, Petrovich is suspected of laundering monies for drug cartels located in: Columbia, Libya, Pakistan, Afghanistan, Syria, Iraq and Sudan. He is also suspected of having provided the bases used in several Arab terrorists attacks.

Improved coordination between the DEA, CIA and ourselves is needed if Petrovich's laundering activities are to be stopped.

Market control.... The New England market is currently under the control of Anthony Voccio, who succeeded his father, Tony Voccio. Over the years, the Latinos, Blacks and Asians have tried to penetrate Voccio's territory. None of these attempts have been successful. However, ROC has greater resources in terms of funding manpower and product accessibility than any of the groups referenced herein. Moreover, whenever they expand their criminal enterprises, Valentine Petrovich has shown that he can make shrewd business and tactical decisions. The ROC infiltration of New York and New

Jersey are prime examples of their superior ability to plan and execute.

RECOMMENDATIONS: (Deleted)

While the Captain and Jake absorbed the memo, Hyde steeled himself for the most difficult part of the meeting.

Tenhagen wanted to know where the Providence police stood in the scheme of things. "Thanks for sharing this information with us, Peter. Can I pass it along?"

"Of course, but only verbally. I'll take the memos back now. It's classified."

Hyde snapped his briefcase shut and leaned forward. "Jake, I regret that what I am about to say will only add to your unfortunate series of sorrows. Last night's target was Anthony Voccio, not your family and friends. He was hosting a celebration in a room adjacent to yours and there was a ghastly mix-up."

Jake's head snapped back as though struck by a blackjack.

Tenhagen intervened. "Peter, it would be best if you laid it all out."

"Certainly. A new busboy was given placards that slide into panels next to the entry doors of each meeting room. The lad speaks a fair amount of English but his reading ability is limited. Confused, he inserted the Voccio placard in your panel. It was a ghastly and lethal misstep."

Pressing both temples with his fingertips, Jake released a long, low moan, his mind churning. *It was a mistake. A stupid fucking mistake. Sheets of drywall and some sound board separated those that lived from those that died. What a crazy, fucked up world.*

Jake's voice was a raspy croak. "How do you know all this?"

"Mr. Voccio talked with me off the record. Tendered that he'd been approached by a New York attorney representing a Russian client."

Tenhagen's cell phone rang and he retired to a far corner of the room.

Jake was curious. "And what did this Russian client want?"

"A franchise to sell drugs in New England. Mr. Voccio told me he declined. No specific threats were made, mind you, but the message was clear. The Russians are coming North, regardless."

"From my years in Europe, I can tell you that the Russians have no qualms about killing entire families. Their ruthlessness has been the key to their success."

"What are the odds of finding the two shooters?"

"A European man and woman were found dead this morning in a coal bin at the gas company. Their Russian made weapons were left lying beside them, most likely as a message to the rest of the Voccio organization."

"And this Petrovich?"

"Not very good, I'm afraid. He's too well insulated."

Jake balled his thick fingers into a fist. He wanted to scream and throw a chair through a window or hit someone, but he didn't have the strength or the voice. "What more can you tell me about him?"

"Maybe we should wait for the Captain before I answer that. Petrovich was my nemesis before I came stateside. The account will take some time."

"He's on his third call. Keep going. I'll fill him in."

Tenhagen must have heard Jake, because he waved an O.K. to Hyde, who continued. "Petrovich has only been in the States five years, but he's already assembled an impressive criminal organization that surpasses anything the Bureau has seen before. The memo I showed you hints at what he's already accomplished in New York and New Jersey. As the security chief for the Russian Parliament in Moscow, Petrovich, like our Hoover, kept dossiers on its key members. When perestroika came along, those in charge were in the best positions to cash in, and they did. Over $200 billion was siphoned out of Russia in five years."

"No wonder they're on their ass."

"With his secret file of dossiers, Petrovich insinuated himself into that lucky group. He came away with about $700 million. Since his arrival in the States, he more than tripled that amount. His most lucrative income producer is drugs, followed by extortion and prostitution."

Hyde looked up at the ceiling. "Sorry, old boy, I must be a little dotty today. I failed to mention his favorite sideline; money laundering. Some of his legitimate enterprises, like his basketball team, have enormous cash flows and that puts him in an ideal position to launder funds."

"Why is this guy still on the street?"

"Petrovich's security and investigative background have served him well. During the last three years, thirty FBI agents scattered over New York and Jersey have tried to build a RICO case. Quite often, the drug merchants are also terrorists. Your CIA suspects that Petrovich is helping several terrorist groups in ways other than money laundering, Like I said, he keeps himself well insulated. To date, he's never been indicted."

A gold cigarette case appeared in Hyde's hand. "Do you mind if I partake?"

"Be my guest."

"One more thing, a lot of Petrovich's line of illicit drugs, like cocaine and morphine, are supplied by his Russian contacts. Criminals disguised as politicians and bureaucrats are now running Russia and Petrovich has positioned himself to profit from that deplorable situation."

"Being that Petrovich is over here, that's some trick."

"Not really. Petrovich kicks back some of his booty to his key Russian contacts. His largess also gives him a place to light, should the law get too close."

"A shrewd bastard."

"The man is a vicious, homicidal barbarian. Those that get in his way pay the ultimate price. No exceptions."

Tenhagen was still holding his cell phone when he stared down at Jake, his eyes moist. "Jake, it's so unfair, but your poor mother passed away a few minutes ago."

It was too much to bear. Profuse beads of perspiration appeared on Jake's forehead and his face took on the countenance of a cadaver. Sitting there on the velour-covered love seat, he was dazed and uncertain as to what was going on inside him. They're all dead. Kathryn, her sister, Liz, Steve, the boys, and now his mother. Realizing that he would never hear their voices again, the scourge of eternal aloneness began to invade every molecule in his body. Death did not frighten him in his mind; there was nothing left for him anyway.

A searing pain followed by chest crushing pressure forced Jake over on his side. He heard excited voices in the distance and could make out the shapes that seemed to be moving to encircle him. He was on an express elevator that was making hurtful unscheduled stops. Each stop hurt worse than the one before and he wondered if he should ring the emergency bell. His instincts for self-preservation begged him to call out, but he was already too weak to move his lips. In his mind, he welcomed the end. *I wonder, do fat boys, like me, get in? If Kathryn's around, that could be embarrassing. How fortunate I was to find my Kathryn and how easy it was to lose her. Fat chance a tub like me will survive whatever it is that's out to get me. Kathryn, did you catch my play on words? Outstanding. This shouldn't take too long and then I'll be on my way. Liposuction, I should have tried liposuction.*

In postponing her interview, Sergeant Maggio had made the right call. Lieutenant Jake Garboosian was having a heart attack.

5

Concerned for Jake's welfare, Tenhagen had Detective Maggio visit him once a week. This was her sixth visit. He'd been lucky. His heart attack had left him unfit for duty. It was warm for early March; 60 degrees. Though she could see darkening clouds gathering in the near distance, a friendly sun felt good on Maggio's face as she trudged up the long walk. There was no response to her repeated rings and she got frustrated. *The bell's working and his car is here. What's he doing? I hear music. Damn him, can't he hear me?* She tried the door and it opened into a small, square foyer. The long, narrow living room ran from front to back and from the foyer, she could see Jake in the backyard.

Watching him through the open French doors, she was totally mystified. He was sitting, unmoving, listening to an old instrumental version of *Sentimental Journey*. As the song ended, he reached over and played it twice more, finally turning it off. There was a childlike look of delight on his face when he saw it was starting to rain. Repeating the same tune was odd enough, but what he did next, made Maggio cringe and bring her hands to her face. Like a priest removing his mass robe, Jake slipped out of his raincoat and she saw that he was wearing a white linen suit. After folding the suit coat over the back of a wicker chair, he draped his tie around his neck, meticulously adjusting the ends so they were perfectly even at the bottom. Looking down and mumbling to himself, he left the shelter of the gazebo and stood out in the rain.

With arms outstretched and sunken eyes searching the heavens, he began to speak. Maggio knew he was a devout member of the Greek Orthodox Church and she wrongly assumed that he was asking for God's help. Soon he was kneeling on the wet ground and it didn't take long before ugly green grass stains began inching up his white linen trousers. In the distance, where the rain had turned to mist, a rainbow arched majestically between purple tinted clouds. Awed, Jake folded his arms tightly against his chest and with his head bowed, he began rocking back-and-forth to the song still playing in his head.

Cool rain ran down his face washing his eyes. Soaked from the soles of his white buck shoes to the finite ends of his long unkempt hair, a new purpose energized his body and he became aware that his mind was clear. No one knew it yet, but Detective Jake Garboosian had just made a life altering decision in an earnest, one-way conversation with his Maker. He raised his head slowly and saw that the rainbow was gone, replaced by a sunless, workaday sky. He smiled, got up and started walking toward the house.

Shaken, Maggio greeted him at the door and he noticed that her lipstick was smeared. "How ya doin, detective? Ya hungry?"

"I'm fine, Lieutenant." He was acting as though nothing had happened and she looked at him in wonder. "And yes, I'm starved."

"I could go for a steak. How's Manny's sound?"

"Sounds good."

"Give me ten minutes."

Dripping water and with his shoes making loud squishing sounds, Jake bounded up the stairs, unaware of Maggio's questioning stare.

Manny's was crowded, but Maggio's badge got them a quiet booth. Over coffee, Jake decided to clear the air. "I must have looked very strange to you out there?"

"It was somewhat unsettling."

"Overcoming my anger has not been easy. Whatya saw was the end of a long struggle."

"It was some ending."

"Yeah, I know. Didya see the rainbow?"

"Yes, it was beautiful."

"Yeah, I got carried away."

"I think it worked." Maggio smiles.

Raising his bushy eye brows, Jake announced, "I'm going back to work next week."

"That's good news. We've all missed you."

Disarmed by Jake's sincerity and apparent normality, Maggio let the incident slide from her memory.

Back on the job, Jake seemed like his old fat self. However, over the next five months, he managed to lose forty pounds. No one noticed because he concealed the weight loss by wearing a back brace that had been padded by an upholstery shop. Doses of prednisone, taken twice daily kept his face puffy. Jake also acquired, illegally, a number of choice weapons from the crime scene of a murdered gun dealer. Officers had searched the dealer's house and had found a dozen revolvers. Experience told Jake that a dealer living in such an impressive home wasn't running a nickle and dime business. He also knew they liked to keep their inventory close at hand.

It was the beautiful hard wood flooring that made the house, and it looked fairly new. Skimming through the dealer's checkbook, Jake found the store where the flooring was purchased. The pony-tailed installer was hunched down on knee pads fitting short oak planks into long dark strips of flooring. "I need a minute. Police business."

Struggling to his feet, the installer popped some M&M's into his mouth and lumbered over. "You put in a floor for a guy named Mason?"

"Yeah, Ronnie Mason, a real jewel."

"How so?"

"There was a big extra on that job and the bum wanted me and the store to eat it."

"What kind of extra?"

"He wanted a hidden floor panel and, detective, I shit you not, that kind of work takes time."

"How big, and how do I find it?"

The installer waffled for the first time. "He finally paid the bill. You got a warrant?"

"You a *Law & Order* TV show fan?"

"Never miss."

"Ronnie Mason was murdered two days ago. His home's a crime scene. I don't need a warrant."

"Am I in any trouble?"

" No, just tell me how big and where."

"Three floor joists wide and eight feet long between the butcher block island and the kitchen sink.

"Thanks."

"Whatever he charged Mason, it wasn't enough," Jake muttered. "Ten men could search this place for a week and come up empty." There were over fifty choice weapons in the hidden cache and everything on Jake's list was there, including silencers. What's more, there were six pristine sets of identifications all with male names. Each set came with a blank driver's license, birth certificate and a Social Security card. Ronnie had expanded his business, and to Jake the I.D.'s were more valuable than the guns. Coming up with authentic documents took time and the right sources, which Jake didn't have.

The media frenzy following the Biltmore shooting had faded, but Providence's Renaissance City billing was left badly tarnished. However, despite the department's strained relationship with the press, everyone, including Jake, had agreed with a local newspaper editorial:

It is ironic that madness and mayhem should shatter the spirit of our city's Christmas Eve. Yesterday, for no apparent reason, eight adults and two children were murdered in our city. For most of us, murder is an abstraction dealt with by others who are paid to do so. However, such a vile act transcends our first line of defense, the police, and speaks to us instead as a community.

For the officers who worked the poignant crime scene, Christmas Eve will never be the same again. For the rest of us, left reeling by the savagery of the crime, we should not rest until those responsible are apprehended and punished. A chaotic world filled with violence and death has turned our hearts and minds to stone. It is easier for us to cope that way. Winter has just begun. We can hide in our warm burrows and do nothing, or we can find the courage to seek out and purge the predators that lay waiting in our midst. Let us act!

Struck by the last two lines, Jake saved the piece and read it often. Knowing that it was hastiness that got most killers caught, he painstakingly re-examined his plan until every imaginable contingency he could think of was covered. On the Fourth of July, two years after Kathryn's death, Jake Garboosian looked into his shaving mirror and said out loud, "You fat bastard, it's time to make things right."

6

Tidying up his affairs didn't take long. A neighbor bought Jake's blue five-year-old Ford and a Goodwill van hauled away a load of personal possessions. What was left fit in the luxury sedan he'd rented from Avis. A solid buyer for his mother's house was already waiting in the wings.

Attorneys in Rhode Island could be notoriously slow in probating the estates they administer and it could take two years before an heir saw a penny. In Jake's case, Captain Tenhagen's persistent urgings resulted in the speedy distribution of assets. Including his mother's insurance, Jake inherited his mother's home and almost $400,000 in cash, stocks and bearer bonds. During the week following the settlement, he sold the stock and closed on the house. The lucky buyer was Sergeant Maggio who got a lovely home at a bargain price. Jake also put in a request for a week's vacation. Another detective agreed to switch weekend duty and Jake had nine consecutive days off.

July had brought a lot of hot sunny days and no rain. Unhappily for some, the weather made it a chore to find parking or blanket space at the Ocean State's public beaches. However, at Bailey's Beach Club, it was a different story. There, every member had an assigned parking space and the beach was pristine and never crowded. To the unschooled observer, Bailey's might not have looked exclusive, but membership there transcended acceptance at Newport's other prominent private clubs including the swanky Newport Country Club. Trim, tall and in his early fifties, Archibald Pope enjoyed three things: sailing his sloop, women and his wife's money.

Urbane and always on the prowl, Pope made adultery an art form. Bailey's was his happy hunting ground.

Unlike most of his law school classmates, Pope had shunned Wall Street and opened his own law office. Over the years, he had committed perjury, destroyed evidence and bribed witnesses, judges, assistant d.a.'s and other lawyers. Now he had but one client: Anthony Voccio, Senior. Archibald Pope & Associates, P.A. were Voccio's corporate representatives and at times they also handled some of his personal matters, like Junior's drunk driving charges. Another firm handled all of Voccio's legal skirmishes. Unscrupulous, resourceful and well connected, Pope could get done what other attorneys thought impossible. Kathryn Garboosian's case was a current example of how far he would go.

During the summer, Pope spent a lot of time on the show-stopping sloop his unloved wife had given him on their tenth anniversary. He could have kept the sailboat at the Newport Yacht Club but he persuaded his wife that the less expensive Wickford Marina had better ocean access. That, of course, was a lie; what he wanted was total anonymity and with his wife being so afraid of the water, he had the perfect set up for his on-the-water tryst.

Pulling into the marina, Pope was in good spirits. Phyllis Stewart was his shipmate for the weekend. On the telephone, she teased him saying she'd never been skinny-dipping. Stewart was forty-four, moneyed and divorced. At a Bailey's costume party, she had worn a bare-midriff blouse and a skimpy skirt. Working with a personal trainer and nutritionist/cook, she had a figure that made Pope's stomach tighten. Handcuffed to his blowsy wife, he had mixed and mingled while hatching a plot that would put him in close contact with his new target. It worked flawlessly.

Standing on the dock, Archibald Pope was caressed by a strong easterly wind. Using a hand to shield his eyes, he saw puffy white clouds sliding gracefully through an unbearable blue sky that seemed filled with promise and expectations. *A steady breeze and a winsome and cooperative first mate. Perfect.* Preferring to do everything himself, Pope used a dock cart to carry some provisions and personal gear to the end of the dock where the boat was tied. As he unloaded the cart, Pope's mind was full of the naughty things he was going to do with the fetching Ms. Stewart. Toting everything below decks, he opened the portholes and hatch in the main cabin and moved gingerly toward the Master stateroom. On the way, he almost bumped into Jake sitting amongst the charts at the navigation station, a long black gun in his hand. "What in hell. You're Jake Garboosian."

"Good memory."

Like a good lawyer, Pope tried to control the situation. "Aren't you in charge of homicide?" Bravado didn't work. "Why the gun?"

Jake pointed at a padded bench seat. "Sit down."

"Lieutenant, I have a friend due here within the hour. Let's call it a day and forget this ever happened."

"First we talk."

Funneled through a porthole, the sun glinted off Jake's gun sending flashes of light in all directions. Pope had only seen silencers on television, and the sinister appearance of the elongated barrel made him nervous. "Are you going to use that thing?"

"Only if you lie."

"How will you know if ..."

"I have an infallible shit-detector."

This time, Pope's voice was more of a distressed-filled plea. "What is it you want to know?"

"Who was bribed?"

Pope thought. *Even if this nitwit's got a recorder hidden somewhere, none of this is admissible.* He decided to play it straight. "The girl, the bus driver, Judge Patrella and the police lab director, John Howard."

"Your accident expert?"

"He received four times his usual fee."

"Who paid?"

"You already know."

"The name."

"My client, Anthony Voccio, Senior."

"Was it expensive?"

"Mr. Voccio has unlimited resources."

Muffled laughter and suggestive cries from a nearby boat prompted Jake to ask, "I see you brought some wine and fresh flowers." Pope had no idea that the flowers will be alive a lot longer than he would. "She a looker?"

The crisis deemed over, Pope relaxed. "Let's say she's well maintained."

"A cozy weekend on the water?"

"I'm still hopeful."

"Achoo! Bad allergies. Must be some mold in here," Jake mumbled.

While Jake fumbled in his pocket for a handkerchief, Pope thought,

I'm going to bury this asshole.

Blowing his nose into the handkerchief in his left hand, Jake took three quick steps and applied the finger-pressure required to fire a .22-caliber hollow-point bullet into the center of Archibald Pope's forehead. In the confined space, the shot made no more noise than a backed-up ship's toilet pump.

Jake dumped Pope's body in the storage space under the bench seat and got underway. Sails down, he motored for two hours to a mooring buoy in Bonnet Harbor. Before abandoning the sloop, he carefully spread a five-gallon can of gasoline around the boat's interior. Since Pope was to be away on a weekend sail, he wouldn't be missed until Monday. A brown paper bag held a simple ignition device lifted from the police property room. *Twenty-two hours should be about right,* he said to himself. Hanging on davits over the transom, the dinghy hid the boat's name, so Jake used the emergency inflatable. Bonnet Harbor was thick with moored boats, but the blazing sun had driven most of the sailors inside. Parched lips and the quickening of his heartbeat caused him to stop and catch his breath. Sitting with the oars dangling, Jake looked around, his haunted mind rife with guilt. He reflected on the cemetery where his family was interred and the guilt quickly dissipated. *Well, now I know how a killer feels. Even in your mind, you have no home. I'd better start carrying a folding chair.*

Instead of paddling to the marina dock, he made for a tiny, rock-strewn patch of beach several hundred yards away. Face covered with a floppy straw hat, he was just another weekend sailor heading ashore for supplies. Jake's fingers were stiff from rowing, but he managed to deflate the rubber boat and get it in the trunk of the rental car he'd parked there earlier. Later, the inflatable and paddles would be sitting at the bottom of a construction site dumpster.

7

Where other areas of Providence had disintegrated into slums, Federal Hill had bent a little and applied some fresh lipstick. The peaceful streets were lined with elms and oaks and all the lawns were healthy and neatly trimmed. But despite its tranquil character, Federal Hill was still the undisputed stronghold of organized crime in New England. Anthony Voccio, The Hill's most prominent resident, was the man in charge.

Voccio had purchased the four two-family homes next to his and had them bulldozed. In their place, he built a five-car garage, a three-room guest cottage and a swimming pool. Bordered by an imposing eight-foot high stone wall, the property had the look of an estate. The exterior walls of the Voccio garage were windowless and constructed out of granite blocks. Inside, the stone was covered with two layers of marine plywood sandwiched around sheets of 5/8 inch thick steel, stolen from the Quincy Naval Shipyard in Boston to thwart electronic surveillance. The end bay of the garage had been converted into an office and security outpost.

Lawmakers and lawbreakers, money men and celebrities of every stripe came to the garage and most of them couldn't wait to brag about it. Voccio held most of his important meetings in the rear seat of his Mercedes. His driver, a guy called Tux, always backed the Mercedes into the center bay and stayed behind the wheel, eyes peeled to the rear view mirror, the fingers of his right hand holding the butt of a cocked gun. Tux was a womanizer and had been married five times. When a *goombah* asked why he was always proposing, Tux had replied, "Because I can afford the rings,

Ralphie. Because I can afford the fucking rings."

Based on the murder of a Voccio associate, Peter Hyde had allowed Jake to read the Bureau's surveillance file on the big man. The file was heavy with entries but light on substance. However, one thing was clearly apparent. There was only one place where Voccio and his son were vulnerable. The last Friday night of every month, Junior and Senior spent several hours at Pajama's, a plush nightspot owned by a Voccio controlled corporation. The club's main attractions were its exclusivity and an endless supply of young, good-looking dancers.

Located in Westerly, overlooking the Pawcatuck River from the Rhode Island side, Pajama's was only thirty minutes from the busy Indian casinos in Connecticut. Over the years, the nightspot had become a magnet for the gamblers who preferred adult diversions over the family fare offered by the casinos. Jake had visited the busy club on two occasions and been impressed both times.

For starters, the place had a tastefully executed, art deco design. Moreover, a pile of cash had been spent on important details like flawless acoustics, professional lighting and quiet ventilation. The appointments were of high quality and the food was surprisingly good. Capable, well-trained male waiters provided five-star service and no one was going around pushing drinks. A stiff cover charge, outrageous prices and a strict dress code kept the riffraff out.

Seven hours after rowing ashore, Jake drove by the club. Only two cars were in the valet lot. After circling the block, he parked several streets away. It was dark, but the club wouldn't open for another two hours. From reading the Bureau file, Jake knew that the manager usually got there early on Fridays so he could "audition" new dancers.

Getting in was ridiculously easy. The rear door was unlocked, but Jake was sure it was left that way on purpose. Inside, he found all of the security cameras shut down. *Probably timed to go on when the place opens,* he mused. Standing outside the illumination from the exit light, Jake sorted out the voices filtering down from the office. Two girls and a man. *Lazy bastard probably left the door open for the girls whose voices he hears.* Satisfied that everything was kosher, he hid the can of gas and inched up the stairs.

Near the top, just before the landing, there was a window made of black, one-way glass. To be safe, Jake ducked anyway. On the landing, he heard a voice that was light, nervous and very young. "We've shown you everything."

A man laughed. "The bottoms."

"On the phone, you said topless only."

"On stage, not up here."

"Mr. Vince, you promised there wouldn't be any of this."

"Any of what?"

"You know what."

"Our dancers make big money."

"We'd have to put out."

"Make a lot or make a bundle. It's up to you."

Jake heard the girls whispering to each other as Vince tried a penalty close. "What's it gonna be girls? Mr. V and his son are due anytime. He sees you dance, you're golden."

You slimy pimp, thought Jake.

"How much can we make as *dancers?*"

"No sex, with those bodies, on a slow night, $600 a night minimum."

More whispers and then the same light voice, "That much?"

Yak, yak, yak. "All right."

"Turn around and drop your panties."

Shuffling.

"Good, nice and firm. Now bend over, grab your cheeks and squeeze."

Wearing a Halloween mask, Jake opened the door and pointed the silenced .22 at Vince. Mortified, the girls were standing there with their hands hanging down over their exposed parts. Vince's left hand moved toward a desk drawer and Jake barked, "Ya wanna die?"

The girls were trembling, too paralyzed by fear to scream. Jake nodded at the two piles on the floor. "Put your clothes on."

The banks for the club's three cash registers were on the desk and the safe was open. "Mr. Vince, put all that nice money into that trash can."

Vince didn't move. "What's the deal? Anthony Voccio owns this place."

"There's no deal. Mr. Voccio's making a gift to a scholarship fund."

"Fuck you."

The custom-made shirt, 75 dollar haircut and Armani suit coat draped around one of those wooden racks that rich men use while undressing is not what Jake expected. "I gotta say, you really know how to dress." The bullet made a nasty little hole in the wall behind Vince's head. "Now move it."

"You crazy bastard, you could have killed me."

"Five seconds."

Holding the can brimming with bills, Vince looked at Jake. "Now what?"

"Put it on the desk and wrap the safe money in that expensive coat of yours."

Vince hesitated. "There's over 40 grand of Voccio money in there. You got a death wish?"

"Five seconds."

Dressed, the girls looked like pom-pom girls who belonged to the best sorority on campus.

Jake growled, "You girls just stupid or is this some kind of lark?"

A light voice replied, "Tuition and dorm fees went way up. Our parents haven't got it."

"Girls, let me clue you in. This is a mob joint. In two weeks, Mr. Vince here would have you hooked on crack and turning 200 dollar tricks."

The other girl finally found her voice. "No way."

"No way, huh? Show them, Vince."

When the girls saw the hidden camera, tears came to their eyes. "You're already dead meat. He's got you on video."

"Oh my God!" the girls cried in unison.

"They tonight's dessert, Vince?"

No response.

"Last call, Vince."

"Ayah, what can I say, the boss likes fresh pussy."

Wide-eyed, the girls began to tremble.

"You girls got the picture now?"

Furious nods.

"Take the can and jacket there and split the money 50/50. *Tell absolutely no one, including your parents.* They'll want to get the police involved and when the slime balls that own this joint know your names, you're both dead. Got that, or are you still too dumb to know what you're into?"

More furious nods.

"Now are you both listening?"

Heads nod.

"Put the cash in safety deposit boxes. *Do not deposit it.* Tap the stash when you need it for school, not some dumb fucking ski trip. Remember, I know who you are and I'll get very pissed."

At the door, the girl hugging the basket to her chest turned and looked at Jake. "What about the video?"

"Trust me, it's history."

Her face told Jake there wouldn't be any 911 call.

"Go, and whatever you do, don't speed."

Since emptying the safe Vince had clammed up. That changed when the door slammed shut. "By the size of you, I figure you've got to be the biggest asshole I've ever run into."

"Yeah, I know."

"You just gave away Anthony Voccio's money."

"You told me."

"He's gonna fry my ass."

"No he won't."

Three silent but deadly bullets struck Vince in his chest so quickly his face didn't have a chance to register shock or surprise. Jake quickly reloaded the .22 and put a match to the raunchy video tape. Twenty minutes after dragging Vince's body into a half bath, he heard loud voices downstairs. Peering out the observation window, Jake saw Voccio, Senior, acting the host. "Make yourselves a drink and get comfortable. We'll be down in a couple of hours."

Voccio smiled at Junior. "Let's check out the new fluff."

Jake had already turned on the stereo, closed the safe and dumped the empty cash banks on top of Vince. When both Voccios were in the room, Jake stepped out of the lav. The silenced .22 made a series of dull phftt's and that was that. Looking down at the bodies, Jake thought of Kathryn and his entire body started to uncoil.

Senior had a roll of hundreds two inches thick. Junior's wallet was stuffed with fifties. Pocketing the money, Jake reloaded for the second time and swaggered down the stairs. With his shirt unbuttoned and sleeves rolled up, a lot of Jake's body hair was showing along with Junior's gold chains. A burly, rummy-faced man was behind the bar playing bartender. Tux sat two stools away, playing with the TV remote and sucking on a cigarette. "The fucking Sox game got rained out. Everything else is shit."

Seeing Jake in the bar mirror, Tux spun around. "Who the fuck *are* you?"

"The new bouncer. Mr. V. sent me down for some Dom Perignon."

Tux turned to the burly man. "Soldier, this guy could probably bounce a pair of fucking line-backers."

Jake chuckled. "I'd have to get in better shape."

Tux snapped back. "We look like servants to you?"

Nodding at the refrigerated case a few feet from Soldier, Jake replied docilely, "The champagne's in there. I've got an ice bucket upstairs."

Tux looked at Jake and then laughed. "Give the fat fuck a break. He's liable to sit on us."

As Soldier opened the refrigerator, Jake shot Tux twice in the face from three feet. Recognizing the telltale sound of a silencer, Soldier turned, grabbing for the gun at his side. He was late. Jake leaned over the bar and noted that the rummy faced man called Soldier had dirty fingernails and bad dandruff. He shot Soldier twice in the head. Needing to take a piss, Jake visited the club's sparkling clean men's room. Feeling relieved, Jake poured gasoline over the upholstered booths and the draperies used to baffle the walls. After tweaking the gas jets on the kitchen's broiler to a slow steady hiss, he walked to the rear door, stepped out and tossed a lit book of matches decorated with the Pajama's logo into a narrow trail of gasoline. There was an instant whoosh and he slammed the door shut. Standing next to his car, Jake looked up and addressed a clear sky bright with stars. *I couldn't let the scumbags slide.*

Intense heat generated by flames ten stories high melted the building and everything inside. Seven hours later, Pope's sailboat went up like it had been torpedoed. Coupled with the death of his notorious client, speculation about Pope's death brought an army of reporters to Newport and the governor was beside himself. The City of Providence had taken the Biltmore press hit. Now, the state was in the headlines.

Jake left the Avis rental in the airport's long term lot. He'd rented the car for ten days using his own name and credit card. From the airport, he took the Holiday Inn shuttle to the motel. A three-year-old RV purchased from a private party in Boston was parked in the rear. Jake paid cash and had registered the camper using one of the gun dealer's fake ID's. With a driver's license and social security card that said he was Hudley Hudson, the ex-detective started driving south.

Overnighting in campgrounds and paying cash for everything, the newly born Hudley Hudson left an ice cold trail. Four days after leaving the Marriot parking lot, Hud, as he liked to call himself, arrived in Key West. About that same time, Captain Tenhagen, visibly upset, was being greeted amicably by Peter Hyde. "Nice to see you again, Captain."

"Same here."

"I must say you don't look on top of the world."

"I'm not."

"Let's hear the worst of it."

"He's sold everything and disappeared."

"He certainly had sufficient provocation."

"Peter, I've got five dead men and a missing homicide detective."

"In London, our splendid tabloids would have described the deceased more accurately as gutter-scum."

"Perhaps, but we're in the media hot-seat and the governor wants answers, gutter-scum or not."

"Captain, you know that everything we do has political implications."

"You're not getting pressured?"

"Sure, but there's not going to be any public outrage. The press will get bored very quickly and move on. Your lieutenant is the real story. A cop gets revenge lead would sell a lot of papers."

"I know, but Jake rented a car for ten days using his own name. Suppose he's up in Maine fishing?"

"An intelligent man, your lieutenant, he has us both stymied for the moment."

"Peter, I realize that, but there's a long list of possibles. Voccio has always been a target and Pope was his man."

"Yes, the Biltmore incident certainly proves your point. However, suppose your bloke has gone bonkers and the judge, girl and that bus driver chap are on his list?"

Tenhagen looked up at the ceiling. "Damn. I can assign a team to the judge, but the other two are out of my jurisdiction."

"I can assist you on that score," said Hyde, swivelling back and forth in his chair. "Whoever did the deed freed up a lot of my manpower."

Tenhagen put his paws behind his neck to cradle it. "Anything from that wonderful lab of yours?"

"I'm afraid not. The fires and ocean currents left us nothing."

"Is that official?"

"Yes, it is. When is Jake's leave over?"

"In four days."

"There is one more thing. I hate to think of the lieutenant as a devious bugger, but I gave him access to our surveillance files on Mr. Voccio."

"I didn't know."

"Between us gentlemen, do you really expect Lieutenant Garboosian to reappear out of the mist?"

"Not after that disclosure."

"My sentiments also. You realize we'll have to list him *Wanted for Questioning.*"

"I know." Tenhagen's heartfelt sigh sounded like a death knell. "I'll keep you posted."

Tenhagen wasn't at all keen about pursuing Jake. Drugs made available by Voccio's organization had shattered hundreds of young lives in Providence, alone, and the captain had two girls in college. In his mind, Jake had done the world a valuable service. When Jake failed to show, an FBI notice tagged him as wanted for questioning in connection with the Providence homicides. The mug shot was the same one on his lieutenant's identification, but there was also a picture of Jake accepting an award from the Mayor of Providence. The notice went on to say that at 5' 10" and 275 pounds., Lieutenant Garboosian stood out in a crowd.

Knowing that it was his bulk that would get him caught, Jake stayed on his high-protein diet and lost another five-pounds. At 235 pounds and without the padded back brace, he was big, but not gargantuan. And having tapered off prednisone, the puffiness in his face was gradually receding. All that helped, but he needed to be unrecognizable. Getting caught was not in Hud Hudson's game plan.

Back in his own office, Captain Tenhagen leaned back and recalled the premonition he had when he hired Jake. A pragmatic man, he wondered if Jake's disappearance was the end or just the beginning. He opted for the former.

8

Key West is the southernmost city in the U.S., and as one might expect, Route One terminated there. Hud Hudson spent two days in Key West. Finding the town charming but a bit tacky and overcrowded, he got in the RV and headed back North. A large coffee and a couple of donuts later, he stopped for gas and a cold six-pack. The thermometer next to the pump registered a muggy 96 degrees. Inside the grungy convenience store, a handwritten card caught Hud's eye: *FOR SALE: Summerland Key. Canal Home and Commercial Fishing Boat. Owner retiring. Good terms. 336-4238.* Notice in hand, Hud approached the tattooed cashier. "Where's the pay phone?"

"Outside. I suppose you want quarters?"

Standing on sturdy concrete pilings well above the eight-foot mean high-water mark, the house was a showcase for neglect. But the canal in back was deep, crystal clear and teeming with edibles like snapper and lobster. Hud, undaunted by appearances, bought it, using the RV as part of the down payment. The seller was a spry, laconic seventy-year-old man with gnarled, arthritic fingers. He lived and fished with Hud and five weeks after the closing, he told his new apprentice, "You learn fast."

Most consider fishing a one-man boat hard work, but for Hud, it was a potent tonic. After a year on the water, he had shed more weight and was finally able to sleep through the night. At the end of the third year, he was still living in solitude, intent on avoiding any unnecessary activity that required human contact. Back in Providence, he was still wanted for questioning. Subtle overtures from the few women Hud met went unnoticed and the guys at the fish-house had stopped trying to fix him up. Weighing in at a lean 180, with his once puffy face deeply tanned and lined just short of gaunt, he was unrecognizable. For insurance, he kept a neatly trimmed mustache and wore dark Polaroid glasses. Woofer was the only link to his past. Unlike Hud, who got seasick when the ocean got rough, the pound dog was a born sailor who liked munching on his master's untouched lunches.

Now, Hud's daily routine was dictated by the time of year. During the summer and early fall months, he caught and sold lobster. The rest of the year he fished. When the weather was bad, he worked on his boat, repaired lobster traps and kept his modest home in shape. Hud had grown accustomed to a monastic lifestyle. He didn't have a single friend; the fish house workers were the only people he saw on a regular basis.

9

Summer in the Florida Keys could be hell. Shirt-soaking humidity and a relentless red sun tended to drive the long-time residents indoors where there was cold beer and air-conditioning. This phenomena was hard for visitors to understand, for on most days, the prevailing southeasterly ocean breeze kept the temperature in the high 80's and low 90's. With winds in the 5 to 15 miles per hour range, summer seas were usually calm, which for the chronically seasick like Hud was a blessing.

A steady drizzle cooled the air, but the lack of a moon was putting a damper on Hud's nightly walk with Woofer. Stepping into a pothole filled with rain water, Hud stumbled forward, cursing, "County can't even keep the damn streets repaired." Most of Summerland Key's residents were snowbirds who came down for the winter. Without street lights and only a smattering of homes occupied, the place seemed deserted and unfriendly.

Unlike the street where Hud lived, Flagship Drive was strictly high end. Walking past a stuccoed pink house with white hurricane shutters covering all the windows and looking unoccupied, Hud heard the faint, muffled sounds of what seemed to him a woman trying to scream. At the same time, Woofer stopped, cocking his head. "Think we oughta check that out, boy?" Moving a little farther down the road where he could see the south side, Hud noticed a thin strip of light bleeding through one of the shutters that covered a ground floor window. Someone had planted the queen palms too close together. Their long, broad leaves were flailing each other in the stiff wind, making bull whip sounds that frightened Woofer, who followed along in his master's footsteps. The light source was at the rear of the house. Halfway there, Hud had some serious second thoughts. *Suppose this was some kind of husband and wife thing. Snooping around like this could get my dumb ass shot.* Woofer sensed something was wrong when his master froze in place. Peering through the crack in the shutters, Hud saw a woman sitting in a wooden lawn chair. A yellow blanket covered her from head to toe and her face was hidden.

Even with their cancerous tans and expensive clothing, Hud pegged both men as repeat offenders. The tallest and raunchiest of the men ripped the blanket away. "Justo, what you think?"

Feeling the bile rising in his throat, Hud forced himself to stay calm. The woman under the blanket resembled those French women he'd seen in television documentaries who'd been punished by the Resistance during WWII for collaborating with the German officer class. The woman's hands were tied behind her and she was bald. Horrible red welts, burns and bruises covered her entire body. Even in the poor light, Hud could make out the scabby razor cuts on her scalp. As she tried to twist away from the man's touch, Hud saw bruised breasts and damaged nipples. A glitzy shopping bag from Sak's sat next to her with a rattan purse sticking out on top. The blanket and shopping bag suggested to Hud that she'd been abused somewhere else.

A bald, thickset man sidled over to the woman and Hud noticed the gun tucked into his belt. "Carlo, better you start warming up the engines. He'll be down any minute."

Shifting his gaze up toward the ceiling, the taller man squinted, "What's the Russian asshole doin?"

Justo shook his head in frustration. "Carlo, no leave empty-handed. Take a couple of bags with you."

Cursing under his breath, Hud watched Carlo trudge out the door, a duffle bag in each hand.

Justo lit a cigar, doffed his shirt and began dragging the remaining duffel bags one by one to the door. He was putting his shirt back on when a third man appeared. He was flat-faced, and unlike the Cuban's, his body had not seen much sun.

"Where's Carlo?"

"Warming the engines."

"Justo, some advice. Don't push it and get stopped."

Justo's eyes narrow. "Why you always bust my balls. I've made this same trip thirty times."

"*Da*, I know, but the coast guard have stepped up patrols."

A broad smile, "I already have the new routes. I'm taking the long way around."

"*Da*, how long?"

"Three days over, two days back."

"*Da*, good. I tell Mr. Petrovich. When you leave?"

"Thirty minutes or so."

Hud thought, *A Russian and two Cubans. They're moving some money offshore, but what about the woman?*

"*Da*, one last thing."

"What's that?"

"The woman?"

"She must die. Mr. Petrovich orders."

"No problem."

Justo's response is found wanting. "What mean no problem?"

"Hammerheads."

From the look on his face, Hud knew flat-face was still confused. "Hammerhead sharks." Justo started drawing pictures in the air with his hands. "I'll cut her a few times and troll her behind the boat. Hammers are eating machines. When they finish, the only thing left will be table scraps and the crabs will munch on those."

"*Da*, Mr. Petrovich will appreciate."

The garage door opened and the sound of tires crunching pea-rock reached Hud's ears. Revulsion and rage washed over him and he thought, *These are some sick bastards. But Petrovich, I can't believe our lives have crossed paths again. First my wife, now this poor woman. He's got to go.*

Holding the woman firmly by the chin, Justo pulled her up. "You'll like the Dry Tortugas. That's where the hammers hang out."

"Nooo," she wailed.

The haunting quality of her outcry caused Hud to wince.

The woman's eyes traveled down to the blanket and bag. Justo laughed, "You won't need those shark bait. Let's go."

Nudged along, she walked unsteadily toward the open door. Hud noted that even with bare feet, the woman towered over the Cuban. Moments later, the downpour hit the woman's raw welts and a frightful scream sliced through the night.

Controlling his fury, Hud took inventory while rapidly scrolling through his options. Unfortunately, the only doable choice could undo his new identity. Knowing that one of the men would probably remain on the boat with the woman, Hud went around to the back and slipped inside the storage room. Someone with a passion for neatness had put up racks with vise-like clips to hold all the fishing tackle and garden tools. Wiping the rain water from his eyes, Hud lifted a black, lead filled fish-bill from its clip. Satisfied with the makeshift weapon, he moved toward the duffel bags.

The hefty duffels were like the kind that servicemen used when traveling from base to base. Hud opened one and saw tightly bound packets of new hundred dollar bills. Clutching the billy, he waited just inside the door. A few minutes later, Justo returned, whistling a popular Salsa tune. Fueled by pent up rage, the murderous blow descended like a sledgehammer squashing Justo's skull, driving slivers of bone into his brain. Blood seeped like heavy winter oil from the Cuban's ears and mouth onto a terry cloth beach towel. Knowing it was too close to home to leave evidence of a crime scene, Hud had planned ahead.

Wearing Justo's baggy silk shirt and carrying a duffel bag in each hand, Hud stepped outside. He checked on Woofer who was cuddled under a flowering hibiscus bush with his head resting on his front paws. "Stay boy. You stay."

Hud dropped the bags alongside the boat under a covered fish cleaning station. The curtains in the main cabin were drawn, but the shadows of life were missing. Hud slipped onboard. The teak deck was slippery, but the steady patter of the rain helped muffle the noise of his approach. From the side plate, he identified the boat as a 58-foot Bertram.

Lying on her stomach, hands still tied behind her back, the captive was being tormented by Carlo who was sitting next to her on the bed in the master stateroom. His long, bony fingers were probing between her legs as his cracked lips grunted, "You like?"

Focused wholly on the woman, Carlo never discovered death approaching. Angling the gun toward the ceiling only inches from the Cuban's head, Hud squeezed. As Carlo tottered like a cut timber, Hud grabbed him by his bloody collar and pulled him out of the woman's sight. Helping the woman sit up, Hud covered her trembling body with a blanket. "You're safe. They're both dead."

Blank, condemned eyes flickered back at him with understanding.

"I need your help."

No response.

Hud tried again. "We gotta take this boat out."

Swaying back and forth very slightly, she nodded.

He laid her back down. "Good. Rest, I'll be back in ten."

In a corner of the storage space, Hud found a wheelbarrow and an old beach umbrella. He stripped the canvas from the umbrella and used it to wrap Justo's body. To keep it dry, the Sak's bag with the woman's purse went into a black trash bag. Surveying the storage room with the painstaking thoroughness of an ex-detective, Hud turned off the lights, locked the door and backed out into the rain. No lights, no cars, no voices, only the steady beat of the waves against the dock. Woofer straggled out from under the hibiscus looking scared. Squatting down, Hud rubbed the dog's floppy ears until he settled down. "Scoot, go on home. Hear me, ya get on home. That'ta boy, Woofer. Good dog."

Storing Justo's canvas wrapped body and the wheelbarrow in the main cabin, Hud returned to find the woman wheezing and struggling to breathe. "Asthma?"

She nodded.

"You have medication?"

Another nod.

He tore open the plastic bag and found an inhaler and a plastic container full of different colored pills. After two puffs from the inhaler, the swelling in her airways began to shrink and her breathing improved. Opening the container, she swallowed two pills.

"How bout some hot bullion? There's some in the galley."

She nodded.

"Good, I'll brew some after I find you some clothes."

A short time later, they were sipping soup from steaming mugs. She had yet to speak and only moved to lift the cup to her lips. She avoided eye contact, but Hud had the feeling he was being sized up. *Can't blame her after what she's already been through. Millions onboard and she's going with a stranger who just killed two men. It's a wonder she hasn't lost it completely.* He checked his watch. It was a few minutes past midnight. Daylight would be on them in six hours. They had to get going.

"There's no moon and it's a narrow channel. I need you to light up the markers. We can't afford to run aground. Are you up to it?"

The resolve on her face told Hud she was capable of helping.

"I found some rain gear." Vacant eyes stared back. "Here, put these on."

"When we get deep enough, I'm going to sink this baby. We'll take the

Whaler back to my place."

Having withdrawn into silent observation, she concluded that Hud was no stranger to violence, that she had no choice but to go along with his plan, and that because of the dead Cubans, their lives were inextricably linked. "Tell me what to do." It's the first time she'd spoken, and her voice was absent of all emotion.

Before disconnecting the shore power, Hud checked the Boston Whaler. The outboard motor looked new and Hud wasn't surprised when the battery and fuel gauges registered in the green. On the bridge, Hud kicked the engines over one at a time and was comforted by their steady purr. One of the boat's three VHF radios was already tuned to the coast guard frequency, so he dialed up the weather on another set.

They threaded their way through the channel at a steady ten knots. Shifting her weight to match the rhythm of the boat, the woman moved the spotlight from marker to marker, lighting each one up like a giant glowworm. Hud clicked off the spotlight as the yacht knifed into open water.

"Nice job."

She released her death grip on the rail and brushed by him. "Some more bullion?" she asked.

"Yeah, thanks."

The rain and clouds had moved on and the inky blackness had been replaced with stars and a narrow moon. A shaking hand held out a steaming cup.

"How deep are we?" she asked.

Hud glanced at the depth finder; "210 feet."

"Why are all the lights on?"

"If the coast guard's around, they'll see us on their radar. Running dark would only make them curious."

There was a new awareness about her and Hud was certain the questions hadn't come from curiosity. She didn't trust him.

Noting that they were making 20 knots without getting pounded to death, Hud was torn by the vision of having to sink such a solid and expensive yacht. "Ya know how to maintain a course?"

"My daddy taught me how to keep a compass heading."

Hud stepped back from the helm, "Keep'er due south on 180."

Afraid to take anything for granted, he hung around and watched for a few minutes. She never wandered more than two degrees off course.

Down below, Hud ransacked the boat looking for items they might need. When he finished foraging, his cache included: bottled water, binoculars, flashlights and a hand–held GPS. The Cubans contributed two wads of bills which he put in his pocket for travel money. Leaving their heavy gold chains, rings and expensive watches, he secured the master stateroom door. After locking shut and anchoring down everything else that he could, he tied the door knob of the main cabin to the deck rail. *That should prevent anything from getting out.* Anything loose topside was put into deck boxes. Storing the duffles and his cache in the Whaler, Hud made his way to the bridge. They were still on course and approaching 300 feet.

As the wind slackened, the air became warm and clammy. Turning the helm over to Hud, the woman removed her rain gear and he noticed that she was a good three inches taller than his 5' 10." Pressing her hands together in prayer, she stared at him with moist eyes. "I was brought up right. I'm a good person." To Hud, the gratitude in her voice conveyed more than her words. *She wants me to know that she's worthy of being saved.*

They were standing within arms length when Hud asked, "What's your name?"

"Jilly."

He was about to respond when the yacht rolled. Reaching for the grab bar over the radar, Hud observed a contact on the scope. "There's a boat out there about forty miles out and she's headed our way."

She watched him intently as he marked the radar screen with a grease pencil. A long ten minutes went by before he spoke again. "They're closing fast. We gotta sink her now."

When Hud opened the seacocks, thick streams of salt water rushed into the engine compartment. Returning to the bridge, he told Jilly, "Go below and get ya personal stuff together."

With the engines turned off, the yacht drifted with the tide and the prevailing breeze. The fathometer read 325 feet, not deep enough to insure the boat wouldn't be found or, even worse, recovered.

When they finally pushed off in the Whaler, running lights could be seen on the horizon. Hud turned the small boat toward land and moved the throttle forward. "Stand up, flex your knees and hold on tight. We're going to get bounced around."

Sometime later, with the cloak of darkness almost gone, they spotted the channel markers.

Out at sea, the crew of the coast guard cutter, *Dauntless,* scrutinized the wallowing Bertram as saltwater streamed off its main deck. It was too late to save the yacht, but they were able to attach a line that played out as the boat headed toward the sea floor. Minutes later, the radar mast slipped peacefully underwater. After the yacht hit bottom, a radar reflector was attached to the line and thrown overboard. It marked the yacht's exact location. When nothing floated to the surface, the captain of the coast guard cutter faxed a cryptic message to headquarters in Key West: *A Bertram, estimated length, 60', has gone down in 325 feet of water. Transom markings covered by sea water. No visible sign of life on board prior to sinking. Attached radar reflector and recorded GPS and Loran coordinates. Circumstances highly suspect as another boat left the scene at a high rate of speed. No debris recovered which is highly suspect. Recommend salvage by navy reclamation vessel.*

After unloading the Whaler, they sat in Hud's compact kitchen, the last ounces of energy gone. Staring out at the peaceful canal scene, Jilly inquired, "What now?"

"Depends on how fast the yacht went down."

"Why would that make a difference?"

"If they find the bodies, we got problems. Petrovich will send people looking for ya."

"Maybe we should call the police?"

Hud knew she was not thinking lucidly. "This Petrovich guy is out one very pricey yacht, two men and a lot of cash. Going to the police just tells him where you're at."

Poker-faced, Jilly just glared at him.

"Another thing, with the bodies and amount of cash involved, you never know what a local sheriff's gonna do. They refloat the Bertram, we've gotta disappear."

"When will we know?"

"Not before mornin."

"We're both beat. Let's yak in the morning. Take my room. There's fresh towels under the sink and the sheets were put on yesterday. The door has a dead bolt. Lock it."

Physically exhausted, Jilly collapsed into bed. Even with the door bolted and a chair under the doorknob, she still felt unsafe, but it wasn't her physical safety that concerned her. He was too quick with the right questions and answers on what to do, how to do it and when to do it. *If he wasn't so gentlemanly and I hadn't seen his fishing boat, I'd swear the man had been a criminal.* Hurting and with her energy depleted, she buried her face in a pillow and began to sob.

The sun had just broken loose over the horizon when Hud got up. After spending the night in his recliner, he fumbled around like a drunk who had attended midnight mass and it took a quick dip in the canal and a cold shower to clear his head.

Starving, he knocked on Jilly's door. "Ya hungry?"

A faint "yes" found its way through the solid core of the door.

"Half-hour okay?"

"Fine."

Jilly looked at herself in the bathroom mirror and comprehended a pale, haggard wreck wearing borrowed clothes. Locking the bathroom door, she did the last thing she wanted to do: turn on the shower. The force of the water on the swollen welts was so painful, she almost cried out. But it was her bald head that brought forth the tears.

The chair slid out from under the doorknob, the door squeaked and Jilly emerged wearing an old baseball cap and some of Hud's old fishing clothes. Her eyes were bloodshot while her lips were almost white.

"Ya like ham and eggs?"

"Just eggs."

Jilly ate staring down at her plate. Not wanting to force conversation on her, Hud finished his second cup of coffee and removed some papers from a waterproof bag. "The Whaler's never been registered. If I remove the console and rip out the deck, we got a wagon to haul our stuff. All we need is a boat trailer."

Although she tried hard to hide it, a wave of mistrust washed over her. "Are you sure we have to leave?"

"That was the coast guard last night. They got to the yacht too late to board, but they marked her. The navy's sending a salvage ship to bring her up."

"How do you know all this?"

"Radio."

"How long will it take?"

"Five or six days. The salvage ship is based in Charleston. It'll take awhile just to get here."

Hud rubbed his jaw. "So far, nobody around here seen ya." He opened the blinds and sunlight poured into the kitchen. "We gotta keep it that way till we leave."

"You got a place in mind?"

"Yeah, Block Island. First, let's talk about the cash."

Jilly thought, *Here it comes.* "What about the money?"

"There's six duffel bags with a million bucks or so in each one. We can split the money 50/50 right now and go our separate ways, or we can stay together and improve our odds of getting away clean. The choice is yours. You decide to go it alone, you can take my truck."

Surprised, Jilly gaped at him, not knowing what to say.

"I've killed. You're still in the clear. I wouldn't fault ya for bailing out."

Not only was he being up front about the money, he'd selected a place that, given their present situation, seemed practical. When she finally replied, the distrust in Jilly's voice was not as strong. "Block Island makes sense, and I'm for staying together."

"All right, then I should visit your place tonight. Where daya live?"

"Kendall."

"Hell, there and back, five hours."

"I'd like my things, but what's the rush?"

"Address books, photo albums and just about anything printed left behind makes it easier for them to find you. They'll get into ya place and they won't need a key."

"But, why today?"

"Cause tonight I can get a van."

Since it rained almost every day on the Florida mainland, Hud borrowed the fish house van for the trip. It took him three hours to go through Jilly's place. When he finished, even the waste baskets and the notes on the refrigerator were gone. There were no shorts or t-shirts in the clothing that he brought back. Everything was long to cover her welts and bruises. Shoes, sneakers, jewelry, scarfs and a big bag of personal items like her hair dryer, also made the trip back to Summerland. She was sitting in the living room when he walked in. "Things go all right?"

"Yeah, real good. Help me unload. I gotta return the van."

10

The next day, Hud worked in the open space under the house, dismantling the outboard motor and getting rid of the parts. Hud's pickup and some neatly stacked lobster traps piled out front hid his activity. By removing the center console, bow railings, bimini top and dive-ladder and adding a streaky coat of dull green paint, the brand-new Whaler became a boat no one would want to steal.

A notice on the wall at the fish house brought a buyer for Hud's commercial boat which he'd priced to sell quickly. Pleased that the fisherman hadn't haggled, Hud gave him his bait freezer and spare equipment. The retired couple next door had escaped to Michigan for the summer and the nearest occupied home was five lots away, so it wasn't difficult for Jilly to remain out of sight. It was impossible to deposit that much cash, so they packed it in six oversized Igloo coolers which fit nicely into the space once occupied by the Whaler's fuel tank and bilge. Deciding that they couldn't park the boat at a motel and leave the money in place, they opted to remove the coolers every night. A removable plywood panel in the deck made the task easy enough and a waterproof boat protected everything else they stowed in the boat. Hud wrapped all the weapons taken from the Providence gun dealer in oil soaked cloths and put them into several waterproof bags. The weapons, along with the fake identification kits, were stored alongside the coolers.

Their last day in Summerland Key was frantic. A fish house worker helped Hud put up the aluminum hurricane shutters. Last minute bills, phone, electric, water and a long list of other things, like remembering to shut off the air conditioning were handled, but it took them all day and most of the evening and at the end, they were both whipped.

It was midnight when they pulled out of the driveway. Common sense told Hud that returning was a big maybe. Once they were in the clear, he'd sell the place. Listing it now would be like putting out a we were here sign.

Watching the roadside mile-markers rush by, Jilly engaged in an ongoing debate with herself. *Was it a whim of fate or her prayers that had guided Hud to that godforsaken storage room? Would they part friends or enemies? Should she take her half of the money and run?*

Hud kept his eyes glued to the road and tried to block out all thoughts of what he was leaving behind. Minutes before leaving, a local radio station reported that the navy would have the yacht afloat by late afternoon the next day. Hud wondered if Jilly realized how dangerous life had just become.

At night, the journey out of the Florida Keys could be hairy. There were no street lights on Route One and even with high beams, the narrow causeways appeared more like paved footpaths. Most of the route on the Keys ran down the middle of a threadlike strip of land straddled by the Gulf of Mexico and Atlantic Ocean. Late at night, without a moon or traffic to light up the road, the 150-mile trip could be a white knuckler. Adjusting to the eerie conditions and wrapped in their own private emotions, neither spoke a word until they were across the infamous Seven Mile Bridge about forty-five intense minutes from Summerland Key. At least once a month, the bridge played host to a head-on that resulted in fatalities.

"Ya all right?" he asked.

"I'm fine."

Withdrawing into their private worlds, no one spoke again until they stopped six hours later in Vero Beach. Bushed, Hud pointed to a Holiday Inn sign. "Long day."

Jilly knew what Hud had to be thinking. In Summerland she had slept alone in his room. He handed her a few of the fifty dollar bills taken from the Cubans. "See what you can do."

Jilly got out without a word and walked into the lobby. She was back in minutes. "First floor in back where there's no street noise."

While he unloaded the coolers and weapons, Hud thought, *Poor girl's still a basket case, she doesn't need me in a bed next to her.* To reassure her, he put half of the coolers in Jilly's room and gave her the keys to the pickup. By the time Jilly had showered, Hud was fast asleep, sprawled across the top of the bedspread in his clothes.

Most of the motels they stopped at had a continental breakfast which usually included cold cereal and fruit. Lunch came from the supermarket: yogurt, nuts, juices, made-to-order sandwiches, bottled water and for Jilly, lots of fruit. For dinner, they sought out restaurants where they could park and still see the boat. Overall, they ate very sparingly and indulged Woofer, who had the king cab's back seat to himself. They paid cash for everything. "No use leaving a credit card trail if we don't have to," Hud cautioned. At his urging, Jilly had destroyed her only credit card and was becoming fanatical about the outstanding balance. "My Visa balance needs to be paid. I've got to do *something*."

"You're dead, remember? Forget it."

"My credit will be ruined."

Hud pointed a finger over his shoulder at the boat. "Ya don't need credit."

Each day took them further away from the events in Summerland Key, but it did little to ease the tension. Hud knew that Jilly was still afraid and stricken by what she had suffered and, sensing that any physical contact, however innocent, might upset her, he stayed clear. Along the way, they stopped at a factory outlet. While Jilly shopped, Hud stayed with the truck. Several hours later, she returned and he noticed that she was wearing new topsiders, a peach colored t-shirt and a baseball cap that had *Paris* embroidered on the front. A pair of skin tight jeans covered Jilly's long, but still discolored legs. A gaggle of teenage boys passed her with ogling eyes and some looks over their shoulders. Hud got out of the truck and secured the bags under the boat canvas. "You look striking. Truly striking." The compliment agitated her and she didn't speak for the rest of the day.

Towing a boat with all that money onboard made the pair rather conservative and they kept the pickup's cruise control set at 58. There was no sense in attracting a state trooper or getting into an accident. To avoid heavy traffic, they usually left their motel around mid-morning and pulled in for the night by three-thirty in the afternoon. They'd been on the road for five days when the *Welcome to Rhode Island* sign greeted them at the bottom of a long hill. For the most part, it had been a difficult trip. Jilly's mood never improved and even the most innocent questions were answered cryptically or not at all. Her reluctance to engage in conversation had made the trip seem a lot longer than it really was.

With the boat in tow, they boarded the Block Island Ferry which charged by the number of axles. On the ride over, they sat outside above the parking deck watching the sun go down.

"Wasn't exactly a fun trip for you, was it Hud? Thanks for putting up with me. I'll try not to be such a bitch."

"Yeah, well, after what you must have gone through, you're entitled."

Her voice was only lukewarm, but Hud took that as an encouraging sign.

"Don't put pressure on yourself. Ya still have a long haul ahead of you."

There was a reproachful silence and Hud figured he'd put his foot in his mouth. It was not the case. She was blaming herself again for all that had happened and that was too big a number for her to handle right now. As for Hud, the pain he'd anticipated returning to the place where he and Kathryn had lived and loved and become one did not materialize. Kathryn would always and forever be with him in his mind and heart and neither distance nor time would matter.

11

Their cottage sat atop a long hill at the end of a dirt road and looked out across the water to the shingled town and the busy city dock. Most days after the morning fog had burnt off, they'd watch the body surfers in their neon-colored wetsuits swim out to catch the Atlantic's cold, gray-green rollers. With no street name and no mailbox, the place was perfect.

Finding a place had not been a slam dunk. Beebe, a vivacious realtor with reckless red hair and wearing enough jewelry on one person to stock a mall kiosk had given them the bad news. "Dears, this is peak season. Even the broom closets are rented and absolutely no one leases for more than three months at a time."

Hud wasn't daunted. "How about we buy something?"

Peering at them over the rim of her tortoiseshell glasses, she advised, "Oh my, not now. The only thing *remotely* worth the asking price is a fixer-upper and that's $1.2 million. And, darlings, come winter, you'd *positively* freeze to death. The place doesn't have a drop of insulation."

Jilly, who hadn't said a word, suddenly burst into tears.

They didn't know it yet, but Beebe, who was high energy, pushy and a tough negotiator was also a softy at heart. She eyed the pale, frail creature in front of her. "My dear, don't you cry another tear. Beebe will come up with something." Beebe *adored* everything and everybody and that outlook had cultivated a wide circle of close friendships. "What to do, what to do?" she said out loud. "Eureka!" Beebe's exuberant shout startled both of them. "Two of my dearest friends are summering in Europe and their vacation cottage is just sitting there gathering dust. They're in a high tax bracket and wouldn't be interested in renting. But, a couple to house sit and take care of the place might have some appeal. Are you able to provide a substantial security deposit?"

Hud didn't flinch. "Of course."

A few days after they'd moved in, Beebe dropped by with a bottle of excellent wine set in a basket of goodies. "I know you're going to *looove* this place," she gushed. After Beebe left, Hud remarked, "She's a hellava gal."

That same evening, the pair stacked the cash on Jilly's bed and started counting. Three hours and $5.4 million later, they finished.

The following week under the name, *The Island Real Estate Investment Trust*, they began the process of depositing their cash horde into savings accounts in thirty-two different banks in Rhode Island, Connecticut and Massachusetts. Hud knew that cash deposits over $10,000 made by individuals were reported to the IRS, so, all of their deposits were for $9,750. It took them four months to bank all the money. For use in emergencies, they kept $500,000 in a safety deposit box in a bank on the island. At Hud's insistence, half the money was in Hud's name, the other half in Jilly's. The local attorney who had done the trust work also drew up wills for each of them. Jilly's father got her share and the Horn family, Hud's.

The summer cottage was custom built and comfortably furnished. Once they were settled, they took long walks all over the island, careful to stay out of the main tourist areas. For fun, they turned the soil over in the dormant vegetable garden and planted whatever the local nursery said would grow. The activity had been good for Jilly to the point where she was more up than down.

Hud was encouraged by her progress. "Come November, we can hit town more often."

Jilly was a dreadful cook, so Hud, with his Greek flair in the kitchen, prepared most of their food. The meals were simple and consistently delicious. With all of their hiking about and Hud's high protein menus, Jilly's muscle tone and physical condition improved to the point where Hud had trouble keeping up with the pace she set. Several times she had readied herself to tell Hud about Valentine Petrovich. But, each time, she stopped short at the last minute.

With an endless supply of restorative sea air to breathe, Jilly considered

Block Island the perfect hideaway, except for one thing…the shock of cold weather. Arriving in mid-July, the pair had experienced three months of delightful weather. But a few weeks before Thanksgiving, a bitter cold front swept in overnight, bringing high winds and temperatures in the mid-thirties. Except for a few respites here and there, it stayed that way for most of the winter.

Beebe constantly popped up in their lives. Several months after they'd relocated, Beebe and a purple-haired lady sat down in a restaurant where Jilly and Hud were enjoying blue plate specials. Beebe waved and blew kisses to just about everyone in the room. It wasn't long before the evening took an intriguing turn. Neither Leno nor Letterman could have outdone the duo on their best night. Adores filled the air and their casual comments about their men friends and town officials had everyone within earshot smiling.

"Benny's simply the yummiest man with oodles and oodles of money. And, spend!"

"There's no question, Mimi will screw any man whose still able to drive."

"Harry hasn't gotten laid since the ice age."

"I wish she'd stop yapping about the damned windmills. Doesn't she ever bake or screw?"

"Bank on this. She's bad and wild. He's an out-and-out stiff. They'll never survive the honeymoon."

Except for a few marginally offensive jaw droppers, the banter found a receptive audience. There was only one problem; no one wanted to leave. Diners kept ordering desserts and more cocktails in order to keep their tables, and the *maitre d's* explanations for the long wait were no longer being accepted by people with reservations. The end came when Beebe got overly animated and let it be known just how much she adored a certain part of Benny's lower anatomy. She said it so clearly and with such dreamy fascination, that the entire place roared. "Lucky Benny," said Hud. "By lunch tomorrow, he'll need a social secretary to handle all the invitations." Jilly followed Beebe with her eyes as she left the room. In her mind, the woman was the most optimistic, keenly alive person she had ever met. *I was like that once*, she thought.

12

Spring had come unusually early to Block Island and it was going to be one of those days that made staying cooped-up indoors unthinkable. When Hud awoke, he saw Jilly sitting in the overstuffed chair where he did most of his reading. Her legs were folded under her and she was staring out the window. "Hud, do you realize that we've never touched, not even casually."

"Did I do wrong? I..."

Jilly put a finger to her lips. "Shhhh, before I lose my nerve. You've never even hinted, but I feel you love and care about me."

"Since Summerland. Jilly, I..."

She shushed Hud again. "After you hear my story, you may change your mind."

Hud shook his head.

"I grew up in the Nashville suburbs. After high school, I was hired by a local realtor. By that time, my too-tall frame had filled out and I had a lot of men on my trail."

"Were you a salesperson?"

"No, I ran the office, such as it was. There were only four salespeople. Anyway, about six months after I started, Mr. Saxon, the owner, showed me an article about a Miss Tall Nashville Contest. He urged me to enter and volunteered to pay my expenses. Said it would be good for business even if I didn't win. Well, I won."

"I've never heard of a beauty contest for tall women."

"There's contests in every state. I could have gone to the nationals."

"Why didn't you?"

"I got a lot of nice stuff but the grand prize was a week in Miami Beach. I liked Florida so much, I never returned to Nashville."

"What about your boss and family?"

"Mr. Saxon had framed pictures of me all over his office and had gotten a lot of local publicity, so he was fine."

"What about your family?"

"My mother took off when I was three, and my daddy raised me. He wasn't happy, but he sent me some money to live on. A week later I was working in a Key Biscayne real estate office."

"Office work?"

"No, most of the time I called fizzbo's. Sometimes when there was a deadline, I helped write copy for the newspaper ads."

"What's a fizzbo?"

"Fizzbo's are homeowners who are trying to sell their own homes. I called, trying to get a listing. My batting average was pretty good. Anyway, six months later, I passed the exam and got my real estate license."

Out of the chair, Jilly began pacing the room. "I enjoyed selling and my height and looks didn't hurt. In two years, I was driving a Lincoln and living in my own condo, mortgaged of course. Sound like a success story?"

"Yeah, what changed?"

"I sold a $9 million estate to Valentine and Tasha Petrovich. At that time, it was the highest price ever paid for a home in the Miami area. All of a sudden, I was the hottest realtor in South Florida."

Pausing at the window, Jilly peered out and folded her arms across her chest. The long silence that followed prompted Hud to chance a comment. "Business must have gone through the roof."

"I worked seven days a week for two whole months and couldn't catch up."

"Ya needed a break."

"When the Petrovich's invited me to their housewarming party, I was working with a travel agent to select a cruise. Hud, I'm not sure I can do this."

"Jilly, keep going, ya gotta get it off your back."

"You're not a sports fan, so you probably aren't aware that Petrovich owns a major media company and a World Championship basketball team."

"I never look at the sports section."

"Well, the housewarming party was set up as a fundraiser for the homeless and most of Petrovich's team were there. About ten o'clock, Petrovich invites me to see what his decorators had done with the guest cottage which is down by an enormous pool and tennis courts."

"Was the party winding down?"

"No, people were still arriving."

Jilly's eyes were fixed on the woods outside and it was obvious to Hud that she was marshaling the willpower to continue.

"Three members of Petrovich's team were in the cottage sitting around with their shirts, socks and shoes off. They were sharing a bottle of vodka. One of the two black men present, a hairy man with lots of gold chains and earrings stood up and said, 'You a fine-looking woman. How tall you, girl?'

The way he looked me up and down frightened me and I blurted out, 'six-two.'

'I ain't never fucked a woman that tall.'

I turned to leave, but Petrovich grabbed my arm and spun me around. 'Gentlemen, meet Miss Tall Nashville.'

I started to struggle, but he had a hand on the back of my neck and I couldn't move. Then he laughed and shoved me toward the men."

Hud nodded his understanding and asked, "Did Petrovich say anything?"

Jilly's silhouette seemed to shrink as though she were hiding from an enemy only she could see. "Here, the bitch is all yours. Show her how the pros do it."

Brushing the hair back from her face with a defiant gesture, Jilly continued. "For the next two hours, they did things to me that were so ugly I could never describe them to you or anyone. No one heard my screams. Petrovich must have soundproofed the bedroom. When they finished, I was tied to the four poster bed with velcro straps. A few minutes later, Petrovich returned with his wife and her friend."

Hud was incredulous. "With his wife and another woman?"

Jilly went on like she hadn't heard, her voice a monotone. "Tasha looked down at me with a pair of scissors in her hand.

'Jilly, I really think you'd look better in shorter hair. *Da*, I'm sure of it,' Tasha said.

She'd cut off an inch or so and stand back and ask the woman 'What you think?

'*Nyet*, too long. Trim some more.'

"When my hair became too short to cut with scissors, she shaved my head."

"What was Petrovich doing?"

"He was sitting in a chair watching and smoking a cigar. I saw a hint of madness in his eyes."

"Jesus."

"Tasha brought a mirror over so I could see myself, and when I started to cry, Petrovich said something to her in Russian and she smiled at me. That's when they started using bamboo switches and what Tasha called 'her naughty toys.' Finally, God answered my prayers and I passed out. I woke up in the house where you found me."

A flash flood of emotions punctuated by pure hate for the Petrovich's and the three players raced through Hud, but before he could say anything, a shrill scream echoed through the room. "I want to kill them all! You hear me? I want them dead, dead, dead!"

With that, Jilly slid to the floor, curled up and began to moan. Gathering her in his arms, Hud rocked her for hours until she finally drifted off to sleep. They were still like that when the sun rose over the tree-line, but by then, they were both in a deep slumber.

13

The spring weather was the tonic Jilly needed. They expanded the vegetable garden and Jilly replanted the flowers that had not survived the winter. Working outside lifted her spirits and gave her skin a healthy glow. Both she and Woofer were a lot happier. There was one nagging problem, Beebe still didn't know if the owners of the cottage were going to spend the summer on the island. Finally, they got the call. "Good news, my darlings, Dee and Ted are going to Spain."

Hud was skeptical. "Ya sure?"

"Of course. They've been invited to stay with friends at a villa on the Costa Del Sol."

"Nice." Hud replied.

That was wonderful news for Hud, whose summer plan was to keep Jilly constantly occupied. And he did. They sailed, fished, body surfed and wandered all over the island and its remote beaches on foot. Since The Nature Conservatory had called Block Island one of the *12 Last Great Places On Earth*, there was a lot to experience. By the end of the summer, the sun had bleached their hair and turned their skins browner than the heavy crust on a rye bread. Jilly was eating well and was finally able to sleep through the night. And, her hair had grown out to the point where she didn't have to wear a hat. Her long buried sense of humor suddenly burst forth and stories about trying to write country songs had doubled Hud over with laughter. "But Hud, you don't understand. Everyone who lives in Nashville thinks they can write songs."

It was late fall and they were fishing on the leeward side of the island where it was warmer. Without fanfare, Jilly reeled in and put her pole aside. "I don't know about you, but I've got rock fever."

"How does dinner on the mainland sound?"

A short walk from the ferry landing in Point Judith, Hud stopped in front of what had once been a bank. Although the putty-colored brick building was fairly large, there were only ten tables in the place and every single one was occupied. Fresh-cut flowers, flickering candles and haunting music added to the ambiance of a place that could have coasted along on its culinary reputation. The grey-haired hostess had beautiful features, but her makeup looked liked it had been applied with a spray gun. *We're in trouble*, thought Hud, as she glanced down at her reservations book. With mock gravity, he gave her his best straight-ahead smile. "We're not in your book."

The hostess laughed. "If you don't mind waiting, I have a cancellation. It won't be long."

Taking in every nuance of the place, Jilly imagined bank customers lined up at the original teller cages that separated the cozy bar from the dining room. Scrumptious food served on fine china and a carafe of reasonably good wine had put a glow on the evening. Jilly's long tapered fingers fidgeted nervously with her linen napkin. "I'd like to go home...to Nashville."

"Alone?"

"No, with you."

Her answer restarted Hud's heart. "When?"

"Before Christmas."

The exchange had caught him off guard. "Could be dangerous."

"I know."

" Jilly, no off-the-cuff stuff. Let me work on it."

"One more thing. It's been 27 months, don't you think it's time?"

"Time for what?"

"Most men can't stop babbling about themselves, you never do. What gives?"

"It's not whatcha call pretty."

She looked at him with concern. "I'll chance it."

The owner, an older man with lots of patience and a sense for important moments, left them alone well past closing. Hud covered everything; his police background, Kathryn's death, the Biltmore and how he had purposely killed five men.

"I'm still wanted for questioning by the FBI."

"Why only questioning?"

"No direct evidence. Disappearing is not a crime."

"I see."

"Have I frightened you?"

"They were horrid people and you avenged their deaths. That Petrovich was involved boggles my mind, but what on earth made you come back?"

"Photos in the Bureau Bulletin identify me as a 275-pound tub named Jake Garboosian. Whata ya think?"

"I can see why you weren't afraid of being spotted, but why Block Island?"

"I knew the place would help you heal."

She reached out and took his hands. "It did."

Squeezing her hands gently, he nodded in the man's direction. "We have to go, he's getting impatient and the last ferry leaves in twenty minutes."

It was chilly on the water, but they lingered outside on the ferry's main deck. When Jilly linked her arm in his, the feeling that had been missing since Kathryn's death returned with a rush.

"You never mentioned any children."

"We tried. It wasn't to be."

"I'm sorry."

"Steve Horn and his family were my only relatives and that's by marriage."

"Hud, forgive me for saying this, but your story makes me want to me see my Daddy even more."

"We've done everything right, so far. Be patient just a little longer."

14

During the following week, a cold front swept down from Canada and the bitter temperatures had kept them inside. Jilly's kept busy packing and reading. It was late, and Hud watched her in the glow from the fireplace. "Can you call your dad tomorrow and make sure he's not going anywhere for the next month? Don't tell him we're coming."

Jilly put a fat book aside. "I'll call at the regular time."

"Don't get upset, but we can't go to your dad's house."

"What do you mean?"

"Random surveillance."

Jilly was confused. "I'm not from your world, Hud."

"Petrovich may have hired a local to watch your dad's place two or three times a month."

"After all this time?"

"Ya cost him an awful lot of money and your dad's his only link."

"Hud, come July, it will be three years."

"Petrovich has to be a nut case. You think time matters?"

"But how. He's based in New York."

"Six hundred a month for a private detective is tip money for a guy like Petrovich."

"God, that's unbelievable."

"That's why it works."

"What's next?"

"That depends on your dad."

Seeing Jilly's puzzled expression, Hud added, "He's gotta retire, move, change his name."

"He's refused, several times. What makes you think he'll change his mind?

"Face-to-face, I'll convince him."

David Barton, Jilly's dad, was one of a dozen purchasing agents for a company that made aeronautical components. She only called once a month and, at Hud's insistence, all of her calls went through the main switchboard where her dad worked. She thought it was overkill, but she went along with it.

"Dad's not going anywhere until late January."

"Good, I'm shooting for December 17."

"That's over three weeks away."

"Were gonna need every minute."

Jilly looked around, that confused look back on her face. "Hud, we don't really own anything."

"Jilly, trust me on this."

The let down showed on her face; she wanted to leave in days not weeks. Hud took the initiative. "First, we trade the truck for a new Mercury Grand Marquis."

"Why a new car and why that one in particular?"

"We're gonna drive to Nashville and the Merc has the same huge, deep trunk as a Ford Crown Vic."

"Then why don't we buy a Crown Vic?"

"That's what cops drive. It'll stand out too much."

That night, from her vantage point on a high bluff, Jilly saw the damp fog creep in over the water. Below, an endless strand of pale green sea grass swayed in the weightless breeze and even with her heavy sweater she felt the cold. Sitting on a long narrow outcropping of granite hedged by a tangle of dormant lilac bushes, she felt the pent-up tension leave her body. She perceived that she was blessed. Hud painstakingly explained all that had to be done and she was overwhelmed by the list. It was obvious that his only consideration had been for her safety and that of her father and she admonished herself for questioning his judgement. And even though Hud loved his dog, Hud was leaving Woofer behind with Beebe. "Island's got running room and plenty of birds and squirrels to chase. We're gonna be livin' out of suitcases for awhile. Things get settled, I'll come back for him."

The bluff had a lordly view of New Harbor and for that time of year there were still quite a few boats tied to mooring buoys. Shimmering in the reflective glow of their gently bobbing anchor lights, the calm water around each boat seemed luminescent. With everything that had happened to her, Jilly knew that every single light had hopes and fears and dreams attached. As she headed back to their cottage, mushy sand from an earlier rain stuck like cake mix to the soles of her sneakers. She never noticed. Her mind was elsewhere.

Standing outside the door to Hud's bedroom, Jilly closed her eyes and slowly turned the knob. Hud was lying on his back, one hand dangling over the side of the bed. She stood stock-still and in the semi-darkness she could hear his slow, steady breathing. For a tall woman, she had a light step and he felt her touch before he knew she was there. She sat down beside him and a perceptible tremor ran through her body as his fingertips reached up and touched her face. Feeling him tremble, she moistensed his lips with hers. Self-conscious of her scarred body, she shed her robe and slid quickly into bed beside him. Neither of them spoke.

Delicate, searching intimacies fueled their pent-up emotions. A gentle hand caressed the scars on her back and her initial fears were extinguished, replaced by a craving to be held. Jilly placed a finger over his lips. "No words." As they lay entwined, Hud's eyes met hers and she fathomed love deep within them. Every fiber of her body came alive, and soon the rhythm of their coupling assumed the steady, unrushed cadence of the waves as they broke against the jagged rocks below. Much later, before the ocean sounds wooed her eyes closed, Hud covered her with a blanket. "Sleep, the morning world is close at hand."

As year-rounders, they knew that by nine the queue for the ten o'clock ferry would be ten cars deep and that all of Aldo's Portuguese sweet bread would be gone. But, Beebe had insisted on seeing them off and she had brought two loaves of the habit-forming bread along with Woofer. As the Ferry pulled out into the current, they waved to each other. Sensing that this was somehow different from their other trips, Woofer unleashed a series of long wails that reached their ears well past the last channel marker.

Bad weather slowed them down and it had taken them two long days to reach Nashville. It was 1:00 in the morning when they checked into the Grand Old Opry Land Hotel. Eight hours later they watched Jilly's father pull into his assigned parking space. They pulled in beside him and Jilly rolled down her window. "Daddy, follow us." Ten minutes later they were in a Denny's having a country breakfast.

"You shocked me."

"We didn't want to attract any attention, Daddy."

Barton was slow to answer. "It's good that you didn't."

"Why's that, Mr. Barton?" Hud asked.

"Well before this week, I never considered myself in any jeopardy."

"What made you change you mind, Daddy?"

"Mrs. Cohen, across the street. She called me to come look at her television. Said she couldn't get any sound. When I got there, she led me to a window and pointed out a car. "Mr. Barton, I'm afraid you're being watched."

"How'd she know."

"Mrs. Cohen's no dummy. She told me she's seen the same car out there, with the driver looking towards my house, twice a week for almost two months since she got the gout."

"Why'd Mrs. Cohen wait so long, Daddy?"

Barton rummaged around in the briefcase that he'd brought in with him. "Because, she wanted to be sure. Damn, I know it's here."

Hud tensed. "Did she get a plate number?"

"She certainly did." Barton brightened. "Got it. Take a look."

The article was two weeks old, and when Hud saw it he raised his eyes at Jilly.

"What?" She asked.

"A minute. This is serious."

When Jilly read the article, she blanched.

Renegade Starters Charged With Rape.

MIAMI: *Karem Zambir, known to his fans as Zammy and star forward, Billy Poe, have been accused of raping Ms. Jocelyn Riley a stewardess for BonAir, the charter airline that transports the Renegades, the championship basketball team owned by media mogul, Valentine Petrovich. A senior BonAir flight attendant, Ms. Riley alleges that the incident took place in the plane's private salon on a flight between Miami and Chicago.*

During a highly emotional press conference, BonAir's attorney, Sheldon Bloomfield, stated that: "As of Monday, BonAir will no longer transport the Renegades basketball team. This decision was not made hastily. Formal complaints involving Renegade players have been numerous, serious and include: harassment of female cabin attendants, violation of FAA flight safety regulations, excessive consumption of alcoholic beverages, use of illegal substances, gambling and destruction of onboard aircraft equipment. Valentine Petrovich, although fully aware of the complaints, has consistently condoned the unlawful and defiant behavior of his players and his culpability will be documented in a civil suit which BonAir intends to file on behalf of Ms. Riley."

A spokesperson for Red Square, Inc., the corporation that owns the Renegades responded stating that, 'Ms Riley's complaint filed with the Miami Police Department is just that, a complaint. It is not an indictment and the men named have not been charged. Accordingly, this office has no comment.' Both players have declined comment. We'll keep you posted on this one!

Not wanting to, Hud pointed to the grainy pictures in the paper. "Those the men, Jilly?"

"Yes. I gave you the other name, Randolf Owens."

Mr. Barton's hand was shaking as he reached across the table and handed Hud another clipping. "This is even worse." Hud read every word and passed the article to Jilly.

MIAMI: *The body of BonAir flight attendant, Jocelyn Riley was found yesterday morning in a drainage canal bordering the parking lot of the Kendall apartment complex where she lived. Police at the scene reported that she was shot three times. Only two weeks ago, Ms. Riley accused two Renegade Players, Karim Zambir and Billy Poe of rape. Her employer, BonAir, a major transporter of professional sports teams terminated their transportation contract with the Renegades and has been providing Ms Riley with legal counsel. Ms. Riley is also BonAir's senior FAA flight attendant training coordinator. Because of her high-profile criminal complaint and work with the FAA, the Kendall Police have requested FBI assistance. Ms. Riley is survived by her father, Gerald Riley, a professor at the University of Miami.*

Their waitress broke the silence. "More coffee?"

When she was gone, Hud said. "What took you so long to let us know about all this?"

"I saw the first article right after Jilly's call and without a phone number, I couldn't contact you. The other piece came out this morning."

"Hud, dad's right. Remember, you refused to give him a phone number for his own safety."

"Yeah, well that decision seems to have cut both ways."

Jilly's hands were wound around her cup so tight that Hud took it from her grip. "This nightmare will never end. Having daddy's house watched all this time, Petrovich must be insane in a way that only the people really close to him, like Tasha, know."

Hud looked at both Bartons. "Jilly's right. He's ego driven and nuts. He's gotta be put in the ground."

Jilly was realistic. "Hud, Petrovich is rich and has people that will kill for him. What can we possibly do?"

Hud's voice toughened. "Leave that to me, you're gonna have to retire and move, Mr. Barton, and right away."

"I'm not eligible…"

"Mr. Barton, between us, Jilly and I have close to $7 million in Certificates of Deposit and T-Bills. So, let's stop bull-shitting around. Pick the place of your dreams and we'll make it happen."

Things were moving too fast and Mr. Barton was badly shaken. "What…what about Jilly?"

"She goes with me. We'll join up with you when it's over."

Mr. Barton was unsure. "How can we possibly do all this so fast and not leave a trail?"

A slight smile creased Hud's face. "Like I said, Mr. Barton, leave it to me. Question. You friends with any Nashville cops?"

15

As it turned out, Jilly's dad didn't know any cops, but the head of security where he worked did. The plate on the surveillance car belonged to Lyle Booth, a private detective whose office was small, clean and tastefully furnished. A secretary ushered Hud into a large office where several Office Depot office setups had been combined to make one impressive layout fitted out with three separate computers.

Mr. Booth saw Hud's awe. "Detecting isn't isn't what it used to be. This stuff saves me a lot of time."

Hud nodded, but came right to the point. "I need ya to find a deadbeat owes me a lotta cash."

Booth's tone was lukewarm. "How long's he been gone?"

"Almost three years."

"That's a long time."

"A beer buddy of mine spotted him in Palm Beach yesterday. It's all in here." Hud shoved a brown letter sized envelope across the desk.

Booth stared at the Bureau Bulletin. "This Jake Garboosian. Does he look the same?"

"My buddy says he's heavier."

"You're kidding."

"What can I tell ya, he likes to eat."

"A road job like this, I get $475 a day plus expenses. I'd need a healthy retainer."

Hud, took out a thick roll of hundreds, and laid it on the desk. "Here's

$10,000 up front, but ya gotta leave tomorrow."

"That's not possible. I have other clients."

Hud laid another $5,000 on the desk. "For the inconvenience."

To his credit, Booth was still wary, "What about the police?"

"No sweat. I want my money not his ass. You find him, call me and the police."

Booth extended a hand, "Mr. Johnson, you just hired an investigator."

"Here's my local number. Leave a message and a call-back number. Fly first class and stay in nice places."

"That's very generous."

"You run low, I'll wire more. I'd start with the better restaurants."

In case Booth was anxious to know who he really was, Hud walked five blocks, cut rapidly through the lobby of a nearby hotel and caught a cab at the stand on the other side.

He knew the detective would probably write up a phony report when he got back, billing Petrovich as though he'd been on stake-out. Hud wired another $5,000 a week later asking the detective to stay with it for another two weeks. He didn't have to plead. Since it was 35 degrees in Nashville, Palm Beach's balmy weather had a lot of appeal.

By the time Booth got back to Nashville, the Bartons were living in a three-bedroom condo on an executive golf course in San Marcos, California under the name Hudson. Priced 25% under the market, the real estate salesman that Jilly called bought her Daddy's house, car and furnishings. To avoid leaving a trail and to keep neighbors like Mrs. Cohen in the dark, Hud rented a van and hauled Mr. Barton's personal items to a UPS shipping center fifty miles from Nashville. Without a moving truck and no forwarding address, Barton's disappearance off the face of the earth threw Lyle Booth and his computers for a loop. *What in hell am I going to tell Valentine Petrovich?*

After they were satisfied that everything was as it should be, Jilly and Hud left town for a long weekend in the country. The narrow country road was empty and with the top down, Jilly watched the trees drift together in an endless wash of greens and browns. The noise of the wind whooshing all around them made a clean sound that shut out everything else. A sudden bump brought her back to the present and she said, "What are we looking for?"

"Lace Hill Road. There's a cemetery with a church next door on the corner."

Ten minutes later she pointed to dozens of granite markers barely visible among the wild tangle of overgrowth adjacent to a boarded up building that at one time could have been a church. "There."

Lace Hill Road was made of hard packed gravel and it hadn't rained for a week. Hud stopped. "Too dusty. I'd better raise the top."

Painted a murky brown and circled by trees, the Wild Flower Inn blended in with the towering oak trees that marked its rear property line. Mint green awning and flowering window boxes said *welcome, you're home.*

"Hud, this is charming."

"Ya like it?"

"Yes, especially the quiet."

The Inn looked out into a deep valley and from their window table they watched the sun move unhurriedly behind the distant hills. A case of nerves had dulled Hud's taste buds and he hadn't tasted one morsel of the mouth-watering veal entree. Fortified with more wine than he was used to, he was still unsettled. His condition wasn't lost on Jilly, who thought, *Everything is so perfect, why is he so subdued?*

As their waiter approached, Jilly kicked her shoes off under the table. "Can I get you something else?"

Hud pointed toward the empty bottle.

When the waiter was gone, Hud slid both hands across the threads of the fine linen and pressed a diamond ring into Jilly's palm. "This belonged to Gram." He paused and looked into her eyes. "I gotta know."

Although the restaurant was in constant motion, Hud felt a stillness that was different from any stillness he had ever known. Time stopped and he cursed himself for the words he'd chosen. The wide, gauzy strips of cloth that covered the windows swayed seductively with the breeze outside and her answer was carried on a cushion of air. "Yes. Yes, I will."

Afraid to shatter the spell, Hud continued to hold her hands. This too tall, too hard on herself woman had captured his heart, and as the guitarist played a moody tango, he whispered, "When we get back?"

"Yes."

Neither of them spoke, and in the waning candle light Jilly felt that she was riding a magical white horse that was floating above a vast layer of enormous silver balloons. Her saddle was heavy with love and commitment and there was a delicious tingling in her body. Closing her eyes she stored the feeling so it would always be there.

Outside, she saw a banana-shaped moon guarded by stars so bright they seemed to melt the sky around them. Jilly hooked an arm in Hud's and they walked down a brick path to a sheltered lilly pond. Their kisses told of unfulfilled longings and their need to be with the one person they could trust and love. Sounds of distant tambourines pealed in Jilly's head and she envisioned piggyback races on lawns so green she almost cried.

Back in their suite, they slow-danced and touched until touching was not enough. "I'll be back." she said.

Lying in bed, Hud thought of how easily love could be lost or misplaced. And how, perhaps because of fate, love had stumbled across his path for a second time. When he opened his eyes, he saw Jilly standing naked in the center of the room, her tall, body marred only by permanent scars. It was the first time Jilly had allowed Hud to see her this way. Her offering to him. Ripples of loving warmth surfed through his body as she sat on the bed and slowly unpinned her hair. Their bodies melted together and all of her past hurts, and his, disappeared.

16

New York City is made up of five boroughs: Manhattan, Queens, Brooklyn, Staten Island and the Bronx. Manhattan is laid out in an orderly grid pattern and most of its inhabitants work in the vertical world of skyscrapers. It's a lot easier to get lost in Queens where the streets have a tendency to go off on weird tangents. Queens' wide sidewalks and streets haven't been overrun by humanity, and the population is not as hard and pushy as the Madison Avenue and Wall Street crowds. With its low-rise silhouette and slower pace, Queens presents itself as a place that is user-friendly.

The Russian Mafia used loan sharking as a highly profitable way to launder their drug profits. Harold Gold, whose forefathers were honest, industrious, early Russian emigres to America and whose father and uncle built, from practically nothing, the business he'd inherited, had been driven by desperation to deal with these new Russians. The business his father and uncle had started with little more than an idea, to learn what their customers wanted and could afford in the way of furniture and give it to them, plus a heavy application of hard work, guts and chutzpah, had grown from a street peddler's stall on Canal Street in Manhattan to the sprawling building that housed the present Gold's Furniture Store, now a business that had fallen on hard times. Not the businessman his father was, and in need of cash to pay off demanding suppliers and creditors, he had turned to these new, cold and ruthless men from the land of his father despite the impossible terms they set for repayment. To the everlasting regret of his family, it would be an action that was to cost him his father's business by foreclosure, and his life by his own hand.

Having acquired the store for a fraction of its value, the Russians had divided the huge store into two units, each with its own entrance. One unit functioned as a private social club that had an extensive Russian menu, a large dining room/bar and a steam room. The other space became the ROC's new 'business office.' Brighton Beach in Brooklyn was the center of Russian life in New York, but it was too far off the beaten track and getting in and out of there was no picnic. With its parkways and interstates, Queens was perfect.

A freak front of warm tropical air had moved into the area, creating patches of fog that slowed traffic down to a crawl. Holed up in a vacant second floor office across the street, Hud had been observing the Russians' comings and goings for three days. Back in their homeland, the Russians had always gotten together at the end of the day to drink vodka, talk and carouse. Old habits were hard to break and the daily ritual hadn't changed. Every evening, the Russians in charge of operations in the other boroughs would turn in their daily take and drift next door to the club. The reassuring presence of all those Russians on the other side of the 'office' and a long period of time without any outside threat seemed to have created a feeling of invincibility, or at the very least an unrealistic comfort level among the men in the business office.

Because of the fog, the street lights had come on early. As the last two 'collectors' straggled into the Russian offices, Hud's senses kicked into acute mode...the street sounds were louder, the neon signs brighter and every movement was seen in a sharper focus. Two minutes later, he strolled casually across the wide street, his weapons thumping rhythmically against muscled thighs. Carrying a large auditor's briefcase and wearing a bulky raincoat, he looked like a middle manager straggling home after an extended day at the office. The two prostitutes who exited the office were laughing and carrying on and Hud got a whiff of booze as they sashayed by him on their way to the social club. Passing by the office window Hud saw one man in the reception area. Business as usual, he thought.

There was a small parking lot in the rear of the building with a loading dock and a set of rickety stairs to the second floor. Placing a 2x4 under the door knob of the club's rear door to keep it from being opened from the inside, Hud took the stairs two at a time. Small, high impact bolt-cutters made short work of the padlock and he stepped into a musty storage space still crammed with furniture. He immediately spread the cans of flammable chemicals that had filled the rest of his briefcase. Standing in the doorway, Hud tossed a match onto a pile of old newspapers. After seeing flames, he hooked the broken padlock back through the hasp.

Forty seconds later, he was standing in front of a pasty faced man who was manning the desk in the reception area. Hud's voice was cordial. "Hi, howya doin?" The man ignored him and continued to chew on a brownie that he chased down with a Budweiser. After a loud burp, he glanced up at Hud. "What you want?"

Hud held out a piece of note paper. "I'm trying to find this address."

"*Nyet*, you leave. No belong here."

Hud acted as though he didn't understand the Russian's command. "Please, just take a quick look."

To rid himself of the stupid American, the Russian snatched the paper from Hud's hand. Hud reciprocated by calmly slitting the man's throat with the small, razor-sharp knife he'd palmed, hidden by the paper.

Putting on latex gloves, Hud took hold of the man's ankles and dragged him into a large storage closet so he couldn't be seen through the window. After locking the front door, Hud opened the door to the main hallway that ran from front to back. Raucous laughter, loud talk and the clatter of glasses filled with ice came from an office at the end of the long hall. Listening intently, Hud tallied the voices. Removing his raincoat and placing it across the top of a fire extinguisher, Hud released the safeties on the two machine pistols and the .357 magnum nestled in his shoulder holster.

Dirty carpeting, shabby, abused furniture and a mass of heads swiveling in his direction greeted Hud as he stepped into the smoke-filled, now deadly quiet room. It took only an instant for the puzzled look on the faces staring at Hud to turn to an awareness of the nature and intent of this intrusion, but within that instant, it was already too late to react. It was a bloodbath. In 17 seconds, 60 rounds killed 11 Russian organized crime members including five from the top echelon. There was no chance to return fire. Fortunately for the people next door in the social club, the stray rounds were stopped by the cinder block filled-concrete wall that divided the building. After filling a laundry bag with cash, Hud donned his raincoat, opened the rear door and was swallowed by the foggy night. Jilly casually picked him up in a rental two blocks away.

By the time the fire apparatus arrived, the entire building was engulfed in flames. Across the street, a large group of club members watched in silence. Queens' police swarmed to the scene and made a pretty good show of putting a high-profile investigation in motion. When the press coverage petered out, law enforcement quietly put the case on the back burner. To the public, bad guys killing bad guys was not a pressing matter.

17

Alden Lensk stood next to his silver Mercedes, his arms resting on the roof. He was staring at the black, burnt out skeleton of the torched social club when the fire inspector said, "Are you the owner?"

"No, I'm attorney for corporation that holds title."

"I'll need that information."

"Give me a card, I'll have it faxed today."

"How much insurance?"

"$1.2 million."

"Will that cover it?"

"*Nyet.*"

"Arson/murder, that insurance money may be tied up for a while."

"Yes, I know."

"Any ideas on who?"

"I've talked to the owners. Nothing."

As the fire inspector walked back to his bright yellow car, Lensk was convinced that Voccio's organization was responsible. Lensk had warned his boss about taking on the Italians. Even so, like many Russian criminals Valentine Petrovich truly believed that everything in America could be had if you were utterly ruthless. Petrovich's methods had worked in New York where greed and jealousy kept five Mafia families in a constant state of turmoil. However, the Voccio family had controlled New England for generations and after his death, Frank "The Brain" Talcone, Voccio's closest associate, had taken over. The Brain made the Russians' attempts to move into New England a three-year nightmare. Shaking his head in frustration, Lensk crawled back into the limousine and dialed a number in upstate New York.

Valentine Petrovich was lying in bed stroking the well-muscled thigh of his wife, a onetime ballet dancer. Except for an initial, "*Da*," he held the phone to his ear. Finally, he said contemptuously, "They're fools, all of them."

Petrovich was incredulous over the boldness of the attack. "I want two armed guards around the clock at our other locations. Four when there's a money drop. Install video cameras and look into buying up all the properties that abut ours."

"*Da*, call me tomorrow."

Petrovich's *dacha*, as he liked to call it, was located in an exclusive enclave of estates on Long Island. Unlike the studious, grinding Lensk, who graduated with honors from Moscow University, Petrovich was a Muscovite who had started his criminal career as a juvenile stealing windshield wipers from parked cars. By the time he was 21, he had 90 people working for him and had graduated to disassembling stolen cars and selling the parts on the black market. Using the profit from his Moscow "chop-shops," the budding entrepreneur invested his profits in Russia's 'New Vodka,' illegal drugs. For Petrovich, it turned out to be a good move.

Her hair still damp, Tasha Petrovich turned over onto her stomach. The mere look of her created a bulge in Petrovich's shorts. Her unrestrained sexuality had done wonders for his awkward potency problem and her facility for erotic language and the imaginative choreography that accompanied her foreplay theatrics had never failed to rekindle his desire.

Valentine Petrovich had never liked women; he exploited them for sex. Tasha Markov, daughter of Russia's General Markov, was in a different category. Petrovich needed her. Petrovich knew about her father's power, about how to use that power, and about Tasha always being there whenever he wanted her. And except for the problems with the Italians, he figured that was all he really needed to know. As she lay there on the bed, naked, her thick hair spread out topsy-turvy, he thought, *Tasha, you beautiful, predictable witch, sleep...sleep.*

Lighting a *makhorka*, Petrovich took several long drags. The smoke from the strong Russian tobacco hit his lungs and his mind honed in on the Queens disaster. With a look of disgust, he flicked the blanket over Tasha and rolled out of bed. After a quick shower, he retired to his study and began making calls.

While holding for an overseas operator, his disgust was drowned with the music from Swan Lake.

To protect his home from the fierce Canadian winds that swept in over Long Island Sound, Petrovich had planted hundreds of white birch trees. Now, the mature trees made a beautiful and effective windbreak. He'd also had triple-pane windows installed. The pricey windows not only kept the cold out they, like the birch trees, blocked out noise. As a result, his private wing was usually an ocean of silence. Seething, he strode back to his bedroom.

Tasha stood in front of a beveled mirrored that served as a closet door. Her reddish hair was down and all she had on was a pair of hooped earrings and a pair of dainty reading glasses perched low on her nose. Before Petrovich could move, she turned and did a graceful revele, going up on her toes and stretching out so he could appreciate her backside. "Ready?" she sighed.

Watching her reflection in the closet's mirrored doors, he could see her nipples beginning to extend. Her glowing, wholesome body inflamed him and he quivered with life. Tasha's mouth was moist and unpainted and when her tongue found the opening between his lips she drove it deep. The one woman whose sexual desires could be even more bizarre than his held Valentine Petrovich with an intensity that was frightening. She whispered "Val" and that was enough.

18

Three weeks after Jocelyn Riley's funeral, Hud called her father and told him he could shed some light on his daughter's death. Intrigued, Gerald Riley agreed to a meeting. Coral Gables is about five miles from downtown Miami and close to the University where Professor Gerald J. Riley taught. The address was an apartment house whose peeling paint and missing light bulbs reflected the owner's reputation for milking his rental properties dry.

As Hud knocked on the door, Ravel's "Bolero" was nearing the end of its relentless crescendo. Since his daughter's brutal murder, Professor Riley had become despondent and the sparsely furnished apartment was a mess. Books, journals, notebooks, bulging briefcases, boxes of floppies and zip discs were stacked haphazardly and Riley had to clear off a chair so Hud could sit down. A suspicious Siamese cat sprawled contentedly under a dining room table that served as a desk, his eyes following Hud's every movement.

"How was your trip, Mr. Hudson?"

"Long. There were lots of delays."

"Bad weather?"

"Yeah, but it still beats driving."

"Not a good time to be wandering around up North."

"We froze up there."

"I'm sorry, can I get you something to drink?"

"Tell ya the truth, I could use a shot of whiskey to warm up."

By the time Hud finished telling the professor about Jilly's experience with Petrovich, each of them had downed a half dozen shots of Crown Royal. Riley was sitting on a lumpy sofa, dazed and drawn. Hud felt sorry for the man. Like Hud, the professor's wife had died at an early age. Jocelyn had given Riley purpose. Now that she was gone, he was a lost soul.

"You're telling me the law will never touch him. That he'll never be held accountable?"

"Yeah, my Jilly and your Jocelyn won't be the last. He's a sick bastard. Jilly wanted to come with me, but I left her at the hotel. Reliving what happened is just too painful."

Professor Riley was 48, but the grey in his hair made him appear much older. He was short, thin as a fly rod and looked anemic. Popular with students, the professor was a classical music and jazz buff who loved cats and teaching. Curious about the professor's grubby beard and noticeable disregard for his appearance, Hud asked, "Ya back at school?"

"No, I tried going back, but I broke down in front of my first class. I'm on sabbatical."

"What da ya teach, professor?"

"I have an advanced degree in Computer Architecture and that's what I teach."

"No research?"

"I was tenured at a leading school of engineering where I spent most of my time doing applied research."

"Sounds like a good deal."

"Our corporate clients and the university did well, but my students were grossly shortchanged."

"How come?"

"Grad students aren't equipped to handle the advanced material that I teach."

Hud was getting an idea. "Ya ever do any moonlighting, Professor?"

"I've received many lucrative offers with get-rich-quick stock options and generous compensation. However, I'm not what you call financially driven."

Disappointed, Hud asked, "No research at all?"

Professor Riley, studied Hud for a long minute. "Why are you so interested in my doing research?"

"I had a crazy idea how Petrovich might be taken down."

"Hmm, in that case, follow me."

The professor led Hud down the apartment's hallway and opened the door to a spare bedroom. Hud stared. The room was lined with folding tables which were packed with an impressive array of electronic test equipment and computers. "This is where I do my private research."

"What kind of stuff are you into?"

"Sorry, I'd have to know a lot more about you and what you're planning."

Having gotten this far, Hud decided the professor hated Petrovich enough to gamble on his discretion, so he related his own story from the beginning to end leaving nothing out.

"So, that was you in New York?"

"Ya, it was. That bother you?"

"Not in the least. Now tell me, what do you have in mind?"

"I've read where hackers can get into just about any system if they try long enough."

"That's total bullshit. The systems I believe you have in mind are encrypted and even a talented hacker couldn't get in. Also, even the slickest hackers end up getting caught."

"How come?"

"Hackers use primitive methods that leave trails."

"Shit."

"Not necessarily, Mr. Hudson. Even the best hackers in the world are mere novices compared to what I'm able to do."

"Why's that?"

"For starters, I've developed software that can break any encrypted code."

"Jesus, good God," said Hud.

Several weeks later, Hud stood next to Professor Riley in his bedroom lab where the greatest bank robbery of all time was taking place. There wasn't a gun or a mask in sight, only the professor's fingers dancing lightly over a keyboard. With a flourish, as though he were leading a symphony orchestra, he dropped his hand to his sides. "Done."

Gripping the professor's shoulder tightly, Hud said, "Mind-boggling."

Sitting uncomfortably in a hard-backed chair, Professor Gerald J. Riley had just stolen $5.2 billion from the accounts of ROC. Total time, 15 minutes.

The Professor's low-end apartment was only a few blocks from a Dunkin Donut shop where they went to celebrate.

Using the university's mainframe, the professor had used his own software to access accounts in eight banks controlled by Russian organized crime in New York, New Jersey and Grand Cayman. Hud's voice was a blend of incredulity, genuine admiration and concern. "I can't believe this is happening. You sure we won't get nailed?"

"You've heard of virtual reality?"

"Yeah."

"I combined some basic virtual reality concepts with the latest developments in artificial intelligence to create a phantom bank. Once the Russian funds were received and transferred to our accounts in real banks, our phantom bank simply ceased to exist. We can't be caught because there is no trail."

Hud said, "Ya make it sound so simple."

"Hud, my PC is tied into one of the world's most powerful mainframes. When the mainframe directed the Russian banks to transfer funds, the electronic signal it sent out also contained an implant which erased forever all, I repeat, all of the electronic documentation that the phantom bank created."

"So, where's the money now?"

"Like I said, the Russian funds have already been funneled to thirty-six real banks where I had already set up accounts. Since all of those banks do at least $25 billion a day in electronic transfers, our deposits will not draw attention."

Hud still looked skeptical, so the professor began drawing pictures in the air with his hands. "All right. Next step. At the close of their business day, the books of the Russian banks I raided aren't going to balance and the search for the electronic transactions that created the shortages will automatically begin. During the search process, the banks' programming protocols will latch onto a labyrinth of electronic trails that my software implanted in their operating systems. Now, it's important to note that these electronic trails exist in a sort of spatial outer-net, however, none of them go anywhere. At random intervals, the trails simply fold back upon themselves and re-multiply. Because of the implants and the fact that my phantom bank no longer exists, all of the trails will forever be dead ends."

"Professor, if they're encrypted, how in hell did you come up with the passwords?"

"That was a slam-dunk. It's well known that the technical people in charge of computer security at the Russian banks all worked for military intelligence at one time or another and they like to use encrypted algorithms to safeguard their passwords."

This was all new to Hud and he responded with a shrug.

"All right, let me explain. Algorithms are complex mathematical jigsaw puzzles that can be used to scramble a password into non-recognizable signals which are called cipher-texts. I could have used a crypto-simulator program or the Cray mainframe at the university which can decipher a billion million algorithms a second, but those methods can be traced back to the source. Are you with me so far?"

"Yep, so far, but don't go too fast."

"Good. Now, most corporate operating systems contain sophisticated blocking programs that will shut everything down whenever there is an attempt to pirate a password. So, one by one, I put each of the Russian computer systems into a sort of electronic trance and in a fraction of a nanosecond, my own software was able to obtain each bank's password voluntarily. Think of it as a sort of remote, electronic hypnosis."

Hud whistled. "Man, oh man!"

Although the professor was not a rich man, stealing for the sole sake of lining his own pockets was something Riley could never justify. "What should we do with all that money?"

"I got some ideas. Tell me what you think."

"Shoot."

"What wouldja think about donating some of the money to women's groups. Ya know for rape prevention, counseling battered woman, that sort of thing?"

"Excellent, I would add groups that are lobbying against drunk driving and deadbeat dads."

"Professor, here's the biggy. All these war on drugs programs are crap. If you saturate a small state like Rhode Island with enough well-paid street cops, the drug problem will go away."

"What are you suggesting?"

"We set up a Foundation and agree to fund an additional 4,000 street cops in Rhode Island as a sort of test for the rest of the country."

"Wouldn't that be too expensive?"

"At $50,000 a year, 4,000 street cops would cost $200 million. Let's say $25 million for ongoing training, administration and some equipment. Another $25 million a year should be enough to gradually bring all the existing cops up to the 50K level."

"So, $250 million a year for how long?"

"I would guarantee ten years, minimum."

"I like it, Hud. I like it very much."

"I'd go one step further. The Foundation sets up four or five technical schools with the best teachers and equipment money can buy. Any kid in Rhode Island who can pass an entrance test in basic math and reading can attend free, with one hitch. If they fail a drug test, or miss three classes without a valid excuse, they're out."

"So, your talking about a place where they can really learn a well-paying trade with a future."

"Right, not some certificate mill that says a kid can repair a fucking jet engine when he doesn't know jackshit about it."

"Hud, those are wonderful ideas."

"Hell, Professor, I didn't come up with any of it. Five years ago I attended a training session given by a black ex-drug addict, who'd lived on the streets for several years. The guy goes clean and earned a master's in sociology. At the end of the session the man got a standing ovation, which almost never happens."

"Wow!"

"One more thing, most of the kids won't have any money. I suggest a $1,000 a year allowance and a $3,500 graduation bonus."

"I don't understand."

"The thousand is so they can eat and afford bus fare. The bonus is so they can buy some decent clothes and transportation. How else you gonna get a job and be able to show up on time? It's all about hope, Professor. About getting a fucking shot."

The professor, who never used profanity, looked at Hud and said, "Let's fucking do it, with one change."

"Whata ya got in mind?"

"The Foundation funds summer camps where any underprivileged kid in Rhode Island can go for two or three weeks."

"Yeah, just getting them off the street will help. Anything else they get out of it is a bonus."

"I'm gonna call Petrovich and tell him that Jake Garboosian stole his money with the aid of a fifteen-year-old hacker. That ought to shake things up a bit. I'll also need about $50 million of that loot to rid the world of Petrovich and his organization forever."

Professor Gerald J. Riley was smiling from ear to ear when Hud finished his explanation. "God help me, but I sure like the way you operate."

Hud felt good, but Professor Riley was ecstatic.

19

Moisture-laden air held in place by an unmoving high pressure system fused with the fierce, unrelenting winds and frigid temperatures had swept down from Canada to form a blizzard of life-threatening proportions. Mountainous snowdrifts covered New York City and visibility was to the point where the sky, the air and the ground were indistinguishable from one another. Once outside one was blind. The cities hulking snow plows were forced to sit idly at curbside. Piled high with dirt and road salt, and with their powerful diesel motors growling in the howling wind, the snow-covered plows looked like humpbacked prehistoric creatures that had been caught in the open. Radio and television stations were running continuous notices warning everyone to stay indoors until the roads could be cleared.

Valentine Petrovich and Alden Lensk were trapped in the Actor's Club that occupied the second floor of a 19th-Century edifice on a side street, two short blocks from Times Square. Before the whiteout conditions set in, the structure's snow-capped spires and ornate domes had looked like a castle in a Disney movie. Now, amid the hiss of the driven snow, the outline of the structure was barely visible. One had to be in the entertainment business in order to join. Petrovich qualified by virtue of his media company.

The club's dues were minimal and the food was good, but the club's dining room was tacky and needed to be refurbished. Even the garish Christmas decorations couldn't dispel the seedy atmosphere. The mood was different in the packed bar where the stranded lunch crowd gathered to drink away the afternoon. Savoring the Cuban cigar he was admiring, Petrovich clipped the tip with a gold cutter and said, "Since we can't leave, let's take a steam."

Petrovich was a steam devotee, and given a choice of meeting places, he would invariably select the club's steam room where he could discuss business and unwind at the same time. Originally built as part of the exclusive private club that had occupied the entire building, the baths, as Petrovich liked to call them, were in much better shape than the rooms upstairs. The floors were covered with a deep purple marble and there were white tiled showers, blue tiled plunge pools, a green tiled steam room for actors and a pale pink room for actresses.

Both men were wrapped in white sheets and sweating profusely as steam poured in through a fancy tulip-shaped vent. "Drink plenty of liquid," said Valentine as he ladled some ice cold water over his head. "It doesn't take long to get dehydrated." Lensk wasn't a bania devotee and he was having trouble getting used to the hot, heavy air.

Alden Lensk had once been a partner in a Moscow law firm. His most potent weapons were a keen mind and hands-on experience with the intricacies of the international banking system. His boss was being too casual and concerned, and that alarmed him. He was right. In one nimble motion, Petrovich stubbed out his cigar and shrugged the sheet off his shoulders, exposing a hairy torso. "Dead ends! Our banks are missing billions and all you can come up with is dead ends!" He'd spat out the words so venomously that Lensk almost stopped breathing.

"I..."

"Shut up, you fool. Less than half the money was ours, the rest belonged to our friends in Moscow. You know what that means?"

Lensk took a troubled breath and spoke with maddening slowness. "There has to be a trail. We'll find it."

Petrovich noticed that Lensk was fighting the heat instead of forcing fluids and letting his body adjust. "Some of our Moscow friends are puzzled. They cannot understand why the best brains in the American computer industry cannot trace our stolen funds."

"We need more time," Lensk pleaded.

Petrovich downed a glass of water then drew another. "Last night I got a call on my secure line. The man who called said he had our money and was in the process of giving it away."

Lensk was disbelieving. "Giving it away?"

"*Da*, to the needy. Among other things, he mentioned that our computer security sucks."

"Our passwords, every thing is encrypted…"

Petrovich held up a hand. "He said a 16-year-old hacker did all the work."

"He's lying. That's impossible."

"You think so?" Petrovich's voice was harsh. "The man said it was the easiest $5.2 billion he'd ever stolen."

Lensk felt faint.

"*Da*, and there's more good news. He identified himself as Jake Garboosian. Not a bashful man this Garboosian, said he'd also done the nifty job on our Queens location.

"The man has to be crazy to confess to all that."

"What should I do, Lensk, call the police and say Jake Garboosian robbed my banks of billions in laundered drug profits and funds stolen from Russia?"

Lensk wiped his brow with a corner of his sheet. "Maybe Garboosian's not his real name."

"Idiot, he told me to the penny how much money he took from Queens and how he killed the two Voccios and their lawyer. Voccio's drunken son ran over Garboosian's wife; and we killed his entire family."

The comment rocked Lensk. "I'd forgotten the name."

"Let me use his words so you won't forget exactly where we stand with Detective Garboosian. 'I'm going to plant you all in the ground and use your friends in Moscow as fill.'"

Physically, Alden Lensk was not impressive. Partially bald, on the stocky side, he supported a paunch that gave him a lumbering gait. His face was florid and puffy, but his razor sharp mind had served Petrovich well. Unending travel away from his wife and children had strained his marriage and he needed pills to sleep. His physique was unimpressive, but because of who he was, people assumed he was a brutal man. They were wrong.

In contrast, Valentine Petrovich was tall, trim and blessed with Shakespearian good looks. Women gravitated to Petrovich, who did little to discourage their advances. Cruelty was the one thing that Petrovich truly enjoyed, but Tasha, his beautiful ballerina, was the only one who knew how sadistic he could be. Luckily for Petrovich, he'd unleashed obsessions in Tasha that rivaled his.

"Lensk, my friend, I have already told our Moscow friends that their money is gone. However, I guaranteed its return within five years with interest of course."

"But, how…?"

"Our crack and ecstasy plants are now on line. New England is the only large, virgin territory left for those products. To survive we must penetrate that market."

"But, without capital…?"

"Tasha has $250 million under her maiden name in Chase Manhattan. That's more than enough."

"What should I be doing?"

"Consider all the bank money gone. I want you in New England ferreting out anyone in authority we can bribe. Police, judges, elected officials, anyone who can do us some good."

Seeing the indifferent look on Petrovich's face, Lensk decided to hold his tongue. "Lensk, I told our friends how hard you have worked and how difficult it has been for your family. Unfortunately, they remember that it was you who set up our banks."

"*Da*, I was the only one with the knowledge and experience."

"There have been comments that my sending the wolf to check on the hen house was very foolish."

"They questioned my loyalty?"

"*Nyet*, they questioned my judgement."

"I have always been loyal."

"*Da*, be assured that you are above suspicion."

Lensk was finding it ever more difficult to breathe. "Excuse me. I have to step outside and catch my breath."

"*Da*, Lensk, you don't look good. I'll join you in a few minutes. There are fresh juices in the alcove next to the door. Drink something."

Hidden by the rising steam, a look of triumph sparkled in Petrovich's eyes. Being accustomed to the role of the ruthless aggressor, the Russian found the current situation unthinkable and unnerving and he thought, *Garboosian, you can change your name and hide, but you're going to die hard and very soon. Lensk, Lensk, Lensk. Well, my friend, after all, you did set the banks up.*

While the icy shower raised goose bumps on his body, Lensk berated himself. *Wolf, loyalty, above suspicion, what is going on here? Does he think I'm a cretin? Am I supposed to wait around until I'm shot in the back?* The avariciousness and brutality of Petrovich's methods were repugnant to Lensk who sat in front of his oversized locker with sagging shoulders and wobbly legs. Devastated over how it was all going to end, he was heartsick for his family. He had to do something, but what?

20

License plates identify Rhode Island as the "Ocean State" and during the summer months, residents take to the water any way they can. But after Labor Day, the beaches start closing and the weekend sailors start hauling in their boats. Newport's Jazz, Folk and Rhythm and Blues Festivals are over and the cottages along the shoreline are empty. After the first cold winds drift down from Canada, even the die-hards begin storing their quahog rakes and fishing tackle. Shortly thereafter, the palate of the state's foliage changes from dark green to the blazing reds and shades of gold that evidence the coming of winter.

The New Year's celebrations were over and Providence was back to work. Silas Hershoff, coffee in one hand and a donut in the other, padded down the hall to his home office. There were bags under his eyes from too much reading and late nights at the piano. He was wearing his usual office attire, bathrobe and slippers, and Hud noted that the nicotine stains on his smoker's hand had gotten a shade darker. For women clients, Sollie shucked his robe for a lime-green jogging outfit and sneakers. Placing his coffee cup down on the first flat surface he came to, Sollie began patting his robe for his lighter when he became aware of the movement of his favorite rocker and the lean figure sitting in it. He turned to run when Hud said. "Howdaya do it Sollie, you never gain a fucking ounce."

Sollie's mouth opened but the donut escaped unharmed. Caught in an emotional bear hug, Hud was lifted off the floor. "You asshole."

Sollie Hershoff's law office was actually two large bedrooms that had been joined together and decorated with white wicker and summery pastel fabrics that mixed well with the pickled oak floor. A white grand piano and wall-to-wall cabinet overflowing with antique porcelain clocks provided solid clues as to Sollie's real interests.

"There's still a "wanted for questioning" outstanding, but I guess you know that."

"Yeah, I know. That's why I'm here."

"You need a lawyer?"

Sollie was sitting on the piano bench, and Hud handed him a money order. "This makes it official."

"The Voccio thing?"

"Nada."

"What can be more important than a possible five-count murder charge?"

"The Voccios are not my problem."

"Nooooo problem, the man says. Jesus Jake, you always amazed me, but the Voccio matter is some serious shit."

"My name's Hud Hudson now, Sollie. Sit down and hear me out."

During the two hours it took Hud to fill him in, Sollie polished off a half dozen vanilla glazed donuts and an equal number of cigarettes. "You come back, you're lean and mean and you lay this incredible story on me. What's the punch line?"

"I've been scanning the *Providence Sunday Journal* on a library computer and I see where you helped get this Tara Lambia elected governor. She any good?"

"She's honest, smart and tough and for this state, that's a first."

"You still on good terms?"

"I can have her here in twenty minutes."

"No, I have to stay invisible. I'm counting on you to make what I outlined happen."

"Tenhagen and Hyde, that could be a deal-breaker."

"They know the turf and I trust them. They'll do it."

Captain Donald Tenhagen had given his secretary instructions to hold all his calls, so when the phone rang he muttered, Who in the hell can this be? A pleasant female voice said, "Captain, would it be possible for you to meet with Governor Lambia at four today?"

"Of course," replied Tenhagen, floored by the request. "At the capitol building?"

"Yes, and captain, the governor requests that you tell absolutely no one about the meeting."

Minutes later, Special Agent in Charge, Peter Hyde, whose offices were virtually across the street from Tenhagen's, got a similar call.

Rhode Island's State House sat atop a hill that began its climb a few blocks north of Providence's Union Station. The official address was 82 Smith Street. Built out of white Georgian marble with one of the largest, self-supporting domes in the world, the State House looked like a scaled down version of the Capitol building in Washington. Since her swearing-in ceremony, a constant stream of obligations had kept Tara Lambia away from the State House. So when she finally sat down at her desk, the single most powerful woman in Rhode Island felt uneasy among the unfamiliar objects and trappings of her new office. Rubbing her hands together to get the circulation going, the governor thought, God it's cold in here. The temperature in Providence hovered around three degrees when the State House heating system went on the fritz. Two portable heaters whirred away, but the room was still uncomfortably chilly. Every once in a while a fickle fan blade would scrape the heater's protective grille and make a racket that was getting on the governor's nerves. She had set aside the day for quiet contemplation, but it wasn't working out that way.

Although there was a calm hush in the governor's inner sanctum, tension reigned in other sections of the State House. After being on the job less than a week, the first woman governor of Rhode Island had created a firestorm of controversy. Her round of post election speeches had sketched out a bold legislative agenda aimed at helping her constituency survive a crumbling economy. Few Americans were in a position to take a vacation. Tourism, Rhode Island's major industry, had gone into the tank and unemployment benefits had skyrocketed. The impact on the state was devastating. Divorce, suicide, street violence and stimulant abuse were off the charts and some of the state's cities were dangerously close to anarchy. Newspaper editorials described the state's situation as grim and perilous.

The afternoon was winding down along with the governor's disposition. Sollie had arrived a few minutes after Tenhagen and Hyde and found them sitting around a conference table. Having worked so closely with Sollie during her campaign, Governor Lambia was familiar with his offbeat wit and other eccentricities, like his dress habits and piano playing antics. However, today Sollie wore a tailored, pin-striped suit and his presentation was anything but slapdash. Five minutes into his presentation, both Tenhagen and Hyde knew they were talking to a man with a vigorous and incisive mind.

After listening to the details of Hud's proposal, the governor asked. "Is the money for all of that really there?"

"You can verify that with a call to Mr. Love at the Hospital Trust Company. Here's the number. I gotta make a pit stop."

When he returned, the governor was pacing the room. "Why does your client want to remain anonymous?"

"He's got valid reasons and I can't discuss any of them."

The governor was cautious. "Peter, any possibility that the funds were stolen?"

"God no. If the money were stolen, it would be the largest theft the Bureau ever handled."

Sollie cut in, "My client is making the funds available to do what we all know needs to be done. This is a win–win deal for the state and everyone in this room. Don't screw it up by getting cute. My client's requirements are non–negotiable. You don't want the deal, I pitch it to the governor of Connecticut."

"Captain, Peter, unless you gentlemen are prepared to retire and take this project on, my decision is moot."

Peter Hyde had serious qualms. "Sollie, why in God's name would a complete stranger to Captain Tenhagen and me make our participation an absolute must?"

"He knows you're both eligible for retirement and he says that you guys have integrity. You have to agree the $200 thousand signing bonus and $250 thousand a year salary is fair."

"That's another thing that bothers me. The amounts seem overly generous."

"Peter, with the amounts of money and responsibility involved, the bonus and starting salary are in line. Check around yourself."

Governor Lambia had been doodling on a pad, now she asked, "When do you need an answer?"

"Seventy-two hours and not a second more."

About the time Sollie was exiting the building, the governor told Tenhagen and Hyde, "Put in your papers or I'll kill you both myself."

21

Five months after the steam bath at the Actor's Club, Alden Lensk sat buckled in his seat, deep in thought. As the plane reached its rotation speed, the pilot pulled back on the yoke and the jet lifted effortlessly off the runway. A leasing company owned the Gulfstream executive jet through an offshore shell company owned by Valentine Petrovich. Because of the private hangar facilities, the jet was kept at a jetport on Long Island. Except for its sophisticated communications equipment, the plane was off-the-shelf and would probably be thought of as spartan by the pampered executives who traveled in corporate status symbols. For the Russians, the Gulfstream provided privacy and a means of keeping the authorities in the dark about their movements.

It was normally a short hop to Providence; however, strong storm cells over Long Island Sound had prompted the captain to take a much longer, roundabout route. Fifteen minutes and 28,000 feet later, they were flying over billowing, sun-drenched clouds in an innocent blue sky. The meeting with Petrovich was only two hours old when Lensk caught himself frowning in the mirror of the Gulfstream's oversized restroom, rehashing what had been said.

"So, what excuses do you have this time?" Petrovich asked.

Petrovich had developed a tendency to erupt lately and Lensk chose his words carefully. "*Nyet* excuses. This Restore Foundation I told you about has already put 500 new police on the street and with the pay increases no one is inclined to take a bribe."

"*Da*, how could they do that so fast?"

"They had 10,000 applications from experienced officers all over the country. They chose the best and they only need two weeks of indoctrination."

Petrovich had only grunted and it wasn't until they were back upstairs having some fresh kielbasa appetizers that he continued to ask questions.

"Is the new governor vulnerable?"

"*Nyet*, she's straight and a doer."

"Humm, too bad. Lensk, if neighboring states copy Rhode Island we're done."

"What should I do?"

"What should you do? What should you do! Not only are we not paying down the money our banks lost, we haven't been buying enough heroin and the Afghans are threatening to shut our friends in Moscow off."

"Why? They already buy tons of the stuff."

"It's not money they're after."

"What then?"

"Missiles."

Lensk's blood froze in his veins. "Nuclear missiles?"

"Nukes, Stingers and Biological."

"It's insane. Osama bin Laden and the Taliban are insane."

"*Da*, but our friends have 20 percent of the country hooked on the stuff. It's not the cash-flow that Markov's worried about. Can you imagine 25 million Russians rioting against the government because they can't get their daily fix? General Markov would be out and so would we."

Markov, Lensk knew, had absolutely no scruples about anything except where it involved great sums of money. In contrast, Petrovich looked like a benevolent second cousin.

Petrovich was both impressed and concerned about the conviction in Lensk's voice: "*Nyet*! This *cannot* be allowed to happen."

"Lensk, Lensk. I agree, and so do our friends in Moscow. They're trying to buy some time." There was no way now that he was going to tell Lensk what was already in the works.

Rain pelted the windows as the plane entered a fringe area of the storm the pilot was trying to avoid. Taking a nervous swig of vodka from a flask in his coat pocket, Lensk returned to his seat where his thoughts turned to the Restore Foundation. Strange, why none of the contributors have ever been named.

Lensk had been a respected lawyer whose family was doing well by Russian standards. Although he had not yet taken up the feral habits of his associates, Lensk knew that through constant exposure he was gradually becoming debased. Lensk's parents had not been party members or part of Moscow's intelligentsia, and they had undergone unimaginable hardships to secure the university education that helped him leave borderline poverty behind. After becoming a lawyer, Lensk and a partner had built a moderately successful practice. Eventually, Lensk had moved onto a more profitable venue as the in-house attorney for one of the partnership's less than respectable clients; Valentine Petrovich. Justifying his deepening involvement in crime was easy. No matter how high up their social standing, just about everybody he met was involved somehow in drugs or in ripping off the government. Lensk had gotten on the money train and his life had gone downhill ever since.

Aware that Valentine and his cohorts viewed cold-blooded murder as a management tool, Lensk broke out in a cold sweat. He was already taking Zoloft for depression, but the periods of melancholy were still increasing in frequency and after the meeting with Petrovich he was paranoid. Retribution was ingrained in the way the American arm of ROC and their friends in Moscow did business. By the time the plane landed in Providence, Lensk had his arms wrapped around his knees and was rocking back and forth like a metronome. He was terrified.

22

Evenings were getting warmer. Summer was on its way and life was moving outdoors. A late afternoon concert at the WaterPark amphitheater had drawn thousands and as the sun set, gas-fueled pots scattered throughout the park's tidal basin spewed flames and white smoke giving the concert a dreamy, Shakespearian mood. The foul river odor that had plagued downtown Providence for decades was gone. In its place were the idyllic and costly WaterPark and RiverWalk, the cornerstones of Providence's massive urban renewal effort.

The concert crowd, cheered by the music, gave Governor Tara Lambia a loud, fervent 'thank you' after she'd presented a sizable check from The Restore Foundation. The symphony board surprised her with a gondola excursion complete with a genuine gondolier, fine wine and a mouth-watering assortment of Italian delicacies. The gondola port was located right there in the tidal basin a scant hundred feet or so from the last row seats. Tara would listen to the remainder of the concert out on the water in the tranquil comfort of the gondola. Tired, but finding the music and the warm, sultry evening intoxicating, Tara turned to her husband. "Well?"

"Are you kidding?Let's go!"

They were escorted by the chairman of the symphony board, who was a veteran of several gondola trips. He was a peppy man who liked to share information. "We're sitting in the first truly authentic Venetian gondola ever built in the States. Isn't she a beauty?"

Tara ran her hand across the wooden armrest of her seat; it felt like a piece of fine furniture. "She's a work of art."

"That she is, governor. That she is."

"She seems much bigger once you're on board."

"The *Cynthia Julia's* 36-feet long but she's light and remarkably fast."

"Impressive. Where did they hide the motor?"

The chairman chuckled. "No motor, just our burly gondolier and one oar."

As they pushed off into the tidal basin, the orchestra was playing a haunting version of the Beatles' "Hey Jude."

Mixing and mingling with the crowd, a middle-aged couple were standing near a refreshment stand slurping soft drinks. When Tara's party was clear of the dock, the couple strolled down the cobblestone walk toward one of the Venetian-styled foot bridges. Halfway there, the man pulled out a cell phone and spoke in Russian. "They're on their way."

Untroubled, the governor's fingers tapped incessantly on the varnished railing. The governor's job had turned Tara into a workaholic, but she was actually enjoying herself. The wine was excellent and a lazy wind was floating the music across the tidal basin and out to the river. *Damn, it's so serene out here. We have to do this again.*

As the gondolier neared the end of the quay, the street lights came on. Knowing the shooting situation had just improved, the pressure building on Gorgi Bololka's brain began to ease. A thick stand of trees and shrubs along the opposite bank had created dark shadows and a troublesome view-shed. Fortunately, the street lights were not yet on and in the twilight and shadows it was difficult for Gorgi to track the slender gondola. Now, with the street lights, he couldn't miss. For a perfectionist like Gorgi, even the best night scopes weren't dependable enough for one-shot jobs.

Most of the police were assigned to crowd control around the concert area, which was now over a mile away from the gondola and another thousand yards from where Gorgi lay prone, sighting in a silenced rifle mounted on a collapsible stand. The morning rain and the warm night had the mosquitoes buzzing around his sweaty head and neck. Immune to the minor distractions, Gorgi checked the surface of the water for signs of ripples. *Good, no wind.* The orchestra was now playing "Jellico Cats." The impact of the silent, high velocity rifle bullet smashed the governor against the side of the fragile boat and it tipped over. On the surface, Tara's husband kept her afloat as blood pumped out of her chest in a small geyser. Holding onto the gondola with one hand he saw her hat floating away in the widening circle of her lifegiving blood. Later, a photographer covering the concert saw the yellow straw hat the governor had worn moving with the gentle current that had been painted red. Better than any words, the picture conveyed the act, the grief and the loss of a good woman. The morning paper and then the national magazines carried the photo on their front pages with a simple caption: Tara Lambia, 1948-2001. The people's governor.

Unknown to those at the concert, two more deadly encounters were taking place within easy walking distance of the WaterPark. The Rhode Island Convention Center was only a few minutes walk from the Foundation's offices where he had delivered another check, but a pesky summer flu and the threat of heavy rain had motivated Sollie to drive. Once there, he regretted his decision. The New England Flower & Garden Show was drawing large crowds and Sollie ended up parking on the uppermost level of the garage. As he was about to lock his door, a man in a raincoat approached him steadfastly. "Mr. Hershoff?"

"Yes?"

The gun was concealed from passing cars by the man's open coat but Sollie could see it clearly. *So this is how it's going to end.*

"Get in the car and slide over to the passenger side."

His senses sharpened, but knowing better than to argue with a gun, Sollie re-entered the car and started to move over. Seeing no one, and mindful that time always favored the target, the assailant fired two bullets into Sollie's head. Pushing Sollie's body to the floor, the assailant covered him with a car blanket from the rear seat.

Minutes before Sollie's murderer exited the parking garage, three men entered the lobby of The Restore Foundation's offices. Two of the men had visited the building before. One man had posed as a recycling contractor interested in obtaining the Foundation's waste paper. The other man presented himself as the manager of a local restaurant trying to drum up take-out business. Prior to perestroika, the three men had been career soldiers in the Russian army assigned to a covert assassination unit. None of the men were impressed by what they saw during their site surveys. For one, anyone could gain access to the Foundation's elevator. Granted, there was a uniformed guard in the lobby, but he was unarmed and appeared to be nothing more than window dressing.

The only person in the executive reception area had been a happy-go-lucky young woman who had taken delight in answering their questions.

None of the men had spotted the state-of-the-art miniature cameras built into the lobby and hallway crown moldings. Not only had their pictures been taken, but their cover stories had also been checked. So when the control room supervisor called Peter Hyde, the Foundation's executive directors were ready.

"Mr. Hyde, we have the three known bogeys in the downstairs lobby."

"Connect me with Violet and Eric."

To make the Foundation's top offices even more secure, it had a dedicated elevator. This arrangement created some useable space behind the walls on each side of the elevator shaft. Peter Hyde had taken advantage of the architectural anomaly by having the contractor build a cleverly concealed access door to the space.

Upon reaching the top floor, one of the men used a telescoping rod to hold the elevator doors open. Music from the elevator's Muzak system poured out into the empty reception area. A hand-printed sign on the reception desk read: *I've gone for coffee. Back in five. Betty-O.* Smiling at their good fortune, the men advanced toward the thick double oak doors that were flanked by stately fluted columns. Seven steps from the elevator, the men were frozen to a stop by a woman's voice and the metallic click of weapons being cocked. "Don't turn around. Lay your weapons on the carpet and step back three steps. Do it now."

Disbelief in how easily they had been waylaid by a woman turned to humiliation and then anger. Aware that the lives of their loved ones in Russia would be forfeited if their mission failed, the three assailants turned in unison screaming something in Russian. Violet and Eric had pre-selected their initial targets and every one of their bullets struck home. It was a turkey shoot that left the two defenders with a sick taste in their mouths.

"No pulses," called out Eric, who was examining the men on the floor. "No vest either."

With Eric's words still hanging in the air, a door opened and Tenhagen and Hyde entered the room accompanied by a woman. The group stopped about ten feet from the bodies and the woman began making a video of the scene. Tenhagen threw a pair of surgical gloves to Eric. "See what you can find."

The woman automatically stopped filming.

After carefully searching the bodies, Eric reported, "Nothing."

Hyde's voice was strident. "Check their waistbands for labels, you never know."

"Knight and Coolidge, Seville Row, London on this one."

"Um, check the others."

When Eric came up empty, Quinn asked, "Weapons?"

Only one man had fired his weapon, but the bursts had ended up in the ceiling. Eric's reply did not surprise anyone. "Uzi's, all reworked for automatic fire."

Tenhagen turned to the woman with the camera. "When you're satisfied, call it in. Eric, Violet, tell it like it happened. We have it all on tape from the start."

When he was told about the debacle at the Foundation's offices, Petrovich went into a tirade. Not only was the Foundation putting more police on Rhode Islands's streets, it was lobbying in Washington for tough new drug and money-laundering laws. Worse, the Foundation seemed to have unlimited finances, and in Washington, money talks. None of this was good for Petrovich's business.

23

High cirrus clouds floated like cotton balls in the bitter cold air as the rusting Ford Crown Victoria moved slowly through the neighborhood. *Bomalay, bomalay, bomalay.* The heavy car passing over the bridge's uneven plank roadway made a reverberating sound that reminded Hud of a song, but he couldn't remember the title. When the echo stopped, the unblemished snow-covered countryside northwest of New Haven came back into view.

Hud had never met Juan Feidor Moralez. Over the years, when Hud was Jake Garboosian, the supervisor of twenty New Haven detectives, Juan's cousin, a physician, had been their go-between. The old Oldsmobile had taken Hud from his hotel to the meeting place. Expecting a lavish estate guarded by combat-booted mercenaries, he was surprised when his driver stopped in front of what looked to be part of an abandoned farmhouse. Built out of clapboards that hadn't been painted in fifteen years at least, the house looked shabby and uninviting. Weeds had taken over the front yard and choked out the grass and shrubs. The road was empty from both directions, but Hud heard the sound of a car that needed a muffler coming from a large barn in the rear of the property. Barren branches from a stand of oak trees were rubbing against the roof of the house and Hud noticed that a lot of the shingles were missing. *Shit, at least fix the roof.*

A tattered sofa and some metal folding chairs were the only furniture in the living room. The windows were closed tightly and the heat was oppressive. Heavy faded drapes held together with clothespins and duct tape sealed out the light. A floor lamp with a yellowed lampshade and a low wattage bulb provided the only illumination and Hud had to squint in order to see. Seated under a greasy ceiling fan in the open kitchen, three men were spooning chili out of styrofoam cups. Cans of Pepsi sitting in a pail of ice surrounded a gargantuan wedge of cheese that was anchored to a cluttered wood picnic table by a switchblade knife. Hud glanced at the kitchen sink. It was clean.

Automatic weapons lay nestled against the table between each man and the hand that reached out to pick one of them up was attached to a wrist the size of a steel I-beam. As Hud's blue eyes became accustomed to the dim lighting, he saw a portly, middle-aged man with shaggy gray hair emerge from the shadows. A chunky build and a small potbelly belied the man's prodigious stamina. He was wearing work clothes and his faltering, uneven gait implied that, somewhere along the line, he had suffered a serious leg or hip injury. Stopping a few feet away, the man who the various gangs selling drugs in New Haven feared more than the police said, "Welcome."

Influenced by Juan's mythical status, Hud didn't know what to expect. However, Juan's friendly gaze put Hud at ease at once. Seeing Hud loosen his collar, Juan said, "The air is on the fritz. Please excuse."

Juan knew the house was a disgrace, but he preferred to meet in settings where he had total control.

"It's been five years." Hud was referring to the time he had sidetracked and eventually dumped the murder investigation of a drug dealer when he was a New Haven detective. The dealer used mobile labs to cook-up the crack and meth he sold to the Voccio organization and the law couldn't nail him. Hud had some preliminary evidence that pointed to Juan as the dealer's killer, but he'd tanked the case for the sake of humanity.

After some small talk, Juan led Hud to a far corner. His tone was authoritative but lacked arrogance. "We're out of earshot. What brings you to my hovel?"

"I need ya help."

"What kind?"

"Dangerous kind."

Juan's mouth barely opened. "Hmm, I see."

While Hud explained what he had in mind, Juan chain-smoked, lighting one cigarette with the butt of another. Juan Moralez had graduated from Duke and had done two tours in Viet Nam. When he came home, New Haven was a dirty, drug-infested sewer. Juan and Bernard High, a black neighborhood activist had formed The Saviors, and had gone to war with New Haven's drug merchants. It didn't help that brain-dead students from Yale University came around looking for the stuff.

"They still gotta reward out for you and Bernie?"

"Twenty-five thousand."

"Anyone crazy enough to try?"

"Twice on Bernie, once on me."

"How is Bernie?" asked Hud.

"He's fine, the rag-tag wannabee's that tried, well you know. Well, anyway, how much?"

"You and Bernie each get 300 thousand. Everyone else gets 100 thousand. I pay all expenses."

"Where in hell you gonna get the money to pay us?"

"It's in the till. Everyone gets 50 percent up-front."

"The Russians have been trying to get a toe-hold in here for the last year, but even after Voccio got whacked, the Italians have been holding them off. With our help, of course."

"Well?" asked Hud.

"I'm in, but I gotta check with Bernie. Where you staying?"

Juan opened a cigar box, took out a cell phone and wandered into another room. On his return, he said, "Bernie and I will be at your hotel at nine tonight."

"Think he'll go for it?"

"You must be kidding, the kind of money you're talking?"

"Seeya at nine. Bring a list of what ya need and who I have to pay."

Juan was about to object when Hud said, "No names. I only need a head count."

24

As they reached the crest of the bridge, Hud gazed down at the sun-drenched harbor and the city by the sea. This was Hud's first visit to Newport in years and the invigorating tang of sea air coming into the car's open windows felt good. Puffy clouds filled the summer sky and a steady breeze was humming through the cables that held the bridge's roadway above the deep blue waters of Narragansett Bay. Far below, waves were crashing against the rocky coastline and Hud could almost taste the salty spray.

At the beginning of the century, Newport had all but cornered the barons of industry market. There, the favored families could summer in splendid isolation. Years later, when the America's Cup races and Newport's annual music festivals came along, everything changed. These days, the town's fame and popularity were its Achilles' heels and the intrinsic civility and glamour of the place had been smothered by an elaborately garnished tourist trap.

As they made their way through the downtown area, traffic started to back up. "Tourists," muttered Juan, who made a quick right down a side street.

"Lots of fudge and taffy makers in this town," Hud observed.

"Makes an inexpensive gift for the folks back home," Jilly said.

Juan made a few more turns and Hud said, "I see you know your way around."

"Newport's not that big and I used to spend a lot of time here hoping some trust fund babe would sweep me off my feet."

Hud laughed. "How did it go?"

"I'm still looking, *amigo*."

In their hotel suite, Hud told Jilly about Moralez and Bernard High and he didn't sugarcoat the situation. Passionately loyal, she sat there, inert, a good listener, silently rejoicing that the man who had almost ruined her life was about to go down.

"Hud, I have to be included."

"No way. Like I said, this is no cakewalk."

When they finally finished talking, it was late and they were sipping white wine. Jilly was going along.

The sign for the Mope Hotel directed them down a narrow blacktop road which very soon turned into a roadway of crushed rock and seashells.

"How far is it?" asked Hud.

"Only two miles but the road is very curvy."

Five minutes later, Juan pulled off onto an unused dirt road full of deep potholes. "I'm glad you rented an SUV," Juan said, braking to a stop. "We're here."

Hud and Jilly looked around, seeing nothing but scrub oak trees and knee-high sea grass. They hid the car with fallen tree branches and headed, single-file, in the general direction of their objective. Loaded as they were with gear, it was slow going. Wading through the grass, they reached a point where they had an unobstructed view of the hotel and quay below. Located on a remote point of land called Sackest Point, the Mope Hotel was spread across the top of a rocky hillside that ran down to Rhode Island Sound. Ninety-eight rickety wooden stairs connected the hotel's guest rooms with the stone-faced quay that served as a swimming platform and dock.

Juan pointed at a boat tied up along side the quay. "There she is."

Wherever the "P" went, it drew oohs and ahh's, and even in Newport where locals considered super-yachts part of the everyday landscape, it was hard not to notice the rakish lines that set her apart. She was built entirely of aluminum and could cruise comfortably at 25 knots. Power wise, her diesel engines were engineered to conserve fuel, and once her cavernous fuel tanks were "topped off" the "P" could go anywhere in the world, nonstop.

"She's got two satellite domes." Hud said. "Where's the chopper?"

In the middle of the boat's helicopter pad, there was a large blue square with the initial "P" painted in gold.

"No idea." Juan responded. "It was here yesterday."

Lying on beds of grass high above the sea, Juan and Hud scanned the hotel through high-powered binoculars.

"Third floor, middle." uttered Juan.

Hud moved his binoculars up a notch and adjusted the focus. "Yeah, I see them."

Juan and his three men, for that matter, had no use for loudmouths. Juan was a quiet, well-mannered man who could go unnoticed anywhere. For those reasons he had warmed to Hud's unassuming, low-key manner. Noting that Petrovich's men were carrying automatic weapons, Juan said, "They're well armed, but too lax."

Unfamiliar with tactical situations, Hud just nodded.

While Juan was squirting some nasal spray into his clogged sinuses, Jilly asked, "What does *mope* mean in English?"

"Sea." said Hud.

"Ah, the Sea Hotel."

As the sun disappeared over the horizon, a sky streaked with splashes of crimson, purple and orange loomed like an abstract painting in constant motion. It was evening when the *"P"* was joined by a wide-beamed, 68-foot catamaran flying the American flag. As three men dressed like yachtsmen left the sailboat for the hotel, two armed men stationed themselves on the bow and stern of the catamaran. Minutes later, as though someone had called, another man was added to the *"P's"* deck watch.

Hud pointed to the large circular object mounted to the roof of the sailboat's cabin. The sailing yacht's air-surface radar was rotating which meant someone was manning the scope. "This is getting stranger by the minute."

Juan's response was cut off by the sound of rotor blades as a helicopter came up over the opposite hillside and landed on the *"P"*. "Three's a crowd." Jilly said as two over-dressed men and the pilot were helped down to the deck.

After it got dark, the afternoon's warm, lazy zephyrs were replaced by a cold turbulent wind. Juan, didn't mind. He had taken the deadman's watch, twelve to four A.M. so the others could get some undisturbed sleep. On the quay, crew members from the two boats had built a fire in an old oil drum and were sitting around drinking and telling stories in languages he didn't recognize. He woke Hud.

"The two sitting against the stone wall are Russians for sure. I'm not positive, but except for the two Americans, the other four are Arabic."

"Hell of a combination."

"Yeah, but Petrovich gets his hard drugs from Russians and they get it from the fucking Arabs."

"How you know all that?"

"An FBI memo."

Juan hated anyone connected with the drug trade. "May I get to piss on their graves."

Rolling back into the sleeping bag he shared with Jilly, Hud said, "Tomorrow night."

During his early morning watch Hud examined the quay, noting the cracked cement and the out of service boats that were lashed down, willy-nilly, in the farthest corner. He attributed the cracks in the quay to the use of salt water in mixing the cement. "Ah Choo!" One of the men on watch let go a mighty sneeze, the sound traveling up the untrammeled bluff with the wind. Hud peeked at his watch; 7:30, and everyone was still tucked in except Jilly who was sitting up with the sleeping bag wrapped around her. "Take the watch, I'm going to buzz into town for some food and hot drinks. Wake Juan if anything starts to stir."

Brushing her hair back, Jilly gave Hud a mock salute.

After dropping off the grub, Hud waited until nine and drove to the hotel. A lackadaisical night auditor was still manning the front desk. "I'm interested in booking your top floor for next season. Might I have a quick look at a room?"

"Sir, all of the rooms on the third floor are suites. I would show them to you, but the hotel's owner and his party are staying with us through the weekend and are occupying the entire floor."

Passing Hud a black and white brochure and rate card, the clerk asked. "Are you a local?"

"Yes, I live in Bristol."

"Then you can knock 20 percent off our rates."

"That's very generous."

"We're pretty far off the beaten track. So, word of mouth is our best advertising."

"How many rooms do you have?"

"Up top we have ten suites, five have ocean views. The second floor has eighteen rooms. Nine of those face the water."

"Are you full?"

"Like I said the top floor is booked. But there are only four rooms occupied on the second floor and two of them will be checking out by noon."

"You wouldn't have a floor plan of the hotel with directions on how to find the place?"

Reaching under the counter the clerk handed Hud a sheet of paper, "It's all here, except that the tennis courts are closed until we can get them repaired."

"How long?" asked Hud.

"They promised to start next week, but they said that five weeks ago."

After five more minutes of chit-chat, Hud thanked the clerk profusely and gave him a crisp fifty dollar bill. "That's for the skinny on the rate break."

Smiling for the first time, the clerk said. "My name is Martin. Book through me and I'll save you another 5%."

How accommodating can you get, thought Hud, as he walked out to the unpaved parking lot.

Back at their observation post, the action oriented Juan asked, "How full is the place?"

"Except for Petrovich and his guest, almost empty. According to the desk clerk, they're all guys cheating on their wives."

"No kids?"

"No, the rates are reasonable, but there's no beach. Those stairs also turn a lot of people off."

While Hud was talking, Bernard High was methodically scanning every inch of ground around the hotel. A wide verandah ran the entire length of the hotel at the back and there were two couples having breakfast out on the deck. From what Hud had shown him, Bernie knew that the entire first floor of the hotel was dedicated to guests' activities. You could swim, steam, sauna, play billiards or dine without encountering a single stair. Looking at a couple struggling up the stairs from the quay, Bernie thought, *Add one more stair to this joint and nobody would stay here.*

One of Juan's men, another black man called Ace, spotted something they'd all missed. Off to one side of the hotel was a dilapidated storage shed which a clothesline strung with blankets had screened the previous day. "They've got two armed men on the ground. They're in the shed."

A few moments later, Juan and Hud responded in unison. "Shit."

Peering through his field glasses, Juan said, "They've got a good angle on the parking lot and the side door. We'll take them first."

By mid-afternoon, Juan's four men were getting restless. Juan had taken the SUV back to town for what he called supplies. Hud passed his field glasses to the man who was getting jittery from the waiting. "Have patience. Tonight is soon enough. Vodka and dessert will help them to relax."

As Hud stretched out on the sea grass, one of the men gave Hud a hard look and grunted, "By the way, I thought there was only going to be one boat. So, what's the deal?"

Hud was irritated by the caustic comment but his response was restrained. "So, you're all getting another 50 thousand for the added risk. Fair enough?"

Good teeth, yellowed teeth, false teeth and a pair that had enough gold fillings to buy a small car smiled back at him. Hud returned the smile, but it was because of what he was thinking, *What a great country, when you can use a bad guy's own money to have him killed.*

Dark clouds and an uncommonly calm ocean sucked up the remaining daylight, and with no moon the night was suddenly black. The man's cigarette made a brief phosphorescent splash as it hit the water. It was midnight and the guard on the boats was changing. Juan had returned with a dozen fragmentation grenades, a fifty-caliber machine gun mounted on a tripod and 1,600 rounds of ammo. His explanation: "We need the extra fire power."

Hud let Juan run the show. "Jilly, you stay here with Ace on the fifty. He'll show you how to feed the ammo and change canisters. Roberto, you and Cup take AR-15's with ten clips and make your way down to the boats. Set up behind that stone wall. When you hear the first shot, take out the stern guards on both boats first. Ace, you and Jilly take out the bow guards, knock out those radio antennas and provide overall cover. Put 200 rounds into each boat to keep them pinned inside. Ace, when Roberto and Cup get back up here, use the grenade launchers. The motor boat gets three, the sail two. Then you all haul ass down to the car."

By the time Juan, Hud and the other two men on the team got to the hotel the wind had picked up and blown away the cloud cover. There was a fat moon in the sky as the quartet approached the edge of the tree line.

Leaving the car, Juan stood stark still inspecting the darkness with the care of a surgeon reading an x-ray. The flash of a cigarette caught his attention. Seconds later two men started walking toward the hotel. "The ground-spotters are calling it a day."

"So early? asked Hud.

Juan responded, "It's getting cold and hard to see."

Hearing the canned music blaring from the hotel's dining room inspired one of the other men to whisper. "Nah. He hears the music and wants a woman."

Sensing nothing sinister in the air, Juan waved them forward. As they entered the hotel's side door, Juan took Hud's arm in a vicelike grip. "We can handle this. There's no need for you to come."

Hud knew it was a hairy mission and that Juan was offering him an out. He also knew that the lives of his new family depended on the mission's success. His response left no room for doubt. With a .9 millimeter Berreta nestled in a shoulder holster, he pointed the AR-15 he was carrying up the stairs. "Let's go."

"All right, but do exactly as I say." said Juan through tight lips.

Hud's nod left no doubt who was boss.

After cutting the telephone wires, Juan's team stood in the concrete stairwell on the third floor. Hud was the only one puffing. They took turns scanning the empty corridor and acquainting themselves with the surroundings. Then Bernie left the stairwell and rang for the elevator.

"No guards in the hall." Juan whispered.

"They must feel safe with men next door in the rooms."

"*Stupidos*," said Juan.

When it arrived, Bernie turned the elevator light off and placed a small block of wood between the doors to hold them open. "Hotel employees are lazy and they hate stairs." he said. After donning ski masks, the men fanned out in the hallway, their soft-soled shoes moving soundlessly over the carpeted floor. With its garish flowered wallpaper, overly ornate wall sconces and deep red carpeting, the place felt like an old fashioned whore house. Since Petrovich had taken the entire floor, there were no civilians to worry about, and in Juan's mind that was a big advantage.

Although she sometimes carried on like one, Tasha was no idle-minded airhead. She was shrewd and when it came to getting her way, "*nyet*" was not a word that Tasha accepted without an ugly scene. Tasha's father, General Markov, had been her husband's springboard to success in the States. She and Valentine shared certain sexual fantasies. Now, in the back seat of the taxi driving her back to the Mope Hotel following a late afternoon shopping spree and a lovely dinner, Tasha shivered with anticipation of the pleasure that she and Valentine would have in bed together with Rita. She felt excitement course through her as the images in her mind heightened in intensity, when, suddenly, the cab slowed and stopped.

"What's wrong, driver? Why have we stopped?"

"Can't be sure, Lady. Could be an accident or a problem at one of the bridge's toll gates."

"How long will be?"

"Don't know. If it's a gate, could be two minutes or two hours. Either way, it'll take a little time."

Annoyed, Tasha called Rita on her cell phone to tell her she'd been delayed.

Rita lay the phone down. Naked, in preparation for the evening's activity, she was quite a package. She was wonderfully built with an attractive latin face and thick black hair that reached down to her waist. Once an American college professor, Rita was a full-time voyeur whose voracious sexual appetites were unfettered by convention. Her elaborate "portrayals" as she called them could be quite intense and always included Tasha. Because it excited her and stripped away her inhibitions, shame and pain were Rita's drugs of choice.

Rita padded over to Petrovich's connecting door and opened it. "Valentine, Tasha just called. Some traffic problem has delayed her. She says she's been a bad girl and will need a good fucking. Oh, if you like, we two can begin now."

"Five minutes."

The sight of Rita naked and the verbal exchange mortified a hotel maid in the sitting room with Petrovich. When Rita closed the door, the maid asked, "Can I serve you something else, Mr. Petrovich? Some cold borscht from the kitchen, perhaps?"

"*Nyet*, you can go. I'll call if I need anything." As the owner of the hotel, Valentine could get anything he wanted, but his favorite snack was Kavaas, a dark Russian rye beer, with plenty of fresh rye bread and cheese and the suite's refrigerator was already stocked. As Petrovich looked out into the darkness at the back of the hotel, he reflected on how he and Tasha were clones of each other. They were both calculating, greedy and vicious at the core, and their relationship, much like Russia itself, was despairing and rudderless.

Juan surmised correctly that Petrovich had taken the center suite with his guards occupying the suites on each side. Two carts stacked with dirty dishes and empty Vodka bottles cluttered the corridor on the side away from the ocean view. Bottles of domestic wines and others with foreign labels Hud couldn't read indicated that Petrovich had given his Arabic visitors the ocean views.

Juan nodded at the center door and Hud knocked.

A man in the room snarled, *"Da,* who is it?"

"Mr. Petrovich, it's room service. I've come for the dinner dishes. Do you need anything else?"

"Nyet!" said Petrovich.

"As you wish, sir," Hud said in a condescending tone. "Should you require anything else, please let us know."

Juan nodded his approval.

While Hud pushed the dish carts down the hallway to block the elevator, Juan's men quietly duct taped battery-triggered acid-packs against the doors of all eight suites. The packs were smallish but the shaped charges were sufficient to burn out the locks with a quiet sizzle.

Petrovich's sitting room was empty, but Hud could hear the unmistakable sounds of sex coming from the bedroom. When Hud cracked open the door, he saw Rita kneeling on the bed, her head buried in Petrovich's lap. Moans and unintelligible noises leaked out of her occupied mouth at random intervals.

Hud had expected to come face-to-face with Petrovich and Tasha, but after Jilly's experience, the presence of the other woman was not surprising. Putting a gun to Rita's head, he said, "Get up."

Standing naked, with her legs apart and her painted toes curled into the carpet, Rita, wracked with fury, spit out, "Peasant bastard!"

Hud was already wired and the woman's outburst inflamed him. Without thinking, he grabbed her by the hair and yanked her head around. When she spat at him again, he transferred his gun to his other hand and slapped her solidly across the face. Stunned and infuriated, Rita looked up at him from the carpeted floor and he saw the tattoo that Jilly had described. She had been with the Petroviches that night in Palm Beach.

Having consumed some wine and over a half bottle of vodka, Petrovich, used to having the upper hand, was a study in indifference. He looked at Hud's masked face, his fuzzy mind trying to grasp the reality of the situation. Viciously spewing out the words, he said, "Who are you?"

"Me? I'm the guy who stole your fucking billions and burned you out."

Petrovich's brain stems must have fractured, because he lunged for the gun on the bedside table, his face contorted by hate. "Youuuu," he screamed. Taking aim like a student on a firing range, Hud fired three times, effectively blowing out the back of Petrovich's head.

Hud heard three thuds behind him. When he looked, Bernie was holding a sound-suppressed Glock, and Rita, with a gun in her hand, was lying dead.

"How?"

"From under the bed. Never turn your back on women like these." Bernie said sadly.

When it was all over, all of the Russians and Arabs were dead and one of Juan's men had a bad shoulder wound. Calling to the man who carried the medical kit, Juan shouted, "Morphine and a field dressing. We'll cover the hall."

While the wounded man was being attended, Hud went quickly through the rooms picking up any papers that looked important. He had just finished stuffing them into a pillowcase when Juan called, "We gotta go."

They poured out of the side door where Ace, Cup and Jilly were waiting in the SUV. As they drove away, two huge explosions shot fiery pieces of both yachts high into the air and sent a 250 miles per hour wave of super-heated air up the contour of the hill. The roof and most of the top floor of The Mope Hotel was blown away instantly and the rest of the wooden structure began vibrating before it burst into flames. When the smoke began to seep into the cellar, the hotel staff who had fled there when the gunfire began, took the cement stairs to safety. Others in the hotel were not so fortunate.

As they drove away, Hud looked back. The sky looked like the grand finale at a small town's fireworks display. "What in hell?"

"The boats must have been carrying high-explosives. Gasoline doesn't have that much punch." said Juan.

Jilly cried out. "Some innocent people must have gotten killed."

Juan looked down, "I expect some did. We didn't know about the boats."

Jilly's mind was flooded with vivid memories of that terrible night in Miami. *Even in death, the bastard managed to kill the unaware, she thought.*

The only way to exit Newport by land was over a bridge. The nearest was a toll bridge, the other one was at the other end of the island. So, 12 minutes after the first shot a fast, twin engine aircraft took off from a small private field only five miles away from the hotel. The plane flew under the radar screen that tracked commercial flights and the short hop back to a grass strip was never detected. Ace drove the waiting van thirty miles to a ramshackle village in Rhode Island that called itself Harmony. Without cable, the place was characterized by television antennas, clotheslines and shabby homes.

The team's prearranged safe house was located on a secondary dirt road hidden by a stand of mature oak and birch trees. Nerves were frayed, and the only one who slept was the man who was wounded and had been knocked out by the morphine. When they'd landed, Juan made a call on his cell phone. "I need you. Thirty minutes."

It was obvious from the medical equipment and supplies that the unlicensed doctor was no stranger to clandestine surgery. He was also very good. "How much do I owe you?" Hud asked.

"For Juan, $3,500."

Hud, went into the bedroom and came back with $7,000. "He'll need follow-up."

After counting the bills, the surgeon said, "He'll get the best."

In her taxi, Tasha, along with everyone else in the stalled line of traffic, was startled by the tremendous explosion. The night sky lit up with fire. On the cab's radio she heard the words from a driver nearer to the scene. "Mope Hotel's on fire. Total destruction!"

In the jumble of Tasha's thoughts that followed, one rose above the others. If Valentine did not survive, if this was not an accident, she would hunt down those responsible. She swore vengeance.

Hours later, when Tasha finally arrived at the Hotel, she was taken to a black body bag. It was Valentine. Composing herself, she called her father. "Val's dead, I want to take over."

25

After a quiet dinner of fresh flounder at their favorite Block Island restaurant, Hud and Jilly went back to the cabin cruiser they'd rented for the week. Jilly was still in turmoil over the possibility that innocent people might have been killed or hurt in the conflagration at the hotel. Hud, meanwhile, spread the papers he'd taken from Petrovich's room out on the bed. With the exception of the maps, every thing was either in Russian or Arabic. The AAA map of the United States had eight cities circled: San Francisco, Long Beach, Chicago, Fort Lauderdale, Boston, Providence, New York and Washington. Having worked drug cases for two years, he knew that everyone in the business, regardless of what country they came from, called methadone "meth" and cocaine "coke."

"Jilly, I don't see one word in this mess that mentions drugs."

"Want me to look?"

"Yeah, I'm going blind."

Hud started putting on his clothes, "Why get dressed now?"

"You read, I'm going to top off the tanks. We're going back to the mainland."

"It's two in the morning."

"This has a bad feel."

The sea was flat, and Hud pushed the throttles to the stops. By 8:15 they had turned in the boat, rented a car, consumed a high protein breakfast and purchased a cheap backpack at a 24-hour drugstore. Minutes later, Hud and Jilly sat in their Buick parked across from the Restore

Foundation Building. When a Mercedes pulled up in front of the building and Peter Hyde stepped out, Hud leaned towards Jilly and said, "Go."

Jilly exited the car quickly. She caught Peter Hyde just inside the Restore Foundation's lobby and dropped the backpack at his feet. "Mr. Hyde, the papers in this bag were taken from Valentine Petrovich and a group of Arabs in Newport last night. Get them to the FBI within the hour."

Before Hyde, somewhat stunned, could react, Jilly was out the door and getting into the car. Hyde, ran out to the curb and got the plate number. Hud had already switched plates with a van parked next to them at the restaurant.

Returning to the lobby, backpack in hand, Hyde was met by a security guard. "Mr. Hyde, Captain Tenhagen asks that you go directly to his office."

Hyde was about to hand the backpack to a male secretary when Tenhagen came out of his office.

"I expect you haven't heard."

"Heard? "

"Petrovich and a group of Arabs were taken out last night in Newport. They've found sixteen bodies so far, two of them women."

Looking down at the backpack still in his hand, Hyde froze. He put the pack down gently on the desk. "Cap, get the building cleared and call the bomb squad. I'll get the Bureau here ASAP."

While the black bomb squad van was racing to the Foundation, two men sat talking in The Old Greek Mill restaurant located in the Blackstone Valley in northern Rhode Island. The area was a mix of rolling farm country peppered with mill villages with strange sounding names like Pawtucket, Woonsocket and Chepachet. During its heyday, the Valley's fifty textile mills spewed chemicals into the Blackstone River and black coal dust into the air. These days, the recycled factories housed trendy boutiques, factory shops and ethnic restaurants. Once the cradle of the American Industrial Revolution, the valley was now a tourist attraction.

Although Mohamed had financed the eatery, on paper it was owned by one of his wife's cousins who had spent five years training in various hotel kitchens throughout Greece. He'd learned well and the restaurant was profitable. Informed of what had happened in Newport, Mohamed had arrived at the restaurant three hours before it opened for lunch. The two men were ensconced in a corner of a small, private dining room where cotton fibers had once been woven into cloth.

"Salud," said Mohamed in a quiet toast marked by the distinctive clink of glass on glass. Both men liked to use Italian expressions, because, as it was Rhode Island, there was always an Italian around. "I'm pleased that you could come."

A lean, reticent man, Salem asked, "Has anything changed because of last night?"

"Everything is fine. Both boats were blown into toothpicks, so there's nothing to find."

"The hotel?"

"Our man called me at six. It all took place in minutes. A professional operation. The explosions from the boats ignited the hotel. It's gone. No papers will ever be found."

A sinister smile crossed Salem's gaunt face, "Except for Providence, we are still on schedule. Allah will be pleased."

Mohamed said. "Our friends in Moscow will be disappointed that Providence will not be hit."

"Four weeks from today we strike the infidels again. They will wait."

Mohamed gave Salem keys to three vans along with an address.

"From here, how far?" Salem asked.

"Thirty miles."

Salem nodded. "More wine?"

"Grasi."

Book Two
Year: 2002

26

Watch Hill, Rhode Island didn't have a supermarket or a drugstore, but that wasn't a hardship for the people who lived there. Venerable Victorian homes sat proudly on low lying hills and you could see the ocean from almost anywhere within the township. A stone's throw across a narrow inlet from Connecticut, the hamlet jutted out into Block Island Sound at the end of Scenic Route 1A, a refuge for those who could afford the pastoral life.

Lensk had become enamored of the small sea coast village and had purchased a home overlooking the ocean. That was last summer. The winter had been unusually cold and windy and all of the windows on the ocean side of the house were pitted by winddriven sand. Now, summer had returned and the house was hot. It had drizzled during the night, and the humidity was high. Lensk fiddled with the new thermostat for the zoned air-conditioning system but couldn't figure it out. He decided to call a repairman later. By the time he finished his third cup of coffee, a fresh breeze came up and the sun was peeking through the cloud cover.

One of Watch Hill's prettiest spots was Napatree Point, a natural promontory flanked by beaches and rolling dunes. Within sight of a lighthouse often painted by artists, the point's calm waters were a boon to families with small children. Sitting in the kitchen of his home, Alden Lensk could see Napatree's east beach, and he was looking that way when a boy on a bicycle threw the plastic wrapped morning paper onto the cement walk. Lensk had taken his family to New York to see one of the final Broadway performances of *Cats* and they'd arrived home as the sun was breaking over the horizon. Lensk's hands shook as he stared at the headline: *Russians and Arabs Murdered in Newport. Yachts, Hotel Destroyed.* He woke his wife. *"Dusha-duske,* Valerie, *dusha-duske,"* he said softly which meant "we must talk soul-to-soul."

Fearing the truth would alienate his wife and daughters he was tempted to continue his charade. However, his love for the specialness of his family won out and he held nothing back. Valerie, who was educated, naturally bubbly and a person who took delight in routine everyday tasks, suddenly found herself dragged into a world so brutal and immoral that she could not imagine its existence. They had talked all day and as twilight waned into darkness a feeling of abject loneliness and isolation so profound tugged at her and made her want to cover her ears and shout, *enough!* Finally, to release her rage, Valerie cursed. "You bastard. You contemptible, brainless, self-possessed Russian bastard!" Haggard, with dark circles under her eyes and her face drawn, she stifled an urge to cry by focusing on the cobwebs and spots of flaking paint on the porch ceiling. Finally, she forced herself to look at Lensk. "Alden, you must go to the FBI and tell them everything."

Lensk sat there in a catatonic stupor.

"Alden, *please* listen to me. You're a lawyer, you have information to trade. The children, Alden. The children."

Her message awakened something in Lensk. "*Da,* but Petrovich's death may have changed things."

"*Nyet,* you must take the chance. We cannot go on like this."

"We have plenty of money and this house is all paid for."

"You idiot, I'm not talking about money and houses. We can't live in constant fear. How long has this been going on?"

"Years."

Years, she thought, unsure of what to say. She took some deep breaths. She felt sick, but behind her blank eyes a mental debate was raging. She had been stupid, plain and simple. *A Porsche and Mercedes, their luxury apartment in Moscow, the travel privileges. She should have known.*

"Petrovich is dead. He can't hurt us." Pleaded Lensk.

"His replacement may be worse."

"I could go to prison."

"Get immunity. Try. You must at least try."

Lensk nodded, and Valerie felt a pang of hope.

Anaesthetized by vodka, Lensk went to bed. It was a warm, sultry night and Valerie ventured out on the porch. In the moonlight, she saw a swarm of seagulls searching for bait fish in the surf line. Pondering the repetitive nature of the ocean, she brushed the hair from her eyes. Before today, her biggest worry was Alden's long absences from home. Now, she knew that he was a criminal who deserved jail. It was odd. The ghastly recriminations she felt were gone, replaced by relief and a sense of purpose. That night for the first time since coming to the States, Valerie Lensk felt relieved of the nerve-wracking tension that had crept up and surrounded her. Watching the gulls swoop down against the prevailing wind, she wondered if it were possible to love someone too much.

27

Los Angeles
July 6...6:30 P.M.

The wind had petered out and it was hot and sticky. Tired workers who didn't have air conditioning at home were in no hurry to get there and the after work hangouts were doing a brisk business. From a bartender's perspective, it was an evening made for one night stands. Fata Ahmed Aza had been in a foul mood most of the day and the oppressive heat hadn't improved his disposition. He had traipsed all the way out to Huntington Beach, and found a vacant yacht slip. "Idiots," he mumbled in Arabic. As he spoke on a cell phone the ugly scar on his chin began to quiver. "The boat's not here."

"They wanted to test the engines and top off the tanks."

"When are they due back?"

"In three or four hours."

"What?"

"Aza, they are trying to please you. Shehli had a good idea."

"Idea? What idea?"

"He's going to pump out the fresh water tanks and fill them with petrol."

"Allah is smiling," said Aza snapping the phone shut.

All the out-of-the-way restaurants Aza favored had a forty-minute wait, so he opted for wine and pizza at Helen Peabody's condo. It took a bottle of cold Chianti, a large Domino's thin crust and a gargantuan salad to ease their hunger pangs. From her teeny kitchen, Helen called out, "How was everything?"

"Your salad was outstanding."

Helen laughed. "It's easy when you live on greens."

"It shows. Now I know why your body's in such gorgeous shape."

"More wine?" asked Aza as he refilled his glass.

"Please." Helen noticed Aza scanning the titles in her bookcase. "Can I get you something else?"

"I'm fine. Stop working and come sit down."

The Chianti and change of venue had done wonders for Aza's attitude and Helen had never seen him so relaxed. She'd been dating the handsome, apparently wealthy Arab on and off for five months. Having decided several months ago that he was the one, Helen also concluded that for a man who did everything well and fast, he was stuck in his ways. Nothing would ever happen unless she took the initiative. Helen wasn't prone to go ga-ga over a man, but she wanted to nail him down, one way or the other. *Some guys can enter your life and screw it up without half trying. I don't think he's one of those, but I've got to know for sure.*

Aza was skimming through a book and said, "I see you like poetry."

"Mostly."

"This is a nice little collection."

Helen looked over and saw that Aza had returned to the sofa and was staring at her. "Please," he said, indicating a place next to him. "The coffee can wait."

While Aza talked he pulled her close and captivated her with poignant memories of his parents and early family life in Saudi Arabia. He liked playing games and every story he told had been invented on the spot. Actually, he'd been born and raised in Afghanistan. Sitting shoulder to shoulder next to him, Helen knew that she had never looked better. The weekends spent at the beach had given her a healthy, bronzed complexion and three nights a week at the health club had done the rest. She was listening with her eyes closed so she could concentrate on his voice, which had a certain lyrical quality she found endearing. The sudden silence caused her to turn and she saw his face as it changed from affection to desire. Wetting her lips, she thought, *It's now or never.* Helen's kiss was warm and loving and tenderhearted and somehow bold. She didn't have to say anything. She wasn't wearing a bra and she could feel the heat of Aza's hand caressing her breast under her baggy cotton shirt. She reached for him and as the tactile pleasure of his arousal reached her nerve endings, her usual shyness was replaced by a shameless rush of desire.

Much later, as they lay naked on Helen's unmade bed, it seemed as though they had been lovers for years, and without thinking, she curved a shapely leg lovingly over his and took him in her mouth for the first time. He had a large member, but he had been so caring earlier that tears ran down her cheeks. As he felt the moisture touch his skin, Aza looked down and saw that her face was aglow with happiness. *Such a stupid woman, he thought. She has been my lover, my cover, my introducer, and my cook and she thinks I'm in love with her. What do Americans call this…oh yes, a mercy fuck.* Coaxing her over on her stomach, he entered her from the rear. When she cried out, he gave her his ring finger to suck on and bite. He tamed her slowly and after a while she began moaning. *Should I kill her? No. After tonight's fucking, my disappearance will send the American bitch to a shrink.* He smiled at the thought.

They were lying in Helen's bed sharing the same cigarette when his cell phone rang. "Yes." he answered.

"I see. A half hour then."

"Helen, I have a minor emergency. Dinner tomorrow. Eight o'clock?"

"Where?"

"Pick someplace special."

She took him in her arms and showered his face and chest with kisses, hoping he would stay the night. He didn't, but neither did she.

When his tan Mercedes left the parking garage of her condo, Helen's car was already parked outside in a guest space. She didn't mind him leaving after having given herself to him so completely, she just wanted to make sure he wasn't married. She'd never been to his home and until tonight, all she knew about him was that he had sold his business abroad and was looking for an opportunity in the States. For the first time he had mentioned his early family life, but nothing new about what he did during the day.

Even at one in the morning the San Diego Freeway was busy. A bon voyage party for a long-distance sailing race was still going on and the Huntington Beach Marina was jammed with cars. Helen found a space on the street. A dark corner behind the cluttered backside of a dockside charter office gave her a good view of the marina and she watched Aza board the biggest yacht she'd ever seen. She became bewildered when all of the men bowed as he came aboard. *What is he? Some kind of Pasha?* One of the younger men took the keys Aza extended and with another man left the yacht. When they got to the end of the dock, she could make out their Arabic features. *At least there doesn't seem to be a woman on board.* Helen's impression that everything was kosher was dashed when the two men returned, loaded down with luggage and briefcases. *The bastard is taking off.*

She was about to go down there and confront him, when another car pulled up to the edge of the dock. Two Arabic looking men got out of the car and scanned every inch of ground as the trunk popped open. Helen dropped down behind an empty oil drum. When she heard the trunk slam shut, she peeked. A green blanket kept whatever they were carrying from prying eyes. The object was heavy and as they got to the dock, one of the men stopped short and put down his end to change hands. The box tilted and the blanket slid off. The large bold letters that were printed on the exposed wooden box alarmed Helen: **DANGER: HIGH EXPLOSIVES.** The Arabs were looking all round and she prayed that they wouldn't see her. *Thank God I wore my navy jogging suit.* Nothing happened, and when she peeked again, the box was being taken aboard very carefully. *What the hell is going on here?* she wondered as she noted the name on the stern; *The Majestic*, Huntington Beach. As she drove home, Helen's face was a mixture of confusion, loathing and fear. When her hands suddenly started shaking uncontrollably, she got off at the first exit and drove to a motel.

As she fussed with the plastic card key, she was still berating herself for being such a gullible ninny. Alone in the hotel suite, every footfall in the hall was a threat, and she constantly checked and rechecked the door locks. Wired and too terrified to be alone, she touched up her makeup and called for the bellman. An hour later, the security man, who was going off duty, knocked on her door. The recently retired Navy quartermaster could tell the woman was near hysteria and agreed to spend the night on the sofa in her sitting room. After he got off the telephone with his wife, he said. "Everything's fine with my G-2."

"She must be an understanding person."

"It's all the time I spent at sea. She's used to an empty bed."

Putting an extra $100 on her credit card for the security guard, Helen Peabody drove directly to the law firm where she worked. It was early and the parking garage was almost empty. She sat with the car doors locked, hands trembling, until two men that she recognized pulled in.

Helen was secretary to Theodore Samuel, a partner who specialized in the purchase and sale of private medical practices and hospitals. He was a thin, reedy man with little personality but, because the HMO's were raising so much havoc with doctors and hospitals, his billings were ten times that of anyone else in the firm. The previous months Samuel had handled the purchase of two large hospitals by an HMO. Both transactions were complex and controversial and the legal fees paid to Samuel's firm were staggering. In the three years that Helen had worked for him, he hadn't made a single spoken comment about her work or personal life. However, the man wasn't a skinflint. She'd received three healthy raises and generous year-end bonuses. Each raise and bonus contained the same note: *You're doing a fine job. Please continue on course.* Her compensation was top secret, but she knew she was the highest paid secretary in the firm.

She'd gotten to the office early, and was pacing the floor in her office when she heard Samuel in his next door office. She opened the connecting door. One glance at her face and jogging suit motivated him to pick up the phone. "Joyce, send down for two glasses of orange juice, two coffees and two bacon and egg sandwiches on wheat toast. Have the order put on Helen's desk, and then buzz me. Helen's going to be late and I'm tied up with a client. Hold all my calls. Thank you."

Mr. Samuel's kindness overwhelmed her and she couldn't keep the tears from leaking out. "Helen, please…start from the beginning and leave nothing out."

By the time she'd finished, they'd polished off all the food. "That hit the spot," Samuel said.

"I feel so foolish, you'll never look at me the same way again."

When Samuel spoke, his eyes were kind. "Helen, as you know I have no family. I feel honored that you thought enough of me to share such a delicate and trying situation."

She looked at him not knowing what to say.

"Helen, you know my car. Here are the keys. Take the back stairs and get on the floor in the back seat. I don't want you to be seen like this. I'll be down in five minutes."

"Mr. Samuel…"

"Helen, this is serious. We must move quickly."

Twenty minutes later, they were sitting across a conference table from the Special Agent in Charge of the FBI's Los Angles office. Two other agents and a stenographer were in the room and everyone was impressed with the details Helen had given them, especially the SAC who said, "John, get over to the court house with Ms. Peabody's statement and get search warrants for the yacht, the home, and the office of the boat's owner. If the boat's leased, get a warrant for the lessee."

The SAC turned to a youngish blond-haired man. "Brooks, assemble a ten-man team and get down to Huntington Beach. As soon as John has the warrants, go in fast and hard with vests and shotguns and have the bomb squad with you."

Mr. Samuel was no wallflower and he had a question, "What about the Coast Guard and Marine Patrol? The yacht could be gone before you get the warrants."

The SAC obviously didn't have an ego problem, because he hit his head with one hand and pressed a button on his intercom with the other,. "Marge, set up an emergency conference call with the heads of the local Coast Guard and Marine Patrol."

After the others were gone, the SAC said, "Ms. Peabody, Mr. Samuel, I believe you just did this country a valuable service and I thank you for it."

Samuel glanced at Helen and saw that some color had finally returned to her cheeks. When she returned his look, he felt as though he had a daughter.

28

Boston
July 6...12:05 P.M.

Ten straight days of temperatures exceeding 100 degrees drove electric consumption to the limit, and the New England power grid had blown a fuse, leaving 3.5 million customers in the early stages of meltdown.

All night the temperature in Bean Town remained in the 90s. Stripped to his skivvies, Miles Lowell Bodington refused to become ruffled over the heat and the lack of air-conditioning. As the lone occupant of a fine Beacon Hill brownstone, such trivial matters weren't worth his time. He had other worries. A refined looking man in his mid-forties, Miles was intently studying a special summary of the week's activity on the various stock exchanges. *Hum, this is strange. The airline and cruise ship businesses are into their peak season but they're being sold short in record numbers. This is nuts.*

A lean, high-energy mover and shaker, Miles Bodington was a standout in Boston social and business circles. In reality, he was a predator whose blue-blooded ancestry and Ivy League diploma provided a model facade for his quasi-criminal activities. Humorless, with a cryptic way of talking, Miles' innate cunning had served him well. For starters, he had murdered his pushy socialite wife in such a clever way that her parents and friends had gone out of their way to console and help him. After losing the insurance proceeds and their accumulated savings on bad investments, Miles, without any qualms, sold off the family treasure hoard of antiques to finance his first boiler room operation wherein he and his merry band of thieves fleeced 4,209 greedy, trusting souls of $272 million.

Now in deep thought, wandering amid the spartan furnishings of his home, he reflected on the odd trading pattern in the shares he owned. All of the theories his criminal mind could envision could not offer him a rational explanation. The reality, though, with or without reason, was that he was down over $18 million on paper.

A stiff late afternoon breeze off the ocean had swept away the fumes left by the morning commuters and the Boston sky was blue. Chain-smoking and scrunched in a deck chair, Miles Bodington studied a lonely formation of billowy clouds moving with the wind. Looking for guidance in a glob of stray moisture cells was akin to a hallucinogenic trip for a man who had boiled the facts of life down to two timeworn credos: "Money talks" and "never play fair." Shrugging, Miles dialed an unlisted number in Cape Cod.

A plummy voice answered. "This is Miles."

"Miles. I have a problem."

"Ah, and what is it?"

"Some 'shorts' and some 'up-ticks'."

"I've been here most of the week. Did you get hurt?"

"Bad."

"Miles, here's a number. Fax me a list. Our usual arrangement?"

"No, triple. I need to know today."

"I'm SEC, Miles, not God. Tomorrow by four?"

"I can live with that."

29

Alden Lensk had stayed overnight at the airport Marriot in Virginia. At the mammoth FBI Headquarters building he asked to see the Assistant Director for International Operations.

"Do you have an appointment, sir?"

"No, but if I could see his secretary, I'm sure he will see me."

"One moment."

Five minutes later, Lensk was escorted by an armed guard to the office of a woman in her early fifties. "Mr. Lensk, what can I do for you."

He handed her a picture of himself, with Petrovich and General Markov. In the background were buildings topped with golden spires. The back of the photo had a list of names and the date.

The woman studied the photo, and picked up the phone. "There's a man out here who says you'll see him if I show you a photograph." There was a long pause after which she said, "Yes, I recognize the names."

Special Agent Joan Loving was five floors down in the cafeteria enjoying her morning coffee when her cell phone rang. "You're wanted, *right now*. Bring Patrick."

Lensk introduced himself and sat down. Clearheaded for the first time in months, he looked at the director and the two agents. He wasn't subtle. "I can save you ten years of work, billions of dollars and lives. But, before I say anything I need complete immunity, citizenship and new papers for myself and family. I do not need funds or relocation assistance, but I shall be allowed to keep all of the funds and real estate holdings that I have now."

During the next half hour, the director's patience and caressive words had no effect on Lensk who was getting impatient. "Mr. Director, to hold this position you must be an intelligent man. I have jeopardized my life and that of my family by coming here. I have invaluable information to trade. Either we do it right now or I will simply disappear on my own."

Only three hours had passed since his ultimatum. To Lensk it had seemed like days. Now he had the immunity deal he'd asked for with all the right signatures in place. But the look on his face showed no sign of satisfaction in getting what he wanted. Rather, his downcast expression held a palpable tinge of paranoia, even terror. Noticing, the director said in a soft voice, "Mr. Lensk, an assistant attorney general will be arriving in a few minutes. Some coffee, perhaps?"

Lensk's smile was wooden. "That would be nice."

Lensk's insights into the workings of ROC in the U.S. and overseas had the resonance of truth not only to the director, but to the other ten people in the room. The scope and enormity of what was already going on and the plans for the future were frightening. The assistant attorney general had an easygoing style and appeared genuinely interested in the welfare of Lensk's family. "Mr Lensk, we appreciate the enormous risk you took in coming here."

There was a glint of uneasiness in Lensk's voice as he responded, "The protection you promised?"

"It is already in place. You will be flown home on one of our planes along with six agents specially trained in these matters. Our field office in New London will provide additional back-up."

Lensk's expression was one of amazement. "So fast," he stammered.

"Mr. Lensk, we made a deal. Your family will have 24-hour protection until you tell us to back off. If you change your mind and want us to handle your relocation we will do so willingly."

"No, just the new identities and protection until we move." said Lensk, adding, "I have documents in two different banks."

"Let's get your family safe first. There will be many more debriefings. Just give me the names of the banks and the box numbers. We'll get a court order to have the boxes drilled."

Lensk, reached for an envelope in his coat pocket. "*Nyet*, here are the keys."

30

Elmhurst, Illinois
July 10...10:03 A.M.

The Zagaskie homestead was located off St. Johns Road, about a twenty minute drive from the Chicago-O'Hare Airport. In the past, the area had been a popular enclave of families with children. The steady decline of the public school system had blunted its favored status and a steady stream of families had moved further out to rural areas of the state.

Having grown up in a farming community, Detective Mike Manus disliked the sterile uniformity of most suburban communities and Elmhurst was no exception. Housing developments, malls and strip centers fed on each other and all of the cookie-cutter franchises were there, along with others waiting to be discovered.

Thinking back to his previous trip to see Leo Zagaskie six months ago in January, Detective Manus recalled bare trees lining the streets and slush deeper than the tops of his boots. He was calling on Zagaskie, a security guard at O'Hare, to investigate the circumstances of a brutal beating that almost took his life. He recalled an ambulance rushing past him, sirens wailing. At the victim's address he'd learned that Zagaskie had lapsed into a coma and was being taken to a hospital.

Recently, Zagaskie, recovered, had called the Elmhurst station house and asked for a detective. Since his name was already linked with the Zagaskie case, Mike Manus got the call. "My memory's been coming back,

Mr. Manus, and I have to talk to someone."

From the glass doorknobs, Tiffany lighting fixtures and low ceilings, Mike figured the house was at least forty years old. The furniture was colonial and the upholstered pieces formed a horseshoe around a fireplace. A golden retriever moved out from underfoot and laid down on the cool brick hearth. It was a cozy room, but Manus sensed a feeling of futility in Mr. Zagaskie. Feeling defensive and unsure of himself the older man selected a maple rocker, which his nervousness soon put in constant motion. "Sergeant, I appreciate you coming out here."

Zagaskie's voice was feeble and Manus wondered why a man in such a weakened condition would need the police.

In her black turtleneck and matching wool pants, Mary Zagaskie looked plain and when she spoke, her voice had the controlled monotone of a convent sister in charge. "It's an extraordinary situation," she explained."

"What is the situation?" asked Manus.

"Leo spent twenty years in the Army and retired as a sergeant. Even with the benefits, we couldn't live on his pension so he took the job at O'Hare."

"I see…"

Mrs. Zagaskie gave Manus a look that stopped him cold. "Have a little patience, Detective. During his patrols around the airport, Leo saw the same man constantly checking his watch and making notes at the various gates. The man came a couple of times a week for three weeks."

"He could have gotten that information from the flight schedules."

"Do you think we're stupid? Please let me finish. The man wasn't interested in flight schedules. He kept going back and forth between the adjacent gates to see if there were aircraft docked there."

"Don't inspectors do that all the time, Mr. Zagaskie?"

"Not often enough, but when they do they have ID cards hanging around their necks. He didn't, so I asked him what he was doing."

Mr. Zagaskie's voice was rapidly fading so Manus slowed down the pace. "What did he tell you?"

"The man was a foreigner for sure, but he spoke English better than I do. Showed me his clipboard immediately with all of the data he'd been writing down. Said he was enrolled at Chicago City College and was doing a thesis on aircraft efficiency. Time it took for a flight to disembark and get the baggage off, that sort of thing."

"Did he have permission from anyone at the airport?"

"He said the Airport Administrator had approved of what he was doing and he gave me the right name."

"Then what happened?"

"I told him to wait there while I checked. My half-ass radio was on the fritz, so I called from a newsstand. No one in the Administrator's office had ever heard of him or the study. Of course, when I went looking, he was gone."

"Exactly what happened when you were you mugged?"

"It was already dark when I got off my shift. They jumped me in the parking lot as I was opening my car door. There were two men and they wanted to kill me."

"How do you know it wasn't a robbery?"

"You get in that same situation, Sergeant, and I guarantee you'll know. I drive a nine-year-old car. Why pick on me? "

"What stopped them?"

"A lady with a German shepherd. She saw it happening and let the dog loose. I can still hear her words." Manus saw Zageskie squeeze his lips together to keep from crying. His wife stood behind him and gently held his shoulders. "Attack, Kate. Attack, Girl. Anyway, they'd already hit me twice in the head and well, you know, the coma."

"I know you're not well, Mr. Zagaskie, but do you recall what the man looked like?"

"Yes, I do."

"Mr. and Mrs. Zagaskie, nothing's happened out at O'Hare during the last six months. However, having said that, I think this needs to be followed up by the FBI, and right away."

Leo Zagaskie's eyes all at once came alive and Manus saw his wife tighten her grip on her husband's shoulders.

31

Brooklyn, N.Y.
July 11...5:39 P.M.

Originally owned and operated by Luigi Delroca and his wife, Anna, Del's Sundries on Remsen Avenue in Brooklyn was a local institution. From the time he was six, Del's had been a second home to Teddy Calvino and he had known every inch of the place from the box-strewn alley in the back to the green and white awning out front. He and his best friend, Albert, were the only ones ever allowed to hang out inside the store. Far from being a typical mom and pop operation, Del's was really a hotbed of illegal activity.

Del's was still acceptably seedy with a well-worn linoleum floor, old hard-oak fixtures and an exotic inventory that included a little of everything. To kids, Del's was the place to buy comic books, cheap kites and a smorgasbord of unhealthy snacks on the cheap. For grown-ups, it was a treasure trove of underpriced merchandise that had "fallen off" the backs of trucks. It was there among the pipe-racks of hijacked designer clothes that Teddy Calvino learned a basic precept...once you got down to the crew level, organized crime was not all that organized. Wiseguys would wander in and out of Del's all day killing time until something jelled. *These guys must be bored out of their fucking minds. No wonder they're always hitting the bottle.*

For what seemed like a long time, Teddy had been slouching in a fiberglass lawn chair. He was nibbling on a candy bar and mulling over what Del's had brought into his life. He concluded that fate had forged his long-lasting bond with Albert and the Delroca's. Because so many of his friends were going to prison, Teddy decided that crime was not only boring, it really didn't pay. Anyway he had something legal going that beat the hell out of heisting cars. Sipping a beer next to him, Albert said, "Watcha so jumpy about?"

"A fare I picked up last week."

Lurching out of his chair, Teddy tossed a rolled up five to Albert and headed toward the front of the store. "I'm buyin. See yah tomorrow at breakfast."

Teddy couldn't sleep that night. Mulling over and over in his mind a decision to do something in the morning that might have life changing consequences left him restless and unsettled. Fearful of awakening the Bosnian refuge family that kept house for him, he tiptoed his way to a bathroom in the former tenement brownstone he'd converted to a single family home.

He submerged himself in a warm bath, keeping the water hot by turning the faucet knob with his toes, and tried to relax. His plan for the morning had exhumed memories of the past both sweet and painful and, struggling with their implication, he finally dozed off, a folded towel his pillow, the warm water his blanket. Hours later, out of the tub, confident now that what he was about to do was the right thing, he looked at his shriveled skin in the mirror and thought, *I'm a prune.*

After begging off breakfast with faithful Albert, Teddy parked down the street from Ellen Roddy's house, six miles and a lifetime away. Married for a short while, she was 56 now and the principal of a high school in the district where Teddy had spent his entire life. He'd picked Ellen up in his taxi at least fifty times in the past, mostly on rainy days when he knew she'd have trouble getting a cab. Because of the way he worked, she'd never recognized him. Today, as Ellen climbed into the back seat of his cab, Teddy knew she would.

Teddy Calvino turned around and Ellen Roddy saw a man who had gone missing from her life for twenty years. Dressed in a beige cashmere sweater and a ribbed turtleneck, to her he looked as loose and lanky as he'd been at 16. She remained composed and by squeezing the handle on her calfskin bag she kept her hands from shaking. "Hello, Teddy. How have you been?"

"Fine, Ellen, and you?"

Ellen Noreen Roddy folded her arms and remembered every detail about the first time she and Teddy had met. However, it was their last encounter that had always haunted her dreams. It was the week after Labor Day, in 1968, and they were both back in Room 212 at Hope High School, where he was 16 and a student. She was a new 22-year-old teacher. She'd been sent at the last minute to Teddy's school and when Teddy walked into her classroom he got the shock of his life. Standing in front of the class was his new homeroom teacher and steady girlfriend, Ellen Roddy. Puzzled by Teddy's presence she glanced down at her class roster and was utterly bowled. She remembered that only two weeks ago in the back seat of his car she'd let Teddy remove her bathing suit top and feel her breasts. She would have gone *all the way* that day, but Teddy had backed off. She stared at him and tears trickled down her cheeks. The questioning looks of his classmates and the awful, unforgettable quiet that took hold of the room shattered Teddy and he felt unclean and sinful. Teddy looked up at her and the torment he saw on Ellen's innocent face was burned into his mind with the unmerciful flame of an acetylene torch. The image lodged there and never strayed.

Not knowing quite what to do, he got up and started toward her but when he got close enough, she punched him hard on his shoulder and ran out of the room. By the time he'd regrouped, he saw her running toward the teachers' room. She had taken off her high-heels and with her head start, she'd won the foot race. He could still see her flashing nylon stockings, the black pumps in her left hand and her tiny fist pounding her side. He remembered the brass alarm gong above the door to the teachers' room and he prayed for a fire drill so she'd have to come out and he could explain. Then he thought of how it would look for her and he ran down the nearest staircase.

The gray-haired woman who gave out late slips was taken back by the shaken, teary-eyed boy standing in front of her. "My mother wants me to transfer over to Classical. It's closer to her job."

"What's your name?

"Teddy Calvino."

"You have a note from one your parents?"

"No, no I don't."

"Uh, huh. What grade are you in?"

His voice was almost inaudible. "I'm a senior."

"You really want to leave all your friends?"

"No, ma'am. I have no choice."

Seeing that Teddy was about to self-destruct, the woman looked to see if anyone was watching. Absent any prying eyes, she filled out a form and slid it across the slippery sheen of the oak counter. "Good luck."

The enormity of what his callous, mindless deception had done to Ellen hit him while he was slumped over the steering wheel and he recalled a line from a song; *Maybelline, why can't you be true. Oh Maybelline, why can't you be true.* Too young to cope, but old enough to understand, his tears finally came.

Because Teddy didn't know a soul at Classical High he was miserable during his senior year and he never showed up for his class picture or the senior prom. Two days after graduation, he left the scene of the crime and joined the Navy.

There was a studied silence before Ellen asked, "Why today, Teddy?"

"I need your help."

It was not the response she'd anticipated, so she probed, "What's it about? What kind of help are we talking about?"

"The kind that could cost me everything."

Because he was driving a cab, she wondered what it was that was so important that he would contact her after all these years.

"Are you married, Teddy?"

"No, I never got hitched."

Over the years, Ellen Roddy had thought often about the young man-boy who had captured her heart. She had dropped two guys already out of college to date Teddy exclusively. Lighthearted, with a flare for clever one-liners, he seemed more mature than most of the grown men she dated. Because he had a snazzy car and enough money in his pocket to take her to nice places, she never dreamed he was only sixteen. The joy and excitement she felt every time she had slid in next to him in the car had never been replaced. A school teacher and a kid who acted like a man and was driving a car instead of riding a bike. *Jesus, he could dance and kiss. I should have known. He blushed too easily.* Sexually, Teddy never pressed her. She would have gone further, but some heavy petting was as far as they got. Ellen had a lot of questions she wanted answers from him immediately, but the expression on his face told her this might not be the right time. *He's in trouble,* she thought.

"All right, where do you want to talk?"

"At my home. It's only fifteen minutes from here."

"Teddy, I think a coffee shop would be more appropriate, don't you?"

"There's a thirteen-year-old child that I want you to talk to."

"I thought you were never married?"

"Her family works for me. She's the only one who speaks English. Her family will be there."

His eyes told her she had nothing to fear. "All right. But will you answer a few uncomfortable questions?"

"Yes, yes of course."

"You really had me fooled, Teddy. The smooth talk, the money, the car. What was it?"

"A three-year-old Rocket 88 Oldsmobile."

"Tell me."

"By the time I was 13, I was hanging out with guys twice my age and I was already street smart. I started using my mother's adult library card when I was eight and I read five or six books a week. I became what I heard around me and polished it with what I read. I'm still doing it and there are some days when I feel like a composite of all that I've seen and read."

"Where did all the money come from?"

"I had a paper route and on Saturdays I picked up the numbers receipts for the *boys*. I had 63 bars and every kind of food joint you can name on my route and they all sold numbers. I got paid 50 dollars for that, plus, I made a small fortune in tips from guys who had scored at the track. But the big bucks came from a little business that a friend and I started.

"You had a business?"

"We called it that, but it was out-and-out theft."

"What?"

"Stealing spoke wheels, spinner hub caps and fender skirts. When I folded the tent, we had 40 kids ripping off stuff that we sold. We had a ball selling the college boys back their own stuff."

"Go on."

"One night I got into a fight over a girl I'd just met outside a beatnik coffee house near the Columbia campus. The jerk outweighed me by 30 pounds, but he didn't know jack-shit about street fighting. Two of his buddies jumped in to save the pasty faced jerk."

"So?"

"They were wearing Columbia University sweat shirts and when they came out, I zeroed in on their car. Later, I followed their car to a frat house and stripped the skirts and spokes. The next morning, I sold the stuff in the high school parking lot for twenty bucks. A lot of money in those days."

"I'll say."

"It took off there and pretty soon with the numbers and all, I was clearing 400 bucks a week."

"My father was only making 130 dollars a week back then," she said.

"My father worked as a spray painter at an auto body shop. He was puking his guts out every night and making 106 dollars a week with no benefits, to keep food on our table. I threw my paper route money and numbers loot in the pot to help out. My father was an honest man. His son was a crook."

"And an accomplished liar."

"Yes, that too."

"How did you hide the car?"

"I rented a garage for 11 dollars a month far enough away so my parents never found out. I stole the plates off a similar car and I paid a guy 50 dollars to get me a legit driver's license."

"I remember, you got asked for an ID a few times, but they always apologized."

The house was furnished with antiques and an impressive collection of art, unattainable on her salary, let alone that of a man who drove a cab. Three adults and a young girl were waiting for them in a spacious, high ceilinged living room that was trimmed with gold-leafed crown molding. The room was awesome, but it was Teddy's reception that impressed her. It was obvious that the gathering was happy to see him back home.

The mother, father and grandmother of the child beamed and spoke spiritedly in a language Ellen didn't understand. Teddy introduced them. After the mother and Sonia, the child, had served some delicious frosted bread and tea, Teddy took out a small micro-tape recorder and turned it on. "This was recorded in my cab."

The 15-minute recording captured a heated conversation between two men in a foreign language Ellen could not place. Only a few words were spoken in English, all of them harmless slang.

"What language is that?" she asked.

"Arabic."

Turning to the child, Teddy said, "Tell Ms. Ellen what your grandmother said."

Like the others, the girl wore quality clothing. Her long-sleeved cardigan flaunted an expensive designer logo and she was wearing the latest in sneaker fashion. "Grandma says that those are bad men on the tape. She says that they want to hurt America. Grandma Sonia says she loves America and Teddy who was kind to bring her here."

"Your grandmother is named Sonia?"

"Yes, I was given her name."

"Does she speak Arabic?"

"No, grandma is very smart and has lived among many nationalities. In Bosnia, as many as three families sometimes share a small apartment where you have to sleep in shifts. She does not understand everything on tape, but she knows enough words to be very scared."

"Thank you, Sonia. Your father will walk you to school now," Teddy said.

Ellen glanced at her watch. "School. I have to call in."

Teddy pointed to a table. "There's a phone."

Ellen called her secretary and took the remainder of the day off. When she and Teddy were alone, she said, "It all sounds pretty dubious to me. Grandma doesn't speak Arabic. How can she really know?"

"I've made a pile of money listening to people in my cab and I've listened to that tape, maybe twenty times. The voices I hear are evil voices, and the anger I hear is real anger. The words America and Americans are mentioned twelve times and that, at least to me, is scary."

"If you're so convinced there's some kind of diabolical plot underway, why not turn the tape over to the FBI?" Teddy hesitated a long time before he spoke. "Ellen, someone has got to be made to understand. I know when something doesn't feel right. I can read people by what they say and how they say it. It's how I made my money. Anyway, I can't go to the FBI."

"Why not?"

"Because of what I do."

Ellen was incredulous. "With a young child in the house, you're still a crook?"

"No, of course not. I've been straight ever since I got out of the Navy and that was a long time ago."

"What then?"

He pondered the question and got up. "Follow me."

Teddy's master bedroom, which took up the entire top floor, had its own elevator that they rode upstairs. Ellen saw a private study lined with books, a huge bathroom, a small but comfortable high-tech audio/video room and two closets that were larger than the bedrooms in some homes. Teddy opened the closet doors and she was astonished to see inside each closet a wardrobe that might outfit the entire cast of three or four Hollywood dramas.

"What in the hell is this?" she found herself asking.

"This is what I do."

"You're an actor?"

"Sort of."

There were coats, jackets, sweaters, shirts, hats, scarfs and every other garment, from Brooks Brothers to western garb and military leftovers. Two walls of shelves were filled with props like a pair of 3-D glasses, a frisbee, some old prescription bottles and various stacks of magazines from porno to philosophy. A pair of crutches, a baby's car seat and a bunch of other stuff hung from hooks. Ellen stared. "This is incredible, but I still don't get it?"

"It's very simple. I make my money by scamming the schemers on Wall Street and these are my tools."

"Teddy, the art and antiques in this place are probably worth over a million dollars. You made all that in the market?"

"Three million is a lot closer and, yes, I made it in the market. But, not the way you think."

"How then?"

"Sit down over there and I'll show you." After she was seated, Teddy set another chair five feet in front of her. "This is the driver's seat. You're in the passenger seat. Got it?"

Ten minutes later, Ellen called, "What's taking so long?"

"Almost ready. When I come out, remember you're my passenger."

Seconds later, a man with a full beard and mop of tangled hair contained by a dirty French beret emerged from one of the closets. His Army surplus jacket was torn at the elbows and a dirty t-shirt declared, *Screw for the Sake of Screwing*. Ellen saw that the apparition, unrecognizable even to her as the Teddy Calvino who'd stood before her just a few moments ago, was also wearing a hearing aid and sunglasses with six-inch long silver wings attached to the sides. Grunting and snapping his fingers to the loud, driving beat of Bo Diddly, Teddy sat down in the driver's seat and gawked at a make-believe young woman swishing across the street. "Will yah look at that body! There oughta be a law."

Teddy looked back over his shoulder. "Now, Ellen, you're one of Wall

Street's premier scam artists and you're upset with me and the messy cab, so you make a demand in a strong manly voice, "Driver turn that music down and skip the commentary."

Teddy turned back around and turned off an imaginary radio in front of him. "Of course, sir. Yes, sir. Very sorry, sir. My apologies, sir."

Teddy paused again and took a Walkman out of his pocket. "Now the magic formula. I put these earmuffs on, which by the way are actually microphones. At the same time I activate the mini tape recorder in the back seat that is so quiet and sensitive that the FBI uses it. Now this middle-aged slicker wants to bed this striking, well-tooled graphics designer in the worst way and he's got his own magic formula…easy money. You got the picture so far, Ellen?"

"Loud and clear."

"All right. Now the guy is relaxed. I'm a dumb, pathetic piece of furniture who can't hear because I've got on these big earmuffs and besides I'm wearing a hearing aid. I push a button on my armrest and a Sinatra ballad comes out of the rear speakers. Mr. Wall Street tries a test kiss. Knowing that this guy can make her some money, the woman sticks her tongue in his mouth and he goes for the kill. 'Honey, you remember how Hillary turned that measly thousand dollars of hers into a hundred thousand in a matter of months? Well, I'm onto something could be even better.'

She strokes the back of his head like he's the financial genius of all time and says, 'You mean I could make some money like Hillary?'

'More,' he says in a matter-of-fact way.

She arches her eyebrows skeptically, 'How is that possible?'

Not one for wasting time, Mr. Street says, 'Think the office can get along without you for the rest of the day? We can get a suite at the Sherry.' She takes out her cell phone, the greatest boon to my business since the credit card, and calls in. Now, this woman may be a looker, but she's no fool. She begins by playing coy footsies and running a polished claw down his thigh and says, 'Now tell me, how can a salaried girl like me increase her net worth?' It doesn't cost him a dime, so he tells her."

With Teddy's performance still hanging in the air, Ellen said, "And that's all there is to it."

"Pretty much. I listen to the tape a few times and check out the one or two companies that are in on the transaction. What the guy on the tape says usually tells me if the deal is for real. I can't really get burned because

I always put in a sell order when I place my buy order. Anyway, by now I know who the phonies are and I never pick them up."

"Are women always involved?"

"Actually that's fairly rare. Usually it's just a couple of shysters hammering out the last minute details of an inside deal or a simple swindle. Stock fraud is such a clean, white-collar crime that it's almost respectable these days."

"You're saying the market's rigged?"

"Not really. The three or four million I make a year is saying that. I ever strike you as the Wharton School type?"

"Not really."

"I rest my case."

"You always pick up the same brokers?"

"Brokers, underwriters, investment bankers and the lawyers who handle the bigger deals. I call them players. I have a list of about forty and I know their habits and favorite watering holes better than they do. I've picked up some of them 30 times and they've never made me."

"You're always different and the cab always looks different?"

"Yes, and I always find a way to block out most of the livery license on the visor so they can't see my name and picture. My looks and personality change every day and there are times when I think reality is slowly slipping out of reach to a place where I can't recapture it."

Despite herself, Ellen had to admire Teddy's varied repertoire, acting ability and flawless execution. By pretending to be an airhead, Teddy Calvino had made a small fortune off the inside information he had overheard in the back seat of his cab. "The punchline?"

"I want you to deliver the tape to the FBI without identifying me."

"Why can't you do it?"

"That should be obvious. As soon as the word got out, I'd be out of business. I can see the headline: *Cab Driver Makes Millions From Inside Tips.*

"Teddy, don't you have any close friends?"

"Just the family that lives with me and only little Sonia speaks English. Ellen, you're a respected high school principal. Everyone knows you. You're the teachers' rep on the school board. I'm just rich. Sonia's whole life would become a nightmare. She's like a daughter. I can't have that happen."

"If that tape has some 'bad stuff' on it, this could be a pretty risky deal for a school principal."

"I thought of that. If there's any trouble, I'll cover all of your legal expenses and any financial losses. If need be, have a lawyer draw up a document for me to sign."

Ellen saw that his hands were trembling and it dawned on her that, with all his money, Teddy had never married and she wondered if he had ever picked her up without her knowing it.

He turned to face Ellen. She fixed him with a stare. "Teddy, have you ever picked me up?"

Even if someone were to threaten him with death, he would not lie to this woman again. "Yes, many times. Usually when it was raining."

Ellen saw a mature, wet-eyed man floating in lonesomeness and she knew why he'd never married. "Teddy, why?"

Teddy's high-energy delivery dropped to a faint whisper. "I'd never dated anyone more than once or twice until I met you. By the time I became so infatuated, I was beginning to stumble over my own fabrications. I tried several times to tell you, but I always rationalized that I was in love and that somehow, someway, things would work out."

"Teddy, you were 16 years old."

"Yeah, going on 25. I grew up fast, Ellen. How many guys you dated ever took you to the race track or on a chartered boat out of Montauk?"

"None. Is it because of me that you never married?"

"Yes. Unfortunately for me, you were it. I'm allergic to the word love."

"I guess you knew when I got married?"

"My mother told me. She read all the announcements."

"Why didn't you throw in the towel?"

"I knew the guy you married."

"And?"

"You were a Rembrandt. He was a finger-painting. I picked him up once with a gal and he gave me her address. They were fooling around in the back, so I drove the bastard all the way out to Kennedy. He started screaming at me and I told the starter he'd stiffed me. He couldn't get a cab back and was forced to rent a car."

Ellen had to chuckle. "Richard was not the smartest of men and in a very short time his discretions became painfully obvious. I'm surprised you didn't hit him."

Teddy's face hardened, but his voice stayed calm. "If he'd been alone, I probably would have killed him."

For Ellen, seeing Teddy again was like awaking from a deep sleep. Having had her almost naked in his arms, she'd expected him to be shallow and brag about it to his friends. Instead, he'd never said a word and quietly transferred to another school. She had banished him from her mind many times, but he just kept popping up. Ellen looked at him and felt a yearning that had never really left her.

Ellen stood up and handed the paper back to Teddy unsigned. His face was so marked by disappointment that she thought he might burst into tears. "I need a ride."

"Home or school?"

"Neither. The closest FBI office. Give me the tape."

"The agreement?"

"I don't need it, Teddy. I trust you."

They drove in silence and when she got out, she said, "Don't wait or call me. When it's all over, I'll call you. It may take weeks, even months. Stay clear, Teddy, you have too much to lose."

Ellen Roddy entered the Bureau's sedate offices and was confronted by a young woman talking to a computer screen that wasn't talking back. "I'd like to talk with an agent."

Still fidgeting with her keyboard, the woman said, "All of our field agents are at a meeting out on the island. Mr. Frederick, our liaison officer will be glad to help you." She removed an unwilling hand from her keyboard and pressed a button. "That's him over there."

Ellen saw a man beckoning to her through a large glass window partially blocked by artificial palm trees. When he opened the door, she was confronted with a slightly hunchbacked man whose pleasant face and bright bubbling manner immediately put her thumping heart at ease. He listened patiently, stopping her at various points to ask intelligent questions and finally, when she was talked out, he put the tape in a clear plastic bag labeled **EVIDENCE.** After carefully filling out the label, he said, "Ms. Roddy, I'll get on this immediately. The Bureau appreciates your help."

Many times, it is the unknowable that can dramatically affect an individual, a city or even a nation. John Frederick was one of the most experienced agents in the office and he was bitter about being left out of the Long Island festivities. *Meeting my ass, it's a fucking golf outing. So, I can't play. So, what. It's a day out of this jail.* Looking at his notes, he recapped his meeting with Ellen. She seems normal. *But, a recording supposedly in Arabic, floating in somewhere from outer space that's deciphered by a Bosnian grandmother who doesn't speak Arabic and has to communicate through a thirteen year old. Give me a break.* Pissed that he had missed all the fun and with the knowledge that at least four persons had handled the tape jaundiced Frederick further. His pen tilted over the boxes on the form where the interviewer had to prioritize his opinion of the statements given by people who walked in off the street. He glanced at his wall clock and, unaware that the tape was a ticking time-bomb, Frederick, without a modicum of hesitation, checked the box at the very bottom; **No follow-up recommended**.

Comfortable that her meeting with the agent would not lead to any sort of follow-up regarding Teddy, Ellen called him the next day. They had an extended lunch and it dawned on Teddy that everything in his life was about to change. However, it would take 24 hours before he would learn how much.

32

Monterey, California
July 14...8:49 P.M.

Having never won the tour, Bruce Howes had just won his third tournament in a row shooting a remarkable 26 under par at Pebble Beach with rounds of 66-66-66 and a mind-blowing 64 played in a thirty-knot wind.

A trim, compact man with a solid swing, he had consistently finished high enough on the money list to retain his tour card, but until his recent run he had never won. Easily recognized by his brush cut and military bearing, the guys on the tour called him "Sarge." Gentlemanly to a fault, and with a husky voice that would have made many a marine envious, Sarge preferred the shadows to the limelight. Unfortunately, the press tent was standing room only. A reporter from *Golf Digest* had the floor. "Sarge, how do you account for your brilliant play these last three weeks?"

"Well, this may sound crazy, but when Bill Rhode, my new caddy, passes me a golf club, it feels like a magic wand in my hand. Every shot has wings and I can see the putt dropping before I take the club back. With Bill on the bag, my confidence is out of proportion to my talent, and *that* has been the difference."

The truth can be dull, and in Sarge's case it would have been a bombshell. The fact that he had changed caddies had been a mere coincidence. Six months before, a middle-aged woman had pressed a napkin spotted with mustard into his hand. *Call me, I know why you can't* win and can help you. *Rene Fabra, 389-2138. It's a local number.* Lots of women came to golf tournaments to meet men. Since male golf fans tended to be better educated and financially secure, tourneys were a sort of a pre-screened dating-pool where making innocent contact was a slam-dunk. *Isn't it a splendid day for golf?*

Having had his share of golf-groupies, Sarge would have tossed the napkin but the 'can' in the message aroused his curiosity. They'd met at a quiet restaurant for dinner that same day and it was obvious from the get-go that she was not one to sugarcoat. They nursed soft drinks while getting acquainted and then she said, "Sarge, it's not the vagaries of the game or bad bounces that keep you from winning."

"How could you know that?"

"Three things. You're reined in by your humble beginnings and feel you don't deserve to win. You only play well in the smaller tournaments where the big guns are absent. And you never do well when you're in contention and playing alongside one of the guns."

Having heard all that before, Sarge wasn't impressed. "So, what's the answer?"

"You lack the 'fuck you' mentality needed to be a winner."

She'd seemed so prim and proper that Sarge was taken back by the language. "None of what you've said so far is a big secret. Your note said you could help."

"Sarge, everyone has an overlay of hidden strength. Some find it. Most don't. I know I can find yours." And she did.

After struggling for years without an equipment contract, Sarge was suddenly a hot commodity. Watching his interview on the locker room monitors, a number of pros began looking cross-eyed at their caddies. When Sarge finally finished up in the press tent and straggled back to the men's locker room, it was empty, so he went directly to his complimentary suite at the hotel which the tournament sponsors had provided. *Funny, when you're winning everyone wants to do something for you,* he thought.

Hani Alnami opened the door, and as usual, her beauty took his breath away. She was the sister of a young Arabic groundskeeper that he'd befriended at his home course in Marin City, located a stone's throw from Sausalito and the Golden Gate Bridge. While on the practice range, Sarge had noticed her brother, Ali, doing all the wrong things on a nearby tee and because of his own humble beginnings, Sarge gave the groundskeeper a free lesson. A month later, Ali introduced Sarge to his sister.

The skimpy purple halter, black leotards and open lips excited him and he drew her toward the bedroom. "Shower first, you dirty old man."

With her long hair tumbling across one side of her face, she reached out and pulled him down on top of her. As they kissed, she slid her leg between his thighs and offered him one of her breasts. Strong, unhurried fingers found him and he felt as though he were free-floating under the lushness and scent of her. Slim, fine-boned and endlessly deep, she was not difficult to please.

Naked, Sarge got up from bed and wandered into the sitting room. It was three in the morning and for some reason he was wide awake and craved a cigarette. Until Hani came along, Sarge had given up the habit he'd acquired while in juvenile custody. He checked his jacket and carry-on bag. Out. *Hanis menthol's will have to do.* He found her leather shoulder bag hidden away under the sofa and he wondered if she was afraid of being robbed while they slept. "The Middle Eastern culture, always protect what you have at all times," he muttered.

Sarge pulled a cigarette out of an open pack laying atop the other items in Hani's bag when he spotted the drugstore envelope bulging with photos. Wide awake now and curious, he flipped through the pictures, all time and date stamped. Several were of Hani, her bare breast pressed against a dark skinned man as she kissed him passionately. That was disturbing enough, but it was the photos of the Golden Gate that unnerved him and caused his stomach to churn. Each shot had notes on the back written in a foreign language. *Arabic,* he guessed correctly. Hani, whose handwriting he recognized, had noted in English the status of the tides at the time of day each photo was taken. *Why would she do that?*

Walking silently as possible to the bedroom door, he watched Hani in deep sleep, her beautiful form and her long hair cascading around her face causing him to yearn for her even at this moment. Returning to the sofa, Sarge carefully felt around the inside of Hani's bag for anything else he might find. From a so-called 'hidden pocket' he pulled a folded sheet of paper. Opening it, he was astonished to see a neatly drawn sketch of the Golden Gate as though viewed from the top of one of the towers. On each leg of one of the two-legged towers were circles that looked very much like…*Oh my God,* Sarge thought, *they look like targets!*

Shaking now, Sarge refolded the sheet, placing it back in the pocket. As he did so, his fumbling fingers touched another piece of paper. Removing it, he found himself looking at a yellowing clipping from an old foreign language newspaper. The face of the man in the center of the clipping was instantly recognizable, *Osama* he thought, *Osama something. How many times had he seen the face of that man, called the number-one terrorist in the world, on the news. Why would Hani have this in her bag?* He looked more closely at the photo. Two young people, a boy and a girl, stood on each side of the man, his arms around them as they looked up to him adoringly. The kids! He focused on their faces and the realization of what he was seeing sickened him. Hani and her brother. Much younger of course, but unmistakably them.

With his stomach doing flip-flops and nerve ends jangling, Sarge returned everything to Hani's bag as close as possible to the way he'd found it, including the unsmoked cigarette he'd set aside when he noticed the envelope full of photos. After replacing the bag under the sofa, he downed a whiskey from the suite's mini-bar. It had only been fifteen minutes or so since he'd left Hani sleeping in the bedroom, but that fifteen had changed his relationship with Hani.

Now, all of the long walks Hani had suggested they take back and forth across the bridge, which she photographed incessantly, along with shots she'd taken from the sailboat he'd chartered at her urging, took on a new meaning. "I know it's always a little rough, but a day on the water will do you good. Sarge, I get very aroused when I'm sailing. Get one with a large cabin."

With a snapshot of the sensual embrace lodged in his mind, Sarge knew he had only served as her cover story. He'd vouched for Ali Alnami when the flight school where he learned to fly had hesitated to rent him a twin-engine aircraft. Ali had become an American citizen and had his commercial and instrument ratings. Renting twins wasn't cheap and the school, worried about getting paid, had called Sarge whom Ali had listed as a reference. Since that first rental was only for four hours, no alarm bells had gone off in Sarge's mind. Had he known that Ali was soon renting the same plane every other weekend he would have wondered where he was getting the money.

An hour ago, he had been on top of the world; now he was a bundle of over-stoked nerves ready to implode. He sipped another whiskey from the mini-bar. *What to do?* he asked himself. Sarge had graduated from San Diego State on a golf-scholarship, no mean feat in a state filled with outstanding golfers. Some rough spots as a youth almost derailed Sarge, who had served two years in a juvenile detention facility for auto theft.

Assigned to grounds maintenance, Sarge found he liked working outdoors. After his release, he finagled a job on the ground crew of a private country club. Well liked by the pro in charge, he took advantage of the free lessons and course time.

Nine months after his first lesson, he shot par. Not very long after that, he broke the course record and attracted the attention of one of the club's board members, Lawrence Winslow. Guided by the pro's glowing appraisals of Sarge's golfing prowess, Winslow became a behind-the-scene financial supporter. Much later, after Sarge qualified for the tour, Winslow's 40-office banking chain became his tour sponsor.

Sarge went down to the front desk and gave the night manager ten dollars to let him make a call from his office. He dialed an unlisted number and Lawrence Winslow's assured vibrant voice answered on the second ring. Having watched the last round of the televised golf tournament, Winslow was disturbed by the hour and the intensity of his friend's voice. "Sarge, for a man who's a shoo-in for a bunch of magazine stories, you seem awfully distressed. What's up?"

"I don't know what to do."

"About what?"

"Not on the phone."

"All right, just give me a key word or two that describes the subject matter. No details."

"The bridge."

Winslow was perplexed, "The bridge?"

Not knowing exactly what to say in reply to Lawrence, Sarge uttered the first thing that came to mind. "Tony Bennet. I think it's going to go boom. My girlfriend's involved and she's in the bedroom upstairs."

Winslow had a high regard for his golfing friend. Once an aimless punk, Sarge's life had changed because of his golf. He was a new person and no one was happier than Lawrence Winslow. Now, Sarge was telling him that the Golden Gate Bridge was in imminent danger. "Don't say another word."

"Right."

"You still at Pebble?"

"Yes."

"Good, my Lear will pick you up at the Del Rey Oaks Terminal in ninety minutes. I'll be on the plane."

"Sarge, please hear me. Don't say anything to *anyone*. Leave your car right where it is and take a cab. At the terminal don't leave the counter, even if you have to piss."

"What about the girl and my caddy?

"We can call the caddy later from the plane. Leave the girl a note explaining that her amorous lovemaking had erased an important commitment from your mind. That you had to leave early and didn't want to wake her. We'll call a florist later and have them deliver a spectacular bouquet with a sweet note."

After hanging up, Lawrence Winslow sat down in thought. Sarge had no pizzazz, but he was not one to trim the truth or build dream houses. Like the fine-grained sand in a well-tended trap, he was consistent and always playable. Winslow picked up the phone and dialed. "Phil, I'm sorry to bother you at home on a Sunday evening, but an urgent matter has come up. I'll be leaving shortly for the Oaks Terminal. Our return ETA is 11:00. I need, no, I must have the top FBI man in town meet our plane, preferably, with the men he has in charge of bomb and terrorist threats. Think you can swing it?"

"Phil, it's nothing like that. I don't need a swat team or a bomb squad."

As the Lear taxied to a stop, Winslow saw Phil Voglin, the head of the bank's security force, and two official looking men waiting on the tarmac.

33

Key Biscayne, Florida
July 14...7:32 P.M.

Knowing the men inside were probably watching her, the dark-skinned Arab woman stretched and shook her long hair. Firm breasts swelled and she smiled. She liked being observed. Putting on a caftan, she let the bottom of her swimsuit fall to the pool deck. She hooked the suit with a painted toe and with a graceful motion flipped it up into a waiting hand. The sun was gone and the air was getting cooler. She didn't mind. A night person, the temperature change ignited her sensuality and put her in the mood for the evening's festivities. As the men studied her walk, she padded across the deck leaving a trail of wet footprints. Closing the wood blinds, her Haitian husband said, "She must have been a stripper in another life." As the Haitian sat down, the lank-haired Arab leading the meeting of the group of men gathered in the room resumed outlining his plan to sink two of America's largest cruise ships.

"The inland waters are wide open. The Guard is out deep playing their stupid drug interdiction games and the marine patrol is too busy writing up speeding tickets in the channels."

As an added precaution, the Arab had leased a Key Biscayne estate with a dock long enough to berth the two yachts that he'd leased. Both boats were already inside the Coast Guard's patrol area, and the marine patrol very seldom fooled with large, expensive yachts. You never knew who the owners were. Having studied journalism at Columbia, the erudite Arab used a black felt-tipped marker to make cryptic notes on the easel paper in front of him. All of the notations were in Arabic. In briefing his confederates, he was using the who, what, where, why and how technique reporters use in writing a story. Since he talked the same way, his guests were getting antsy. With a bored, empty-eyed stare, the only non-Arab in the room said, "Isn't this overkill? We've been through it and rehearsed it a dozen times."

"We can't practice enough. We only have one shot."

The fine silk and bold colors of the Haitian's flowing robe were quite striking. He was a physically imposing man whose white teeth flashed whenever he grinned. "I know the drill is necessary, but nothing has changed since this morning's run through."

"No, there is a big change. The water tanks were pumped this afternoon and have been refilled with an additional 4,000 gallons of petrol."

"Outstanding," said the Hatian with a dazzling smile.

Dressed like prosperous businessmen, the Arab men were constantly bemused by the Haitian's dress. The Haitian wore robes because his own following expected him to do so. His sing-song way of speaking was also a put-on that he used to disarm those he wished to exploit. With an intellect superior to everyone in the room, the Haitian was thinking, *For once the Arab fanatic has come up with something sensible.* Even though he had attended Oxford, like all Haitians the man was highly superstitious. In the hills surrounding Port-au-Prince, he witnessed firsthand, rituals that had marked his life forever. Whenever the Arab's comments got on his nerves the Haitian would roll his eyeballs up until they were almost white. At the same time, his body would stiffen and begin to tremble. The deep, tortuous moans that seemed to slither from his throat made the Arabs' blood run cold. Seeing the look on their faces, the Haitian had all he could do to keep from laughing in their faces.

Though for the Haitian, it was no laughing matter. His Arab wife with her drug connections in the Middle East had made them rich. Although they were getting paid a small fortune for their service, they knew it was payback time. The Arabs in the room were fanatic Osama bin Laden followers, but the Haitian and his wife were not being asked to sacrifice their lives. The mission did not require that they do so. They had already been reimbursed over a million dollars for the anticipated loss of their cigarette boats.

"The pickup is the tricky part, so let's go through that segment one last time," said the Arab leader.

Heads nodded, no one in the room wanted to die needlessly, and the pickup was the only sticky part of the entire mission.

"Alu, take us through, step by step."

The youngest of the group, Alu, rose. "After leaving the dock we all don our color-coded life preservers. We observe the no wake rules. When we receive the signal for *The Coming* we increase our speed to 15 knots riddling the fuel farm and containerized cargo facilities as we run by with .50 caliber machine gun fire and launched grenades. On the mark, we turn in unison until our yachts are facing the center of each cruise ship. At 1,200 yards on the radar, we set the automatic pilot. If the boats continue on course, everyone except the helmsmen jump from the rear dive platform to be picked up by their assigned cigarette boat. After we've all jumped clear, the helmsmen go to full speed. If the auto pilots hold, the helmsmen jump at 400 yards to be picked up by the boat set aside just for them."

"Perfect, Alu. Rashed, take us through the remainder of the destruction phase."

The oldest of those assembled, Rashed looked more Slavic than Middle Eastern. "When the yachts strike their targets dead center, the 3,000 pounds of dynamite in their bows and their maximum fuel loads along with the massive fuel tanks on each of the cruise ships will cause a blast strong enough to raise the ships out of the water and break them in half. Even as they sink, they will continue to melt. The initial blast of super heated air will not only kill everyone on board, but anyone within 200 yards of the vessels who is not underwater at the time."

"Well done, my friend. Khafan, the pick-up." Khafan had volunteered to be one of the helmsmen. He saw no greater glory than to die for the grace of Allah. He did not plan to jump, but he went through the drill for the sake of the others. "Except for the boats picking up the helmsmen, each cigarette boat will pick up four men according to the colors of their life jackets. All of the cigarettes have pre-arranged routes back to marinas where vans will be waiting. The cigarettes are expendable and they will be docked close to or alongside large privately owned yachts so when the charges planted in them go off they will kill more of Allah's enemies." The thought of killing more Americans seemed to give Khafan such great pleasure that he beamed. "From the marinas we drive five miles under the posted speed limits to our safe-houses. Once there, we wait for further instructions. The houses are fully stocked for a month's stay."

The Arab leader knelt on a prayer mat and bowed. "Allah is looking down on us with favor and promise. We are ready for *The Coming*."

34

Washington
July 29...2:01 A.M.

A gentle drizzle had hung over the city most of the day, cooling things down. But in the windowless office she had requested, Marta Wentworth, maiden name, Marta Kamus Daoud, didn't know it was raining. With the exception of a few catnaps on a cot in her office, she had worked slavishly at her bank of computer consoles for twenty hours, slogging through endless megabytes of information. As her neck began to stiffen, she knew a migraine was on its way. *It will be moving soon,* she thought. Slowly, as it always did, the pain began to intensify and drift down into its customary position. Within an hour, it felt like a red-hot icepick had been thrust through her head from behind her left eye. The throbbing agony was steady, but whenever she looked at a screen a stabbing jolt of excruciating pain made her look away.

The top student in her class at Brown University, with an IQ off the charts, Marta was one of the FBI's most potent assets when it came to fighting terrorism. Having lived in Europe and various Middle Eastern countries for twenty years, she could speak and write in Arabic, French and Spanish. She also liked to work alone without a secretary. *Too distracting, and I keep weird hours,* she had once commented. She wasn't even listed in the Bureau's internal telephone directory. With the exception of the assistant directors, she was the only agent with the FBI Director's home hotline number.

Items had been trickling in from the field for several weeks and for the first time since the van exploded in the World Trade Center garage, the pressure squeezing her brain had brought on a migraine. When the report from the Special Agent in Charge of the San Francisco field office flowed across her screen, she made the call. It was 2:13 in the morning.

Becoming more woozy by the minute, she chose words that would get the director's immediate attention. "Sir, this is Marta. I think we should go red immediately."

"Red. Marta, did you say red?"

"Yes sir, and right now."

Had anyone else called with that same request, they would have been grilled for an hour. To his credit, the director didn't hesitate. "Marta, call the communications supervisor, I want every assistant director assembled in the main conference room in one hour. I'm assuming this is a terrorist threat with a tight timeline?"

"Yes, sir. It definitely is."

"In that case, have communications get hold of everyone else that should be in the room. I'm authorizing you to select the people you want to be there."

"Got it. One more thing, I think the White House should be notified immediately and the Chief of Staff at a minimum should be here. Perhaps the Director of the CIA also."

"I've never seen you this forceful on anything before, Marta."

"Sir, it's going to be big."

"How sure are you?"

"Very sure, sir."

"I'll call the White House and Langley from the car. Tell the kitchen we'll need a lot of coffee and orange juice. No food. I want everyone alert."

Although the White House Chief of Staff and CIA Director were not available, the assembled list of titles at Marta's meeting was impressive, including the number-two man at the CIA along with the head of the White House Secret Service unit and the President's Advisor on Foreign Relations. No longer slim after so many hours spent sitting at computer terminals, Marta was not an attractive woman. Looking drawn and gray, she was fighting off nausea and the briefing she gave was a ragged affair. She had explained her condition up front, but those from outside the Bureau weren't moved. To them she looked like a walking zombie.

Referring to some notes as he spoke, the CIA Assistant Director was brutal. "Mrs. Wentworth, you got us all down here in the middle of the night to deliver a disjointed presentation because of a Brooklyn cabbie who likes to play act, a San Francisco golf pro with a police record and some Polack from outside Chicago who just got out of a six-month coma." He paused to glance at the yellow legal pad. "Oh yes, then there's the woman in L.A. who's pissed because the Arab she's been screwing has a yacht and is taking off without saying goodbye. There's also the tip from the yet to be identified source that there's been some strange trades made lately. Let me remind you that there are probably a hundred strange trades every day on the exchanges. That's why we have the SEC monitoring unit and *they* haven't said boo."

The CIA man kept his eyes riveted on Marta while he sipped some orange juice. The only *legitimate* information you've mentioned was given by the Russian, what's his name…"

"Alden Lensk, sir." Marta said.

"This Lensk gave us all a good deal of information about how the drug deals and money laundering between Russia and Afghans work, but he never produced any hard facts dealing with terrorism."

"Sir, the Russians get most of their illegal drugs from Afghanistan and some of that money helps finance the Taliban and bin Laden's terrorist network."

"Where's your proof?"

"It's a logical assumption, sir. The Arabs killed last week in Newport were meeting with the head of ROC in our country. Why were they here? Arab drugs are always funneled through Russia so the leaders there can get their cut."

"Maybe the Arabs were tired of getting paid less by going through a middle man or, in that instance, a middle country."

"Sir, the explosion that destroyed the Arab yachts was so powerful it also blew away a hotel over 300 feet away on top of a hill. The boats had to have high explosives on board."

"Enough exploding gasoline can accomplish the same thing."

"With all due respect, sir, I checked. Even if their gas tanks were full, the concussion from those boats would have blown out some windows and that's about it. They *had* to be packed with explosives."

"Marta, investigators and divers are still on the scene. Let's see what they find before we go overboard on this."

Following the CIA man's lead, the Secret Service chief said, "To be candid, this is all supposition from individuals with no real credibility. In the case of the L.A. woman who was scorned by her lover, her statement appears biased on its face. When your agents showed up, the yacht was gone and those tied up on the other side of the dock said they'd gone fishing, for what was it, Big Eye Tuna. The president is not going to scare the crap out of an entire country based on what I've just heard."

Overcome by a feeling of foreboding, she thought, *Who appointed these clueless imbeciles and why can't they connect the dots?* Their words cut Marta like a sword wielded by an executioner, an intense wave of pain doubled her over and she fell to her knees.

In the Bureau's own infirmary, they told the FBI director that Marta was dangerously dehydrated.

Looking down at her inert body, the director was shocked by her appearance. "What's all this?" he asked, pointing to the tubes going into her arm.

"Because of the pain, we had to knock her out with morphine. The IVs will control her blood pressure and up her fluid levels. She also has pneumonia, and that small bag is feeding her antibiotics. She'll be fine in day or two."

"Is the morphine necessary? We need her input as things develop. She can stay here and use a laptop."

"You want her dead or alive, sir? She was minutes from going into shock when she got here."

"Jesus!" said the director. "Those stupid bastards. I'll have an agent posted outside her room. Nobody except your staff goes in without my permission. She's to have complete rest."

"Now you're talking my language, sir."

When he returned to the conference room all of the people who weren't FBI were gone. "Marta's going to recover, but they had to knock her out. Forget what the CIA and White House said. I want ten agents on each side of the Golden Gate Bridge within the next two hours. If it's going to be hit, it will probably be during rush hour."

A short, stumpy agent with a beard, spoke up. "Have them watch for vans or trucks with rental plates or markings. All of those should be stopped and inspected. We may need some state police help for that. Also, they should pull over anyone who looks Middle Eastern. And, remind our agents that it's the ones who smile the most that usually do the damage."

"I'm convinced we're going to get hit. Call everyone in, even those on leave. I want 20 agents at all of the airports in the cities Marta mentioned. I want them roving and overseeing the check-points operated by the rental cops. "

The stumpy man spoke up again. "Sir, I'd get the SEC out of bed and have some fresh teams of agents reinterview everyone Marta mentioned. I've known Lawrence Winslow, the golfer's friend, for years. He's a superstar in California banking circles, and a man who doesn't believe in fairy tales."

"Everyone hear that? Let's get on it."

With the feedback he received from his White House staff and the CIA, the president took the previous night's junta in stride. He was enjoying his favorite dessert, strawberry cheesecake, when the Director of the FBI finally got through to him in the White House dining room. By then it was too late.

35

West Palm Beach
July 26...5:30 A.M.

Salem Abar, along with nine other Arab men, had operated a golf course and driving range in West Palm Beach, Florida for five years. All the Arabs who worked at the course had wives and children. Six more Arabs worked in Mohamed Jarrahi's Greek restaurant in nearby Jupiter. During that time, the Arabs, with the exception of Mohamed, had taken flying lessons. Florida's weather was ideal for flying, the terrain was flat and there was an abundance of good flight schools.

The owner of the school where Salem and several of his men flew was a golf nut who had eagerly traded flying lessons for free golf and range privileges. The golf course was in excellent condition, but best of all, the greens, cart and range fees were reasonable. Members of the local high school golf team could play golf free after 3:00 p.m. and were allowed to use the driving-range anytime. Salem Abar was also generous in dispensing gift certificates for local fund-raisers and the resulting goodwill endeared the Arabs to the community. All of the Arab men who worked at the course and restaurant lived quietly in adjacent neighborhoods with their wives and children.

Salem and Mohamed, along with the fifteen Arabs who worked for them, had earned their instrument and multi-engine ratings for propeller-driven aircraft at five different flight schools within a 50-mile radius. After they had a sufficient number of solo hours in their log books, they often rented aircraft for weekend trips. Renting multi-engine planes every other week is an expensive proposition, but no one at the flying schools ever gave a thought to where the men were getting the money to pay for the aircraft rentals, especially when the Arabs always brought them boxes of delicious Greek pastries and snacks. During practice flights they sharpened their skills, flying simulated missions over some of the sites that were targets of their hate. Trusted members of an Osama bin Laden terrorist cell, they were religious fanatics who had pledged their lives in behalf of the Jihad that bin Laden had conceived five years earlier.

To his neighbors and suppliers, Mohamed was a hardworking stiff who cut his own lawn and drove a four-year-old Chrysler. No one would have guessed that he was exorbitantly rich and the man that bin Laden had entrusted with the plan he'd blessed as *The Coming*. Three months earlier, without fanfare, Mohamed had closed on the sale of his restaurant and, apart from a two-week transition period, he'd retired from the business. His dedicated all-Arab staff and their families had remained together, supported by Mohamed as though they were still working in his restaurant.

Except for Mohamed and Salem, all of the men had entered the States on temporary two-week visitors' visas. The INS did not have the manpower to keep track of all the hundreds of thousands of those who came to America each year on guest visas, so the men working for Salem and Mohamed simply faded into the woodwork. With the exception of Mohamed, none of them knew that bin Laden had over 1,200 operatives planted throughout the United States and Europe. Like many of the businesses owned by bin Laden's followers, the restaurant and golf course were owned by corporations that filed legitimate federal and state tax returns. All of their payroll and sales taxes were paid on time and all employees and their families were covered by an Aetna health plan.

Three days before Marta Wentworth raised a red flag, the Arab pilots departed Florida in their rented aircraft for small private airfields close to their midwest and east coast targets: Chicago, Washington, New York, and Boston. There they would make their final preparations for the attacks. Meanwhile, pilots in an al-Qaeda cell in California were readying their aircraft for an attack on the Golden Gate Bridge in San Francisco.

The golf course conglomerate that had acquired Salem Abar's Florida course two months earlier took over hours after the last terrorist's plane left.

San Francisco...July 29...11:45 A.M.

Despite the best efforts of the FBI, four apparent soccer-moms driving different American-made vans with at least two children in the front seats made their way through the makeshift checkpoints on each side of the Golden Gate Bridge. The carpeting and head liners had been removed. The vans were then lined with plastique explosives two inches thick in some places. The seats and arm rest were solid plastique. Cell members trained in car upholstery worked for two weeks putting the vans back in apple pie order.

As the vans, two on each side of the road moving in opposite directions, came alongside the tower on the San Francisco side of the Golden Gate, they veered suddenly and jumped the curbs that protected the pedestrian walkways. Working swiftly, the women tied and locked chains from their car bumpers to the thick poles that supported the free-standing light poles only feet from the tower.

Waving their arms frantically, the children sat down in the center of the road, backing up traffic all the way to the downtown section of Sausalito. Seconds before the Arab mothers pushed their plungers, they touched their hands to their lips and threw kisses towards their children who smiled and waved back.

Flying at maximum cruise power, Lotfi Moged sat trembling in anticipation. All joy had been taken from him long ago and his anger at Americans had the unshakable fervor of the radical religious fanatic. A walking pig sty with dirty, scraggly hair and a crooked, mocking smile, he was the kind of man who would let his wife work to pay the rent. He hadn't shaved for several weeks, telling his wife that there was no point in doing so. It was only his dedication to bin Laden and Allah that had kept Moged going the last few years. Now he was drunk with power, drunk with the anticipation of victory and drunk with the sense that his miserable existence would at last serve some useful purpose. On takeoff, after the wheels had retracted into their wells, Moged savored a feeling new to him: glee.

With the knowledge that on most mornings an ocean of fog envelops the bridge, Moged, fearful that fog would spoil his chances at the target, began to sweat, so much so his undershorts became damp. In flight, fog is a great equalizer and Moged had barely squeaked through the flight test for his instrument rating. As he approached the target area, a scornful smile lit up his face. The early morning fog crept away and the city by the sea glistenened in the distance. Moged observed the ferries on their way to Alcatraz Island, but it was the 48-story Transamerica Pyramid that drew his attention The building reminded him of everything he hated about the untroubled, fresh-faced Americans wandering around the hilly city. Just the idea that some of those he was about to kill worked there made him salivate.

When he beheld the bridge's magnificent, ferrous orange outline and the spreading line of brake lights in the distance, Moged's indifferent eyes grew larger and he screwed his lips around the soggy, unlit cigar in his mouth. The bridge's skeleton reminded Moged of the bridge model he purchased for his son at a flea market. Built with a fifties erector set, the seller had wanted 30 dollars for the rusty relic. He'd paid five. "All Americans want to do is get rich," Moged muttered, setting his bloodshot eyes on the target, a long open-air tunnel filled with six lanes of backed up traffic. Even closer on, the cars and trucks were out of scale and the people looked like toy soldiers; *A herd of roadkill.*

When it opened in 1937, the bridge's daily traffic count was sparse and state officials were faulted for overbuilding. These days, over 160 thousand cars, along with bicyclists and walking tourists by the thousands, jammed the six-lane road and the protected ten-foot wide sidewalks on each side of the roadway. Moged noticed that the tops of the two mammoth towers were still wrapped in light canopies of fog.

Suspended in his bosun's chair 720 feet above the turbulent water, partially hidden in the white cheesecloth-like clouds, Ron Johnson, "Crash" to his friends, held a spray gun with an arm that would make most body-builders envious. In the white painter's coveralls he called his flight suit, and with his safety harness and lifelines secured, he dangled in space so close to heaven he playfully poked at the sky as if trying to touch the invisible presence. Usually a happy-go-lucky person, Crash's Monday morning started on a bad note. The place where he got his morning fix of *café con leche* was closed for a funeral and the notepad in his locker where he kept track of how much paint he applied each day was missing an entry from the day before. *Was it 3 gallons or 3 1/2 gallons?* He couldn't remember and it bothered him. Crash was one of the ten men and two women who painted the bridge year round. It took ten thousand gallons of epoxy-based paint a year to stay ahead of the salt-filled Pacific air, and Crash was the kind of man who liked to know if he was doing his share.

Forever a man who wanted to fly, Crash was in his natural element, the sky. He loved being up there, like some men love being Marines. From his precarious perch, he noticed that the boat anchorages and best picnic tables at Angel Island were already taken and that the sailors he had labeled the old farts were approaching the starting line for their weekly race. Had he been working below the roadway, Crash would have seen the long dark shadows of the sharks that follow the freighters. Too lazy to use the onshore grinders and dumpsters, some of the freighter captains ordered the food scraps dumped overboard knowing the sharks would make a meal without anyone being the wiser. One captain, flying a Korean flag, had made the mistake of dumping while his boat was passing directly beneath Crash's work station. "Bombs away," Crash laughed, letting loose a steady stream of paint. Three gallons of epoxy redecorated the vessel, just out of the shipyard after a refit. The ship's officers and crew rushed on deck. Looking up, they saw a man giving them the finger, yelling, "Littering is a misdemeanor, you assholes."

There was one particular shark, about 18-feet long, that hung out in the waters between the two towers. Everyone on the paint crew called him Gus. When a friend left the paint shed in the morning, you were obligated to say something like, "Now Billy, don't you fuck with Gus today." Most job applicants didn't last an hour on the paint or inspection crew's mandatory pre-hire walks that took them up one of the bridge's main cables. The combination of 90-story height at the top, the movement of the bridge sideways and up and down, and the sight of the sharks prowling below scared the living shit out of most of them.

The pay was good; 18 dollars an hour to start. Crash was making 29 dollars with a good health plan and a month's paid vacation. During his ten years on the paint crew, he'd personally seen 76 desperate souls end their lives by jumping from the bridge. Hundreds more had been saved by passersby who either tackled them or talked them down. Crash knew every expansion joint in the bridge and he'd noticed that most of the suicides leaped from the joint closest to the bridge's center. *Need to have someone in civvies hang out around that joint,* he often thought.

Now, suspended under one of the main cables so he could work on it from underneath, he felt like a movie director on one of those boom cranes. Looking down, Crash saw the four vehicles jump the pedestrian barrier, the women with the chains and their kids scattering into the center of the road and sitting down. The scene was completed when he heard the prop–driven engines of the two aircraft. Seeing them approaching fast from opposite directions, he knew instinctively that they weren't there to show off by flying underneath the bridge. A bright man, Crash also knew there would never be another notation in his locker notepad. Snapping the paint sprayer to a hook on his safety belt, he blessed himself, pressed his mike button and began singing in a low melancholy voice. *I left my heart in San Francisco, upon a high and windy…"*

Heading to the trucking company she used in San Francisco, Lida Seto sat stalled in traffic annoyed by a teenager on the sidewalk whose boom-box was playing the vulgar rap crap she hated. Sitting next to her in the pickup was her thirteen-year-old daughter watching a boy who had stopped on the bridge to take pictures. Lida was a plain but talented Japanese woman who restored old "dobby horses" rescued from merry-go-rounds. Lida knew that her fear of the bridge was unreasonable. Her husband, Jeff, often pooh-poohed her when he was driving and she had her eyes locked shut. However, trapped between the center spans, she could feel her heart beginning to pound. When the spaniel in the jump seat barked, Lida looked around and saw Moged's plane. She tried to grab her daughter, but Lida's seat belt was fastened. Before she could unbuckle, the pickup was lifted off the ground by four almost simultaneous explosions. Pressure from the blasts blew out the eardrums of all the people with their vehicle windows open. Lida's daughter had her tinted window closed, but the shock wave cut it off at the sill and it struck the child in the face. As Lida Seto's truck began sliding downward behind the vehicles in front of her, she put her arms around her unrecognizable daughter and closed her eyes. The spaniel continued to bark.

Juana and Roberto Perez worked for the City of San Francisco as trolley car operators and on their day off they usually biked over the Golden Gate to Sausalito. They were only eight hundred feet from safety, when the bridge was hit. They'd biked for two hours before starting their jaunt across the bridge and had slowed down the pace to rest and enjoy the view. Roberto yelled, "Peddle, Juana, peddle hard!" Three hundred feet from the end of the bridge, the sidewalk beneath them began to vibrate and tilt downward. Roberto stopped and when Juana slowed next to him, he swept her off the bike. "Run, Juana. Run for it."

Knowing their immortal souls are at stake, Roberto experienced a clarity of thought that he had never known before. He could taste his wife's homemade candies and the smell from the hot dog wagon of his favorite vendor on United Street. As Juana prayed in Spanish for their salvation, Roberto thought of the hand-me-down car she drove and promised himself to get her a new one. He also promised God that he would give up the on-again-off-again gambling that had plagued their marriage from the start. A mere 50 feet from their objective the bridge collapsed into the bay. Roberto lunged out grabbing his wife by the waist with one arm, hooking his other arm around the steel bars of the pedestrian handrail. There were screams and blood all around them as others were cut down by random pieces of cable that scythed through bone and tissue like a whetstone-honed meat cleaver.

The mass of twisted cable tempered the Perez's impact with the cement abutment allowing Roberto and his wife to hold fast to the railing. The piece of railing still attached to the place where the bridge started was 50 feet long. They were dangling by a thread 170 feet above the abutment's base which jutted out 30 feet from the cement wall. Sadly, all of the inch-thick cables hanging down around them were out of reach. The Perez's feet found support on the railing and they hung there, afraid to move lest they break the threads that stopped their death fall. With dread, Roberto watched the scene below them as the sharks in their feeding frenzy turned the water blood red.

"Don't look down," he told his wife. They were still hanging there when the veil of bay fog moved in off the Pacific. The warm rays of sun were suddenly gone and it began to get cold. "Roberto, we'll never survive the night."

"We're going to make it."

"I'm getting very weak."

Fearing his wife might let go to save him, Roberto removed his thick belt and fastened it around her waist. He hooked his arm through the belt and then through the railing. "If you go, I go."

Through the remainder of the day, Roberto and Juana heard the chilling clamor of cries from those in the water. The pool of fresh blood had drifted out to sea on the outgoing tide where sharks thirty miles from the bridge detected the scent. Roberto observed the convoy of dorsal fins approaching like hundreds of surface-running torpedoes making their run. When the convoy arrived, even those fortunate enough to have found refuge on a piece of floating debris became fresh prey.

As the night wore on, Roberto felt Juana's body weight cutting into his arm. Encased in the cold fog and with his own strength beginning to wane, he fought off the ghost that tried to sap his will to live. The intensity of the light beam blinded Roberto for a moment and then a voice amplified by a bullhorn said, "Hold on, we're sending a basket down. Ten minutes. We're going to keep the light on you, so close your eyes until I give you the word." Juana Perez continued to pray long after they were safe. After taking her to a nearby shelter and downing a hot meal provided free by a local restaurant,

Roberto, a changed man, returned to the bridge site to help out.

The bridge's two towers support two main suspension cables, each three feet wide in diameter. Dedicated al-Qaeda cell members with degrees in engineering had correctly determined that taking out one tower would bring down the entire bridge. Though he was the least talented of the pilots in the group, Moged's aim was perfect and the solid twin engine King Air jammed with explosives and extra petrol impacted the targeted span at 300 miles per hour 20 feet below the roadway. Seconds before impact Moged saw the stupefied faces of motorists staring out at him. His visions of flying body parts and rotting bones gave him great comfort in death. Two minutes later, a Piper Aerostar hit the other leg of the tower, moving at 312 miles per hour. The handsome aircraft was piloted by Ali Alnami, the greenskeeper that Sarge, the golf pro, had befriended.

Prior to the blasts, two fully laden freighters yawing and rolling in opposite directions had passed under the bridge. Beyond them, 62 brightly colored sails of the Senior Captains and Mates Club added a kernel of cheer to the bay's bleak appearance. There was a 21-foot limit on the size of the boat one could race, so the club's fleet paled in comparison to the expensive sailing yachts that raced and cruised the bay on weekends. The club's weekly race was a fun thing for active retirees and the winning crew got a free lunch.

While still a mile from the bridge, widower Mort Gurnick shouted orders to his last-minute crew member, the younger sister of a friend who was sailing on another boat. The woman's tight shorts and skimpy halter had Mort so distracted that he trailed the fleet. An excellent sailor who almost always placed in the top five, Mort took his last place position philosophically. *The price of beauty, Mort. The price of beauty.* As they approached the next marker, they watched in amazement as the planes flew into the tower. Mort, a retired Naval officer, knew what would happen if the bridge went over. "Duck, I'm coming about!"

As the tower began to lean, Mort observed the elements of weight, gravitational acceleration and kinetic energy coming into play. He grabbed the radio mike. "All boats this net, turn your stern to the bridge, drop sail and turn on your engines. I say again. Turn your stern to the bridge, drop sail and turn on your engines. Maintain maximum speed away from the bridge and prepare for massive wave action. Don't wait! Do it now!" Hearing his words, the woman immediately began locking down hatches. In the end, it was Mort's expert seamanship, his fastidious maintenance and their last place position in the race that saved them.

Absent any load, the bridge and twin towers weighed an awesome 840 million pounds. As the supporting cables snapped and melted, the span leaned toward the point of least resistance, San Francisco Bay. Helped by the 20 to 25 knot winds and the weight of the gridlocked vehicles, the tower submitted and the 4,200-foot-long span plunged 487 cars, 158 pickups, 18 motor homes, 32 RV's, 56 trailer-trucks, 8 tanker-trucks, 18 motorcycles, 108 bicycles and strolling pedestrians into the frigid, treacherous water 220 feet below. Within minutes, the bay became a butchering ground for hundreds of sharks that honed in on the 1,811 men, women and children who had landed helplessly in the sharks' domain.

Riding the tower down, Crash heard the agonizing screams, the frantic barking of dogs and the pitiful screeching of cats, who like their owners, knew they were about to die. He saw cars and trucks hit the water, split in half and explode, the occupants tossed through the air like rag dolls to the waiting sharks. Beneath him, bicycles, pocketbooks, cameras, hats, lunch bags, backpacks and hundreds of other objects temporarily filled the air. Along with the flames and smoke from the six terrorist detonations and the miles of cable rocketing out in every direction, Crash viewed the scene as a jungle and hoped that the barbaric perpetrators burned forever in hell.

The Golden Gate Bridge was held up by two massive cables each three-feet thick. Together the cables contained 80,000 miles of steel wire woven into thousands of strands 7,650 feet long. When the strands snapped, many of them rocketed into space for almost a mile in every direction. The first victims were the two freighters and sailboats that were within reach. Some of the men and women on deck of the freighters and sailboats were killed outright by the slashing wires. When the morass of wire became tangled in the props of the freighters, the captains had to stop their engines.

Nearly a thousand gas tanks, including those of eight fully loaded gasoline transport trucks, ruptured when they hit the water and something like 185,000 gallons of burning gasoline were carried by wave action over a wide area. Once the flames reached the ensnared freighters, the lifeboats and cargo stored on their decks ignited. Five minutes later, as a TV helicopter hovered dangerously close, both freighters detonated in successive fireballs.

Mort Gurnick looked back, but did not panic when he saw the tsunami building directly behind them. He had sent his mate below and tied himself to the helm with two lifelines. The little boat rode the wave to its crest where it perched as if on the fulcrum of a see-saw. When the prop broke clear of the water, Mort cut the engine so it wouldn't throw the prop. As they surfed uncontrollably down the face of the giant wave, he turned the little diesel back on and regained some steerage. The boat struck the trough of the wave like a submarine on a crash dive and kept on going until the only parts of the sailboat showing were the cabin roof and the mast. Clutching the solidly built helm in a death grip, Mort held his breath as the water buried him. Thirty seconds later, the boat's positive buoyancy and the dependable diesel shot them back to the surface.

Wiping salt water from his eyes, Mort saw the undamaged towers, but the Golden Gate Bridge was no longer there to welcome the world. Except for the burning freighters, he did not see any other boats including the one that his mate's sister was aboard. Mort cut the engine and drifted. The marina where he had tied his boat wouldn't be there, so where was there to go?

The bridge's critical mass, loaded down with another 4 million pounds hitting the water created a tsunami which in Japanese means "harbor wave." The wave that formed was 39 feet high and moved toward the shore at 180 miles per hour, well under the 110 foot high, 900 miles per hour waves generated by tsunamis created by natural means like underwater earthquakes.

Donny Andersen had spent forty years as a ferry boat captain. For many of those years he ran a prison boat out of Alcatraz until it was shut down. Nowadays, he skippered a yellow and white ferry that hauled tourists back and forth to the same island. As Donny came out of the Seaman's Chapel on Fisherman's Wharf, he instantly knew something was very wrong. The fat gulls and pigeons that made such a clamor feeding on tourists' pretzels and other morsels were gone, every last one of them. Using his hands to shield his eyes from the sun, he studied the bay. Spotting the wall of water, Donny began running toward the closest high-ground, Ghirardelli Square. As he ran, he pointed with one hand and screamed, "Wave, wave, run, run!"

Stragglers or those who didn't comprehend or who assumed Donny was another crack-head on a tear, soon heard a *Schhhhh, Schhhhh, Schhhhh* sound coming from the bay. As it approached the shoreline, one of nature's elemental sounds, that of a wave cresting, became an ear-shattering roar. The shallow water and confines of the bay increased the wave's height dramatically and its stored energy was magnified many times over. The transfer of the unleashed energy to whatever stood in its way on land would be no contest.

Fisherman's wharf and the Embarcadero's Pier #39 with its wooden fishing village vanished. Hundreds of boats of every size and description ended high up on the steps of Ghirardelli Square or against the first building the wave had not knocked down. Donny was hit by a wall of water from below as he reached the relative safety of the square. Squashed onto the cement, he was stunned for an instant, but reached out for anything that would keep him from being sucked back into the bay. His hand found the root of a lamp post and he wrapped both arms around the base. He lived. Aside from those killed when they were cast from the bridge, three thousand eight hundred souls on land were drowned or had perished in the fires and toxic fumes started by the tsunami as it leveled every low-lying building in its path. Sitting up, with his back against the wall of a store, Donny Andersen could only think of one word to describe what he saw: Apocalyptic.

Long Beach...July 29...11:46 A.M.

The fifth largest city in California, Long Beach, is home to the area's most famous tourist attraction the *Queen Mary*. Fata Ahmed Aza had chosen Long Beach as his target for a different reason. With its constant stream of oil tankers and freighters, Long Beach was one of the busiest ports on the Pacific Coast and the crude oil pumped from the tankers fed the nearby refineries. In addition, some of the city's most vital assets were located at the water's edge.

Feigning steering trouble, the captain of Aza's 108 foot-yacht had wrangled permission to tie up along side an oil tanker that was waiting its turn to be pumped out. "I've called for a tug. We should be out of your hair in fifteen minutes. My hydraulic steering is so hairy, I'm afraid to take her all the way in." The captain and executive officer of the tanker were both ashore, and the engineering officer violated a company rule in order to help a ship in distress. No one noticed the yacht's captain and skeleton crew motoring away in a rubber dinghy concealed by a tug boat going in the same direction. Twenty minutes had elapsed since the leased yacht had been abandoned and through his binoculars Aza could see two officers on the tanker's bridge taking stock of the situation. With his men safe in the rear of the Ryder Truck, Aza checked his watch, waited thirty seconds and flipped the micro switch.

Loaded with 20 more of the wooden boxes that Helen Peabody had seen that night at Marina Del Rey, the explosion of the yacht started a chain reaction that ravaged the Long Beach waterfront. Fully loaded tankers, oil storage tanks, freighters, tugs and pleasure boats blew up. Millions of gallons of crude oil and other fuels liberated from the ships and dumped into the water spread the fire across four miles of highly developed waterfront. The intense heat and pressure reached out and destroyed the Long Beach's Convention and Entertainment Center where 8,000 people were attending a home and garden show. All of the sea creatures at Planet Ocean, the complex of shops and restaurants at Shoreline Village and the *Queen Mary* were consumed by fire. The major hotels that catered to convention goers along with scores of smaller tourists facilities, homes and commercial buildings ceased to exist. To Aza, the holocaust and the tragic loss of so many lives was a lovely thing, so well executed, so right.

New York City...July 29...2:45 P.M.

Before sunrise that morning, in a damp Gladstone, New Jersey hangar that smelled of old oil and burnt out engines, Salem and his pilots loaded the five multi-engine aircraft rented for the period with a pre-calculated amount of high explosives. With their oversized tanks topped off with AvGas, the Arab men were flying megaton missiles. In order to carry the explosives and extra fuel inside the plane, some of the seats had been removed and anything else that added an ounce of weight was ripped out. Today, the Arab pilots were wearing baggy tunics instead of shorts and t-shirts. Since every ounce of weight reduced their payload, they would strip down to their boxer shorts before takeoff.

Privately owned, the airstrip had only one runway and no control tower. Salem had checked the weather on his computer earlier and flying conditions were perfect. He'd also filed flight plans for all of the aircraft in his group. With all of the last minute details completed, the rented hangar suddenly became very quiet. The Arab men rolled out their prayer rugs and knelt, facing east toward the holy city of Mecca in Saudi Arabia. For a group of men about to die they were calm. Dog-eared Korans, the holy book of Islam, lay beside each man. They had all made the required pilgrimages to the city of Mecca, the birthplace of the prophet Muhammad, and the thought of that experience provided solace.

To Salem, the fervor of the pilots' prayers reflected their belief in the righteousness of bin Laden's Jihad. All the Arabs except for Amed Resem were of the Sunni Muslim sect which dominated Afghanistan. Amed was a Shi'a Muslim who spoke both Dari and Pashtu, the languages spoken by 85 percent of the those who live in the country. A mean-minded man,

Amed tried hard to keep his blazing anger hidden under his practiced, have-a-nice-day face. But now, with their goal in sight, Amed's heaving chest and restlessness betrayed the eager anticipation of one of Allah's devoted warriors about to be released from all restraints and set free to engage an enemy whose prosperity and lifestyles he had come to hate. Amed knew that over half of his country's 25 million people were illiterate. Most would be lucky to see their 46th birthdays. The wealth he saw around him in America was an incessant thorn in Amed's side and he thought about the Americans who spent thousands each year just on golf. A rich man in Amed's village was someone who earned 3 dollars a day.

Their prayer rites completed, each pilot, in different ways, felt forever free. Salem could sense the tranquility, see the euphoric expression on their faces, even Amed's. He knew that all were ready to give to Allah the ultimate gift, their lives.

He passed out a typed list of the radio frequencies for the air spaces each of the pilots would be entering en route to their objectives. "Have you all completed your pre-flight checks?" Salem asked.

Nods.

"Weight and balance is critical. Has anyone loaded *anything* that would change things?"

Heads shake.

"Remember, maintain normal radio contact until you're in sight of your target. Fly straight and level, Allah is waiting."

Before the men and one woman boarded their aircraft, Arab wives took possession of their clothing and valuables. The tearful good-byes and comforting words one would expect were not present. The families had made their peace long ago and some of the wives had their own missions to carry out. Donning their new aviator glasses, the pilots waved to their loved ones and took off ten minutes apart.

At the controls of his Mitsubishi Mu-2 heading for Manhattan's Wall Street, Salem's mind drifted back for a moment to the time when he and his brothers, dressed in black, were sprinting through a thick line of trees in a field in Turbat, near the coast of Palestine. They heard the music of a small combo playing on the deck of a lakeside home, a party in progress. The brothers' mission was to kill three men who had betrayed their leader, Osama bin Laden, These three would be meeting in a boat shed 200 yards from the party house in an hour. Osama wanted them dead in a manner that would cast blame on the Americans. There was no moon and the lake was silky smooth. The open ground between the wall and the boat house hadn't been mowed for many weeks and with the summer rains, wild flowers and weeds had flourished. As they climbed over the low wall, Salem noticed that nature had polished the granite stones on top. Halfway to their objective, powerful searchlights lit up the entire area. Salem and his brothers were trapped in the open and the sounds of crickets mixed with the stream of lethal gunfire from the house. Salem Abar envisioned his entire family and the men he was assigned to kill standing around his grave. They were holding umbrellas and there was polished granite all around.

The crackle in Salem's earphones broke the spell. "This is Larry."

Salem checked in with the other pilots by radio and cell phone and except for "Larry", everyone was on track. Salem had picked the name, Larry, from skits in the old *Bob Newhart* show. He sometimes chuckled when he thought about it and today was no exception. "Larry, what's your status?"

"I was running a little hot. I'll be back on track in five minutes or so."

"Good, you don't want to miss the party."

When he saw the New York skyline Salem checked and everyone was on station. Nine minutes later he keyed his mike button and said, "Allah is calling us. Atonement is at hand." Other pilots on the same radio frequency heard snippets of the terrorists' conversations, but since Salem's pilots were speaking mostly in Dari or Pashtu, no one understood what was going on.

At 2:45 P.M., Tuesday, June 25, 2002 the New York Stock Exchange was having another hectic day. A day trader standing next to his runner griped, "Shit, Billy, I can't wait for the fucking bell."

At that very moment, Salem Abar's old but fast MU-2 made a sweeping turn a mile above the slip-stream of a TWA flight on its final approach into Kennedy. Salem had flown the same course five other times but without the steep dive angle he was about to execute. The controller at Kennedy who was tracking the TWA plane saw Salem's unauthorized move and tried to make radio contact. Salem laughed and turned up the volume on his CD player. As Elvis's "Blue Suede Shoes" rocked away, Salem Abar pushed the wheel forward, lowering the nose.

To make absolutely sure Salem hit his target, a New Jersey cell member had squeegeed a five-foot wide strip of neon yellow paint around the perimeter of the Exchange's roof. Employed as a supervisory night janitor, the dependable Arab hid the long-handled squeegee and paint on the roof over a two-week period. Then, the night before Salem's attack, he'd simply poured the paint out of the cans in long strips and squeegeed it across the roof's flat surface. To helicopter pilots who flew over that morning, it looked as though the roof were being repaired. To Salem, the shiny yellow paint eliminated any chance of hitting the wrong target. There was no sorrow or remorse in Salem's mind as his plane gathered speed. Afraid of flying the wings off the aircraft he inched the throttles toward the stops. At 340 miles per hour he slid the side window back a notch and the roar of the straining engines filled his ears. He felt the three-point seat belt cut into his flesh as the snowballing acceleration and steep dive angle pushed him forward. He sliced through the tiny panes of glass that made up the roof's skylight dome and at 363 miles per hour Salem screamed, "Allahaaaaa!"

Loaded with explosives, AvGas and 200 pounds of incendiary phosphorus, Salem's plane contacted the center of the trading floor and the pressure from the horrific detonation pushed out the walls, allowing the roof to collapse. The flames, intense heat, flesh-eating phosphorus and thousands of knife-like shards of glass knifing through the air had killed almost everyone in the building. The crushing weight of the fallen roof finished the job.

Within minutes of the destruction of the NYSE, the remaining aircraft in Salem's squadron struck the United Airlines planes docked at the crowded La Guardia Airport's gates and the American Airlines planes parked at busy John F. Kennedy. Hitting the waiting Boeing 757's and 747's broadside, the explosions created a domino effect which leap-frogged from gate to gate until the two terminals no longer existed.. Fragments of metal and glass coupled with lung-searing heat and noxious fumes killed everyone within 300 feet and destroyed 22 fully loaded aircraft that were taxiing to and from various gates.

When the ground under the planes melted, the heat reached underground fuel lines and they erupted in a chain of blowouts that ran all the way to the off-field fuel storage tanks and the other terminals. The resulting blasts turned hundreds of planes into piles of cinder and black smoke. Shock waves from all the explosions sent debris into the parking lots and garages where the chain-reaction of exploding cars eventually collapsed the parking structures.

The intense heat limited what the firefighters could do, so they focused on containment. Almost blinded by black smoke and wearing oxygen masks, they put a constant mist of water over the area to stop wind-blown ashes from starting fires in nearby residential and commercial areas.

Meanwhile at Yankee Stadium, it was all sunshine and blue sky. The Yankees were leading the Seattle Mariners 2 to 1 in the top of the second inning when one of the TV cameramen picked up two low-flying planes. He shouted into his face-mike, "Planes! Planes heading for the stands!" The Arab aircraft cleared the left field and right field walls by fifty feet and blew up against the structural poles supporting the bleacher seats in back of both dugouts, causing the bleachers to collapse and killing 14,800 fans and everyone on the Yankee and Mariner teams, from the bat boy and girl to the managers. Hundreds of cars in the parking lots were hit by debris and the same domino effect that had befallen the airports did the rest. Twelve thousand cars disappeared as the explosions melted the asphalt and blew large craters into the earth.

Mohamed Jairahi had booked suites of rooms on the top floors of five New York hotels including one at each airport. There, he and four of the Arab wives videotaped the attacks and devastation. In his commentary, Mohamed said, "All was normal until Allah's soldiers thundered down on the blasphemous infidels. The sturdy buildings we saw a moment ago have collapsed like tissue paper and everything inside has been incinerated. Allah be praised. When the dust finally settles, it will look as though Allah has cast a shroud of thick gray soot over the marbled castles considered so impregnable only minutes ago.

The smoke you see on your screen is hiding the remnants of the New York Stock Exchange, once the pinnacle of world finance. When the smoke clears, it will look like a doll house crushed by a wandering camel. See the useless army of ants scurrying around in their colored hard-hats and little white masks? They and the spider web of fire hoses and cables strung out in the streets are as useless as the Americans who have retreated from the unbearable heat. They can do nothing to stop Allah's wrath. America has been violated and even from here, thirty stories above Allah's carnage, I can sense their fear and humiliation. Death has come to the infidels and the Jihad, with Allah's guidance, has emerged victoriously.

The gates of paradise have opened to our brothers in arms. They are standing next to Allah looking down at their handiwork. Allah has embraced them and set off the thunderclaps you hear in the back ground to honor and welcome them."

Later, in his own home studio in New Jersey, Mohamed would strip in the thunderclaps.

When the Mayor of New York flew over the airports two hours later, there was nothing to see. Kennedy and La Guardia had ceased to exist. Everything was gone; commercial and private aircraft, terminals, hangars, rental car facilities, everything. Substantial portions of the runways where the underground fuel lines had exploded looked from the air like moon craters.

Moving through a gray, rising cloud of soot and debris, the whirling blades of the sleek Sikorsky helicopter seemed to be hunting for the faceless, remorseless monsters that had reeked such havoc on the innocent. Homegrown from birth, the mayor recoiled from the sight of thousands of charred bodies below. *We'll never find them all,* he thought. The chopper circled Yankee Stadium where the mayor was a regular and the words *take no prisoners* lingered on his tongue. By the time they finished viewing all of the impacted sites, the mayor had regained his composure. An essentially decent man with a first-rate mind, the mayor was mindful of what had to be said. His message was unadorned and painfully honest. "We have been mortally but not fatally wounded. The attacks can never be justified. We are no longer untouchable. The amount of damage is staggering. Recovery will be slow and we must be patient and help each other. For the sake of humanity, we must take into our homes those who are wandering the streets with no place to go. We must pray for our dead, our dying and our wounded. There is no instant fix that will make the pain and sorrow go away." Then the mayor's voice became hard-edged. "We are going to war with evil in the form of terrorists. We must not rest until this planet is rid of their kind."

Fort Lauderdale...July 29...2:48 P.M.

Earlier that morning, Mary and Salvador Pina, who'd flown from their home in Kansas City to Fort Lauderdale, Florida the day before, waited expectantly in Terminal #2, Port Everglades' newest embarkation facility with its immense waiting area and dramatic view of the harbor. They were two among thousands of passengers who would soon be allowed to board the magnificent 15-story-tall cruise ship, the *Maharajah*, the newest, largest and most glamorous cruise ship in the world, on its two-week maiden voyage across the Atlantic.

For Mary and Sal it would truly be the trip that dreams are made of, the one they believed would never happen and, amazingly, it was all free!

As they waited, Mary reflected on the events that made it possible.

On a day during the week of the American Society of Travel Agents convention in Kansas City, John Moody, a local travel agent and long time customer of Sal and Mary's barber shop, visited the shop bringing with him a distinguished looking elderly gentleman who he introduced as Henry, a friend who was attending the convention.

Sitting in one of Sal's antique barber chairs, with Sal's scissors clicking away at his full head of white hair, Henry looked around the shop, smiling broadly at the amazing display of museum quality and quantity of photos and artifacts that spanned the history of the cruise industry.

Sal told Henry the story of his collection which grew from the gift of a poster by a customer many years ago to its present size. He told him of his and Mary's lifelong dream, thwarted over the years by one or another of life's more pressing needs, to some day accumulate the means to take their dream trip.

Following his haircut, Henry walked around the shop for a closer look at the display, pausing to read with interest the notes Sal had written about each item, some of which filled Henry with poignant memories. Preparing to leave, Henry complimented Sal and Mary. Helping him with his topcoat, John said, "What did I tell you, Henry, isn't this place something?" Henry Richardson, Chairman of the Board of Palace Cruise Ships didn't reply immediately; seemingly lost in thought. Outside in the car, he said, "I'm glad you brought me, John."

Not long after that visit, Sal and Mary received in the mail an envelope whose content made them gasp with surprise and disbelief. They held in their hands a formal, engraved invitation from Henry Richardson, Chairman of the Board of Palace Cruise Ships, to be his special guests at the company's expense on the maiden voyage of their new cruise ship, the *Maharajah*.

John Moody confirmed that the invitation was genuine, identifying the chairman as the gentleman he'd brought with him that day. He did not tell them that, gracious and generous as the offer was, valued at about $24,000, the chairman was a hard nosed businessman who knew his publicity department would make maximum use of his gift to this couple as a public relations tool. The company would get tons of copy in the media that could be expected to generate lots of new business.

Sal and Mary could not believe their good fortune. All the sacrifices they'd made in their lives to help their children and other members of their family through hard times; all the vacations given up so they could care for Mary's mother during fifteen years of illness before her death last year; all that hardship was now to be rewarded in fairy tale fashion, helped along by the wonderful bon voyage party thrown for them by their family, friends and loyal customers who made it possible for the Pinas to buy new luggage and wardrobes.

Later in the day, in their luxurious stateroom on the *Maharajah*, the Pinas finished putting their things away. They had already done some exploring on the ship, finding it difficult to take it all in at one time. The ship, and everything about it, was stunning. The stateroom itself, with its portside verandah was a startling contrast to their home in Kansas City, still the same cramped second floor flat Sal's parents had lived in for so many years.

In the quiet room, Sal and Mary stood facing each other, holding hands and looking deeply into the other's eyes. As if by magic, the years rolled back to the days of their courting over 25 years ago. The same sweet urges of that time welled up in them again, so fully and naturally that, without words, but with the innocence and intimacy of lovers discovering each other for the first time, they silently renewed their vows of love and though it was early in the afternoon, they made love.

Waking, Sal looked at his watch; 2:35 p.m. Still in a magical haze over what happened between him and Mary, he put on his slacks and stepped out on the verandah. He stood for a few minutes at the railing drawing deep breaths of fresh air and enjoying the view. He could see the *Maharani*, the slightly smaller sister ship of the *Maharajah* docked nearby, taking on baggage and fuel for its departure two days hence.

A tugboat pulled up alongside the *Maharajah* and a harbor pilot boarded. Half the great ship's mooring lines had been cast off and Sal could hear the whir of the bow thrusters turned on but not yet engaged.

As Sal began to turn back to the stateroom to wake Mary, something caught his eye, something that seemed out of place. A small flotilla of cigarette boats and two yachts had circled about in the harbor, their bows now directly facing the *Maharajah*. What were they waiting for, he wondered?

Just then, the first of the fuel storage tanks ignited sending thick black smoke and flames spiraling upwards. The noisy din from the thousand or so passengers waving goodbyes on the starboard side became a palpable hush followed by total pandemonium. A frightened Mary joined Sal on the verandah and they watched in horror and disbelief as the two yachts and cigarette boats began moving, no, racing directly towards them. They watched as those aboard the yachts jumped overboard to be picked up by the trailing cigarette boats. The yachts were about 200 feet apart bracketing the midship position of their stateroom and the ship's main fuel tanks.

The full force of what was now inevitable hit the Pinas with a clarity that was near-mystical. Their great dream would never be a memory. They held each other in a tight embrace, uttered the last words of a prayer and gave their souls over to the mercy of God.

The ship's whistle was still tooting a warning when a cataclysmic detonation lifted the *Maharajah* out of the water, breaking it in half. Port Everglades provided berthing and passenger facilities for 19 cruise lines. With two million passenger moves a year, the port was a national symbol of tourism. At the time of the attack, ten other cruise ships were docked at the port's other embarkation terminals, and all, including the *Maharani,* were incinerated by the firestorm.

The terrorists' attack on the fuel farm detonated over 200 storage tanks full of gasoline, jet fuel and heating oil in a chain reaction that created a lethal firestorm. The roaring wind of fire and suffocating heat consumed everything within a mile radius including eight super-tankers and 124 petroleum hauling trucks in various stages of unloading and loading. In fifteen minutes, Southeast Florida's primary petroleum port was gone; and so was the only source of jet fuel for the busy Fort Lauderdale/Hollywood, Palm Beach and Miami International airports. The raging firestorm spread out to feed on the extensive containerized cargo facilities and the businesses located on the fringes of the port.

On the *Maharajah* alone, 3,622 passengers, 1540 crew and 1,489 well-wishers on the dock perished. The total number of lives lost in the attack was staggering. Property damage and clean-up costs were so extensive it would take months to fix the costs. Moreover, South Florida's tourist-based economy had been dealt a crippling blow that would take years to heal. Arab planners had not anticipated the firestorm and they were jubilant that night when they learned that Port Everglades had ceased to exist.

Boston...July 29 ...2:43 P.M.

The sky in Bean Town was the same pale blue as that over New York while terrorists' planes smashed into commercial aircraft docked at the

Delta and Continental Airlines gates at Logan International Airport. The Harvard University School of Law and three nearby buildings were leveled. Devastation at Fenway Park where the Red Sox were playing the Cleveland Indians mirrored that of what was going on at Yankee Stadium and Wrigley Field.

Chicago...July 29...1:46 P. M. Central Time

Although the weather in the windy city was overcast with scattered slashes of lightning, all of the terrorist aircraft hit their assigned targets. At Chicago-O'Hare, two suicide aircraft rammed into fully loaded planes at the airport's international gates. Other planes attacked the Chicago Mercantile Exchange and Wrigley Field where the Cubs were out-playing the Braves. To achieve the maximum number of deaths, the terrorists had carefully figured America's three time zones into their planning. The 1:30 p.m. time at Wrigley fit the mold perfectly.

Washington...July 29...2:45 P.M.

In the cramped cockpit, Fila Khan thought of her mother. With no husband, Fila doted on her mother and gave her a bonsai tree as a parting gesture. From the time she was ten, terrorism had been Fila's stock in trade. Her handlers then had used her sweet-looking innocence to cause the deaths of seven adults and two children and the maiming of many more passengers on a city bus in a Jerusalem suburb. Entering the bus with the small but powerful explosive device tucked within the raincoat over her arm, she exited two stops later, the device left unseen and secure under her seat, timed to go off four minutes later.

Her proud mother's roomful of curios were grotesque reminders of the places where Fila had practiced her grisly profession. At 24, she was the youngest and best pilot in Salem Abar's group and had been given the honor of selecting her own target. Based on a three-day visit, Fila chose the Washington Monument, the one symbol she felt could be totally laid to waste by a single aircraft.

The Israelis had killed her brother, Waleed, and she blamed the Americans. Fila was not a martyr. She was a thoroughbred killer who wanted revenge, and that revenge had to be personal. The Washington Monument filled the bill.

Fila's doleful eyes and whiplike body attracted a steady stream of men, such as her flight instructor, who had fallen in love with her. She was wild and fanciful in bed and she used that prowess to manipulate the men who could do her and her cause some good. To Fila, American men were pale albinos who were easily fooled, and she hoped that the monument would be full of them when she made her run.

Four miles from her objective, across the placid water of the reflecting pool, Fila saw the Lincoln Memorial and she knew that somewhere up high, Satan Alai was about to start his dive. Scanning the sky, she made out the other pilots in her group approaching the Jefferson Memorial, Capitol Building and Reagan International Airport. Nawaf Waile, whose target was the White House, was nowhere to be seen. She wondered if he had lost his nerve. A virile, handsome man, all of Nawaf's talk about morality and mortality sat like camel dung in her mouth and she had brushed off his advances with undisguised scorn.

Clad in a bra, panties and scuffed sneakers, Fila Khan locked her steely glare onto the Washington Monument through the ever present cloak of polluted air. Even as her breathing became shallow, she continued to chew on the bagel she'd been nibbling on for the last hour. A mile out, she noticed the red aircraft warning lights built into the monument's pyramidal top. Without any wind, the flags that ringed the monument drooped limply against their polished brass poles.

Two hundred yards from impact, the platinum lightning conductors at the tip of the monument were plainly visible and she was surprised at how many there were. Fila's slim, strong fingers steered the 300 miles per hour bomb into the center of the monument, shearing it in half, creating two separate fountains of death.

Indiana limestone, and marble brought in from Colorado and Tennessee could not protect Lincoln's statue from being desecrated. The nation's inspiring symbol of humanity, carved from crystalline Georgia marble, disintegrated when Satan Alai's plane slashed through the Lincoln Memorial's weakest point, the roof, and scored a direct hit.

Flying low over the Tidal Basin, another terrorist's aircraft leveled the awe-inspiring Jefferson Memorial which was built on carefully constructed landfill. The U.S. Capitol escaped unscathed when the pilot of the largest and most expensive aircraft in the group undershot his target and crashed instead into the green dome of the Library of Congress, extinguishing irreplaceable books, records and other priceless documents forever. The thunderous fulmination propelled lethal debris scything over a wide area; however, it was the Supreme Court building on the other side of East Capitol Street that was decimated. There, three Supreme Court Justices and over 50 staff members were killed.

Since the terrorists wanted targets that would either be badly wounded or totally annihilated, they passed on the massive Pentagon and instead chose the War College-Fort McNair located at the muddy confluence of the Potomac and Anocostia rivers. The desecration of the War College and its library, the largest military collection in the world next to Great Britain's, was a brutal body-blow to active and retired U.S. military officers around the world.

The remaining terrorists guided their aircraft like laser-controlled torpedoes into boarding gates at the Dulles and Ronald Reagan airports. A mechanical problem with his starboard engine forced Nawaf Waile to land at a small rural airport in North Carolina which did not have a maintenance facility. Knowing that he would not be able to meet the mission timetable, Nawaf simply walked away from the plane. Shortly thereafter he boarded a Greyhound bus bound for Atlanta where another cell took him in. Still laden with explosives, the abandoned plane was soon in FBI custody.

The attacks on some of America's most lasting and meaningful symbols was so diabolical that, to civilized people, it was almost inconceivable. However, no one outside of the White House yet knew that the President of the United States, Jeffrey Lodge, and the Secretary of State had been assassinated and that other American cities had suffered catastrophic damages.

At nine that evening, Marta Wentworth finally opened her eyes and saw her husband and the FBI Director looking down at her. She'd been out for 17 long hours. Their expressions bared their souls. "How many?" she asked.

The Director took her hand. "It was bad. Very bad."

Marta closed her eyes and wept.

At home later that night, her husband cradled Marta awkwardly in his arms as if she was the most precious thing on earth. Something incomprehensible had overtaken them and tore into their hearts and words could not express the hurt. The next morning, she caught him standing in front of an open window and she felt the freshness of the air. She heard the rain rush down the roof into the clutches of the aluminum gutters, making tinny musical noises as they hit bottom. *Those are love chords, the ones that are hard to find and difficult to replace.* And then her mind flashed back to the previous day and she began to weep once more.

San Francisco...July 30...5:25 A.M.

Mort Gurnick finally woke up and found his haggard-looking shipmate still asleep in the rolled up jeans and the bright, lime-colored sweatshirt she'd put on after they'd docked. There were no more ferries. Exhausted, and with the harbor in turmoil, Mort tied up at the Alcatraz Island dock. To avoid waking his shipmate, he got up slowly and tiptoed his way topside. Night was waning and the boat was beaded with moisture from the fog.

Mort looked forlornly in the direction where the Golden Gate once stood. Even though the visibility was nil, Mort knew that without the bridge and waterfront, San Francisco would never be the same. Because his radio antenna ripped off during their plunge down the great wave, he was unaware that heavy concentrations of unhealthy hydrocarbons still blanketed five major U.S. cities.

A Coast Guard boat tied up alongside and the captain filled him in. Having been a dedicated Naval officer, Mort had a sensation that he had been hacked to death by a machete and the blood was running out of his body. By the time he'd finished having coffee with the captain, Mort pictured himself living in a country that would soon become fond of the dark. Given some provisions and ordered to stay put, Mort's perspective began to change as the day progressed. A sharp Coast Guard electronics technician jury-rigged an antenna for Mort's radio in nothing flat; however, reports about the shark attacks sent his shipmate into an inconsolable state. "Mort, my sister was aboard one of the missing boats. Oh God, Mort, she may have been eaten by sharks!"

By nightfall, a sleeping pill and two stiff shots of bourbon provided by a sympathetic couple on another stranded boat knocked the distraught woman out cold. After covering her with a blanket, Mort sat out on deck and found himself looking for the bridge that was no longer there. By the time the moon was high in a night sky strewn with brilliant stars, Mort Gurnick was the same ferocious, untamed warrior who had served so valiantly aboard a ship of war.

He watched the lights of the rescue vessels still prowling the harbor and was reminded of unplanted gardens, of sackcloth and ashes and the letters he had written to the families of shipmates who had died next to him in battle. The wind had come up and the whitecaps seemed to be dancing under the fullness of the moon. Like a man with a sandwich in his pocket and nowhere to go, Mort paced the dock. Drained emotionally, he stopped in his tracks and thought of the woman sleeping below. He cursed himself for wallowing in self indulgent grief. *You asshole!* he cursed. *She's heartsick and alone now. She's going to need help. Help her.*

It was the middle of the night and she was sleeping, but Mort was not stymied. He had to do something useful and positive and had to do it now. The sailboat rolled slightly as he went back aboard. His mind was a blur of raw emotions and memories and he couldn't remember the damn name of the whatchamacallit he was trying to find. Finally, he spotted what he had been searching for, the ship's log. With a stubby pencil he recorded the time and date and made a simple entry. *Clear skies, visibility excellent. Wind 25 to 30 knots out of the west. Boat secure.* He closed the log, put on his old deck shoes, and began to clean the boat.

36

The White House
July 29...2:42 P.M.

Once he got rolling, Ziad Ahmed didn't like to dillydally. An enigmatic 24-year-old, Ziad had whizzed through law school with honors. Currently he was enrolled in an MBA program at the University of Maryland in College Park. He and Jiahi Shehlia, a member of his cell and his lover, lived in a small Georgetown apartment that had a view of the muddy Potomac River. His mother was Norwegian, and with his long blond lashes and golden hair tied in a ponytail, Ziad did not look like an Arab.

As they cruised toward their target in the spiffy motor home, Ziad rubbed the garnet ring his father had given him and his tendency to dwell on the past took hold. He saw his father warming himself by a fire in the mountains near Kabul. The Afghans were fighting the Russians back then and the United States had been the Afghans' benefactor. The tawny hues of the rough Afghanistan terrain came into view and he saw his father coasting down a long, tortuous road guided by the hand of Allah. Now he knew that Allah was with him. He'd left the campus early and had rendezvoused with Jiahi at a prearranged location. Now, he and Jiahi sat in the parked motor home close enough to the White House to allow them to get there at the prescribed time.

"How?" President Lodge asked.

"Heart attack."

"He was a dreadful man and I have no sympathy for the no-good bastard. Ironically, his shrew of a wife is worse. Anything else?"

"I had dinner at the Palm with the Whip last night."

"And?"

"I think the pre-school bill has a shot."

"That sounds highly improbable. Are you sure?"

"With one hitch. That damn relic of an Army base in his district that the GAO took apart. He wants the report dead and buried."

"Tell Congressman Sturgis, I hear anything about that report it's his ass."

The president paused to take a call, but said aside, "Jerry, all-in-all that's good news."

Fighting the temptation to slick back his hair, a habit the press and Saturday Night Live had picked up on, the president buzzed his secretary. "Helen, this damn chair has embossed the seal on my back. Where did it come from?"

"Mr. President, The chair was a gift from John Tunny."

Tunny was not only a good friend of the president, but a fund raiser par-excellence. "It's beautiful, but the carving's too deep. Get it replaced. I'll talk to John."

"Ten minutes."

"Thank you, Helen."

Holding up a dark blue cup trimmed in gold the president asked Jerry Cohen, "Want some?"

"Sounds good. Got any danish?"

"Over there."

Putting down the file he was carrying, the White House Chief of Staff sashayed over to the silver coffee service that had been set on a table next to a window. His presence always improved the president's mood and this morning was no exception.

"Jerry, you know something?"

"What, Mr. President?

"Sometimes you walk like a woman on the make."

"So?" Jerry chuckled, waiting for the punch line that never came.

Cohen, enjoying his coffee and danish break, looked out the Oval Office window across the Rose Garden and the vast South Lawn where the president's helicopter took off and landed. The wrought iron fence on Constitution Avenue was already lined with tourists peeking and photographing the distinctive, elliptical-shaped structure that is the Oval Office. He noticed the mobile television unit with its satellite dish pull into the parking area reserved for the media on Ellipse Road. As though he had been cued from the wings, Cohen saw a burly White House Security Officer heading toward the converted motor home to verify the press credentials of the occupants. He was there when Ziad emerged smiling on the sidewalk with a professional-looking video camera that encased a .357 Magnum. Dressed in khaki pants with the call letters of a local station stenciled on his baseball cap, Ziad looked like a typical cameraman.

In the Oval Office, Jerry Cohen sensed danger when a dark-haired young woman raised herself through a hatch in the roof of the mobile unit. He stiffened. Steadying herself, the woman paused and casually flounced her hair. Seconds later, she raised an object up through the hatch. At first, Jerry thought it was one of those long-barreled telephoto lenses. However, when she swung the object around he recognized it as a stinger missile. Then things happened in microseconds. Seeing the girl with the weapon, the officer went for his service revolver, but Ziad's laser-aimed bullets shot him down.

From her vantage point, the woman could see over the eight-foot high wrought iron fences that ringed the White House grounds. She had a clear shot. In no time, she brought the weapon to bear and fired. For Cohen, time slowed to a waltz. "Noooooo!"

Startled by the ear-splitting wail, the president looked up. He saw Jerry drop his cup and stumble as he tried to turn and run toward him at the same time. Two Secret Service men outside the door heard Jerry's scream and burst into the room, but the missile was already on its way. Whoomph! As they drew their weapons the room exploded.

The three-inch thick, clear composite sheets of space-age material that stood guard in front of the White House windows were undetectable from the street. Mounted in heavy, stainless steel brackets embedded in concrete, the shields were the primary defense against outside attacks. However, ten years of daily exposure to the elements had eroded the shield's innate tensile strength. The manufacturer of the composite knew what the ravages of time and the elements would do, but had never passed that information on to the Secret Service, which after five years of regular testing without seeing any noticeable change in strength, had stopped checking. Unfortunately, the shields had not yet reached the threshold where they began to break down.

When the stinger missile hit, the defective shield exploded into dust, sending forward a concussion which contained enough lethal kinetic energy to blow the shatterproof window out of its steel jam. Like some sort of deadly, oversized frisbee, the window sliced through the far wall and through Helen, standing frozen in place at the sounds from the president's office. Thousands of steel splinters from the shattered window jamb and shield shot through the offices like bullets from a gattling gun, decimating staff working 90 feet from the point of impact.

Eyeing the carnage, the first Secret Service men who entered the room knew immediately that everyone was dead. As the White House medical team and several agents tore through the door, the eerie stillness gave way to pandemonium. Structural engineers later calculated that the unwanted chair had catapulted the President through the far wall of the Oval Office at over 120 miles per hour, embedding both him and the chair in the wall on the other side of the corridor. All of the heavy draperies in the room had been sucked from their mountings, leaving the Oval Office bathed in bright sunlight. The explosion had scorched the exterior wall around the window and, to onlookers, the wall had the visage of an abstract painting done in different shades of white, black and a filthy gray.

With the explosion, all eyes turned in disbelief and horror toward the White House and away from the TV van. Using the distraction and ensuing pandemonium to their advantage, Ziad and Jiahi, in the vehicle, stripped down to the shirts and walking shorts they wore beneath their clothing. Looking like typical tourists, they slipped out of the unit's rear door and melted into the crowds gathering at the scene. Walking calmly, they turned on Constitution Avenue to 20th Street, four blocks away. In the shadow of the Federal Reserve Building, they got into a black Mercedes sedan. The car was chauffeur-driven and had diplomat plates stolen earlier from a local garage that serviced most of Embassy Row's limos. As they pulled away from the curb, the two changed clothing again, Jiahi donning a conservative Ralph Lauren suit. Within minutes, Ziad looked like a prosperous young banker.

"Did you get the infidel?" the driver asked.

"Jiahi hit the target. If he was there, he's dead."

They could see the driver's mirth in the rear view mirror. As they drove away, massive numbers of emergency and police vehicles, sirens blasting, coming from all directions converged with real TV mobile units on the way to the scene. Seconds later, Ziad and Jiahi heard their converted motor home explode on schedule.

The Secret Service had whisked Vice-President Barbara Bennet away from her home while she was about to change clothes for a dinner engagement in New York. Everything had been laid out on the bed, but the President-to-be was still in her bathrobe and slippers. Barbara pointed and a female agent scooped up every thing on the bed. She pointed again. "The shoes."

Sitting there in the nude, in the back seat of the armored limousine, Barbara Bennet still possessed a rare dignity and understated elegance. Sitting across and next to her as she donned her undergarments, the Secret Service agents looked away and made failed attempts at small talk. After shimmying into a black satin sheath, she turned and lifted her long brown hair. "Zip me up," she asked politely of one of the male agents. Months later in the break room, the female agent in the car's front seat had a great time telling a stylized version of the incident. "After seeing all that bare skin, Felix's fingers were trembling so bad he couldn't get hold of the zipper."

Sworn in two hours later at the White House, Barbara Bennet, no relation to William Bennet, the one-time Secretary of Education, became the first woman to hold the nation's highest office. She was only 52.

37

State Department
July 29...2:43 P.M.

The method Judy Price, birth name, Bola Nahad, chose to kill the Secretary of State was not original. She had studied the *Godfather* movie video many times and her husband even videoed and analyzed her rehearsals. Primitive and practical, the unadorned scheme circumvented all of the Secret Service's security measures.

Except for the few agents who took the Metro area subway to work, many of the White House Secret Service staff were tied up in major traffic jams created by a slew of sudden accidents and the police and emergency vehicles that blocked key roads into the city. The afternoon shift was going to be short-handed and the senior agent at the White House was not happy.

"Bobby, you got an update?"

"We're still undermanned."

"Damn, this is getting more squirrelly by the hour."

"Larry, whatever else slides, I want the president covered."

"I've already made some assignment changes."

"Good."

"How long before we can get her out of here?"

"They may have more stingers. No one wants to chance it."

"Keep it tight."

"Roger."

Kismet was kind to Judy Price. In the end, the traffic jams and the Service's sudden staffing shortfall made her assignment easy.

Martin Rhine watched as the 45th President, surrounded by Secret Service Agents, was sworn in, then immediately spirited away to a secret location. Sporting a healthy tan following his recent two-week vacation in the Caribbean, the silver haired, always elegant and regal-looking Secretary of State, was considered by many to be the brightest of the deceased president's cabinet.

Having worked closely with the White House staff for years, Judy was well known to the two Secret Service Agents who stood in back of Rhine. Influenced by her effusive, warmhearted greeting, the agents, already frazzled by the weight of sharply increased levels of stress, relaxed for a moment. Hired for her unmatched talent for stringing words together overnight, Judy had been employed as one of six speech writers Senator Lodge used in his presidential campaign. With a gift for making almost any position sound tenable, she quickly became the senator's chief wordsmith.

A widow, she had a young daughter just starting school and she told the agent who interviewed her that she wanted to be home when her daughter got home. Working as a freelance writer out of her home in Bethesda, she either faxed or overnighted her work to the senator, which in the eyes of the Secret Service, made her a contractor and not a member of the White House staff. Contractors got far less scrutiny. At one time Judy had been a senior editor with a respected political journal and her employer had vouched without reservation for her character and dependability. Born in Afghanistan, Bola Nohad migrated to Italy where she changed her name and became a citizen, using false papers obtained for her by a bin Laden cell based in Milan.

A beautiful girl, Bola, now Judy, looked more like 20 years of age than the 15 she was when she met the American who would become her husband. A month later, he took her with him to New York. Two weeks after she graduated from Princeton with honors in literature and creative writing, she sent her husband on a short errand. As planned, he was killed in an unwitnessed accident made to look like a hit and run. She had played the grieving widow to the hilt. Seven months later, their child was born.

Her articles on America's social ills had appeared in every major magazine and newspaper in the country and the FBI had relied very heavily on her writings, always heavily slanted toward law and order, in establishing her bonafides. As a result, Judy Price was never thoroughly checked out by the Federal Bureau of Investigation.

On this occasion, Judy had been called by the Secretary of State to draft a speech that the new president would give that evening at seven. It was a daunting task, but she had agreed. Escorted by an agent, Judy entered Martin Rhine's impressive suite of offices at the State Department.

"Have you got it?" Secretary Rhine asked.

"Yes, yes I do." Her shaky voice, tired, somber looks and long grey dress matched what the agents expected. Inside, she was a coiled snake, ready to strike.

"Come here, girl."

Judy's angular features creased into a tight, fading smile. *Perfect,* she thought, *having the lamb invite me to the slaughter.* In the investigation that followed, agents would agree later that handing the speech file to the agent had been a nice touch. It kept him occupied for a few moments and diverted his attention. The agent scanned the boilerplate title page that read: *The Pennycandystore.* Draft: July 29, 2002, by Judy Price for President Barbara Bennet.

As she entered the secretary's outstretched arms, Judy removed her glasses. It was a natural movement one would expect to see in preparation for a hug. His body heat warmed her and she thought, *Hum, I should have worn cotton.* Like a drowning person, she clung fast to Martin Rhine while she severed his jugular vein with the knife-edged temple of her eyeglasses. Using a succession of files, each one finer than the one before, Salem Abar had painstakingly honed the undetectable plastic shiv to surgical sharpness. Hidden by her hair style, the makeshift weapon was undetectable. Paying no mind to the gusher of sludge-like blood that covered her and Secretary Rhine's snowy-white shirt, Judy kept sawing away. Knowing it was already too late to save the secretary, a burly, sloop-shouldered agent carefully shot Judy Price twice in the side of the head. As the bullets penetrated her skull, the agent's mind focused on one thought: *We fucked up.*

38

The White House
July 30...7:45 P.M.

The rain had tapered off, but it was gloomy out. Having risen before dawn, President Bennet, the 45th President of the United States, had a hectic first day. That night, she invited Mrs. Jean Lodge, the late president's widow, to supper. The president had always admired Mrs. Lodge and the two women had forged a close personal relationship during the campaign for the presidency.

"Barbara, honey, you're fresh meat. They're out there right now deciding the best way to drag you down. Want some advice?"

"Jean, I'd be grateful for anything you can pass on."

"Always stay on the offense, needing to defend yourself is a no-win position."

"No exceptions?"

"Honey, I hope you're a quick study. Elected officials on the defense come across as whiners. The public *hates* whiners."

"*I* hate whiners."

"One more thing, don't dillydally. Once you know what has to be done, go and don't give any of the clowns on your cabinet any maneuvering room. Give them marching orders or cut them loose. At a time like this, you'll have to keep the lid on some of your honey-tongued back stabbers."

The moon was still high when the president slipped out of bed, leaving her husband snoring away. After downing two aspirins, she slid back between the warm sheets. There, her mind locked on Jean and some of the comments she'd made during their talk. *Action and offense, action and offense, action and offense.* Finding it impossible to keep her mind from churning, the president sat in a warm bath and started making calls. Lots of them.

The quick, early morning get-together with the executive housekeeper did not go well. Wanting to assert her authority early on, the executive housekeeper said sweetly, "Excuse me, Madam President, how long do you think Mrs. Lodge and her family will be with us?"

"A month, perhaps longer."

"Madam President, you may find that time-frame inconvenient."

Just as sweetly, the president responded, "My husband and I are moving out to Camp David this weekend. While we're gone, Mrs. Lodge's family is to receive *everything* and *anything* they request."

The chaos caused by Osama bin Laden's unwarranted savage attacks and the chilling assassinations of President Lodge and Secretary of State Rhine had paralyzed the nation. At 9:00 the previous evening President Barbara Bennet had addressed the nation and most of the free world. Her initial comments focused on calming the country and what was being done to save lives and restore America's symbols of commerce. But it was the president's final statements, that, in our instant-information world, told the world there would be no compromises:

"Fellow Americans, since the First World War began, over 2.5 million Americans have been killed, wounded or reported missing on foreign soil protecting us. Many of us have pictures of these brave men and women in our family photo albums.

Today, on our own soil, 46,000 lives were lost and tens of thousands more were injured. Over 550 American aircraft and two of our country's largest cruise ships were totally destroyed. Two of our most important stock exchanges were leveled. Over $1.8 trillion in damage was done and that is just a preliminary estimate. The final total, if we factor in what is happening to our economy, may exceed $5.5 trillion. But just as important, the enemy took away some of our most beloved and priceless national symbols. War has been declared on the United States and under the Emergency War Powers Act I am taking the following initial steps to insure the safety of our citizens:

Except for emergency vehicles, all air, motor and water traffic is suspended for two days until security can be put in place to guard our nation's bridges, tunnels, airports and waterways.

Our armed forces all over the world have gone to combat status and we are already moving assets to strategic positions in the Middle East. Other battle groups are gearing up for their departures.

Reservists, including those in the Coast Guard, are called to active duty.

All immigration into the country is canceled for a minimum of two years. Immigration staff will be shifted to assist in the tracking down of those who have remained in this country illegally.

I have ordered the Army to seal the Mexican and Canadian Borders and the Coast Guard and Air Force to close unauthorized sea and air access.

All illegal aliens who do not report to the U.S. Immigration authorities within 72-hours for deportation will be imprisoned and assigned to a clean-up work details for a minimum of two years.

All commercial aircraft will carry armed marshals and or military personnel. Security of all major airports is now and will remain the responsibility of the FBI. During the next nine months all contracts with commercial security firms will be terminated at the convenience of the government.

To reduce the amount of vehicular traffic that must be monitored, car pooling is herein declared mandatory and the use of mass transportation encouraged. Prices of gasoline are hereby frozen at the levels they were prior to the attacks.

The terrorists who committed the monstrous acts on our country did not try to hide the fact that they were followers of Osama bin Laden, who has declared a trumped-up Holy War on our country. My message to the Taliban government and al-Qaeda networks throughout the world is this: You have declared war on the United States and you will pay the ultimate price for your actions. There is no acceptable diplomatic solution. The United States is mobilizing and our coming is just over the horizon.

No, the United States is not going to indiscriminately launch missile strikes against the innocent Muslims who neither support nor believe in bin Laden and the ruthless, drug-dealing Taliban regime. But, however long it takes, or whatever the costs, we will, with the cooperation of the world's civilized nations, wipe out every terrorist camp and kill every terrorist on the face of this earth, regardless of where they choose to hide. Those who provide refuge and support will suffer the same fate.

Now, as Americans, we must ask ourselves. Did 2.5 million Americans die so that the rich and powerful can manipulate our lives through their control of our democratic ideals? Because of the obscene amounts of campaign money they provide, special interest groups and an expanding cadre of greedy multi-national corporations own our elected representatives. As a nation, we have paid a dreadful price for their greed. With callous premeditation, a relatively small group of lobbyists and attorneys have pawned our future and usurped our ability to act. Had the correct safeguards everyone in government knew were needed been put in place, perhaps the carnage we have suffered could have been avoided.

Our duly-elected representatives have not protected our borders, our airports nor the bridges and tunnels that are our economic lifelines. Their paid-for compromises and lack of guts have let drug monies influence a good part of the world and put us all in jeopardy. It is time to change all that. Tomorrow I will formally request that our legislative bodies repeal, immediately, our campaign financing laws and that all future elections at the state and national levels be financed by public monies. As Americans we must all demand this change, and now.

There are many other initiatives underway that simply cannot be divulged, lest they be compromise our objectives. I ask the media to restrain the rhetoric and act responsibly during this trying time in our country's history. There is too much real work to do and we cannot squander time in endless press conferences. My press secretary, Brenda Swaysland, will conduct a daily briefing which will include all of the information that can prudently be shared with the public. Regaining our economic vitality and social promise will take all of our strength as a people. Best we harness and channel our outrage for the national good. The heinous acts of the Taliban have taken many of our loved ones. Pray for them.

Most of us understand that timing can mean everything or nothing depending on how well you are prepared to take advantage of a given situation. Well, the time has come to protect the 250 million Americans who pay the freight and I would advise anyone who thinks differently to move aside. There will be no trials or pardons and any person or group that acts against America's interests will be dealt with swiftly and without mercy. Thank you for your attention this evening. Good night.

It took only a few hours for the president's speech to be condemned by every minority group whose immigrants were affected by her new immigration policy. Especially vocal was the Colombian Ambassador to the United States who called President Bennet a "wanton, dangerous and seductive demagogue." An hour later, the president ordered the ambassador and his family out of the country.

Outraged by the immigration ban, a group of politically active Cubans in Miami blocked the interstate highways in Miami as they did during the ridiculous, press-fueled, Elian Gonzalez affair. Mollycoddled by the last two administrations, the activists sought to use the situation to further their own agenda. It was a bad move. Within hours, national guard and army troops had run tanks over 100 vehicles crushing them into scrap metal. Three hundred Cubans were arrested and taken under tight security to Eglin Air Force Base from where they were proscecuted for endangering public safety.

Despite outcries from the politicians and minority groups, independent surveys told a different story. An overwhelming 92% of those polled felt that President Bennet's actions and remarks were right on the money. And, something else happened that was never anticipated. For the first time in 60 years, military recruiting offices were overrun with young men and women wanting to enlist. After studying the polls and reading their flood of e-mail, elected members of both political parties began re-tuning their positions on immigration and campaign financing.

39

The White House
July 31...8:20 A.M.

Slashing rain beat down on the bunker as the last man around the table offered his input. President Bennet knew what was going through their minds and she didn't blame them. The two assassinations had eliminated the hardliners that the terrorist and their drug merchant business partners feared the most. Now, they were dealing with an untried woman. Problem was, she had all the polls, and therefore most of America, with her.

Osama bin Laden had taken credit for the attacks and there was already enough hard evidence to substantiate his claim. President Bennett's first official Cabinet meeting had moved along rapidly and despite the late hour, no one seemed tired. After everyone had spoken, the president said, "You've all made your views known. First, anyone in this room who makes anything but a 'no comment' statement to the press will be removed from office."

The duplicitous director of the CIA, Phillip Ramsey, shouted, "This is outrageous."

The president nodded to the two navy commanders, both lawyers, stationed at the door. "Mr. Ramsey's tenure is terminated. Brief him on the consequences of opening his yap to the press."

Picking up the phone, she said, "Joan, send in Admiral Rolley."

Admiral Rolley was a front line war hero respected for getting the job done and done fast. The president shook his hand and introduced him. "Ladies, gentlemen, the Admiral has come out of his brief retirement to serve as the Director of the CIA."

The room was now dead silent. One thought ran through everyone's mind: *She already knew that Butterfield was a loose cannon and had to go.*

"Now that we have the entire team on board, I want you to understand that we are not going to fight this war on CNN so you can sell a book. So keep a low profile. The legislative branches will be kept informed, but only through the key committee chairmen. As you should all know, surprise is a huge advantage in war and for the next three weeks, I would prefer that the terrorist organizations and drug lords think we're cowed and completely muddled about what to do."

"Just what are we going to do?" asked the president's paunchy National Security Advisor, caustically.

"Mr. Lloyd, drop the attitude and take off those dark glasses so I can see your eyes. Margaret, please pass out the agenda. Before we're through here today, a decision will have been made on each topic."

Lloyd scanned the agenda index, and was impressed. Everything was there.

Eleven hours later the Chairman of the Joint Chiefs, a man who lived for the greatness that had never found him, rubbed his gimpy leg and said. "Is Afghanistan the last stop?"

"No, it's only the jump-off point. Work with the CIA to prioritize the other countries involved by the level of threat. Command centers, missile launch and storage sites, communications, military installations, bio labs, the whole kit-and-caboodle. General, I know innocent people are going to be killed, but I do not want a civilian bloodbath."

"What countries are we talking about?"

"You don't know?"

A wolfish grin crossed the chairman's face. "I see."

"There is one important issue that we have not discussed. All those nukes and bioweapons stored in Russian bunkers scare me to death. The country has been stripped of its productive assets and if they start selling the stuff to the wrong people it could be catastrophic. I'm taking on that project personally."

The looks from her fellow Democrats around the table were not friendly. It was Barry Goldman, the Senate Majority Leader of the opposing party, who came to her defense.

"Gentlemen, ladies, the president has served on the Intelligence Committee, the Armed Services Committee and the Foreign Relations Committee. I'm not crazy and I value the safety of my family. I not only agree with her decision to handle the Russian situation personally, I also agree with her agenda."

"But, Mr. Goldman…"

"Please let me make one more point. Does anyone in this room except the president speak and read Russian fluently?"

Silence.

While she had their rapt attention, the president said, "Osama bin Laden has the resources to disappear at will and turn up somewhere else with a running start. It's his way of slapping us in the face. We should also keep in mind that the war he has blessed as a Jihad has three facets: Terrorist acts, anticipatory terror and the weakening of those things that can only operate if integrity and trust are in place. I'm talking here about law, banking, our financial markets and the media. His main weapon here is the proliferation of illegal drugs and the harm that drug money does buy. We have to stop this bastard cold."

The strength of the president's resolve and her advance planning had thrown most of the Cabinet off balance. As her lacquered nails tapped the table, she said, "I expect everyone in this room to be working 12-hour days until we're out of this mess. Now, let's get to it. No more lip service. I want action!"

The president's decisiveness had infused the room with great energy and the National Security Advisor, who had been the president's most formidable critic, thought she was tougher and more resilient than he had ever hoped to imagine. *The woman has guts,* he thought. Searching his mind for the right word to describe her, he came up with a four-letter word that fit….*icon.*

40

Washington
August 8...1:35 P.M.

Around the country, key Republicans were phoning their major contributors. The new president was being massacred by the media and they wanted the money-men to help finance the slaughter. President Bennett had been in office for over a month and had not made a single public appearance. Brenda Swaysland had issued a brief statement to pacify the press: *President Bennett and her Cabinet are working on an overall plan that will address the attacks and the impact on our economy. She urges everyone to be patient.* Unfortunately, patience is not a journalistic trait and within a week, the press was awash with half-baked rumors and speculation. Some of the headlines were brutal: *President in Self-imposed Exile; Lodge's Widow Won't Give Up President's Bedroom; Untested President Waffling and Aloof.*

Through her aide, Mrs. Lodge put out a press release that articulated her family's gratitude towards the president's help and compassion. Feeling slighted, the entrenched Washington press corps ignored the heartfelt message. In Georgetown, a four-dollar cab ride from the White House, a senior Republican congressman slapped his legislative assistant on the back.

"By the time this is over, her own party will want her impeached."

"Why the low profile? She should be on the tube."

"She's a greenhorn."

"Come on, she has advisors who can prep her."

"By hiding out at Camp David, she's put herself in a box. She's dead meat."

"Congressman, with all respect, she handled herself well enough to help get Lodge elected. And her initial talk went over well. Look at the polls. She can't be *that* naive."

"Campaigns are all show. This is the real deal. Have you seen yesterday's numbers?"

"No, I haven't."

"Since her speech a week ago, the bitch is down 18 popularity points. Bennet's a lightweight who hasn't got the stuff."

The festivities in the congressman's hotel suite reminded his wife of a Super Bowl party. The Republicans had stage-managed the president's absence from the spotlight to the point where one widely quoted pundit wrote: *"Without question, President Bennet's address is a watershed event. Along with her future, the survival of the Democratic Party is also on the line. Does the president have what it takes? Only time will tell."*

Moved by the president's kindness toward her predecessor's widow, the congressman's southern-born wife looked at him with utter disdain. "John, you're starting to tick me off." Her tone was cutting and there was a furious expression on her face. "I wouldn't gloat if I were you. Wouldn't it be funny if she sandbagged you all?"

Brandon Fletcher, a Republican senator who was much more pragmatic than his Georgetown soulmate, was holding forth in his spacious corner office in the Rayburn Building. Finished inside and out in white and pink marble, the building was the most expensive publicly financed structure ever built in Washington or anywhere else.

With his red suspenders and lumpy pants, the senator was a caricature of a back-room politico and, like many of the old time pols, Brandon Fletcher was long on clever, short on intellect. The foxy senator was livid. "What the hell is she planning? I can't get a fucking word out of anybody."

"Senator, she's put the lid on."

"Screw the lid. I thought we had people inside?"

"We do. They're either in the dark or afraid to talk."

Looking wild-eyed at counsel, Fletcher hissed, "We're uninformed and everyone's sitting on their ass thinking she's some kind of dunce. She's not. We could get fucked and I mean big time. We have to put her on the defensive."

Reacting to Senator Fletcher's tirade, counsel responded sheepishly, "How do we manage that?"

The feisty chairman of the Senate Finance Committee waved his fist.

"You're supposed to know all the angles. What about her use of The Emergency War Powers Act?"

"Mr. Chairman, the fact that our country's been attacked and is currently broke is not debatable. If you accept that, the President's use of the emergency act is not only proper, it's probably mandatory."

Mindful of what he knew about the senator's unscrupulous tactics, counsel was not surprised to see him grin. "Get the goods on the bitch and get it fast."

"Senator, I..."

"Take her fucking life apart, hour-by-hour if necessary. Who did she screw? Is she fucking someone on the side now? I hear she undressed in the back of her limo. Check into that first."

"Senator, the president is married."

"So what."

"Senator, this is very distasteful. We're talking about a President whose got her back to the wall. Her background's been checked and rechecked by pros. I can't..."

Cutting counsel off, the senator screamed, "Don't you fucking get it! Either we get her or she gets us! I want that bitch burned at the stake. Now get your ass out there and find me a fucking blow torch!"

When Chairman Fletcher's door closed, a thin, prudish-looking man entered from a connecting office. "What a jerk. Everything we had planned is in limbo and your counsel wants to play nice-nice."

"If Lodge was still around, Bennet would still be a nobody."

"Maybe, but right now, she's a somebody who could cost all of us a fortune."

"Conrad, you're a pompous ass. You mean it's costing you and your mucky-muck clique a fortune."

Conrad's piggy eyes and indulgent smile made Fletcher want to puke. "Can anything be done to slow her down?"

"Right now?"

"Yes."

Not one for offering limp, untried excuses, the chairman explained. "Conrad, there are only two sure ways to derail a president."

"And what might they be?"

"Death and disgrace, they never fail. Since we are limited to the latter option, neutralizing President Bennet will take time. Tell your cronies to sit tight. In the long run, we'll fry her ass."

41

Nashville…October 26…8:15 P.M.

Donald Tenhagen and Peter Hyde had experienced many changes in their lives since the murders of Governor Lambia and Sollie Hershoff and the assault at the Foundation. For one, both families had moved into the high-security condominiums in the same complex as the Foundation's offices and whenever they went out they were always escorted or trailed by someone from the Foundation's expanded security staff.

Accompanied by Violet Evers, Peter Hyde, former Special Agent in Charge of the Providence FBI branch and now co-director of the Restore Foundation, caught up with Jilly and Hud at the Oxford Repertory in Nashville. They had watched the last act of the dress rehearsal from the shadows in the back of the theater waiting for the casts and crew to leave. The Hudsons, standing on the set with the theater's creative director, were thunderstruck at seeing Peter Hyde striding down the center aisle accompanied by a wisp of a black girl. Life for the Hudsons had been slow and sweet of late and the sudden appearance of Hyde and the girl was a jolt, possibly even a threat, to their new life.

As Jilly and Hud turned towards Hyde, he saw the smile on Jilly's face rapidly dissolve into an expression of shock, bordering on fear. Always the perfect English gentleman, he held up a hand. "I'm here on an errand and bring you nothing but good tidings. This young lady is Violet Evers from the Foundation's security staff. Please accept my apology for barging in on you."

There was a jubilant undertone in Hyde's voice and Jilly, who was sure the pair had come to arrest Hud, relaxed. Hud, as usual, remained composed.

The house and stage lighting had been turned off and the only illumination came from a small strip of black, can-like objects hung from a boom above the stage. Noting the high, domed ceiling, Hyde commented, "Hard to believe this place was once a department store."

The director beamed with the enthusiasm of a man who knows he has the ultimate toy. "It had five floors before it was gutted."

"You'd never know it."

"It's old, but very well built."

"Those moldings, were they hand carved?"

"Oh yes. Unaffordable at today's prices."

"I read where you had financial problems?"

"Yes, several years ago, the Rep almost folded."

"How so?"

"A most disastrous season of controversial, poorly staged offerings. Reviews were beastly and there were scads of empty seats. Patron support dried up. I'm told it was a nightmare."

"Sounds like it. And now?"

"Thankfully, we're playing to standing room only."

Nodding toward the set, Hyde offered, "This is really something."

"Thank you. Our set designer and his staff outdid themselves on this one."

"I gather you're doing *Annie?*"

"It's *the* showcase piece for our children's group."

After the director left, Hyde said, "Nice man."

"And an exceptionally talented and gracious man," said Jilly.

"That certainly comes through, Mrs. Hudson. May I ask what got you into theater?"

"The Rep was broke and Nashville, with all its entertainment facilities, was lacking a theater program for children."

"I never knew you were a theater buff, Hud."

"Peter, children's theater can be a positive force in a child's life if it's done right."

"What do you do here?" Hyde asked Jilly.

Jilly gave a wan smile. "Hud and I provide any funding that's needed and in return we have show, budget and casting approval."

"And the theater board went for the deal?"

"It was Desmond's idea."

"Your director?"

"Yes, we initially hired him as a consultant."

"To look the operation over?"

"Yes. He told us that without total control, the Rep was doomed and we'd be throwing our money away. "

"Based on?"

"The board of directors had too many conflicts of interest."

"I expect he knows his stuff."

"Desmond's sharp *and* honest. The board tried to bribe him."

"Ah, and so you hired Desmond as your in-house director?"

"Yes."

"Why the casting approval?"

"Board members can put casting pressure on a director...hire so and so, she was great in whatever. Auditions can end up being a farce. Desmond believes talent should dictate who gets hired."

"Uh-huh, please forgive my naivete, but what would stop Desmond from hiring his friends and favorites?"

Jilly's smile broadened, "Every so often we bring in an independent casting director to monitor auditions. Desmond's not deceitful, but he's a pushover for a sob story."

"Is it worth it?"

"Of course. Regardless of how good the script, or the sets, it's the casting that makes the show. When performers know there's a level playing field, you get a much better turnout for auditions."

"I'm curious. How does Desmond feel about being second guessed?"

"Hud spelled everything out when he was hired. It's a moot point."

Being a Londoner, Peter Hyde loved the theater and he thought, *What a remarkable change. From homicide detective to wanted man to producer.*

Intrigued by the vast open space above the stage, Hyde made the mistake of looking up. Squinting painfully, he exclaimed, "Those are some kind of lights!"

"They're klieg lights and they're extremely powerful. Be careful, you can damage your eyes."

"Now please tell me. What is all that other stuff up there?"

Pleased by Hyde's interest in the theater, Jilly explained. "That vast area above us is called fly-space. All the stage lighting, rigging, scenic drops, flying mikes, what-have-you are hidden up there where the audience can't see them."

"I've never been on a real stage before."

"Right now you're standing on the proscenium, which is the apron part of the stage. That extension above us is called the proscenium arch."

Looking to where Jilly was pointing, Hyde's early feeling that they might be dilettantes evaporated. *This is no casual plaything. It's a calling,* thought Hyde.

Outside the Oxford Repertory Theater, three men gathered unnoticed at the locked stage door. In just moments they disabled the theater's security system with freon gas and used acid to burn out the lock in the wooden door. They entered silently and made their way to the area at the back of the stage.

Tasha Markov had guessed from the first that there might be a connection between the killing of her lover, Valentine Petrovich, and the hundreds of millions dispensed by the Restore Foundation that came into existence shortly after his death. For some while now she had men and women who had been trained by the disbanded Russian KGB observing and filming comings and goings at the Foundation. One of her operatives had photographed Jilly in her encounter with Hyde at the Foundation, and had taken a shot of Hud behind the wheel of his parked car. Something stirred in the operative's mind.

Not long before, one of Juan's crew, flush with cash, picked up a high-priced call girl at an upscale New Haven hotel. Unfortunately, the girl he chose for the evening was "sponsored" by ROC. His tongue, loosened by liquor and the girls statuesque looks, the crew member bragged about his adventure at the Mope Hotel. Tortured before he was killed, he gave them a description of Jilly and Hud.

Looking at Jilly and the man she drove off with, Tasha's operative was certain they fit the description. He followed them to their hotel. With ease he learned their names, their address in Nashville and the flight number of their plane to the music city the next day. He reported this information immediately to his immediate superior.

On orders from Tasha Markov, the three men had been sent to assassinate Hud and Jilly. One of the men had been aboard their flight to Nashville and for a few days discreetly observed the pattern of their daily activity. It was decided that the theater presented their best opportunity. Jilly and Hud often lingered there long after everyone else had left.

Seated at the cluttered director's table in the front row of the theater, Hyde and Jilly continued their conversation. Hud listened patiently, but suddenly interrupted, "Peter, if you're not here to arrest me, what is it you want?"

"As I said, I'm here on an errand. But first, I wonder if you would indulge my curiosity?"

"Wadda ya wanna know, Peter?"

"Everything."

While the trio sat there in the semidarkness looking up at the set, Hyde lit an English cigarette and clouds of smoke momentarily hid his cherubic face. Jilly, who knew the story, was still left open-mouthed as Hud related everything from the Voccio hit to their harrowing adventure in Florida and the attack on the Mope hotel. The entire account was much more Byzantine than Hyde had ever dreamed possible. The Russians, too, were absorbed in Hud's story, pausing in their movement towards the stage entrance, unable to believe their luck. There would be a big bonus for those who ended the lives of Valentine Petrovich's killers.

When Hyde saw Violet, the Foundation's sharpest and most experienced bodyguard, remove her stainless steel .9mm Taurus automatic from a shoulder holster, he followed suit. Violet had picked up the creaking sound that wooden floorboards make under pressure from a heavy weight. She assumed it was a man. Signaling the others for quiet and, listening intently, she heard other sounds of movement in the area of stage.

No, it's three or possibly even four men and they're spreading out. Lowering her voice she put her hand on a piece of equipment.

"What's this for?"

"It's a remote console that enables the director to control all the stage lighting without someone up in the tech booth."

"Is it working?"

"See the green light. It's still on."

The small, sunken orchestra pit that was directly in front of them drew Violet's attention. Brass railing separated it from the aisle, but there was space enough between the bottom rail and the floor for a person to roll under and into the pit.

"Where does that door lead?" Violet asked, pointing to the door in the pit.

"Backstage."

The Russians deployed, taking positions on both wings and the entrance to center stage. They were experienced, taking the time needed to let their eyes adjust to the darkened conditions of the theater's interior. Hyde heard a safety being released and nodded to Hud who threw the master switch on the lighting console. The cumulative and sudden candlepower from powerful border and trough Kleigs, Fresnels and ellipsoidal spots created a blinding burst of light between the Russians and the front row of seats. On cue, the four of them rolled under the table and down into the orchestra pit where a low-ceilinged tunnel behind the door took them backstage. With the din of AR-15's ringing in his ears, Hud called 911 on his cell phone. "The Rep Theater. Three or four men. Automatic weapons. Shots being fired. Hurry!" He kept the line open so the dispatcher could hear the gunfire.

Downstairs, under the stage, there were rooms for dressing, costumes and props. Smaller spaces had been set aside for a good-sized laundry, stage manager's office and general storage. Violet queried Hud, "Any weapons down here?"

"There's some swords and spears in the prop room."

"Real or fake?"

"Both."

"Peter, prop room. Bar the door as best you can. Jilly, Hud, use the spears. Is there a circuit breaker down here?"

Hud pointed to an antiquated panel that used fuses. "That's it there."

"You've got two minutes before I kill the lights."

Noises at the top of the stairs prompted Violet to unscrew the main fuse thirty seconds sooner. She put the fuse in a pocket and disappeard into the dark. In the pitch blackness of the prop room, Hud and Jilly were glad that Hyde was a cigar smoker who always carried his silver-plated lighter. Before turning off the cell phone, Hud told the dispatcher, "We're in the prop room below the stage."

Violet smelled the man's cheap aftershave before she heard the first footfall on the metal step. The man withdrew and there was a long pause in which Violet surmised that the men were staring at each other, wondering if their prey were armed, and deciding who should lead the way. With practiced self-control and intense concentration she identified the sound of leather rubbing against the rough stucco wall of the tunnel. *Classic pincer move*, she mused.

Carefully removing her shoes, Violet dropped down into a prone position behind a stack of sandbags that, before automation, were used to raise and lower the scenic drops hidden in the vast fly-space above the stage. Very carefully, she put four extra clips on a piece of cardboard next to her. She was ready.

A split second after she flattened her body to the cement floor, the Russian in the tunnel sprayed the room with automatic fire. Violet targeted in on the long lick of flame coming out of the Russian's weapon and fired. *Bam, bam!* Pause. *Bam, bam.* He was wearing a Kelvar vest and the first two shots hit him in the chest. Anticipating that he might be armored, Violet's last two bullets blew away most of his throat. The only sound of his death was the dull thud of the rubberized AR-15 hitting the ground.

Even though she had eleven bullets left, Violet ejected and pushed in a fresh clip. The Russians heard the police sirens outside and knew they were trapped. They tossed a flashlight down hoping it would draw fire and give away the shooter's position. Violet never blinked. Lying there on the floor, the flashlight's yellow beam only served to improve her odds. Suddenly, both men free-fell down the stairs. Hitting hard, they tucked, rolled and came up firing. Anticipating the move, Violet had pressed her face to the floor to hide the whites of her eyes and protect her "night vision." When she heard them pop their clips, she raised her head and used the sand bags to steady her aim. She didn't miss.

"How'd they get in?"

"They froze the system with freon, Captain." said the Nashville detective. "Then used some kinda acid to eat away the wood holding the lock."

"Acid, freon. Whata these guys, chemists?"

"Had to be pros, Captain."

"Obviously they never made the majors. Who took them out?"

The detective gave his captain a quizzical look and nodded towards Violet. "The girl talking to Jimmy."

"Billy Bob, you got to be screwing with my head. She looks like high school."

"Cap, she's combat trained. Won a medal in the desert fight."

"That little thing did all that shootin'? Hard to believe, Billy Bob. Hard to *believe*."

Gesturing toward the three black body bags, the detective replied, "Not really, Captain. Twelve of her last fourteen shots hit home."

The Nashville captain looked at Violet in awe and shook his head. "A .9mm against three AR-15's. Billy Bob, you all make sure that little girl there isn't hassled by anyone. And Billy Bob, I do mean anyone."

It was a life-changing moment and Peter Hyde became very formal. "Mr. and Mrs. Hudson, I was sent here to hand you this envelope. It contains a document which extends complete immunity to both of you. It was executed by the Attorney General of the United States and has been duly recorded in the court house records in Washington. Additionally, any and all references to Jake Garboosian and Hudley Hudson have been purged from all law enforcement computers around the world and of course, you are no longer wanted for questioning."

"Whose idea was this?" Hud asked.

"Actually, it was the idea of the FBI Director."

Hud was stunned. "Why?"

"The yachts that you and whoever took out at the Mope Hotel were earmarked for detonation at the Providence Gas Company docks which you know are on the river close to the downtown area and the intersection of two of the state's most traveled interstate highways. As you know, the abandoned factories around the docks have been converted into shops, apartments, condos and office buildings. If the gas company had blown, the entire area would have gone up with it. Conservatively, at least ten thousand souls might have been lost, not to mention the massive physical destruction of property and a two-year transportation mess costing tens of millions to unravel."

"Sounds good, Peter, but I read the papers. The Bureau and the CIA took the bows for that one."

"Well, old chap, there is one other thing. A Navy diver found that each yacht you sunk at the Mope Hotel had a round stainless steel ball attached underneath its hull. Together they contained suitcase-sized nukes potent enough to level a good portion of New England. They hadn't been armed or they would have blown when the yachts went up. The nukes are something else entirely. What we once perceived as unthinkable is now a constant peril to us all. You saved millions of souls."

"Russian made?"

"Of course. The country is slowly starving and the gangsters are running the show."

"So they've started selling nukes?"

"I'm afraid so."

"What's being done?"

"With President Bennet running the show, plenty. Oh, that reminds me. The Bureau's been keeping an eye on you two since you got to Nashville and they know Jilly here is back trying to write songs again. President Bennet asked me to give her this personal note."

"I think I'll calm down a bit before I read it, Peter."

Now it was Hud's turn to be curious. "How did you find out about Newport?"

"Gerald Riley. Your most ingenious idea to steal the Russian's billions and give it to law enforcement and needy kids was another factor in your favor. By the way, the professor is your biggest fan."

"He turned me in?"

"No, he helped us after the attacks with some computer software he'd developed. Smart man, that professor. Anyway, he was the one who mentioned the possibility that under the Emergency War Powers Act you qualified for, let us say, special treatment. Our Director agreed. You saved a lot of lives, Hud."

"Were any civilians killed in the Mope Hotel deal?"

"Yes, three."

"How is Captain Tenhagen these days?" Hud asked.

"Getting to be more of a pain every day. If you're thinking that you've disappointed him, please, banish the thought forever. That blessed story about you being his curse has gone the way round and he's elevated you to sainthood."

"Give him my regards."

"Done."

For the last year, Jilly had used tranquilizers to battle one anxiety attack after another. She steeled herself for the worst. What she was hearing sounded unbelievable. Hyde's face showed he understood their relief. He looked hard into Hud's eyes and the silence in the theater became deafening. Hyde got up, put on his overcoat and put out his hand which Hud took in his. "Good luck with the Rep."

Halfway up the aisle, Peter Hyde heard his name and turned. Jilly was standing in the aisle, her troubled face a heart-wrenching display of relief and genuine gratitude. Tears streamed down her cheeks as she called out, "Mr. Hyde, break a leg."

After Hyde left, the Hudsons just sat there. Finally Jilly said, "Let's take a walk."

"Where?"

"Anywhere, it doesn't matter."

And, it didn't. The third act was over. They were free.

They exited the theater by the stage door and once on the sidewalk, they set out taking long, energetic strides that only those who are free can enjoy. So many thoughts hit Jilly at the same time: adopting children, song writing and spending more time with her father. After a mile or so, Hud felt queasy. He sat down on a school yard bench and leaned back against the chain-link fence gulping fresh air into his lungs. His mind filled with reflections of the innocent people he'd killed. He looked at Jilly and was surprised to see fresh tears in her eyes. "What's wrong?"

She handed him the president's personal note. "Nothing, my love. I'm just so very happy."

Hud read: *Dear Jilly, My FBI Director knows I'm a country music fan. So, I hope to be hearing some of your hits someday. I've taken the liberty of having the wonderful people at C.F. Martin reserve one of their new D-50 Deluxe Edition guitars for you on a complimentary basis. Martin's only making fifty D-50's and the sample I saw was breathtakingly beautiful. Even the heel cap is a work of art. Like all Martins, the tone is flawless. Enjoy, and keep on writing!*

Jilly and Hud linked arms and began walking back towards the theater and their car. Traffic was heavy and it was beginning to drizzle. They still made it home in record time.

42

Federal Hill, R.I.
October 28...10:45 A.M.

Close to a million people live in Rhode Island's 39 cities and towns. Providence, the capital, is the state's largest city, with a population of about 150,000. What most people like about Providence are its size and location. One could walk to just about any place in the downtown section without a lot of effort. A reasonable cab fare would take one anywhere else within the city limits. Boston is only an hour's drive and Amtrak trains make the trip to the Big Apple in the time it takes to grab a snack and take in a movie.

ROC considered Providence a pivotal city in the expansion of their growing drug empire. Mohamed Jarrahi liked Providence because a suitcase bomb would level the entire state and then some. A nuclear suitcase bomb would demolish the Naval War College and Base at Newport, the Submarine Base in New London, the insurance industry in Hartford, two major naval shipyards and New England's financial center, Boston.

It had rained hard the night before and the roads were still wet and slippery. Because the unmarked car kept hitting potholes hidden by large lakes of water, the detectives in the car couldn't drink their coffees. Maggio was considering alternative routes when her partner pointed to a sign. "Cut through the park."

Situated between Broad Street and Elmwood Avenue, Roger Williams Park & Zoo was an oasis of connecting lakes, towering trees and greenery. Not only had Maggio learned how to play tennis on the park's clay courts, her first romantic encounter had taken place in the woods next to the park's amphitheater. That was back then. Now, Maggio took her nieces to the park's zoo. The zoo had over 900 animals but, like a lot of other children, Maggio's nieces had fallen in love with the penguins that inhabited the artificial icecap in a freezing exhibit room.

The two detectives had been called by an established Federal Hill realtor who had leased an expensive home to a swarthy couple with Italian names, Michael and Roberta LaRosa. Used to well-to-do clients who treated him like one of their lackeys, the realtor was pleasantly reassured by the couples' innate civility. Unbeknownst to the realtor at that time, her likable clients were settling down under false colors. For starters, they were Arabs and their story about buying a business was a barefaced lie. They were setting up a clandestine base of operations for their leader, Osama bin Laden, and they had two nuclear suitcase bombs hidden in the basement of their new residence. They had been trained in Afghanistan and had spent three years in a cell outside Rome.

Fluent in Italian, the LaRosas made friends easily. They began their weekly contact ritual with dinner at Gracie's on The Hill. Their next stop was the bocce courts. Bocce, a traditional Italian game that looked somewhat like bowling when obsered, was played outdoors on clay courts. Just as Providence is the only city in New England to have an Italian Consular's Office, Federal Hill was the only place in the state to find bocce played late into the night on lighted courts. Roberta actually liked watching the game.

Since they both loved wine, Gasbarro's pre-1900's liquor store on historic Atwells Avenue was also an obligatory stop. Lombard Gasbarro, the current proprietor, was the La Rosas's wine advisor. "You see this bottle? Only 16 dollars, but it comes from old, established, Primitivo vines. The vineyard in Puglia is quite small and everything is done by hand. I know this because I was there. Now you take home and enjoy."

"Lum, you know my taste…"

"Mrs. LaRosa, it's sensuous with a deep provocative ruby color and personality so passionate that you will love…"

"Lum…Lum, stop already. You're getting Michael all excited."

Part of the LaRosa's unique contact ritual was a brief visit at the

Poncellio Funeral Parlor. Nicholas Poncellio, the owner's son, had handled the funeral arrangements for a member of their cell who had died of cancer. The family-owned business was being squeezed by corporate-owned funeral homes and the LaRosas always popped in to hear Nick Poncellio's latest harangue. "Michael, they use phony videos to sell overpriced boxes that a few heavy rains will turn to sawdust. They're thieves, Michael, high-pressure thieves!" Having paid $7,000 to bury their associate, Michael wondered who was the bigger thief, the corporations or Nick Poncellio.

The LaRosas always ended their trek of Federal Hill, listening to old standards at the Blue Grotto's piano bar. The verve and emotional pull of Carlo Danza's voice had set the Grotto's mood for five years. His real name was Marwan Ahmed Arai and he was the LaRosa's cell leader responsible for all al Qaeda terrorist activities in New England under the direction of Mohamed Jarrahi.

Everyone had a C.D. story, but the one Roberta liked the best revolved around a gorgeous woman who had been wooing C.D. all evening. Even so, when C.D. decided to play an extra "thank you" set, the woman vented. "Lover, I don't wait around for men; men wait around for me." Well, her haughty tone must have hit C.D. the wrong way because without looking up he said to the bartender, "Herbie, better call this lady a cab cause I'm taking *The A Train*."

During his second break of the evening, Carlo Danza would go to the rest room and leave coded messages for Michael LaRosa. In a short time, the LaRosas became friends with a widening circle of acquaintances, which was important because it helped build an unsuspecting wall of security around their activities

At the realtor's Cranston office on the other side of the park, Maggio and Jack Cross, her partner, sat and stared at each other. The realtor sounded sane and he didn't have a record. The office was clean and he'd been in business for twelve years without attracting the attention of the Better Business Bureau. In the Providence metro area those were mighty big pluses.

Maggio did all the questioning:

"Mr. Johnson, how long ago was the lease signed?"

"Eight months ago."

"For how long?

"One year with an option to renew for two more."

"What are they paying?"

"Thirteen hundred a month."

"Sounds pretty steep for Federal Hill."

"It's about right for the size of the home."

"What prompted you to drive out there?"

"They haven't paid the rent for two months."

"Could you tell if the LaRosas furnished the home?"

"There were mattresses on the floor in two of the bedrooms. The living room was furnished with a couple of beanbag chairs and a television set."

"That's it?"

"Except for all the litter."

"What makes you so sure this is a police matter?"

The realtor unlocked his desk and handed Maggio three sheets of paper stapled together in one corner. "This."

Maggio scanned the papers and her face paled. "Where was this?"

"Inside an empty pizza box. It fell out when I accidently kicked it with my foot."

"Are they still living there?"

"There's food in the refrigerator and a lot of cash on the counter. I expect they're out somewhere."

"Mr. Johnson, an FBI agent will be here within the hour or so. Should the LaRosas contact you, act as if nothing's happened and call us immediately."

Back in the car, Maggio said, "Jack, we got a problem. Stop at a pay phone."

"Between us and the car we got three phones."

"Not for this we don't."

"Who ya gonna call?"

"The captain. We need the Bureau, and right now."

The two detectives drove out to the Arab homestead immediately. Their timing was impeccable. Five minutes later a van pulled in behind them and four men approached their car. They were wearing blue windbreakers with Water Dept. stenciled on the back. Maggio rolled down her window and one of the men said, "Anything?"

"Nothing."

"Got the keys." Maggio handed over several keys with a piece of paper. "Keys and alarm code. The keypad is to the right of the front door."

"We're going in. There are three more teams nearby. Clear the area. There's a green van on Ivory Street. They're expecting you."

Clipboards in hand, a pair of FBI agents walked up the front walk while the other two went around to the back of the house. Two hours dragged by before there was any news. The three Bureau agents manning the communications van were wearing headsets, so the detectives couldn't hear what was coming through from inside the house.

"Right, bomb squad ETA, 60 seconds."

"All units converge. Converge."

The third agent in the van only had one ear covered. "Well?" Maggio asked.

"It's not good."

"Was it for real?"

"Yes."

"What can you tell us?"

"The Arab man and woman came back a few minutes ago. We have them in custody and the situation's under control."

"Will they talk?"

"They're already spouting the Koran. Allah's emissaries, the normal crap. We'll be lucky to find out their real names."

"That it?" asked Maggio.

"Sorry, Washington is already running the show long distance."

They had let her keep her clothes and cosmetics, and Roberta LaRosa had coated her lips an arrogant orange. Dressed in a black leather jacket and brown slacks, she managed to look both crass and mannish. She'd been in custody for four days and moved twice. No one had even questioned her, which went against everything she had been conditioned to expect.

On a bright, sunny morning on the fifth day, a skinny, homely woman wearing sneakers and a Chanel suit walked into the room where Roberta was chained to a chair. "How are you this morning, Mrs. LaRosa?"

Incredulous at the sight of what she considered an ugly looking matron, Roberta LaRosa said, "The FBI actually hired you?"

"Roberta, my name's Furgerson and my salary's paid by the CIA."

"Is this some kind of joke?"

"Roberta, I'm thinking more hush-hush than ha ha."

"You look like an ad for a fucking laxative."

"Let's not waste any more time. Please watch the monitor in front of you."

When Roberta looked, her face drained of color. Her entire family in Afghanistan was on the screen. Thirty-five of them, all told. From 6 months to 84 years old. She even recognized the building where they were standing. It was her family's home. Furgerson pressed a button on the device she was holding and a microphone descended from the ceiling to a point directly in front of Roberta. "Go ahead, say hello. There'll be a little delay because of the live satellite bounce."

Roberta said nothing.

Another button was pressed and Roberta could hear her family talking in Arabic.

"Roberta, here's the deal. I want the names, addresses and codes for everyone in your cell and for anyone you have ever dealt with since you started working with the al-Qaeda and Taliban."

Silence.

"It's real simple. Until you tell me what I want to know, one of your family members will be shot every three minutes. After we run through your relatives, we'll start on Michael's. After that your friends and neighbors. We'll kill everyone in the village if need be. The choice is yours."

"America has laws. You can't do this."

"Listen up you cowardly imbecile. Under the Emergency War Powers Act we can level your entire country. By the way, those black armbands attached to your biceps will tell us if you're lying. Well?"

When Roberta did not respond, Furgerson took the mike in her hand. "John, start with the oldest and work your way down."

"How much of a gap?"

"Three minutes starting right now."

Furgerson left the mike open and never said another word. Twelve minutes later, the wailing and pleading overcame the lies drummed into Roberta's head and she broke.

43

Standing in the hospital's sunroom, Robert Cabral looked much older than his 56 years. His gray hair was slicked-back and there were purple-colored splotches on the back of both hands. Nonetheless, his manner and speech exuded confidence. President Bennet noted his Hermes tie and grey, impeccably tailored seersucker suit. "It's been a while," he said.

Ever upbeat about her energetic administration, the President knew her top expert on terrorism, Robert Cabral, was the missing piece. Badly wounded in the attack on President Lodge, Cabral had already spent three months in the hospital recovering from an extensive amount of surgery. The finest doctors using the latest techniques had put him back together. However, he would be permanently and frightfully disfigured.

A brief conversation with Cabral's primary physician had helped the president get a hold on a nagging riddle.

"Madam President, Robert Cabral is not sick."

"Then why does he look sick?"

"Anyone who drops sixty pounds is going to look different, and Mr. Cabral was terribly overweight."

"I know, but if everything is so peachy, why isn't he back at work?"

"Bob has excellent medical insurance and as long as he keeps fabricating symptoms, the hospital and I have no choice but to keep him."

"Seriously?"

"Dead serious. There's too much potential liability. If something unforeseen should happen, we're on the hook."

"I don't get it. You would think he'd want out of here."

"He does, but he's tormented and afraid."

"What's he afraid of?"

"You've seen his scars. Bob thinks he's a freak."

President Bennet was stunned. Bob Cabral had more actual combat experience than anyone in the White House. "Jesus."

"The scars on the side of his face and scalp can't be hidden like the ones on his body."

"What about a head piece?"

"It would help, but he turned the idea down flat."

"Why?"

"Who knows? Bob's self-image is severely impaired. Once that mindset is grooved, no amount of therapy can undo it."

"Has he seen a psychologist?"

"The sessions were a waste of time. He was predisposed not to listen."

Bob Cabral was surprised by the President's visit, but he wasn't prepared for what she had to say. "Get packed," she said briskly. "I need you."

"What? No, what a beautiful morning how are you?"

"I'm serious. The country is in jeopardy. So, let's go."

Certain she was kidding, Cabral countered, "Maybe for Halloween, Madam President."

With a quick move, the president ripped the magazine out of Cabral's hand. "Spare me the Halloween bull. I haven't got time to play games, especially with a grown man as bright as you."

"Madam President…"

Opening Cabral's closet, the president started tossing stuff on the bed. "Enough! You think you look ugly? Wear a hat. Let's go."

And he did.

44

Several days after meeting with Robert Cabral, the president was sitting on a love seat wearing a Japanese kimono and pair of old sweat pants. Her arms were wrapped around her knees and she was rocking back and forth like a metronome. She had maintained the same, steady motion for hours as though any change would bring forth tears. Her husband was sitting in an overstuffed chair watching her.

An energetic young woman who'd worked in the White House at the time of the attack had died from an infection after a long illness. At the cemetery, President Bennet noticed an older man assisted by a young boy. Tears came to the man's eyes as the casket was being lowered. Not knowing the man, but sensing his immense grief, the president and a Secret Service agent approached him after the graveside service. "Thank you for coming, Mr...."

"Lou Lou, Mrs."

"Was Julie a relative?"

"She was a my friend, Mrs."

"I see. Would you all like to join us at the White House, Mr. Lou Lou? We're having a quiet supper in Julie's honor."

"That's a nice. Thank you, Mrs. I can't stay out very long these days." Grief was chiseled on Lou Lou's face as he took her hands in his. "My wife sends her prayers. She's very sick."

"I understand."

"Make them pay, Mrs."

Lou Lou's eyes had bored into her as he spoke and the president knew she was talking with a man who definitely believed in retribution. Acknowledging his gaze with a weak smile, the president said, "Thank you for coming, Mr. Lou Lou."

The president couldn't get the old man out of her mind. He'd called her Mrs. and that had made her feel personally connected to his grief. "Still thinking about Lou Lou?" the First Man asked.

"Yes. Julie must have been very special to him. You had to see his eyes."

He handed her the latest polls. "You're doing well."

The president went on a media offensive and her messages were riveting. Sensing a reasonable way out of the quagmire, Americans responded. Across the country, like miserly twenty-watt bulbs, the first sparks of optimism began to sputter and glow. Women loved her as their own because, in their heart-of-hearts, they trusted her to do what was right and just and sensible. Those close to her were aware of her uncanny ability to see strength where others only saw weakness and that gave her a leg up in a world dominated by men. Bottom line, she was simply a force unto herself with that indefinable quality that makes great leaders out of those who are propelled to center stage by circumstance.

However, the president's plans had also infuriated and galvanized some of the world's most powerful interests, and even her staff and closest supporters worried that she might have overreached. For those about to lose their influence or the source of their unearned wealth, she had.

Despite efforts by her political rivals to delve into her past, the truth was still buried. Now that she had prevailed, they would be digging deeper and honing in on the missing pieces that she had glibly explained away. To those who had forfeited command, the new president was merely an over-the-counter hangover remedy. She was an anomaly, a one-night stand, whose sizzle would dissolve sooner rather than later. They had the wherewithal to watch, unseen, in the dark shadows. Over time, they would ferret out her secrets, her weaknesses and her hidden passions. Once known, they would destroy her.

Throughout the world, snug in their palatial lairs and well-hidden by their bland anonymity, some of the diabolically evil types targeted by the president smiled. Others who operated out in the open, protected by their private, well-equipped, well-paid armies and the politicians they had bought, laughed. Faced with what sounded like possible extinction, this unsavory group was not that alarmed. To them, the president's plans were academic. The president's optimistic words spoken so confidently meant nothing. Yes, all the polls said she had made an honest connection with the American public, but making good on her promises was another matter entirely. Politics was a foul, sorry business and her detractors would never let her get off the ground. Smug in their beliefs, they sat around and joked about quicksand, beautiful women, skiing, the price of gold and their cravings for immortality. Should President Bennet become a nuisance, well, there were ways.

President Bennet's storied journey and the events that had propelled her into the Presidency were as unlikely as they were remarkable. Honing in like the Stinger that could have taken her life, those events had become a force of their own, coming and going with deadly consistency, snipping away the threads that held her life together and threatening to devour her will to go on. It was safe to say that no one who voted for President Lodge could have ever imagined the precipitating events that vaulted her into the ultimate office. During the next three years, the President's fortitude would be continually tested beyond the limits of human endurance.

After her husband retired for the night, President Bennet thought of all the happiness they had shared during their short married life. Tears flooded her eyes and although there were several security people in the house, she felt as though she were permanently marooned on an uninhabited island surrounded by an ocean of sorrow.

Too many nights with too little sleep had dulled her judgement and sapped her energy. To function coherently, she had to stop her mind from churning nonstop and get some undisturbed sleep. Putting on a sweat shirt, the president took a long walk around the White House grounds accompanied by three Secret Service agents. Between turns around the manicured lawn she managed to plow through the sadness and despair. She would fight.

Epilogue

Professor Gerald Riley

Martha Wentworth received an unexpected windfall in the form of a padded envelope delivered to her office. A terse note had been scribbled on the brown covering: *TO: Mrs. Wentworth: This package contains an item that will be useful in the president's initiative to resolve our country's terrorist and drug problems.* The package had already been cleared. Inside, Marta found several computer disks and a long explanatory letter written and signed by Gerald Riley.

This advanced software created by Professor Riley had enabled the Bureau and CIA to break terrorist codes, trace and track their funds and in some cases to "steal them" just as the professor had done with the banks used by the Russians. After the usefulness of the disks were authenticated, the Bureau Director asked the professor to come to Washington and work with Martha. The Bureau Director cinched the deal by offering Riley the novel privilege of attending a high-level staff meeting on the growing terrorist threat. After introducing Professor Riley and explaining his contribution, the director's voice took on a knife point edge. "From now on there is to be no leniency. Let's ferret the scum out, take their money and send them to hell."

Gerald Riley continued to fund the Restore Foundation and other worthy causes with the money he'd stolen from the banks owned by ROC. Busy at his job with the FBI, he had hired a Providence law firm to monitor the Foundation's activities. The Priority Mail envelope that arrived at Riley's modest home in Washington contained a transcript of a local television show. Riley smiled as he read the piece:

Rhode Island Caves on Lottery

Three days before a lawsuit by The Restore Foundation was to be filed, a special joint meeting of Rhode Island's state legislature found a way to replace the millions in state lottery monies that should have gone to education over the last three years. According to the Foundation, state officials illegally diverted lottery monies which were budgeted to fund Rhode Island's school systems. Instead, the funds were used to finance various dubious projects that benefited the supporters of the state officials responsible for the diversion. To establish accountability for the lottery funds, attorneys for the Foundation had prepared a civil suit alleging fraud and malfeasance by those involved.

Unions representing the state's teachers and police officers had already made it clear that they support the Foundation. By now, most of us are aware that The Restore Foundation has poured unprecedented amounts of money into Rhode Island's educational and law enforcement activities. At last count, 1200 neighborhood foot patrolmen and 900 new teachers have been added to the state's roster, all funded by the Foundation.

The Foundation's educational grants also provided $175 million for the purchase of new books, equipment, teaching aids, plant improvements and new schools. Additionally, the Foundation has established several highly regarded "vocational boot camps" where students can get their high school diplomas while obtaining job skills. As an incentive, students who graduate receive monthly stipends to tide them over until they start receiving weekly pay checks. Since most of the enrollees are high school dropouts and juvenile court referrals, the instructors act more like drill sergeants than teachers. However, the camp's 82 percent success rate is impressive, and graduates of the camps have nothing but praise for the training they received.

Not only is the Foundation funding all the above currently, they have pledged to continue the same level of support for the next three years. During that time, the state is required to accumulate reserves sufficient to continue funding what the Foundation has started. And there is the rub. Both the Foundation and unions know that without the lottery money, the chances of the state building the reserves are nil. On the other hand, contributions are still pouring into the Foundation's coffers.

Unlike our federal government, which seldom monitors what the states are doing with our grant money, The Restore Foundation's hard working co-directors, Donald Tenhagen and Peter Hyde demand strict accountability. Any city or town that accepts Foundation money is subject to independent audit, not only to ensure that funds are being used for the purposes for which they were intended, but to make sure that those managing the funds are doing a good job. With the recoupment of the lottery funds, and all of us keeping tabs on the state's fiscal activities, there is a chance that the strides made by the Foundation will not be squandered by those we elect to office.

Two years after the article appeared, Donald Tenhagen was elected Governor of Rhode Island. At the discretion of Gerald Riley, Peter Hyde continued to run the Restore Foundation as sole director.

General Gregor Markov

Gregor Markov was unquestionably one of the most powerful men in Russia. Serving as the Vice-Chairman of Parliament and being the majority owner of Russia's only major airline, he could manipulate government policy to serve his own ends. But even stronger leverage came from his position in the not-so-secret *troika* that had stripped Russia of its productive assets. Gregor was imperious, brutish, clever, very persuasive, absurdly rich and Russia's prime mover in building the immense drug trade with his country's old enemy, Afghanistan. He had also been Valentine Petrovich's mentor and protector.

Tasha Markov had lobbied hard for the right to take over her husband's illegal business interests. In a few minutes, General Markov would pronounce judgement. From the increasing noise of the sounds below, Tasha could tell that the party downstairs was in full swing. *Nothing like a party to break the ice,* she thought. Sitting across from his daughter, Gregor casually nursed his drink. While his stubby fingers played with the swizzle stick in his glass, he said. "It's done, with one small-minded wrinkle."

"What sort of wrinkle?"

"Petrovich invested heavily in legitimate business. Some of these enterprises are not only highly profitable, they are also complex and difficult to oversee. Your new associates insist that stewardship of those enterprises be my responsibility. I could not say no."

Privately, she thought, *I bet you couldn't, you greedy, lying bastard. That's what you suggested and they couldn't refuse.*

Keeping her poise, she replied, "That seems reasonable."

"*Da*, it is good that you agree. Everyone will be pleased."

Tasha knew that dealings with her father's associates were fraught with dangers, so she asked. "Anyone in particular have a problem with me getting involved?"

"*Da,* Victor Kristoff. He controls Azerbaijan and now his own worldwide narcotics contacts."

"What's Victor's problem?"

"A closed mind. He thinks the job is too tough for a woman."

"Even a woman with your blood in her?"

"*Da.*"

"Well, screw him." She cursed.

"Tasha, Tasha," her father grinned, "He's a handsome specimen, but I don't think that would be wise. Give it time. He'll come to you."

Quickly regaining her composure, Tasha said, "I'll try to cope."

"Excellent. Now what about Lensk?"

The subtle change in the general's voice told her that her father was testing her judgment." I suggest we cross him off our *To Do List* and focus on what really matters. We can catch up with him at some later date, when it's more convenient."

From the look on her father's face, Tasha was confident that she had passed the test.

"Excellent, my dear, truly excellent. Now, about the woman you brought with you?"

"What about her?"

The General pointed to a wall monitor which showed an extraordinarily striking woman entering the grand foyer. "I want to talk with her."

"Talk?"

"Why not?"

"Moscow's overflowing with young girls for hire."

"I know. The entire country's a red light district."

"And you're responsible."

"*Da,* I know that too. But I still want that woman."

Tasha was seething. "I have plans for her."

"You invited her?"

"*Da,* I want to impress her."

"*Nyet,* your face tells me you want to punish her."

"She played kissy-kissy with a friend of mine."

"Don't despair. My long-term plans are quite punitive."

The tiniest of smiles creased Tasha's lips. "I'll send her up."

A man of few scruples and hardened by his own vanity, General Markov didn't hear his daughter. He was still watching the monitor.

Downstairs, Tasha asked one of her father's friends to point out Victor Kristoff. He steered her toward a man standing alone next to the harpist. When he saw her, Victor stared at her and smiled roguishly. There was a sort of barbaric Nicolas Cage look about him that excited her, so she extended her hand. Twenty minutes later, they sped away in his car.

Upstairs in his study, General Markov asked, "Do you know who I am?"

Since she was there to kill him, Ribe Viborg was well versed on the general. He was the undisputed leader of ROC activities world-wide and a supporter of terrorist activities in countries that supplied his organization with illegal drugs. "Certainly, you're the most powerful man in Moscow."

"I understand you're a Dane."

"Yes, blond hair and all."

"Walk over to the fireplace and take off your clothes. I want to see *all* of your hair."

Although the General's guards had done everything but disrobe her, a coy smile crossed Ribe Viborg's bewitching face. "Aren't you going to have me strip-searched first?"

"*Nyet*, a body and face like yours should not be shared with lackeys."

With her face to the blazing fireplace, the woman did a provocative striptease that made the General less cautious than he usually was with women he was going to bed for the first time. "Turn around and let me see your breasts." Her large, firm pendulums made the General's eyes glaze with anticipation. "Come sit on papa's lap."

She tunneled into the General's mouth, and could feel him respond. When she withdrew her tongue, he took her breasts in his large paws and slumped back in his oversized chair. Feigning passion, CIA agent Ribe Viborg leaned away from him and made two quick moves. With a knuckle protruding from a closed fist, she hit the General in his windpipe, crushing it and cutting off his air and ability to shout. Then, in one swift motion, Ribe's hand snatched the General's gold letter opener off his baroque styled desk and embedded it in his heart. Eyes wide, the general looked down and saw the blood spurting from his chest. Then, with his arms dangling over the sides of the chair, he closed his eyes and died.

Wanting privacy, the General had shut off the monitors in his office, so Ribe took her time getting dressed. *I don't think the general was into quickies*, she thought, removing his key ring and wallet from his pockets. One of the keys fit his desk and she went through each drawer, putting aside papers that looked interesting. A few minutes later, after scouring the office, she muttered, *Shit, no safe.* Ribe put the papers, the documents from his wallet, the money and his $48,000 diamond studded watch into her oversized handbag, knowing that the guards outside wouldn't dare search the general's new whore. She opened the door, snapped the lock and stepped out into the hall. The guards gave her boorish looks of approval. It took Agent Viborg ten minutes to reach the broken-down hangar. The airstrip had been abandoned for years, but the runway was still sound. The hangar doors were open and the engines were running. They were airborne in minutes.

Alden Lensk

ROC was only a memory to Alden Lensk, who was now a full-time government consultant and an American citizen. Instead of relocating to the other side of the country, Lensk had changed his name and moved his family to the small coastal town of Niantic, only forty miles away. Up early for his morning run, Lensk was greeted by a damp, unforgiving cold. The morning sky was a palate of greys as the first cold front of the fall season moved into the area. Donning a heavy woolen sweater, he stepped off the porch and headed toward town.

Though it was still in the embryo stage, Alden Lensk was vastly grateful for his new life. Passing an opening in the trees where one could see the ocean, he tried to discern where the sky ended and the water began. His eyes were not good and he couldn't. Lensk took his jogging seriously, and his dedication had paid off. He felt better and had shed over 20 unwanted pounds. A mile beyond the town line, his runner's form was still intact. As he rounded a sharp bend in the narrow, winding path, a man and woman stepped out of the bushes in front of him. Suddenly, recognition dawned and he stopped abruptly. Mouth agape, he stood in disbelief. Not 50 feet in front of him, Tasha Markov, General Markov's daughter, stood smiling alongside a bearded man with a weatherbeaten face. "Cold morning for a run, Lensk," she said.

Lensk wanted to flee and hide, but his legs wouldn't cooperate.

Tasha Markov's lips were painted a weird shade of purple and, dressed in a black leather jacket and pressed purple slacks, she managed to look both crass and mannish. Zeroing in on Lensk over Victor's shoulder, she said, "You killed him, Lensk."

Feeling queasy, Lensk tried to brazen it out, "What are you talking about?"

She shrugged off the question and there was venom in her voice when she replied, "Victor, this is Alden Lensk, the slime I told you about."

"*Nyet, nyet,* you make mistake. "

Tasha's face went still. "*Nyet,* it was you."

Seeing Lensk flinch, Victor added, "You have a nice home, *da?*"

With that question, Victor might as well have shot Lensk in the groin. Fighting off the awful weariness that stems from complete resignation, Lensk's mind flashed to thoughts of his family and he wondered if they would be next. As though she had read his mind, Tasha drew out a Walther pistol. "Victor and I are going to enjoy meeting your family, Lensk."

Lensk snapped and lunged at her.

The awful cold that ran through his body reminded Lensk of how his daughters had endured Moscow winters: *Two layers of underclothes, cotton shirt, corduroy pants, heavy argyle socks, sweater, leather shoes, fur-lined boots and gloves, muffler, ear-muffed hat and a heavy wool outer coat that weighed a ton whenever it got wet. And, everything had to be put on and taken off every time they left the house.* As his blood pooled beneath him, he felt its warmth and closed his eyes.

Hendersonville

Although the Hudsons had purchased a farm in Hendersonville outside of Nashville, Hud still got the *Journal* mailed to him from Providence. The Restore Foundation was always in the news, but it was an editorial that drew his interest:

The Second American Industrial Revolution championed by Wall Street has not panned out and the nation's economy has slowed to a painful crawl, locked in an ever deepening recession. The Fed's drastic reductions in interest rates to artificially prop up the stock markets have not worked. Bowing to political pressure to save the greedy bastards on Wall Street, the Fed has succeeded in cutting the income of millions of retired workers and savers dependent on interest income by two-thirds, forcing them to curtail their spending drastically on anything but necessities.

We have learned some tough economic lessons the hard way. Among them: You need a real industrial base to survive hard economic times and grow an economy. Steady drops in America's exports of goods and the steady rise of imports led to an imbalance of huge proportions that our government chose to ignore.

Another lesson that might or might not have been learned, only time will tell, relates to the stock market. It was ultimately an obscene deceit and disservice on the part of government, the Securities and Exchange Commission and brokerage houses, to allow millions of hard-working Americans to continue to be lured into a market uprooted from its fundamentals and living on a fantasy of hype and hope. The markets rewarded the unscrupulous brokerage houses and clients who bought in cheap, earned huge fees and profits and got out early, but betrayed those investors in for the long run. The only other winners were the informed speculators who had inside information. Wall Street had essentially become the nation's casino. And many who could least afford it paid the price.

This economic impact and huge costs of rebuilding resulting from the attacks, along with the big tax cut passed in 2001, has seriously weakened the United States' financial position. Allowing their fiscal decisions to be jaundiced by those who finance their election campaigns, our elected officials have put the final nails in our economic coffin and we are now sliding into a depression. This debacle is not a one-sided affair. Republicans and Democrats must share the blame.

If you remember, in 1999 and the first half of 2000, our economy was on fire and Wall Street was euphoric. Then, Americans decided that the Internet was not the Second Coming, that they didn't need a faster computer. The prices of gasoline and electricity were eating up their paychecks and when President Lodge took office corporate earnings were already showing signs of erosion. Then came July 29, and the world changed.

In our own city, the Plunder Dome scandals are steadily tearing Providence's city government apart. Just yesterday, Mayor Cianci's top aide and the second highest ranking official at City Hall, Frank E. Corrente, was indicted on federal charges of attempted extortion, conspiracy and mail fraud. As taxpayers, we must ask ourselves, when is enough, enough?

Pouring another cup of coffee, Hud wandered into the cedar-lined family room and slouched down into his favorite chair. Back when he ran homicide, Hud knew that everything in the city went through Frank Corrente. He also knew that, like a pack of coyotes, the Feds would swarm all over Corrente, trying to turn him against the mayor. It was SOP for public corruption cases, and more often than not, the tactic worked.

For months, a flurry of *Journal* articles about critical misplaced evidence, missing high-tech equipment and a number of fuzzy deals regarding the sale of seized vehicles by the Providence police department had bothered Hud. On the other hand, many of the articles praised the performance and integrity of Governor Tenhagen and his staff. Teresa Maggio, who had broken the Plunder Dome debacle, was often praised for her investigative prowess. Informed and ambivalent, Hud gulped down the rest of the coffee and headed for the shower.

The Hudsons had converted part of an old horse barn on the farm into a comfortable room where Jilly wrote her country songs. Mornings were reserved for writing lyrics. Some nights, when the mantle of the moon was it's brightest, the incredible sound of the Martin guitar could be heard a long way off. Late that night, listening to her from the wrap-around porch, Hud could tell that Jilly was down. The music was vibrant, but her voice was a mournful wail that stilled him.

Carry me across the valley, make the river part. Take me home where I can dream. Where angels rest their wings and the high mountain air is always clear. Mend my soul, heal my heart. That sweet country music is all I need to hear.

Our love was far too easy and way too soon. Hold me close, my love, lie and promise me the moon. Those distant drums and tambourines are what I really fear. Mend my soul...

Hud heard her change the song's phrasing and even some of the words, but the music still embraced pain. Unable to bear her suffering, Hud went inside and shut the door.

Iraq

Located thirty-five miles from Baghdad, General Homad Sherik's hidden compound overlooked Lake Buharyrat which was fed by the Tharhar River and a small backwater village. The village's only attraction was a covered bridge that had been commissioned by the general, who was a closet Clint Eastwood fan. Using timeworn boards from several old hay barns, the bridge looked identical to the one shown in *The Bridges of Madison County*.

Up early for his hour with a personal trainer, the general was greeted by a damp, unforgiving cold. Absent sun and with no leaves left on the trees, the cheerless day was dispiriting. Standing on a hidden patio, General Sherik sipped a fresh glass of orange juice and watched the waves race toward the shore. The lake was over ten miles wide and with the constant wind, there was always wave action. The dependable cycle gave Sherik great comfort and on those rare occasions when the wind abated he was always more difficult. Being both a callous and careful man, he was resolved not to do anything haphazard or rash at the meeting he was about to chair. As though on cue, his cell phone rang and a familiar voice said, "General, they're all assembled."

The general had mandated that the complex be missile proof and insulated from electronic surveillance. Telephone lines had been run inside a special coaxial cable that couldn't be tapped and there were miniature-sized video monitors and alarms hidden everywhere. Camouflaged by the natural terrain from the air, the massive complex was buried 50 feet underground and was immune to detection by satellites and spy planes.

General Sherik had abandoned his casual attire for a three-piece pinstriped suit and now he looked like a successful lawyer. Upon entering the room he flashed a carnivorous smile and thanked everyone for coming. His tone was reassuring. "My brothers, except for some last minute details, everything is in place. Your assistance will merely insure our success. America is mired in economic quicksand and their problems with Muslims throughout the Middle East are getting worse every day."

The men around the table traded knowing glances.

"Let me read you a communique I recently received from one of our most trusted and established agents."

My general, America is weak and their economy is in shambles. Every social indicator shows the American family unraveling at breakneck speed as home foreclosures, bankruptcies, divorce, drug usage and unemployment have reached all-time highs.

Without anyone at home to keep tabs on them, America's overindulged young are entertaining themselves to death on such trivialities as sports, movies, television and computer games. The stupidity of the American youth defies understanding, for they have also provided the drug merchants with seven straight years of double-digit growth. America's showy, nonproductive drug war has cost American taxpayers hundreds of billions, and what had once been a problem is now a plague. Incredibly, the 28 government agencies involved in America's so-called War on Drugs have been unable to stop a bunch of uneducated Third World country drug lords. This incredible situation reflects the lack of resolve and misguided judgement of those who run the American government.

The American military and intelligence forces are undermanned and unprepared. If they started tomorrow, it would take the Americans a minimum of three years to reposition themselves for the aggressive actions contemplated. And that assumes that their political leaders have the will to act swiftly. Your humble servant, Jamel.

Of course, Jamel was not the Iraqi agent's real name. He had been educated at some of America's finest colleges and currently held a high-level position in the State Department. Rubbing his leathery shaved head with his hand, General Homad smiled. "You see, even Jamel, who has lived among the Americans for over twenty years, agrees that the time is now."

Around the table there were nods of conviction.

"Good, I'm reassured that you agree."

With disarming sincerity, and a mellow tone, the high-level emissary from Iran said, "General, the American carriers must be taken out in the first strike. Are you sure of your capability to accomplish that feat?"

To the general, the question was a kick in the groin. Years of painstaking effort had gone into the planning and preparation of the attack and this man had the audacity to ask such a question. Fighting off the weariness that stems from dealing with fools, the general's face was a mask of civility as he thought, *The Iranians will eventually require more damage control than they're worth. After it's over, they too, will become disposable.* "Your Excellency, I can guarantee you and everyone else in this room that as of now we can neutralize the entire American fleet."

Finding himself straddled between rage and melancholia, the general raised his arms wide. "To Allah!"

The exuberant chorus of voices that responded washed away the general's ire.

"To Allah!"

A cold rain, accompanied by the peals of thunder, greeted the Iranian as he left the airport for the royal palace to give his report. He looked up and watched the dank, foreboding layers of amorphous clouds move in and take over the sky. Moving his lips in silent prayer, he said, "Allah, give me guidance. Is this a praiseworthy end?"

Moscow

Valentine Petrovich's old cronies in Moscow were ex-communists and gangsters now posing as bureaucrats and elected officials, and it was because of them that corruption was infecting every aspect of Russian life. A thriving black market, widespread tax evasion by wealthy individuals and major companies had made the collection of taxes a national joke. The combination of an eroding tax base and the systematic theft of U.S. Aid, had crippled the Russian government and drugs, violent crime and prostitution were out of control. Although food was scarce, vodka, Russia's "Green Snake," was still plentiful and deaths from alcohol abuse and drunk driving were a national disgrace. In this climate of wanton criminality, Petrovich's friends had come out winners.

The stress on Maynard Orlin after the Arabic attacks on America caused him to lose over 20 pounds. Victor Kristoff and Tasha Martov had married and returned to Russia, leaving Orlin in charge of ROC operations in the States. Since taking over, the revelations about Petrovich's illegal activities had rocked the basketball world and the league board had forced Red Square to sell the franchise.

Orlin's face was gaunt and his crew cut had grown out into a mane. As he approached customs, he was wearing jeans and a New York Mets warm-up jacket. The customs agents at the Moscow Airport took their jobs very seriously and they were trained to look for passengers who displayed certain nervous characteristics. As the agent studied his passport, Orlin kept his eyes on the agent's face. *Let's see who flinches first,* he thought. With a studied flourish, the agent handed back the passport. "Welcome back to Moscow, Mr. Orlin."

Orlin walked across the crowded concourse to an airport bar. Inside, the ceiling was festooned with propellers taken from old aircraft. Seated under the prop of a Boeing B-25 was the man he sought. Pointing to a rattan chair the man said, "I understand it's Orlin these days."

"*Da*, Moche. Maynard Orlin."

Moche grinned. "How does a beer sound?"

"*Da.*"

As they drove to Orlin's hotel, Moche nodded toward a line of cars at a service station. "That's the only place for miles that actually has uncontaminated gas on hand."

"Has everyone arrived?"

"*Da,* they're waiting for you."

Orlin and Moche walked slowly from the National Hotel next to the Kremlin, across Red Square toward Alexandria Gardens, a flamboyant indoor shopping center that combined baroque architecture with the glitzy storefronts of Gucci and Cartier. Elsewhere, Russia was rusting and rattling itself away. Crime and corruption had run amuck and the Russian people had given up the hope that had helped them persevere throughout their country's violent past. Crime, sloth, gutted buildings, malaise and alarming unemployment marked a sad, dysfunctional society on the brink of death. Only Russia's cold, vulture-like bureaucrats, gangster politicians, and new, well-heeled entrepreneurs could afford to shop at the Gardens. No one else had any rubles.

The glass-domed roof of the structure was a city block long, supported by an exposed spider-web of intricate steel pillars and girders that had taken on an odd patina that only nature could bring about. Deep carpets of moss curled out and around the trees and foliage and blooms so vivid and healthy they might have been painted by Gauguin. At night over 200 thousand tiny white lights sprinkled among the trees gave the Gardens the feel of a magic forest in a child's book.

On the third level of the mall, the Natural Cotton Boutique's windows and doors were covered with brown paper and a sign said, *Closed for Renovations.* The sign had been there for over a year. Inside, Victor had built a comfortable secure space within a space. He'd informed Tasha that, "Bears hide in caves."

"But we're so exposed here."

"*Da*, but we can see what's coming and everything needed to survive is available in this building. Besides, no one would dare bomb this place."

Victor's greeting made it clear that he was in charge. "Orlin, we thought you wouldn't make it."

"*Da*, travel is difficult these days."

Victor spoke reassuringly. "My friends, lets get started."

Rubbing his shaved head with an arthritic hand, Mexican General Ario Hidalgo spoke loudly, and vehemently. "The American president must be killed!"

Victor frowned, but nodded for the general to continue. "Before, the chances of getting caught at the border were slim and getting caught was a mere inconvenience. There were lawyers, plea-bargains and bribes. Now, our drug carriers are taken to the nearest military base and shot. So far, fifty of our best carriers have faced military firing squads. And carriers by the hundreds have just disappeared on their own."

A Colombian with a moustache, black wire-rimmed glasses and bad acne chimed in. "In my country the American Air Force has already reduced our production by half. Even at night the bombs continue to fall. There is no respite."

Victor inquired. "Political pressure has not worked?"

"Our *presidente* threatened to reduce oil production. President Bennet told him face-to-face, 'Do that and I'll see you and your family dead in a week.' Of course she denies this, but I know it is true."

Everyone in the room was astounded, except Orlin, who kept his face blank as he spoke. "It's no idle threat, my friends, the lady wants *everyone* connected with our business dead."

Orlin's mind raced. A Russian, educated in America, he'd known things were bad. With supplies way down, the price of hard drugs had gone through the roof. Demand was way down. However, killing the American President, bitch that she was, would only make matters worse. Law enforcement and the military had gotten the green light and they loved her way of doing business. Clinton was a pussy cat. President Bennet was a raging leopard on the hunt. Find them, kill them, take their assets and destroy their fields and production bases. The American public had taken the civilian casualty reports in stride. The bitch outfoxed everyone on that one. In a nationally televised speech she had laid it on the line. "It's them or us, and in that context there is only one sensible choice."

Orlin sensed Victor's concern about killing the American President and he said, "Victor, perhaps a report on what's going on inside the White House would be useful."

Glad for the change in emphasis, Victor said, "An excellent suggestion."

Orlin rose and addressed the group like the CEO of a small company running a staff meeting. "Using the Emergency War Powers Act, the President fired just about everyone at the Drug Enforcement Agency who held a top management position because of his political connections. The Marine Corps general she appointed brought his own staff with him. He's tough, organized and loyal to President Bennet. My source, who is 100 percent reliable, told me the American President means every word she utters, and he pointed to Kabul as an example."

Leaping up from his seat, Mohamed Jarrahi said, "The fucking camel-haired bitch. There is no more Kabul! Her air force leveled it and then she had it bulldozed flat."

"You just made my point," said Orlin. "Because Clinton and Gore lacked any guts or common sense, Osama went too far. Way too far. Did bin Laden think he could trash America and just walk away? Mohamed, your leader is so addicted to killing Americans he has lost all perspective. He threatens our very existence yet you come here seeking help? I live in the States. Believe me when I say Americans are enraged. Remember, it was bin Laden who had President Lodge and his Secretary of State killed."

The same Haitian who had provided the cigarette boats in the Miami cruise ship attack got to his feet. He was dressed in a tailored houndstooth coat and had the natural presence of a born statesmen. "I was led to believe that Miami was the only target. It was total insanity to destroy what Americans hold most dear. And killing the president will not solve our problem. There's only one thing that can make a difference."

The Colombian who hated blacks, smirked. "And what's that."

"Oil."

Nods.

Orlin held up his hand. "Our Haitian friend is right, but there is a complication. President Bennet wasn't elected by the oil companies, the banks or the American Bar Association. Next week she is going to make an announcement which raises the legal driving age from sixteen to eighteen. She is also going to direct the auto companies that within 24 months, every car and pickup they make will have to get 33 miles to the gallon, no exceptions. Along with that she's planning to expand America's mass transit system tenfold within ten years."

"If that is true," said the Oxford-educated Haitian, "she can say fuck you to foreign oil."

"It's true." replied Orlin. "She'll be on television next Wednesday at nine."

Mohamed Jarrahi, who Victor considered almost as deranged as bin Laden, not only rose, he stood on his chair like some kind of prophet looking down on the masses. *Crazy bastard*, Orlin muttered to himself. "Nukes and bio, Victor! Russia has nukes and bio stockpiles! Your top people are making billions. They can threaten to sell them. Iraq and Iran would love to own a few. So would we."

The Haitian looked at the faces around him and saw no alarm. *What fools* he thought. Then he looked at Victor and was comforted.

"Please." said Victor, addressing the Arab still standing on his chair. "Please sit down and listen." The Arab sat. "I was privy to a meeting last month in Paris where Russia's leadership cried about their money problems to President Bennet. They hinted that if Russia's money situation was not solved they might have to sell some of our nukes and bioweapons. It did not go over as they had anticipated. Perhaps you are unaware that President Bennet speaks fluent Russian. She told them point-blank in Russian that if one missile or one bioweapon from our stockpile was ever used on U.S. soil, she would have every one responsible hunted down and their nuts cut off. And, Mohamed, she promised that their families would also be hunted and killed. She called it personal accountability."

"Camelshit," said the Arab.

Victor took out an enlarged photograph and handed it to the Arab. "You think so?"

The group traded smirks while waiting for the Arab's reaction. They saw his eyes widen and his hands begin to shake. All at once he covered his mouth and ran for the restroom. Then came the sound of a man puking out his guts. The Colombian picked the photo up from the floor and the blood drained from his face. He was looking at bin Laden's third in command who had been reported killed in action. He was hanging by a meat hook in front of a large American flag. His nose and ears were gone. One eye had been gouged out, his balls were missing and both legs had been cut off at the knees. A standard ranger combat knife had been thrust deep into his mouth. His legs and a chainsaw lay in a pool of blood under his body.

Victor waited until everyone had seen the picture and when the Arab returned, he said, "Osama bin Laden talks of reprisals. Don't delude yourselves. Forget any notions about how far President Bennet will go. I know from Orlin that, with her, there are no taboos. Remember, Bennet has never denied that she ordered General Markov killed."

The Arab's diverticulitis had acted up and he was in pain, however, he still wanted an answer. "Well, *Victor*, is a deal for some nukes or bio possible?"

"Mohamed, right now the top priority of the men running Russia is the absolute protection of our missile and bio supply. They have already got the missiles we sold to Iran and Iraq back."

"How is that possible?" the Colombian spat out, sarcasm and disbelief dripping from every word.

"Actually, it was quite easy. The Russians lied and said the missiles were defective and had to be replaced. Very sorry, no charge, updated versions, more powerful and so on. The lies worked. Forget about the nukes and bio, it's not going to happen "

The Colombian, still sickened by the pictures, changed the subject and addressed Orlin. "Is immigration going to start loosening up?"

"While she's President, you can forget immigration. There won't be any."

General Hidalgo was beside himself, "I want that Marine general killed."

Orlin could understand Hidalgo's wrath. The Marine general had taken the president's comment about *ferreting the scum* out literally. Within sixty days, over a thousand predators directly involved with the international drug trade along with their confederates: chemical suppliers, pilots, piggish bankers and crooked lawyers had been killed in raids or executed by the general's combat troops. A third of those killed were from Mexico.

"General Hidalgo," Orlin said, "The Marine general is the first one the Americans have had in charge who coordinates with the DEA, CIA, Customs, Coast Guard and the rest. He's not a grandstander and he lets the agency heads take all the glory. The general has three people on his staff just as capable as he is. Killing him would serve no useful purpose and would only make things worse."

The Haitian shrugged eloquently, and his deep baritone drowned out Hidalgo's hollow laugh. "Orlin, I hear rumblings that certain countries will not even be allowed be to visit in the States. Is this fact or fiction?"

"Fact. The floodgates are being closed. Within the next month, no one from Afghanistan, Pakistan, Iran, Iraq, Columbia, Sudan, Viet Nam, Cuba, Haiti, Puerto Rico, the Dominican Republic or any of the Bahamian islands will be allowed to visit."

General Hidalgo sneered, "The uproar will bury her."

"I think not," said Orlin. "She's not letting anyone in until they get all the bad guys out. The public will buy it because it makes sense."

Tasha, who sat well in the background, had not said a word, but now she traded knowing glances with Victor. A change was taking place among those in the room. It was gradual but there. This was the moment for Victor to make his statement. Speaking with conviction, Victor said, "My friends, for us the drug business is dead and in a very short time it will be buried. To continue means annihilation. The words zilch and zillion are as far apart as you can get, yet they follow each other in the American dictionaries. If we continue, we will end up with zilch. My friends, forget the zillions and invest what you already have in legitimate enterprises."

Both Victor and Tasha had expected an uproar, but after what the group had seen and heard there was a minimum of fuss. The perceptive Haitian was the first to speak. "We go our separate ways then?"

"Da," said Victor. "It's time to go our separate ways."

They filtered out of the meeting at ten-minute intervals. Each of them would have to explain to their masters the reasons behind the major decision reached at the meeting and they dreaded being the bearers of bad news. The Russians had declared a new era was upon them and their submissive acceptance foreshadowed the fear they felt in their hearts for themselves and their countries.

The Fisherman And His Wife

In the Arabian Sea, nine miles off the coast of Rarachi in Pakistan, a wiry old fisherman looked through his well-worn binoculars searching for the telltale signs of feeding fish. It took a lot of work to drop the net, and a bout with pneumonia had weakened him. Better to find the fish first, then drop the net.

The wind was light, and ripples in the water reflected the sun in the fisherman's face. In the distance he saw swirling columns of smoke where there should have been only sea. Strange, he thought. As he watched the smoke build and billow out, the ripples turned into waves and before very long, he saw random splashes of whitecaps. He put his hand into the water and kept it there as if he were feeling for a pulse. His grandfather had done the same when they were out fishing in these same waters. Then, he was an unpaid helper barely five years old. Scooping up a little water in the palm of his hand, he tasted it with the tip of his tongue as though looking for a clue. It was fine. *Why the whitecaps?*, he wondered. Arami, his wife, had made him lunch of cold potato soup, goat cheese and stale rye bread. He ate, and the gentle rocking of the boat lulled him to sleep.

Midway through a dream of the days when fish were so plentiful he could fill the boat in hours, not days, he was shaken awake by a wave that nearly capsized his tiny boat. Hands with deep cuts and purple splotches grabbed the gunnel and hung on. Bewildered by what he saw, he sat back on his haunches. No matter where he looked, there were American and British flags flying from warships. The sky was dark with aircraft looking like flocks of birds flying south for the winter. Not 200 feet away, an American destroyer had put a small boat over the side and armed men were heading his way. *I'm going to die,* he thought. As the boat drew near, a man yelled to him in his native tongue. "Fisherman, we are here to take you out of danger. Do not be afraid. We will take you and your boat aboard and see you safely to port. Do you understand?"

Shocked, the fisherman nodded his head vigorously.

"Do you have any weapons aboard?"

This time, the fisherman shook his head even more vigorously.

The Americans had been kind. His fragile boat was handled carefully and they fed him and gave him two large sacks of food for his family. An Arabic-speaking doctor gave him a large bottle of pills. "Your heart rate is too high. Take one pill a week. That's a year's supply." Before he left, the crew of the ship passed the hat and gave him what it would have taken him three years to earn. The doctor gave the fisherman an old shirt and said, "Friends of the Taliban will kill you if they find out about the money. Tell no one, including your wife."

The fisherman bowed his understanding.

"There is a great storm brewing far off-shore," said the doctor. "Take your boat and family and go up the river as far as you can and wait it out."

By the time the fisherman and his wife were anchored far inland, the storm's expanding underbelly was picking up almost two billion gallons of water each day…the volume of a force-five hurricane. Where and when the storm would land was anybody's guess. Regrettably, the forest fires raging out of control in Angola had filled the sky with microscopic ash that obscured the pictures taken by satellite. It was not until two days later, when a navy airplane was lost, that the potential intensity of the storm became known. Telemetry data beamed back to the control center by the plane were so incredible that the experts looked at the information with jaundiced eyes. Had the sensitive onboard equipment malfunctioned? Unfortunately, by the time things were sorted out, an unusual set of circumstances had doomed the coast of Pakistan.

When the savage and unforgiving storm hit, the fisherman and his wife were over 90 miles inland in a small inlet surrounded by jagged outcroppings of lava rock and a few sparse trees that provided some windbreak. The American food was sealed in watertight bags tied with clothesline, and their water supply was kept handy in plastic jugs. They had covered the boat with canvas stretched tight from gunnel to gunnel to form a low tight roof, so crawling was the only way to move around the boat. Fortunately, the canvas let in enough air so they could breathe. They lived that way for two days.

Thirty miles from Rarachi, floating bodies began to appear. When they finally reached the mouth of the river, the stench of death was overwhelming. Piles of reeking debris and broken boats blocked the entrance to Rarachi, so they tied up to a large freighter that had broken in two on a sandbar. The ladder had fallen loose and they climbed the stairs to the main deck, working their way up to the top of the superstructure. Rarachi was gone. The old fisherman turned to his wife. "Arami, my beloved wife. Allah has spoken."

Pakistan

Mohamed Jarrahi drove like he knew every curve, which he did. The tires of his pickup truck made a crunching sound as the chains dug into the hard-packed snow. He did not like bringing bad news to Osama bin Laden. The Russians had been cowed by a woman. He shook his head in disbelief. The Russians would not be selling any nuclear or bio-warfare weapons to bin Laden or any other terrorist group. The sun flashed off rock-strewn hills creating countless shades of gold and amber that dazzled and blinded. At times, Mohamed felt like a nomad. In other moments, as now, driving in the open and approaching bin Laden's hideaway, he considered himself fresh prey for the American planes flying overhead. His worst fears however, leading to the growing sense of apprehension and terror within him, were reserved for his encounter with his master.

With information provided by the Russians, American planes were methodically sealing caves that the Taliban had used for years. The bombing went on unabated 24 hours a day. The lack of sleep and the perilous trip had dulled Mohamed's judgement. Arriving at bin Laden's lair, he needed rest.

Anchored to a deep barren slab of rock 326 feet above the sea, the rugged Pasni lighthouse had emerged unscathed by the typhoon that had ravaged the Pakistan coastline. Jutting out from the land into the Arabian Sea, the remote station was there to warn ships of the jagged rocks that made up the vast area of shoals around Pasni. Over 100 years old, the lighthouse was built from local unpolished stones that had been gathered up and mortared together. Because it was only 116 feet high, the rose-colored structure was only 16 feet thick at its base. However, the structure's elevated site and powerful Frensel lens cast a beam that could be seen more than 20 miles away.

A stiff wind blew powdery snow against Mohamed's boots as he stood outside the pickup looking up the lighthouse wall. He glanced down at the rusted out Land Rover tucked in close to the lighthouse, out of the wind. Mohamed was stalling and he knew it. An unshaven, squalid-looking man, familiar to Mohamed as one of bin Laden's elite bodyguards, opened the rugged door of the lighthouse and saw a bleary-eyed face atop a weary body sagging from fatigue. The man was well known to Mohamed and they hugged. "Welcome, my brother. Our master has been waiting for you. Unfortunately he is resting. I suggest you eat and do the same."

After some food and a brief sleep, Mohamed, somewhat refreshed, was bidden to enter his master's room. Osama bin Laden sat in an oaken chair eating ice cream from an earthen cup. The room was spartan, lit by candles whose warm glow made the gaudy pink walls seem more friendly. There was a sensual languor about bin Laden that Mohamed had never seen. A wanly beautiful girl sat on a stool close to bin Laden, speaking to him softly as Mohamed entered. Their muffled words ended abruptly and the girl moved off into the shadows where she sat on the floor, legs crossed, eyes looking down at the dirty carpet. The girl's heart-shaped face put a thought into Mohamed's mind that almost made him smile. Osama had not been napping. He'd been with the girl and she had done more than rain kisses and gentle caresses. Waving Mohamed to a seat, bin Laden's stained teeth showed as he casually squashed a bug with a rolled up newspaper.

Mohamed saw the comprehension in bin Laden's heartless, smoldering eyes and a shudder went through his body. "Mohamed, you have failed." His senses sharpened from the three hours of sleep, Mohamed did not let the sinister undertone in his master's voice unglue him. To show weakness now could be fatal. "I beg your indulgence. Threats from the American President have the Russians in a panic. As you predicted, they have returned to their cowardly ways and offer us no help."

The transition from hunter to hunted had not weakened bin Laden's resolve, but the relentless pursuit had worn him down, physically and mentally. He was rail-thin. His once commanding voice had taken on a reedy quality. The deep moles on his drawn, shrunken face looked like craters. To Mohamed, he looked like a hollow-eyed junkie. Bin Laden had recently begun to have bursts of instability marked by unrelenting ranting that could go on for hours. Osama's shrewd Arab mind was still intact, but some of his inner circle had begun to worry. Bin Laden's lukewarm response, rather than the fury he expected, gave Mohamed hope. "It is of no real concern. The Iraqis have enough to do the job twice over. Russians believe paranoia is the key to their long-term survival." There was no finger pointing. "My expectations failed to consider the Russian mentality. How inconsiderate of me."

To an astonished Mohamed, the words and voice of his master sounded very much like those of one already resigned to his defeat.

Politics, and his continuing program of *anticipatory terror* against America ultimately killed Osama bin Laden. Tired of bin Laden's constant threats and concerned with the collective agony of innocent Muslims who were starving to death, President Bennet put unbearable pressure on the Pakistani government. Already under risk of anarchy from groups of miscreants who chose to believe bin Laden and with the clerics demanding more power every day, the Pakistanis had given the president the exact location of Osama bin Laden and his inner circle in the Pasni Lighthouse. Secret electronic surveillance measures by AWAC planes and high-flying stealth bombers monitored the conversations at the given location and compared the voice prints there to those in bin Laden's recorded speeches. They matched perfectly.

Timothy O'Leary, call sign Acid, and his wingman, call sign Fossil, were flying *down on the deck* just before dawn, 100 feet above the green water of the Arabian Sea, well below the radar pulses that could detect their approach to the lighthouse. A thick-jawed Irishman, O'Leary was one of the best aviators in the U.S. Navy. The picture taped to the wall of his stateroom on the carrier indicated that his wife was a stunner and that their two girls had her genes. At the moment, O'Leary's mind was focused on keeping his single seat F-18 Hornet from taking a swim. When they'd been picked for the single most important mission of their careers, the airwing commander told them. "You're both hard asses, but you seem to have some sort of telepathic connection with your targets. Don't screw this one up."

Have to hand it to the wily bastard, O'Leary thought. *Hiding out in the open without any missile or anti-aircraft cover. Who wouddathought. And those lying bastards, the Pakistani fuckfaces who gave us all that crap intelligence. Lucky we got a president who doesn't give a rat's ass about the niceties of diplomacy.* Everyone in the president's cabinet had gone apeshit when she ordered the immediate destruction of the television station that aired bin Laden's video messages. O'Leary had applauded her guts.

To avoid being sighted visually, the mission had been planned to the minute, and that minute was almost upon him. Absent flak, missiles and enemy fighters, Acid and Fossil considered the mission a milk run.

On the catwalk at the top of the lighthouse, Saeed Bamihamad squinted into the rising ball of red fire that was the sun. Saeed, bin Laden's personal cook of ten years, saw the planes and stood rooted in disbelief. His prayers to Allah had been answered. From their low approach he knew they were on the attack. He could easily have sounded the alarm and everyone would have proceeded down the emergency elevator to a series of rooms carved out of solid rock, nine stories underground. The Pakistanis, who had designed and built the space, boasted that bin Laden's sanctuary could withstand a thermonuclear attack. *So what if it could,* thought Saeed. *What would it matter?*

Once a true follower, the thrall of his master's myth had worn thin and

Saeed had come to see the man for what he really was; a cunning, cowardly ghoul who used the vulnerable and naive to do his evil bidding. Bin Laden's expensive public relations flacks and media contacts in the Muslim world made him look like everyone's favorite uncle, but Saeed had overheard too much over the years. The man was a bloodthirsty piranha with a penchant for American blood.

Saeed's desire to poison and kill bin Laden and those around him had been born two-months ago during prayer in a humble Afghanistan mosque. As he cradled his Koran, he saw his hands become streaked with blood. Curiously, the Arab men on each side of him sensed his alarm, but when they looked, they saw nothing wrong. Minutes later, Saeed's hands were spotless and he began to relax. Then, high above him he heard the sounds of wings cutting air. The soaring sound built to a crescendo. Saeed could hear it echoing through the mosque. Then an unworldly voice, with an edge like cut crystal, reverberated through the Holy place: *Saeed, you've known for some time, yet you continue to nourish the monster. Don't temporize too long. There are limits. Do what you know in your heart you must do.*

The sound of soaring wings stopped abruptly. No one else had interrupted their prayers to listen to the sounds, only him, and for the first time in his life, Saeed was truly terrified. Now, watching the planes climb to attack altitude, he was reminded of an old Arab saying, *'As-sabr muftah al-faraz,'; patience is the key to paradise.* Since the mystical episode at the mosque, Saeed had been beset by an overwhelming need for atonement. He had tried unsuccessfully to obtain enough poison to kill his master and those close to him, but bin Laden had become more paranoid then ever and even after ten years of service to the master, Saeed's every move was scrutinized. Eyes bright with happiness, Saeed waited patiently at the railing as death approached.

O'Leary keyed his mike one time to let Fossil know that the 'Go' signal had been confirmed. Everyone was still inside the lighthouse. The sensitive eavesdropping equipment could pick up the inhabitants' breathing patterns. Sighting the lighthouse, O'Leary keyed his mike twice. Immediately, both aircraft banked right and climbed to 2,500 feet. Practiced eyes scanned digital displays while deft hands guided fingers to the correct buttons and switches. Reaching the desired angle of attack, O'Leary and Fossil locked the lighthouse on their target–displays and fired one smart bomb each.

Banking sharply to starboard, they pushed their throttles forward to gain altitude. Coming around, O'Leary looked through his canopy and a saw a smoking pile of rubble. They hit the target a second time, driving two more bombs deeper into the target mass.

O'Leary broke radio silence and spoke to Fossil. "Time to pelt and melt."

Fossil, who had grown up in Odessa, Texas, drawled, "Roger that."

On their final run, each aviator dropped a Fuel Air Explosive, one of the Navy's most gruesome and controversial weapons. The detonation of high octane gasoline ignited by timed flares sent fiery, mushroom-shaped clouds sky high, sucking out all the air around the target while incinerating everything within a half mile. Circling around in a wide pass, Acid and Fossil viewed a surreal scene. The lighthouse was gone, replaced by a deep crater surrounded by scorched earth and molten rock. Black smoke from the bombs turned saffron-yellow and was thrust, by pressure, five miles into the atmosphere.

In his digital cocoon, O'Leary opened the Hershey bar's wrapper with his teeth and pointed his aircraft toward home. As un-hip as they come, like Fossil, O'Leary was a solid family man who knew that if the people running the show weren't vigilant, drugs and terrorism would do them in someday. He and Fossil had just killed the most wanted man in the world, and he felt righteous. Both aviators felt high from a ceaseless flow of adrenaline. Not exactly the emotionally expressive type, O'Leary had a hard time keeping the lump in his throat out of his voice. "We're done, let's go home."

"Roger that."

Like O'Leary, Fossil could also be a smart-aleck around his bosses. A shy, modest man, he wore his warriorhood lightly and was the favorite officer among the enlisted men and women who orchestrated the controlled madness on the carrier's flight deck. He knew that bin Laden and his followers could never be pacified. They had to be killed. If his cockpit hadn't been so tight that its sides chafed his skin, Fossil would have knelt in prayer. Not for those he just helped kill, but for those lost because of one evil man. High-time pilots with Fossil's skills were being recruited like never before by the airlines and they were offering big bucks. Six months ago he'd opted to stay in the navy. Now he knew. No amount of money could match, never mind beat, what he felt now.

The sun was climbing as Fossil leveled off into his shotgun position five miles behind and eight-hundred feet higher than O'Leary. Unsnapping his oxygen mask, a toneless Texas voice began to sing:

There's a bend in the sky
Where the clouds never cry
There are clouds that I know
Where all love has to go
Except, inside out or upside down
Clouds and love...have no real bounds

The rest of the song brought thoughts of his wife and their three boys. Being a navy wife was no picnic. A lot of unbridgeable water separated them for long periods of time, but his wife knew that on land he'd be eaten alive by the monotony of everyday life. He was where he belonged.

With the exception of the carrier's three senior officers, everyone on duty assumed the aviators had been on a routine mission. Landing on a moving aircraft carrier twisting and turning through the sea at 25 knots or more is a daunting task that takes skill and steel nerves. In reality, all carrier landings are controlled crashes. O'Leary's approach was right down the chute and his tail hook made an "okay" third wire landing at 160 mph. Five G's of force threw him forward against the straps. He quickly taxied the plane out of the way where the yellow shirts took over its care and feeding.

O'Leary had his canopy pushed back when he heard the whine of Fossil's engines increase. Applying full power at touch down was SOP just in case an aviator was unlucky enough to miss all four wires.

Fossil had come in a little high and caught the second wire. Acid waited for him on the lee side of the oxygen storage tanks. Like O'Leary, Fossil was not the quintessential badass pilot that the movies liked to glamorize. Acid knocked Fossil's landing. "Losing your touch."

"Yeah, I was making a sandwich."

The airwing commander half-stood when O'Leary and Fossil entered his stateroom. "Well?"

Expecting a flip reply, the commander was surprised by O'Leary's subdued answer, "Done, Skipper."

A bottle of Irish whiskey and three glasses sat on the corner of the commander's desk. It was strictly against Naval Regulations to have booze onboard ship, but there were rare exceptions. "Join me?"

Both pilots were still chilled from the short time they'd spent on the flight deck and the smooth liquid warmed them. Glasses clinked and thanks were given as the U.S.S. *Theodore Roosevelt*, fondly known as *The Big Stick*, plowed through 20 foot seas.

O'Leary and Fossil were disappointed to see the commander remove the bottle and lock it in the bottom drawer of a file cabinet. As he stood, the commander noted their chagrin. "Try and sack out as soon as you unwind. There's a briefing in three hours."

Both pilots were perplexed, "Briefing, what for?"

U.S.S. *Theodore Roosevelt*

Folding chairs were added to the regular seating in the ready room in order to accommodate all of the carrier's aviators. Taking the podium, the airwing commander held up his hand for them to remain seated. A one-time top-gun in his own right, he wasn't keen on formality. After O'Leary and Fossil landed, the ship changed course and thoughts of home were on everyone's mind. One look at the commander's face killed that notion.

The room quieted and became respectful. The commander said, "Gentlemen, ladies, in an hour we'll be at battle stations. Our target is Iraq. Intelligence has confirmed that when Saddam learns of bin Laden's death, he will use *unwarranted execution* as an excuse to launch a number of biological and strategic nuclear strikes against the United States. Fortunately, we have been able to verify that the weapons in question are still in Iraq. Our job is to see they never leave."

All gum chewing stopped and the room became a morgue. "I know what you're thinking. How reliable is the intelligence? In this case, I can assure you it's 100 percent."

Fossil spoke up. "We're in this all by our lonesome?"

"We have three carriers already on station and the British have two."

The room stirred. Six carriers; this was big.

"What about the rest of NATO?" asked O'Leary.

"We'd lose the advantage of surprise. Saddam would have time to crank up his propaganda machine. At this point, Saddam doesn't know that bin Laden's dead."

A senior aviator rose. "Sir, with five carriers already on station, don't you think the Iraqis know we're coming?"

"This mission wasn't planned yesterday. Those same carriers have been holding joint training exercises for over a month now."

O'Leary rose. "Sir, how are we supposed to keep the Iraqi weapons from getting out?"

"Our initial strikes will take out every airfield, roadway, railroad line, bridge and donkey trail in the country. Next, we'll be hitting their military bases, germ warfare facilities and nuclear storage and assembly plants. If we have to, we'll seal every cave in the country. We'll be operating around the clock, and just about every supply ship, guided missile cruiser and destroyer in the U.S. fleet is only a day or so away. Our orders are to nail Saddam and the rest of the nut cases around him to the wall."

The commander had his hearing aid turned all the way up and he heard Fossil murmur, "President's gonna catch all hell on this one."

Unfolding a sheet of paper, the commander looked at Fossil. "This is a short excerpt from the talk President Bennet will give this evening: *Since the Arab attacks on July 29, I have warned repeatedly that the United States will never again sit back and let another country invade our soil and take American lives. Iraq has chosen to ignore those warnings and they are paying the price.* Questions, gentlemen?

Bob Dias's next book will deal with Jilly's emergence as an award-winning writer of country songs and President Bennet's unwavering war on terrorism and the international drug trade. Because of the dramatic changes and pressures on the music industry, Jilly's side of the equation rivals that of the president in terms of intrigue and surprises.

Real Words

Country Songs by Bob Dias

Release
No Real Bounds
Lost Love, A Help Wanted Sign
Blanket of Love
Soldier
Loosey-Goosey
Mend
Jilly
Zero to Zillions
There's Love in the Wind
Let Love Find My Room
Hard-Packed Ground
Rooms To Go
You Know Better
Internet Cowboys
Last Change Ranch
Chili Stop
It Won't Happen Again
Love's Bargain Bins

Inspired by *The Pennycandystore*, the lyrics to the foregoing songs are included as a bonus to the reader. Professional demos of the songs were recently completed at the **Sound Control Studio in Nashville, Tennessee**. Hopefully, they will find their way onto the CD of your favorite country vocalist.

All songs are copyrighted by Robert M. Dias and represented by the **Welk Music Group, Nashville, Tennessee**.

RELEASE

Male Vocal
She has the heart of an angel
A manner so fine
Everyday brings us closer
It's the magic of time
Her touch so caring
It fills me with life
For me there's only one woman
My loving wife
Lost in a darkness..that can almost be touched
Still tortured by demons.. with the power to crush

Duet Chorus
Seems we've been married forever
Love aging like a fine wine
With the world so out of focus
Together...we walk life's thin line.
Joy's never easy to come by
We see only blue skies
We released all the things that hurt us
Released..before love passed us by

Female Vocal
He was lost in such darkness
His heart I couldn't touch
He was tortued by demons
He needeed me so much
So he released all the hurt
From a heart frozen with pride
And poured out love's music
That was locked deep inside

Repeat chorus (And double the last two lines)

Copyright © 2002 by Robert M. Dias. All rights reserved.

NO REAL BOUNDS

Stalled in traffic...looking down
Pails of rain flood the ground
A liquid sky...flat like tin
Protects the clouds from eyes within
I take a walk inside my head
There's our home...our canopy bed
I miss our green valley...that much I know
Starting over's been rough...my spirits are low

Chorus
There's a bend in the sky
Where the clouds never cry
There are clouds that I know
Where all love has to go
Except, inside out or upside down
Clouds and love...have no real bounds

There must be a cloud...where angels go to play
When I think of you there...a thousand hurts melt away
I hear the laughter of angels...I reach up to the sound
But my hands come down empty
Clouds and love...have no real bounds

Repeat chorus

Bridge
Perched on a cloud...in the first rays of light
You speak and I listen...God shows me you're all right

Repeat chorus
I know there's a cloud...where angels go to play
When I think of you there...all my hurts melt away

LOST LOVE, A HELP WANTED SIGN

He was a shy Montana country boy
With a slow, heart-warming smile
She was a fast-track big city girl
Who'd never had to walk a mile
He was best man for the groom
She was standing up with the bride
He took a chance and asked her to waltz
She said yes...he looked pleasantly surprised

After that they danced all the slow ones
And seemed lost in a blissful trance
Each time their bodies would meet
Is this passion or true romance
He whispered how much he loved horses
That he was born to the quiet life
She said that was something she'd dreamed of
She looked away...and tears filled her eyes

Chorus:
He said, "Love can be lost...
And love can be found..."
She said, "I've never found true love...
In this big neon town..."
He whispers, "I think life is a two-ticket show...
Lost love, an unwanted, help wanted sign..."

She's known the gloom in the cold city dawn
When all its hopes and compassions are gone
And in this place full of millions
She feels so alone
He said, "Then come see my mountains...
Where your heart can still run free..."
And his loving kisses...offered her...the key

Forget logic, reason or thought
Love just happens...it can never be bought
There are a few second chances
And precious little time
The ice-carved angel...slowly melting
With all of her fears...they are...left behind

Repeat chorus
Copyright © 2002 by Robert M. Dias. All rights reserved.

BLANKET OF LOVE

Across the valley on the canyon's rim
She saw a fragile moon turn crimson and dim
Next to her holding a warm slender hand
Her reason for living…an ordinary man
No worldly possessions…no luxury car
Just a pickup truck and a beat up guitar
She felt the ring and his eyes asked will you
She pressed it on her finger and said
Yes…yes I do

Chorus
Their flames fit the fire
Passions simmered with desire
Ever so young…ever strong
Wrapped in the blanket of love
Their lives would never go wrong

He worked summers as a high mountain guide
Very little money…just liked being outside
But his flannel shirt gave their families a start
He thought money troubles would tear them apart
Genuine love is both painful and sweet
All-night conversations on how to make ends meet
Wicker baskets of dreams…warm apple pies
Good people struggle
But good love won't die
Hard-working men…know all the real songs
In the blankets of love
It's forever one

Repeat chorus
Repeat last two lines of chorus

SOLDIER

My blood's running out and my body's running cold
I'm lying here dying only nineteen-years old
From a terrorist bullet in the faraway dark
No future of marriage or children in the park

Astride a magnificent horse dressed with gold filigree
A halo of angels smiling all around me
Heaven bound souls soaring through a white light
Ma, I know you can't see me, but I'm waving good-bye

Chorus
Ma, I can hear it
I'm at peace, I don't fear it
My last rising sun lights up the sky
Ma I can hear it
I'm at peace, I don't fear it
A moment of grace and this soldier will die

Oceans of voices serenade the stars
Singing with musicians
Strumming twelve-string guitars
Legions of harpists play crescendos so serene
That the notes of the flutist are magical-dreams
Lemonade waterfalls gush from the sky
Wide rivers of goodness, bring tears to my eyes
Webs of emotion hang from skyscraper trees
Stars flicker like candles in a magical-breeze

Repeat chorus
Add to the end of chorus:
Ma I can hear it
I'm at peace...I don't fear it
A moment of grace, this soldier will die

LOOSEY-GOOSEY

I was shootin' pool and drinkin'
When down from the blue it came
The message that needs no messenger
The voice said "wind up the game"
You've led a pretty good life
So there's no need for doubt or fear
No calling...no packing...no fretting
You need no earthly gear

No problem, 'cuz I don't have much now
'Cept my faithful pick-up truck
Wish I'd have known that today was the day
I'd have left it to my Uncle Buck
And maybe I'd have gone fishin'
With my sometimes best friend Ray
But in the kingdom there's no loosey goosey
So I best be on my way

Chorus
Heaven's waitin' everybody
Heaven's waitin' it's a glorious day
There's no loosey-goosey
No warning who goes or stays
Goodbye my sweet Annie
Seems my number's up today
No more loosey goosey
It's my judgement day

Won't be punchin' in tomorrow
Hope they'll miss me on the line
No need to worry about Billy
Cousin Willie will treat that dog fine
And please forgive me Annie
No wedding this spring like we planned
And there's no more loosey goosey
Hello heaven goodbye earth for this man

Repeat chorus

MEND

Carry me across the valley
Make the river part
Take me home where I can dream
Mend my soul, heal my heart
Where angels rest their wings
And the mountain air is clear
That sweet country music
Is all I need to hear

Our life was far too easy
Our love was way too soon
Hold me close, my dear love,
Lie and promise me the moon
Distant drums and guitar strums,
Tambourines are what I fear
That sweet country music
Is all I need to hear

Stay on busy sunlit roads
Avoid old worn-out men
Their goodness is all gone
It will hurt you in the end
Heaven above is waiting
And the stars are getting near
That sweet country music
Is all I need to hear

I see purple sundown sky and
Your candy-yellow shawl
And there's memories and comfort
Familiar as those red-rock walls
Remember our love dear
And dry up those tears
That sweet country music
Is all I need to hear
That sweet country music
Is all I need to hear

JILLY

Jilly, you train horses for rich people
I write music from the heart
You got used to high livin and we drifted apart
Now, the van is my home...I'm wearin yesterday's clothes
Sleep as late as you want...let's see how it goes

Somehow a rich seam of love...got lost in our haste
Come out of cold storage...we'll plea-bargain the case
No glib conversations...no lukewarm replies
Lets narrow it down...and leave out the lies

Chorus
Well...I'm working at a Wal-Mart
Sleepin in a parking lot
I play my guts out every night
One of these days I'll get it right
Jilly...oh Jilly
Give me some time and I'll come back for you

He's just a cardboard imitation...the walk-away type
Jilly, please believe me...he'll never love you as a wife
Shed your party clothes...good intentions aren't enough
Like a well tended garden...I'm livin dreams out in the rough

Jilly open the windows...there's no shape to the wind
And when trouble comes a runnin...always hold out for a win
We can't dance in separate rooms...or rain kisses on what's past
We're just two imperfect people...with a love that has to last

Repeat chorus
At the end of repeat chorus add:
Yes, I'll come back for you

ZERO TO ZILLIONS

Wet grass stained your knees as you tried to explain
You never noticed...you were in too much pain
Climb mountains of pink sugar
Enjoy water-colored skies
It's a punching bag world
So it doesn't pay to cry
Unmade beds and laundry
Versus life on the go
What could be better
Than a baby-blanket of snow

Chorus
I've gone from zero to zillions with a guitar and a hit
Got a workingman's heart
So I'm no ego trip
Gone almost broken
Feelin cold like a stone
I'd give it back tomorrow Jilly
If you'd only come back home

Line your pockets with love
Keep change for the bus
Find a juke boxy diner
Happy songs are a must
Country roads can be dusty
Unused love turns to rust
It's an iffy situation
When there's no one to trust
No comedies, no tragedies, no sugar-coated plays
A sandwich in your pocket
Won't make it go away

Repeat chorus
And repeat last two lines of chorus

THERE'S LOVE IN THE WIND

Male Vocal
Lost in a darkness that can almost be touched
I stumble and fall…Jilly makes a big fuss
She's my guardian angel…we've been married ten years
She likes chili, hamburgers…and ice cold beer

Female Vocal
We bought a small farm
Where love can't get lost…
Hud says big mortgages…make work the boss
Watch for rainbows…and moons that don't lie
You'll need those memories…as life passes by

Duet Chorus
Life's full of tears and constant doubt
Roll with the punches…that's what life's all about
Open the screen door…let the night come in
Listen hard…to the cries of the wind
Give yourselves second chances
Life's compromises…not all out wins

Male Vocal
Benson is a backwater
No sidewalks…no malls
We lead a simple life…our favorite season is fall
Decisions are easy…when you have no choice
Jilly gave up singing…after losing her voice

Female Vocal
Hud's a wonder…so tender yet bold
Tucked in beside him…I never feel old
Still goes around barefooted
Never watches the time
Deep lines mark his face…body's worn just like mine

Repeat Chorus
and add the lines below to the end:

Open the screen door…let the night come in
Listen close for the love in the wind

LET LOVE FIND MY ROOM

Candles flicker
Lost stars scratch the moon
I have to wonder...
Is it me or too soon
Got to hold on...
Let love find my room
Have to hold on...
"Til love finds my room"

Have a few fond memories
Lots of regrets
Emotions stored neatly...
On a make-believe set
Time passes...love's never around
I'm lost... I want to be found

Non-repeat Chorus

So give me a taste
Of an authentic life
Replace the grays..
With pastels and pure whites
24-candles...
Only one wish
Let love find my room...
It shouldn't happen like this

My make-believe man...
There...on a make-believe set
It's only a dream...
There's real heartbreak ahead

24-candles
Only one wish
Let love find my room
I can't go on like this
Let love find my room
Nooooo...I can't go on like this

HARD-PACKED GROUND

Neighborly eyes...
Warmed a dazzling smile
But after two Coronas...
She'd shed her disguise
Returning my love...
With excuses and lies

Now love's all gone
Pain's leaned on in
I need a fresh start
A place to begin

Chorus
That red-hot sun
Always finds its way down
While the fiery sky
Lights the hard-packed ground
Workday's over..everyone's gone home
Nothing there for me
'Cept despair and alone

Her feelin's weren't real...
They were nothin' like mine
We were never together...
She was only passing time

But hey...there's a brand new band
Down at Chance's Cafe
Might meet a lady
Who'll take the pain away

Ending
The red-hot sun
Always finds its way down
While the fiery sky
Lights the hard... hard...hard..hard-packed ground

ROOMS TO GO

Outside on the cold steps
The raindrops feel like stones
Inside the walls are bare
All the furniture's gone
I know now I shouldn't have left you
So many times…home all alone

I was a guitar player…in a touring road band
A beat-up electric Fender…cradled in my hands
Music was my dream
But I didn't see her plans
Now my life's a lonely desert
And there's no real land

Chorus
The sign on the truck says…'Rooms To Go'
How many times can one start over
I really don't want to know
Walkin through this empty house
My heart is aching so
She's not coming back
Now I need 'Rooms to Go'

Music swam in my heart
Fingers danced across strings
She didn't hear the music
My songs became meaningless things
God send me an angel to help play this last song
I'm tired, weak and forlorn

Bridge
You can't keep love's fires burning
From the back of a Silver Eagle bus
I double-crossed myself
Thinking love would be enough

Repeat chorus

YOU KNOW BETTER

Rumors are flyin that I'm foolin around
Another long-distance driver
With a love in every town
The hiss from the tires says I'm a miss
An unwelcome card
That always skips the kiss

They say the bolts that hold us together
Are coming apart
That I'm a rough...bitter man
With a diesel for a heart
An unstable rig...no substance...no pride
A sorry hauler...who'll cast you aside

Chorus
But, you know better
You know better
I know you do
Rigs in the shop
There's nowhere to go
Put some soft music on
Let's dance real slow

We toil every day...enough jobs to survive
The price of fuel...eating us alive
They say I'm in the slow lane
With no chance to pass
That it's a bad situation
That our love will never last

Repeat chorus

INTERNET COWBOYS

Sally was an angel flying asleep in the rain
She needed summer in her life
His clever e-mails brought pain
There were cloudbursts of deception
Sunny pictures made of smoke
His digital promises..a cruel..no mercy joke

There were long candlelight dinners
Romantic walks in the park
She took him at face value..and opened her heart
Too trusting and absent sin
Soft...desperate lips...invited him in

Chorus
Beware of Internet Cowboys
Made from discarded spare parts
Once they get in your mailbox
They never stop
They're horrible men,
Who prey on lonely unselfish hearts

A practiced liar..said he worked every day
So, it turned into takeout and overnight stays
Months of cold-eyed kisses..tore Sally apart
She pressed for answers
He sighed with boredom..and downloaded her heart

A delicate woman..Sally couldn't bear alone
She tried to call..his laptop tied up the phone
Wearing brown sensible shoes
Decked out in cool pristine white
Sally's finger squeezed a hair-trigger
A monitor darkened..Sally walked into the night

Repeat chorus

LAST CHANCE RANCH

The rain tumbles down from a dirty city sky
Tunnel traffic isn't moving at all
The diesel fumes are burning my eyes
At least it blurs the grafitti on the walls
Beside me a once familiar woman
Now a stranger from too much champagne
Brown eyes the size of gumballs
Her heart knee-deep in pain

She prefers the black-tie crowd
Loves the city's maddening pace
I can see that I am losing her
There's no love left on her face
One more long and troubled silent night
Leads us into a dry cleaned day
Can I convince this once forgiving woman
That I can mend my deceiving ways

Chorus
My mind wanders to how it all happened
Too little patience, no reason or circumstance
Now our love is in its last season
God I pray for one more second chance
Yes I pray that there is a vacancy…
At the Last Chance Ranch

Bridge
She goes to our room the door closes
An invisible do not disturb on the door
Is hope just as dead as romance is
One more chance to even the score

Repeat chorus

CHILI STOP

My throat was dry ..it was sticky ..getting dark
Chili Festival today..I wheeled in and parked
Lots of good food and a fine country band
Everyone knows each other...
It's a strange...hard-case land
She senses my discomfort...green eyes lend a hand

She was no raving beauty... wore a one size fits all
But her presence rocked me...and I took the fall
On the makeshift dance floor ...
Engulfed by comforting sounds...
If love were water... I would have drowned

Chorus
Fix cars for a livin..live under the hood
Exchanging dreams and addresses never did me any good
Drive a bike on weekends like the 360-view
Roam the back country roads..looking to find something new

Hands round my waist... we head out of town
The wind whooshes by..love that's been found
In the waiting dark..the heat of gentle hands
Loving lips brush my neck...
I'm in a strange welcome land
It's a mystical moment...for a long, lonely man

Flushed and elated...her head against my back
It's a newfound feeling..a fresh, green track
I stored it for a life
There's not a doubt in my mind
That the girl holding on... will soon be my wife

Repeat chorus

IT WON'T HAPPEN AGAIN

Sleepy winds and scratchy music
Stir the stillness of the night
You gave me unwavering love
I gave you cold persuasive lies
You believed all my sweet talk
Until your heart broke and died

In the mist before dawn..we wait for the sun
Empty beds and unused pillows
Silent vows made on the run
Funny..you never read the fine print
How can love be so numb

Chorus
There was a room with a candle
Where we danced in the dark
No compass to follow..no reliable charts
I keep turning the pages
Counting my sins
It's always my fault
It won't happen again

A poisoned pen marks your hand
Hours fall..sweep into the next
You were always ambitious
Welcomed life's relentless tests
Hardened and resilient
You'll survive to love again

Sunrises hesitate..but never forget
Only time provides comfort
From life's long-shot bets
Forgive...and get on the plane
We spent our second chances
For you it's a brand-new game

Repeat Chorus and add:
Yes, it's always my fault
It won't happen again

LOVE'S BARGAIN BINS

She's so gorgeous..that eyes roll and dance
The lilt in her voice...offers urgent..steamy romance
Her love however ...is a bloodbath of hurt
She's an ice-pick in the eye
Who'll cut up your best shirt

Her dark roomy eyes...soak up body heat
When she rips you..it's all proper and neat
One ripple of laughter..she's got her way
There's a long list of wounded..who thought her innocent play

Chorus
She does me more harm than good
Believe me..I'd leave her if I could
It's her nature..she has to cheat again
But after being with her
Other women..seem like love's bargain bins

She's a danger..a high wire act
Full of bleak blind alleys
And heart-breaking pacts
Lightning slashes my heart..slanting rains drown my soul
Like the others..I'm just a fool

I eat cereal from boxes..stand alone in the rain
My life's an ongoing crime scene..in tragic real-time
She's acid and freon..I'm a mellowed-out wine

Repeat Chorus